Implode
Hollows Bay Trilogy (Book two)

E.K Hunter

Copyright © E.K Hunter 2023

All rights reserved.

This is a work of fiction. Names, Characters, Places, Businesses, Incidents, and Events are fictitious. Any resemblance to actual persons, living or dead, or actual events is purely coincidental.

No part of this book may be reproduced in any form or by any electrical or mechanical means including information storage and retrieval systems, without written permission from the author, except for the use of brief quotations in a book review.

Cover By: Getcovers.com

Edited By: Hunter Author Services

Created By: Atticus

To my fur babies.

Thank you for keeping me company when I was locked away in my writing cave, even if one of you did keep farting and distracting me.

Foreword

Readers should be aware that this is a dark romance with morally gray characters and contains the following topics that may be triggering for some readers:

- Torture
- Murder
- Drug abuse/overdose
- Suicide references
- Dub-con (Mild)
- Familial death(s)
- Kidnap
- Sexual assault (Touching)

This book ends on a cliffhanger.

Playlist

Fragile- Kygo
Never Be The Same- Camila Cabello
Roses- The Chainsmokers
Stuck With U- Ariana Grande & Justin Bieber
Love On The Brain- Acoustic- Veronica Bravo
Heroin- Badflower
Poison- Rita Ora
Antichrist- Holly Humberstone
11 Minutes- Yungblud & Halsey
Beneath Your Beautiful- Labrinth & Emeli Sande
Vampire- Olivia Rodrigo
Haunting Me- Loveless
See You Later (Ten Years)- Jenna Raine

Prologue

The sun beats down, heating my skin and warming my body all over. I'm in heaven, this must be what heaven is like. Waves crash softly on the powdery sand, the gentle noise helps to relax me. Tall palm trees line the beach, the vibrant green of the leaves a vivid contrast against the light blue sky.

I don't know where I am, nor do I know how I got here, but I don't care, and I'm certainly not complaining. It's peaceful, peace like I have never experienced before.

A squeal draws my attention. I slowly open my eyes to find Angel playing in the crystal blue sea. She swipes her hand across the surface of the water and a huge splash hits a shirtless Kai in the face. He laughs his deep laugh that stirs butterflies in my belly, and he gives her a genuine smile, one he normally reserves only for me. It's a sight to behold, and I can't help but smile over at the two of them.

He pounces on Angel and she squeals again as he pulls her into his arms and lifts her above his head.

"Kai put me down!" Angel giggles, her words aren't mumbled like they usually are. I don't understand why though, I don't remember Angel getting the cochlear implant she so badly wanted, and if she did get it, then she shouldn't be wearing it in the water.

I don't give it much thought as Kai launches Angel into the air, she flies high before crashing down underneath the waves, disappearing for a long minute.

Panic starts to creep into my body but her head bobs back up and she laughs so loudly that it echoes all around the beach, filling the air. I can't help but laugh, causing both Kai and Angel to look over at me.

"She's awake!" Angel cries, and Kai smiles his heart-stopping smile at me which I feel all the way to my core.

She grabs Kai's hand and starts pulling him towards the shore, telling him to move faster. The second Angel's toes hit the sand, she drops his hand and runs over to me, flinging her arms around me and soaking me with salty water.

But I don't care, if anything, the water cools my heated skin. I throw my arms around her and pull her into me, holding her so tightly that I don't think I'll ever let her go.

I smell her hair, her usual raspberry scent just about detectable underneath the salt of the ocean, and I breathe in deeply, inhaling as much of it as possible. It's a smell I will never get enough of.

She smells like home.

"Kai's been teaching me how to swim underwater," Angel beams as the shadow of Kai falls over us.

I look up at him, a strange feeling coming over me, it feels like I haven't seen him for such a long time, and I realize how much I've missed him.

I drink him in, his black hair that's shaved around the sides but messy on top, his strong jawline that's usually clean shaven, but now has smatterings of dark stubble, and those eyes, those all-seeing, intense dark eyes which have flecks of gold in them.

My eyes travel down his body, over his broad tattooed chest, over every solid muscle of his firm body, and over the black ink that covers both his arms from shoulders to wrists. If this place really is heaven, then Kai is a god.

"Let me see my girl," *he says after a minute of me gawking at him. Angel reluctantly steps out of my grasp and I let her go, the need to feel his hands on my skin overwhelms me.*

As soon as Angel moves, he swoops down. I barely have a second to prepare myself before his mouth is on mine, his full lips tasting exactly how I remember as he claims my mouth. His arms wrap around me as his tongue meets mine, the two of us pouring every little emotion into the kiss. For some reason, it feels like it was a lifetime ago that I last felt his mouth upon mine.

After what seems like an eternity, he breaks our kiss and steps back but still gives me the smile I love so much. It's only then I notice Angel isn't standing where she was moments ago, my brows furrow as I look around the beach in concern. She's nowhere to be seen, and the once clear blue sky has turned a deep dark gray as storm clouds roll in, the waves now crashing powerfully onto the shore. In the distance, thunder rumbles menacingly.

"Angel?" I say, but the words don't come out, they lodge painfully in my throat.

I look back to Kai, but now he isn't there either, neither of them are anywhere to be seen. Fear works its way through me, my heart pounding fiercely against my chest.

The thunder roars again, only this time it's much louder indicating it's close, so very close. I call out again, but still, my words don't come out. I try to stand from the bed I've been laying on, but my body won't move, and suddenly, everything hurts. Pain rolls through my body making me nauseous, my vision grows blurry as darkness crowds around me.

I fight against it, but I'm so exhausted, and I start giving into the black hole that is trying to consume me. Just as my eyes are closing, hands come towards me. They belong to a masked man with eyes as dark as the night sky.

I scream, but nothing comes out.

And then the darkness finally sucks me in.

Chapter 1

Kai

The smell hit me the second the door to the dark room opened. Not the smell of death, death has a distinctly pungent smell to it.

No, this was the smell of dirt and sweat, of piss and shit, and all other delights a body produces after being locked away in a dark cold room for days without any food, no sleep, and the constant threat of death hanging over your head.

The human body is an incredible machine all the time it gets what it needs to survive: water, food, and sleep. But removing one element can quickly fuck it up.

That's why I'd made sure Jane Timpson was given small glasses of water every eight hours, enough to make sure her body didn't start to shut down, but not enough to keep her from the cusp of delirium.

Dehydration can be dangerous, and as much as I wanted the woman to suffer, just as I was suffering, I wanted her lucid enough to tell me what I needed to know.

Where the fuck was Danny?

If I was honest, I was on the fence as to whether she was involved in his deceit. Yeah, the phone he had been using to communicate with my enemy had been found in Jane's handbag, but there was a possibility she was another victim in Danny's twisted game. He could have set her up to make it look like she was involved.

Until I'd interrogated her *personally*, I was keeping an open mind.

It had been three days since everything I thought I knew was turned upside down. Three days since my cousin, Miles Wolfe, cracked the phone we'd discovered in Detective John Anderson's backyard. When Miles had analyzed it, he'd found only one number saved in the contacts under the name 'D'.

Anderson had been smart enough to delete all the messages between him and D, but not smart enough to delete the number. When Miles had explained all this to me, I couldn't help but think back to what Isaac, my private investigator, had said.

It seems like someone is leaving you little breadcrumbs to follow.

Being the tech genius he is, Miles traced the location of D's number, only to find it was at the care home where Jane's mom was a resident.

The same place Jane was visiting right then.

His initial theory was that Jane was the sole culprit in feeding information back to Anderson. Determined to catch her in possession of the evidence, Miles headed straight to the care home where he and Jane's protection detail, Matthew, detained her and searched her bag. Lo and behold, the phone was in there.

But when Miles unlocked the phone, that's when he realized Danny was the real culprit. Anderson may have been smart enough to delete the messages between the two of them, but Danny wasn't.

In the hours after the crash, Miles showed me the phone, and I sat for the rest of the night reading the messages between the two of them. Danny had shared every little detail about my operations, my business plans, and of course, how much Riley had come to mean to me.

If I had any doubt that it was Danny behind the messages, I only had to look at how they were written to prove it was him. Danny *despised* texting, he couldn't be bothered half the time so would always shorten words. Every message to Anderson was written exactly the way Danny sent his messages to me.

When Miles wasn't able to contact me because there had been a problem with my phone, he'd instructed Matthew to take Jane to the cell, and that's where she'd been since.

I hadn't been to see Jane before now, I hadn't trusted myself not to snap her neck the second I laid eyes on her. But Miles and my closest friend and associate, Hendrix Becker had. They both reported back the same thing, either she was a really good actress or she genuinely didn't have a clue about Danny's betrayal.

Apparently, she'd been horror-struck when Miles told her what had happened in the middle of West Bay, where the car carrying Riley and Angel had been hit by an armored truck, and Danny had kidnapped Angel. If it hadn't been for the fact that I was minutes away with backup, who the fuck knew what would have happened to Riley.

The constant image of her unconscious form hanging limply in my arms had stopped me from sleeping more than a couple of hours these last few nights. I was so scared I would lose her.

The girl who made my black heart beat again.

Jane's cell was dark, damp, and freezing. It was located in the basement of my apartment block, next to my torture room. There were no windows, and the only door that would have allowed her exit was surrounded by two armed men at all times of the day. They had been stationed there since the minute Jane had been thrown in there on the off chance Danny was stupid enough to try a rescue attempt.

But there was no trace of the fucker.

I had ordered raids on every property linked to him, and no stone had been left unturned. Much like the ghost who killed my brother, Danny had disappeared into the night, taking Angel with him.

Hendrix, Miles, and I were working day and night to find Danny's hideout, not just to find the traitorous cunt, but for when Riley woke up, her sister would be ready and waiting.

But we were failing fucking miserably.

Perhaps it was for the best my Star hadn't regained consciousness, if she woke to find her sister missing, she'd be devastated.

After the crash, I held Riley while Hendrix drove us straight to Dr. Harris' private hospital, and while the doctor was assessing the extent of Riley's injuries, Miles set about hacking into the city's camera network to find the route Danny had taken.

The camera footage showed the Audi being plowed into by the armored truck, followed by Danny getting out and dragging Angel from the back seat.

The little girl had been kicking and punching, trying her best to get free as he dragged her away from the wreckage and Riley. Fear was etched all over her face as Danny eventually hauled her into his arms and carried her down an alleyway.

It was less than a minute later when Miles, Hendrix, Frank and I arrived at the scene.

After watching the footage, I'd punched a wall and split my knuckles open out of sheer frustration at how close we had been to stopping Danny. More infuriatingly, at the moment when the four of us arrived at the carnage, the camera footage had been cut. There was no trace of where Danny went after that.

Miles was still hacking private cameras across the city, but it was taking fucking time, time we didn't have, and the longer Danny remained out there, the longer he had to get further and further away from my clutches. You could get halfway around the fucking world in three days.

I had a million and one unanswered questions, but no matter how many times I went over the facts, the answers remained unknown. Why had Danny taken Angel when Riley was the target? Why had his car been ambushed if he was working with my enemy? Why had it been three days, and yet he hadn't made any demands in exchange for Angel being returned unharmed?

But there was so much of this nightmare that didn't make sense. Theo had been murdered several months ago when he was lured to his death. A Detective by the name of John Anderson knew something about Theo's death, if he wasn't directly involved in it. Then, when Riley and I had been at a charity ball, Anderson made an appearance and tried to kidnap her, telling her someone wanted to meet her, and she was going to be leverage in order to get to me.

Who that *someone* was, I had no fucking clue. And I was pretty sure that *someone* was going to strike again, and soon if I didn't find out who the hell they were. That was without mentioning the involvement of a gang known as The Stags who ruled Huntsville, a city on the other side of the state. Somewhere along the line, they had been brought in to help overthrow me.

Talk about a mind fuck.

As I stepped into the cell, the light from the corridor illuminated the small room. My eyes fell on the tiny frame of Jane Timpson who was sitting in the furthest corner of the room. Her knees were tucked up to her chest, and her arms wrapped around them, trying to stop the cold from seeping into her bones.

At my arrival, she lifted her head. Dirty streaks stained her cheeks from where she had been crying, and heavy bags lay underneath her eyes, probably from lack of sleep.

As a torture technique, whenever Jane started to nod off, my guards were instructed to play white noise as loud as possible in her cell to prevent her from sleeping.

One way or another, I *would* break her.

Her face was gaunt, malnourished even, her mousy brown hair was thick with grease, and the room stank from her body odor. The waste bucket in the corner of the cell was almost full, adding to the stench and making me want to gag.

I didn't feel an ounce of sympathy for the woman. In fact, my hands twitched with the need to make her feel pain. I didn't make it a habit to hurt women, only when needs must, and this was a time if ever there was one.

I wanted answers.

I stared down at her for the longest minute, allowing the bile rising in my throat from the foul smell to settle. It also gave me a minute to control the rage that was vibrating underneath my skin. I was usually in control of my emotions, I never acted without thought, except when Riley was involved. But the last few days had been the hardest of my life, and I was finding it increasingly difficult to not fly off the handle at any little thing.

I feared the only way I would regain the power to control myself was for Riley to wake up and be back in my arms where she belonged.

"Mr....Mr. Wolfe," Jane broke the silence, daring to speak before she was spoken to. Her voice was croaky, her lips pale and cracked from dryness. She couldn't meet my eyes, her head dropping to her lap, but I wasn't sure if that was because she was shit scared of what I was about to do or a sign of guilt.

I could understand what Danny had seen in her, there was something vulnerable about her, even before her current pitiful state, something you couldn't help but want to protect. She had a sheltered upbringing that made her naive in adult life, and despite Danny being a vicious motherfucker, he had a caring side to him. He wanted to protect those who were weak. Or, at least, I thought he did.

Danny had been a victim of the system growing up, abused in practically every care home he had ever stayed in until he was old enough to protect himself. He was my best enforcer, my most savage ally, but give him a tiny woman with doe eyes, he was a goner.

I'd seen it between him and Riley, the bond they had developed in the short time she had stayed with us. As much as he had never said it, he had come to see her as family. I honestly believed he would have given his life to protect her.

How wrong I had been.

"Hello, Jane," I replied coolly, honing in on my skill to keep emotion out of my voice.

"Have you come to let me go?" she asked feebly, although it was a waste of breath, she knew what the answer would be.

Despite my nostrils protesting from the increasing smell, I took a step forward, and while she didn't raise her head to look at me, she did tuck her feet further under her body, knowing I was moving closer.

A coiled snake ready to attack.

"What do you think?" I replied with a hint of venom in my tone.

Slowly she raised her head, her eyes finally meeting mine. They were filled with sorrow, and for the first time, I could see why Hendrix and Miles both believed she had nothing to hide.

"Mr. Wolfe, I know you think I had something to do with what Danny did," she said quietly, holding her nerve as she stared back at me. "But I promise you, I didn't know what Danny was up to. I...I love Angel, if I knew anything that might help you find Danny, I would tell you. I just want to go home."

Sadly for Jane, she wouldn't be going anywhere for a long time.

"I'm going to ask you this one time, Jane. Where is Danny?"

Great big tears slid down her face as she swallowed several times before answering. "I don't know."

I thought the time alone with no food, no sleep, and limited water would have broken her by now, but she wasn't quite there yet. I still wasn't convinced of her innocence.

It was time Jane met the real Kai Wolfe.

I smiled at her, a truly menacing smile, and her eyes widened in fear. Without warning, I reached down and grabbed the fragile woman by the throat, slamming her against the wall and pinning her to it.

She immediately bucked against my hold, her hands flying to my hands to pull them away, but she had zero strength in her muscles. As she opened her mouth to breathe air into her lungs, the smell from her breath hit me.

She fucking reeked.

"Don't fucking give me that, you know where he is," I snarled in her face, spittle landing on her cheek. I loosened my grip fractionally, enough for her to let out a pained sob.

"I don't....please, I don't know where he is," she choked out. I squeezed again, holding her long enough for her lips to turn blue. Jane needed to see the stairway to heaven to understand just how fucking serious I was about killing her if I thought for one second she was lying to me.

"You expect me to believe you spent all that time with Danny but didn't know what the fucker was up to? Didn't know he was planning on betraying me? Didn't plan on helping him?"

Again, I let go enough for her to take big gulps of air. Tears fell from her bloodshot eyes as resignation washed over her.

She finally knew she was going to die.

"Mr. Wolfe, I give you my word, I had no idea."

I released her throat and she sank to the floor, her knees buckling under her weight. The second her ass hit the floor, she cowered into the corner as far as possible, whimpering like a beaten puppy.

I was wasting my time. She didn't know anything.

Willing to play my final card to get her to talk, I crouched down in front of her. She bravely met my eye, pure hatred reflecting in them.

"I'm going to give you one last opportunity to tell me everything, or I promise you, Jane, I will personally march my ass into Sunnybank Residential Home, and I won't just put a bullet in your mom's head, but every single member of staff who looks after her will receive the same treatment. Tell me what you fucking know about where Danny is!"

She let out a pained cry of despair as hate-filled eyes turned to pleading ones.

"Please, Mr. Wolfe," she whined. "I swear to you on my mother's life, I don't know anything."

Jane was an only child. She had spent the majority of her adult life looking after her mom. If Jane had no regard for her own life, she would have done anything to protect her mom, including giving up Danny.

Sighing, I stood, confident she knew fuck all.

"I'll make sure my men bring you some food and give you access to a shower and some clean clothes, you fucking stink." I gave her my back and started walking towards the door.

"Wait!" she cried, scrambling to her feet. Her knees buckled, but she held herself up with a hand against the wall. "I told you, I don't know anything, I just want to go home."

I didn't acknowledge her. Instead, I walked out, slamming the door behind me, and listening to her wails as I walked back to the elevator. I needed to head to the gym and beat the living shit out of the punch bag, imagining it was Danny like I had done every day since I had learned of his disloyalty.

While I was confident Jane didn't know anything, I wouldn't be letting her go until I found Danny and had irrefutable proof in my hand she was not involved.

As I reached the elevator, my phone started ringing. I took it from my jacket pocket, my heart rate spiking when I saw who was calling.

"What's up?" I asked urgently, a mix of panic and hope in my voice.

"It's Riley, Mr. Wolfe. She's awake."

Chapter 2

Riley

Thunder continued to rumble around me as my eyes slowly opened. It took a few seconds to focus as the nightmare faded away. It had been playing on a constant loop that I couldn't wake up from, but now I was coming to, I couldn't remember what it had been about, only that it ended in darkness, leaving me terrified.

The first thing I noticed was how dry my throat was. The second was that there was a man in my room I didn't recognize. Panic reared to life, and as I tried to pull myself up from the bed in a pathetic attempt to protect myself, my head spun. Pain rolled through my entire body, making me wince.

"Riley, try not to move. There's a good girl," the man said soothingly and was beside my bed in an instant. He placed a warm hand on my shoulder and stared down at me with kind eyes. Relief washed away a smidgen of the panic when something in my brain told me I knew this man and he had helped me once before. My gut instinct told me I had nothing to fear from him.

He was a small man in both height and stature. His graying hair was receding, and the gold-framed glasses he wore were almost too big for his face, making his eyes look huge.

"Riley, I don't know if you remember me. I'm Doctor Harris," he said. The name rang a bell, I had a vague memory of him carrying out an examination on my throat when someone had tried to choke me.

The memory of being choked alerted another part of my brain that I was parched.

"W-water," I croaked out and tried to reach for the jug of water on a nearby table but all I managed to achieve was sending more bolts of pain through my body.

Questions spun in my head about what the hell had happened, why was I in so much pain? But I could barely speak, and it hurt my scratchy throat when the word came out.

Water first, questions second.

The good doctor obliged. Pressing buttons on a remote, the back of the bed I was lying in lifted so I was propped up into a sitting position. The doc poured me a glass of water and handed it to me, gratefully I took it but only managed a few small sips. The cool liquid felt like heaven against my burning throat.

The spinning in my head slowed as I sipped my drink, and I took the opportunity to look around the room. The crisp white walls, the thick black curtain covering huge windows that I somehow knew overlooked the city, the soft velvet silver chaise lounge at the end of the bed. It was all so familiar but I just couldn't think why.

There was an exception though. A chair was at the side of my bed which *felt* out of place, like someone had been sitting next to me, watching over me while I slept.

For some reason, I found that comforting.

As I gazed around the room, my eyes landed on a stand holding an IV bag, the tubes of clear liquid trailed down until eventually, it led to a cannula embedded into the back of my hand that was holding the glass of water.

Not really comprehending what in the world was going on, I reached over to put the glass back on the side, but as I twisted, blinding hot pain shot through my shoulder. I looked down to find the arm not connected to the IV drip supported by a sling. The doctor, who had been fiddling with the IV stand, quickly turned and took the glass from me.

"You need to be careful, Riley, your shoulder was dislocated. It's going to be painful for a while," he said in his soothing tone.

Dislocated shoulder?

What. The. Fuck.

"How the hell did I dislocate my shoulder?" I squeaked as the pain started to recede, probably thanks to whatever liquid was now trickling out of the IV bag and into my veins. Dr. Harris raised a graying eyebrow at me as a look of concern flashed over his wrinkled face.

"Can you tell me where you are, Riley?" he asked softly, perching on the side of my bed. He tried to keep his expression neutral but there was a hint of worry which gave him away. I cast my eye around the room again, and slowly, pieces slotted into place.

Kai Wolfe.

The deal.

Falling head over heels for a monster.

"Kai's penthouse," I muttered as the memories of the last few weeks flooded back into my head, overwhelming me. I squeezed my eyes closed to block them out, but they came at me like a freight train.

Kai.

Toby.

Kai killing Toby. My old friend who had taken me under his wing when my sister and I had first arrived in Hollows Bay. I hadn't seen him for over five years until he suddenly appeared in Sapphire, Kai's club. I thought it had been a coincidence, but it wasn't. Toby had been sent by the leaders of his gang, The Stags, as part of a plan to kidnap me.

Despite everything I learned about Toby's involvement with the plan, I begged Kai not to kill him, but he did, breaking my heart in the process. I had been so pissed at Kai that I locked myself away in this very room, but I'd reached a decision to stop sulking and speak to Kai about everything that happened.

And then......*nothing*.

"Can you remember what happened?" Doc Harris asked when I opened my eyes again.

"I....I was in my room, this room here. I was angry at Kai." I stared at the wall, replaying the images of me sulking on my bed, cursing Kai, and regretting the moment he walked into my life. But at the thought of Kai, an overwhelming pang of missing him flooded me as questions circled through my throbbing head.

Was he ok?

Had something happened to him?

Why wasn't he here?

"Please tell me what happened." Tears welled in my eyes as emotion got the better of me and the sense of dread deepened in my belly.

Something bad had happened, I just didn't know what.

"I think we should wait for Mr. Wolfe to arrive, Jacqueline has gone to contact him. In the meantime, I'd like to examine your shoulder."

My shoulders, *my good shoulder,* slumped with relief to hear Kai was on his way. Not having the strength to argue and insist the doctor told me everything now, I gave him a small nod of acceptance.

As the doctor started his examination, I distracted myself from the pain by thinking about Kai. The man who had bulldozed his way into my life, offering the chance to change my sister's life in exchange for me being his for six months.

Granted, those weren't the exact words he used when he offered me the deal, no, he said I would work for him. But I knew Kai now, he never had any intention of me working for him, he just wanted to use the time to get me to fall for him.

And it worked.

Boy, did it fucking work.

I hated him to start with, *really* hated him. But then he showed me another side to the monster everyone thought he was. Don't get me wrong, Kai *was* a monster.

But he was so much more.

Protective, loyal, and I never thought I would say this, but somewhere deep within him, he had love to give.

At some point, my hatred towards him turned to something entirely different, and before I had a chance to protect myself, I fell into his bed and allowed him into my heart.

But why did that feel so wrong right now?

As the doctor was explaining that I would have to rest my arm for a couple of weeks, and have physio on my shoulder, a soft knock on the door interrupted him, making my heart jump into my throat.

Kai.

Trepidation raced through me. Kai hadn't come to see me in the days that followed the incident with Toby, he'd left me alone to stew. The memory of him sneering at me, and telling me he had manipulated me into growing feelings for him reared its ugly head. I tried to push it away, but self-doubt grabbed hold of it and held onto it like a goddamn lifeline.

Dr. Harris looked at me expectantly. I hesitated for a moment before I gave him a nod. Maybe it wasn't Kai, he didn't usually knock when he wanted into a room, normally he just strolled in.

What Kai Wolfe wanted, Kai Wolfe took.

"Come in," Doc Harris called, and without hesitation, the door swung open, and in stepped the man who had changed my life.

And not necessarily for the better.

The man who equally drove me crazy with his intensity and arrogance, but made me feel desire like I had never known before, even if I had been manipulated into feeling things for him. It didn't matter now, those feelings were there, and they were very real.

He looked different from the last time I saw him. Kai was always a vision of perfection, neatly groomed, impeccable suits, and full of confidence. He walked with a swagger, strong and sure of himself. With the air of danger that surrounded him, it was clear as day why he had the reputation he had. He was not a man to be messed with.

But the man who walked into the room was a million miles away from the one I was used to.

He was broken.

Kai looked tired. Older than his thirty-five years. Dark bags sat heavy underneath his eyes, and where he was always clean-shaven, he now had dark stubble growing on his chiseled face.

And didn't that make him even more handsome?

Gone were his smart suits and crisp shirts, instead, he wore a black t-shirt and black jeans. I'd never seen him look so casual before and that unnerved me even more.

He stepped into the room, his eyes immediately finding mine, and the second they met, his tensed body relaxed, almost as though he had been holding the weight of the world on his shoulders until this moment.

"Thank fuck," he sighed, running a hand over the mop of hair on his head. But he didn't make any move to come further into the room, and for some reason, the feeling of dread, the feeling that something bad had happened, grew monumentally.

Neither of us said anything, we were locked silently staring at each other. A mixture of different emotions swirled around in my head and my heart. I wasn't angry with him for killing Toby, not anymore. I'd denied it at first, but deep down I knew why he had. He was protecting me, and how could I be angry about that?

But instead of anger, anxiety took its place. Anxiety as to why I was in bed with a pounding head and a painful arm, and anxiety over the bad feeling that was growing the longer I stared at him. Somewhere mixed in was relief that he was okay, physically, at least. He was practically vibrating with tension which was most unlike the Kai I had come to know.

It was only when Dr. Harris cleared his throat that I remembered he was in the room with us and I dragged my gaze away from Kai.

"Right, well I'll leave you two to talk." He crossed the room but paused as he was about to leave, stopping to address Kai. "Please try not to upset Riley, Mr. Wolfe, she is still suffering from the concussion and it would be wise not to get her worked up."

Concussion?!

That at least explained the throbbing in my skull. Seriously, what in the fuckety fuck had happened?

A rumbling emitted from Kai's chest that sounded very much like a displeased growl, but he didn't say anything, just gave the doctor a nod of his head. Dr. Harris gave me one last look which was more of a grimace than anything else before he left the room, closing the door quietly behind him.

Kai took a tentative step toward me and I noted the hesitation, but he seemed to shake himself. In three big steps, he reached my bed and bent down to kiss me gently on the top of my head.

"Fuck, Star. I was so worried." His lips brushed against my hair as he spoke, sending delicious tingles down my spine. I closed my eyes, reveling in the feeling of his presence as his scent wrapped around me.

It felt like I was home.

"How are you feeling?" he asked as he pulled away and sat in the chair next to my bed, grabbing my cannulated hand and holding it in his.

I was used to Kai being dark and broody, but he was more intense than I had ever seen before. His dark eyes, almost black in the low light, scanned over the parts of my body that weren't hidden under the blankets before they returned and bore into mine.

"Like I've been hit by an eighteen-wheeler," I replied honestly, because now I was more with it, I was beginning to feel every ache and pain, and my entire body hurt. "Kai, please tell me what happened."

He sighed loudly and sat back in his chair but didn't drop my hand. His thumb ran over my knuckles, just like he would do whenever we were in his car. It was like it was his way of reminding himself I was really there.

"What do you remember?"

I sighed in frustration. "I was in my room, angry at you for everything that had happened with Toby." His eyes hardened before I quickly added, "but I realized maybe I was being unfair. I didn't want you to kill Toby, but I accept you had your reasons. I wanted to talk to you, I think I was going to come and find you, and then.....nothing. It's just darkness."

He was silent for a moment but his jaw clenched, his teeth grinding. I knew him well enough to know he was taking a few seconds to compose himself, and something told me now was not the time to push.

"It's probably best if I start from the beginning, but I need you to stay calm, you're hurt enough as it is."

The penny dropped as soon as the words were out of his mouth.

"Something has happened to Angel." It came out as a statement of fact as opposed to a question because I didn't need him to answer. I knew in the pit of my stomach something had happened to her.

Tears sprung to life as a solid ball of emotion clogged my throat, my mind conjuring all kinds of awful things that could have happened to her. "Please Kai, tell me what the hell has happened to my sister."

"Danny's taken her."

For a happy moment, I didn't understand what the problem was. Danny was Kai's friend, not just his friend but a loyal employee. He was Angel's friend, he was *my* friend. Danny had spent time with Angel over these past few weeks, he'd grown to adore her, like most people did when they spent any time with her. He wouldn't hurt her, of that I was sure.

Kai's words didn't register because I didn't understand what the issue was, if he'd taken her on a day out or something, so what? It wasn't like he hadn't done it before.

"I...I don't see what the problem is," I said, still not grasping the problem. His thumb stopped moving over the back of my hand and instead, he gave it a gentle squeeze. He took a deep breath, almost as though he was trying to give himself the strength to get through what he was about to say. Again, it was most unlike Kai, he never showed anything resembling empathy or remorse.

"Three days ago, I made the mistake of leaving you here with Danny so I could visit my private investigator. I never thought for one second that I would be leaving you with a traitor." My jaw dropped open as Kai spoke slowly, *carefully*, but full of determination to get the story out, no matter how much it was going to hurt me. "Danny took the opportunity to tell you I had ordered him to take you to a safe house. He loaded you and Angel into a car to take you fuck knows where. But on the way, there was an ambush. The car you were in was hit by an armored van, and as a result of the crash, you dislocated your shoulder and received a concussion." He paused as I gaped at him, the words taking time to sink into my brain.

"Danny managed to pull himself out of the car, but you were trapped. It was on its fucking roof. He managed to get Angel out, and then he took her." Kai grew angrier, and then he jumped from the chair as though his ass had been lit on fire. He slammed his hand against a wall, making me flinch before he growled out words that made my heart shatter into a million tiny pieces.

"He left you there, Star. He left you there to be taken while he kidnapped Angel."

Tears slid silently down my cheeks, my head refusing to comprehend his words. Kai stood with his back to me, his head tipped up to the ceiling as his whole body shook with rage.

His words kept circling around in my head.

He kidnapped Angel.

He kidnapped Angel.

"I'm so sorry, Riley, he's got her, and I don't know where they are."

His words broke as he turned back to look at me, waiting for my response. But how can you respond when your whole world has been flipped upside down and stomped all over?

Angel was missing.

Even before we had run away and started life in Hollows Bay, Angel had been my only priority. My parents used to joke that I should have been her mom because of how much I fussed over her. I loved that little girl more than life itself, and all I wanted for her was a life where she was happy. I thought I was doing the right thing by agreeing to Kai's deal. All we had to get through was six months and she would have had everything that ordinarily, I couldn't have given her.

I never thought in a million years that all I would be doing was putting her life in danger.

"Say something, Riley," Kai said stoically. I didn't know how much time had just passed. It could have been seconds, it could have been hours. The only thing in my head was a memory of Angel's face, and of how terrified she must be.

As the tears cascaded down my cheeks, words I wanted to say churned in my head but I couldn't force them passed the lump that was lodged firmly in my throat.

When I didn't say anything, he stepped towards the bed and took my hand again. But instead of the usual warmth I felt when Kai touched me, all I felt was fire. Fire that started in my fingertips and spread into my hand before traveling up my arm. My skin burned, and pain like I had never known before took over my entire body. I snatched my hand away, Kai's eyes widened as if the fire had spread into his own body.

"Don't touch me," I hissed, venom in my tone. My eyes narrowed on him, hatred oozing out of every one of my pores.

This was *his* fault.

I may have made the deal, but he was the one that had brought this upon Angel. Him and his fucking criminal ways, his bullshit *'nothing can touch me'* attitude, and his quest to find out who had killed his brother. Well, now his ways had caught up with him, yet Angel was the one who was suffering the consequences.

"Star-" he began, but the use of my nickname was enough to finally push the words out.

"No, you don't get to call me that anymore. You don't get to be anywhere near me again," I snarled. My hands shook with rage as my words turned from quiet angry words to shouts of pure hatred. "You did this to her and I will *never* forgive you. I fucking hate you, Kai. I wish I'd never met you!"

My body twitched with the need to get the fuck out of bed and inflict as much physical pain on him as possible, but I could barely move from the pounding in my head. Kai recoiled at my words, but I didn't care, I meant every single one of them.

"I'm doing everything I can to find her, Riley, and I promise you, when I do, Danny will not live to see another day."

I didn't want to hear another word from him, I wanted him to get the fuck away from me. There was nothing he could say to stop my blood from boiling with rage.

"Fuck sake, Kai. Don't you see this is what started all this mess in the first place? Are you so arrogant you can't see that people want to kill you for all the shit you and your family have done? That Theo's death was probably in retaliation for something *you* did to piss someone off?"

At the mention of his brother's name, his lips curled into a snarl and his fists clenched. But I didn't care, I hoped the mention of Theo caused him as much hurt as I was feeling.

"Riley, I know you are feeling-"

"Don't you dare fucking tell me how I'm feeling!" I roared, the movement jolted my shoulder causing white-hot pain to shoot through my arm. But I didn't wince, in fact, I relished it, as for a few seconds, it took away the pain in my heart. "Your brother was killed because you and him are nothing but criminals. Angel is innocent, she's just a little girl, Kai, she doesn't deserve any of this shit."

That was all I could say before the dam broke. Tears fell like a waterfall as deep wracking sobs consumed me, making it hard to breathe. The pounding in my head worsened to the point I thought I was going to be sick.

My baby sister was out there somewhere in the big wide world, no doubt scared shitless, and not knowing what the hell was happening. Danny wouldn't be able to communicate with her, he wouldn't know the things to do to calm her down when she was scared.

She needed me.

I didn't know how much time passed as I sat in bed sobbing. Kai didn't make any move to comfort me which was for the best, if he touched me again, I wasn't sure I would be responsible for my actions, dislocated shoulder and concussion be damned.

Eventually, exhaustion took over and my sobs slowly receded. My head throbbed, my shoulder ached, but it was nothing in comparison to the anguish I felt in my chest. When my eyes cleared from the tears, I found Kai leaning against the wall and was momentarily surprised to see his own eyes were watery. I couldn't look at him for more than a second.

A tiny part of me wanted him to wrap me in his arms and tell me everything was going to be okay, but the bigger part of me wanted to get as far away from him as possible, knowing that nothing would be okay until I had Angel back with me.

"I'm going to get her back, Riley. I promise you," Kai said softly when my tears dried up and I could do nothing but stare at the wall.

Although he was only standing a few feet away from me, it felt like we were on different continents. I turned to look at him, holding my nerve as I told him exactly what I needed to say.

"When you get her back, we are done. Fuck you and your deal, Angel and I are getting as far away from you and Hollows Bay as we can get, and I promise you, Kai, I'll never give you a second thought again."

He didn't respond, his nostrils flared as he turned on his heel and walked out, closing the door behind him.

The second I was on my own again, the tears spilled down my cheeks as my entire world imploded around me.

Chapter 3

Kai

"I think he is dead, Boss," Miles said grimly as I brought my bloodied knuckles down again on the mangled body in front of me.

I hate you.
I will never forgive you.
I wish I'd never met you.

Riley's words repeated over and over in my head as I pounded my fists into the dead man. It helped to take some of my anger and frustration out, but it was nowhere near enough to quell the storm raging inside me. When she uttered those words, she destroyed the peace I had become used to since she entered my life.

The fucker in front of me deserved every punch, and when I finally stopped hitting him, his face was totally unrecognizable.

Lyle Winters worked for the city council, operating public cameras throughout the city. It had been Lyle who wiped the cameras after the ambush. It was his fucking fault that Danny had managed to get out of the city untraced.

Standing over his dead body, I wiped my hands on the rag Hendrix passed to me, and I was pissed to see the skin on my knuckles had split. Blood, bone, and brain matter covered the concrete floor in my torture room at the basement of my apartment block. It was going to take a hell of a lot of cleaning to get rid of the mess, I'd probably have to pay the clean-up team extra for this one.

"Get rid of this fucker, and get the cleaners in here to clean up, I want this place sparkling," I growled as I headed towards the door, leaving Miles and Hendrix to clean up my mess.

The pair of them had been in moods that equaled my own foul one. It wasn't just me Danny had betrayed, we may not have all been blood, but we were a family and he'd betrayed them too. They wanted a pound of his flesh as much as I did.

Miles had spent the last few days holed up in his room doing whatever he could to recover the camera footage. He'd been hacking private cameras so we could find one fucking clue as to where Danny was. He had traces on Danny's phone, his bank accounts, and even his fucking emails. If there was any sign of Danny resurfacing, Miles would know about it.

Hendrix had been tapping up his sources and interrogating anyone who had previously worked with Danny, along with leading the raids at the properties Danny owned, but despite their best efforts, we were no closer to locating him.

I knew Winters wouldn't have had any information about where Danny was, he wasn't important enough, but he was able to shed some light on who had paid him to wipe the footage.

Anderson.

Anderson had threatened Winters' family, the same way he had threatened Victor Griffin's family. Detective Anderson was becoming more and more of a pain in my ass, and yet he was like a fucking ghost I couldn't pin down. Miles was using every trick in his bag of skills to trace Anderson but both he and Danny had gone to ground, no doubt together, plotting their next course of action to destroy me.

They need not have bothered. The girl upstairs hating my guts was doing a fine job of destroying me all on her own.

I stormed out of the room, intent on heading upstairs to shower and change out of my bloodied clothes when Hendrix followed me out.

"Problem?" I barked at him when he stopped in front of me. I didn't particularly like it when my orders were ignored.

"Worried about you, Boss," Hendrix said after a moment's pause.

"Nothing to worry about," I snapped, glaring at him.

He sighed and dropped his head. "I just think everything with Theo, and now this with Riley, it's taking its toll on you. I've never seen you beat someone so brutally before."

The image of Winters' caved in head flashed before me, followed by Theo's dead body lying cold on the ground with his throat slit, before quickly morphing into the image of Riley's limp body in my arms as I carried her into Dr. Harris' hospital. I blinked my eyes, clearing the images away.

"I told you, there is nothing to worry about. I just want to find Danny and bring Angel back so we can focus on finding the cunt who dared to cross me when they killed my brother."

"I know, Boss, and we are throwing everything we have at it, but you not thinking clearly isn't going to help. Why don't you take a few days away from it all, spend some time with Riley?" Hendrix replied.

My hands curled into fists, eager to spill more blood.

"You think I can take time off from hunting down the fucker who killed my brother? Not to mention finding the traitor who will die for betraying me," I spat back at him with nothing but pure venom in my voice. He must have heard it too as he took a step back and raised his hands as if surrendering.

"I didn't mean to offend, Boss, I just thought taking some time might be good to clear your head."

I was getting impatient, the blood was beginning to dry on me, and I desperately wanted to shower and get out of the clothes I was wearing. I also wanted to check in on Riley. Not physically, I hadn't gone near or by her room since she told me to leave her alone.

That hadn't stopped me from dipping into the camera feed that was in her room whenever possible.

"I don't need to clear my head, Hendrix, it's right where the fuck it needs to be. Now, I thought I gave you an order to get that shit cleared up or do I need to repeat myself?" I glared at him, making it super fucking clear that if I had to repeat my demand, it would be with my fists turned on him.

"No need to repeat, I'm on it." He spun on his heel and walked back towards the room.

I watched him go, irritated with everything. With how slow it was trying to gather information on who killed Theo, with finding Danny. With Riley thinking she could just up and walk out of my life when her sister was found.

She was wrong.

She might be pissed at me now, but there was no way in the universe I was letting her go.

Riley was *mine*.

It might take time to fix things between us, and I wasn't against locking her up until she saw sense if that's what it would take. I'd given her space after the debacle with Toby and she eventually came around, all she needed now was a few days to see sense that she and I were meant to be.

I'd give her a few days alone, mainly because I knew she couldn't leave the house and she also needed time to heal from her injuries. But as soon as Dr. Harris gave the okay, I'd be paying my girl a visit and laying it out for her in no uncertain terms that she wasn't going anywhere.

The door slammed shut behind Hendrix and I headed up to my apartment to clean up and get my Riley fix, even if it was only from a small television screen.

Several hours later, I found myself sitting at the bar in Sapphire nursing a tumbler of whiskey. It was the first time I had left the apartment and I had done so reluctantly, I didn't like being away from Riley. I trusted Miles to look after her though, and as much as she refused to speak to me, she was at least talking to him.

The club wasn't open for another few hours and there were only a handful of staff milling about, restocking the bar, and preparing for the night's entertainment. I'd paid a fortune to secure a performance by a world famous DJ, and the night was a sell-out. I only stopped to make sure everything was going smoothly, but on seeing the bottle of whiskey sitting on the countertop, I helped myself and poured a glass.

Why the fuck not, I owned the place after all.

After Toby admitted he had been let into the club by one of my bar staff, an idiot called Terry, I had Issac run background checks on every single employee who worked for me. Isaac found another two staff members at the club who had tenuous links to gangs across the country, and while I was sure they weren't anything to worry about, I wasn't taking any chances and had promptly sacked them.

Terry wasn't so lucky in just being sacked, he paid with his life for his part in letting Toby into my club.

As I finished pouring my second glass, Kimmy scurried out of her office carrying a clipboard, her brows pulled together in worry. I'd poached Kimmy from Indigo, a club that, funnily enough, I now owned. I couldn't fault Kimmy as the manager of Sapphire, she ran it like a dream, and there were rarely any issues she couldn't handle on her own.

Spotting me, she made a beeline over to where I sat and clambered onto the stool next to me. I wouldn't class Kimmy as a friend but she was probably the closest thing to being something like a friend aside from Hendrix and Miles.

And once upon a time, Danny.

She was also one of the few people who didn't call me Boss or Mr. Wolfe, and one of even fewer people that could get away with calling me out on my bullshit and not finding themselves staring down the barrel of my gun.

"You look like shit," she said with a hint of teasing in her tone. She reached across and swiped the bottle and a clean glass from the stack that was waiting to be put away and poured herself a shot.

"Good to see you too," I grumbled back. She smirked and then pushed the clipboard under my nose.

"I've finished interviewing for the two new replacements. There's three that would be suitable, do you want me to give Miles their names so he can check their backgrounds out?"

I scanned down her clipboard, a list of names crossed out with the exception of three I didn't recognize.

"Email them to me and I'll ask Isaac to check them out, Miles is up to his eyes at the minute," I said and pushed the clipboard back to her, instantly forgetting the names I'd just seen.

"Sure thing," she replied before taking a sip of her drink. She started scrawling some more notes over the paper and I tuned her out, letting her do whatever it was she was doing.

Kimmy was a pretty woman, with short black hair, and stunning light blue eyes. She had a gorgeous figure, all tits and ass, and a tiny waist. It was her looks that attracted me to her in the first place. I tried to hit on her, only for her to turn me down. I wasn't used to women turning me down, they usually threw themselves at me, but Kimmy took great pleasure in telling me not to be offended by her rejection. It wasn't a personal slur, she simply preferred tacos to hotdogs.

Her words, not mine.

"I heard about Danny," she said tentatively after a few minutes of silence. Just hearing the fuckers name boiled my blood. I downed the rest of my whiskey and slammed my glass down on the counter.

"Yeah." I couldn't bring myself to say anything else, his betrayal stung like a bitch, and there was part of me that still couldn't believe he would do it. After everything I'd done for him over the years, he betrayed me by working with my enemy.

"I did not see that one coming," Kimmy said, more to herself before following my lead and downing the rest of her drink.

"You and me both."

"How's Riley doing? I heard she took quite a hit in the crash."

Kimmy had spent some time with Riley on the night she had not so coincidentally bumped into Toby, and Kimmy had told me after that she really liked Riley, that she thought she was a good match for me. I happened to agree.

"Dislocated shoulder, concussion, and fuck knows how many cuts and bruises," I reeled off Riley's injuries as I stared at the row of spirits lined up behind the bar. Kimmy took the hint, pouring another glass for me but didn't refill her own.

"Sheesh," she replied with a grimace. "She'll be okay though, right?"

"She'll recover from the injuries, but that's not the issue." I turned my gaze on Kimmy to find her staring back at me with a face full of sympathy. "She's devastated about Angel. She spent the last five years of her life protecting that girl, doing whatever was needed to make sure she was taken care of. I don't know if she'll survive if I don't get Angel back soon." I finally voiced the concern that had been playing on constant repeat from the minute I'd found out Danny had taken Angel, how would Riley go on living without her sister?

She couldn't, that was the truth of it.

Riley had sacrificed her happiness to protect her sister and give her a decent life. Look at the deal she made with me. Never in a million years would she have given it a second thought had I not offered something that would benefit Angel. If that was taken away from her, Riley lost her purpose in life. She'd lose herself completely before she would have an opportunity to find something else to keep her going.

No matter what, I *had* to get her sister back.

"Do you have an idea where Danny might be keeping her?" Kimmy asked carefully, correctly reading that I was a silently raging bomb likely to explode at any minute.

"No."

"You'll get her back, Kai. You have the resources and the power to find her, it might take a bit of time but I know you won't stop until you do," Kimmy said quietly. I appreciated her vote of confidence, even if I didn't believe it myself.

"Yeah, but at what cost? Riley already hates me." Fucking hell, even I heard the pity in my voice. I downed my drink but this time slid the glass away. As much as I wanted to get shit-faced, it would do no good, all I would achieve would be a fucking hangover from hell. "She wants to leave when I get her sister back."

The words burned like acid. I hadn't told anyone that Riley said she intended to leave when Angel returns, it was like if I didn't say it out loud, it wouldn't be true. But Kimmy was one person I could be honest with, and right now, I needed to purge the words from my head, otherwise, I was going to drive myself crazy.

Kimmy was quiet for a minute, her eyes burning into mine and several times her mouth opened as if to say something before closing again.

"She's hurting, Kai. We all say things we don't mean when we are upset," Kimmy said eventually, keeping her gaze fixed on me. I gave her a shrug of my shoulder.

"Doesn't matter. She's not going anywhere," I told her firmly.

She paused for a moment, but in true Kimmy style, she had no problem calling me out on what she thought was bullshit. "You can't keep her as a prisoner if she doesn't want to stay."

I opened my mouth to reply, to tell her I would do *exactly* that, but she held up a hand, silencing me. I glared at her expectantly.

"Look, I know you do things your way, and I'm sure what I say will go in one ear and out the other, but hear me out." She was suddenly all serious, business-like rather than a friend offering advice. "Riley might think she hates you at the minute but she is hurting. If you lock her up and refuse to let her go, she will genuinely hate you. It might be the hardest thing you will ever have to do but if she wants to go, you have to let her."

I let her words sink in. My instant reaction was to tell her to mind her own fucking business, but something entirely different came out.

"I can't, Kimmy. I can't let her leave me." My voice wavered as for once, just for a moment, I allowed myself to show true emotion to someone other than Riley.

I scrubbed a hand down my face and swallowed the lump that had formed in my throat. "How can I let go of the girl who has made me feel something for once in my life? How can I let go of the only person I trust more than anyone in the world? She's been in my life for less than two months, and yet I can't imagine surviving a single day without having her in it."

Kimmy surprised the hell out of me by placing her hand gently on top of mine that rested on the counter and gave it a reassuring squeeze.

"Sometimes Kai, you have to do things you don't want to do. Sometimes you have to be selfless so the person you love can be happy."

Love.

Other than Theo, I wasn't sure I loved anyone else. He was the only person in my life I loved, and not just because he was my brother. He was my best friend, my confidante, someone I would have died for. I certainly didn't love my father, he was a cruel bastard who made my life hell. And my mom, I know I loved her but she was my mom, it was a different kind of love.

Love wasn't an emotion I was capable of, and I certainly didn't deserve it. My feelings for Riley were something I'd *never* experienced before, and not having anything to compare them to, I didn't know whether it was love. But the second Kimmy said those words, it was like I had been struck by a bolt of lighting, and I knew without a shadow of a doubt that I loved Riley.

I loved her with all of my cold black heart.

I didn't reply to Kimmy, what the fuck was I supposed to say back to that anyway? After a few minutes of silence, she gave my hand another squeeze and muttered her apologies, telling me she had to get ready for the event. I barely acknowledged her, my head was fucked with everything spinning around again and again until all I could think of was Star.

I ached to go home and gather her in my arms, to smell her hair that always smelled of strawberries, to kiss her soft lips. How could I ever contemplate living the rest of my life without her in it?

At some point, I moved to my office as the evening got going, but even in the quiet of my office, I couldn't stop the noise in my head, not helped by the memories of the night I fucked Riley over my desk.

Kimmy's words played on repeat until they were so firmly lodged in my brain, the only way to remove them would be via a lobotomy. I warred with myself, the stubborn part of me refusing to even consider letting Riley go, while the other part of me argued that all I wanted was for her to be happy. Even if it meant not being in my life.

I was a selfish prick, I knew that. I had always grown up with the attitude that if I wanted something, I took it, and it had always worked for me. But now I had something as precious as Riley, all I wanted was to make her happy, nothing else mattered.

The noise only stopped when, after several hours of pure torture, Kimmy's words finally sank in, and I reached a decision that cracked my black heart straight down the middle. Sneaking out the back door, I drove home despite the whiskey swimming in my veins.

My head was quiet for the entire journey, almost as though a feeling of peace had settled over me for the first time since the ambush. I abandoned the car in the garage, giving a brief acknowledgment to the armed guards who were stationed there. Instead of heading to my room where I could check on her from the monitors, I headed straight to Riley's room.

Her room was in darkness thanks to the heavy curtains drawn across the windows, but a lamp on the bedside table cast a soft glow across her tiny body. She was tucked up under the blankets, and I was pleased to see she was no longer connected to the IV drip. I crept over to her and sat in the chair next to her bed.

She wasn't asleep. I'd spent hours watching Riley sleep, and I knew her breathing pattern when she slept. Right now, she was awake, but she kept her eyes closed which made it easier for me to say what I needed to say.

Gently, I picked up her hand and held it in mine, admiring how small and fragile it seemed in my big palm.

"I just wanted to say I'm sorry for everything," I started, keeping my voice barely above a whisper. She made no sign of acknowledgement and I wondered how hard it was for her to stay pretending to be asleep. "Meeting you was one of the best things that has ever happened to me. Before you, my life was full of darkness, and I didn't give a fuck about anyone. But the minute I laid eyes on you, everything changed. You were a glimmer of light that grew bigger the more time I spent with you."

I paused for a few seconds, taking a deep breath and resisting the urge to shut the fuck up and change my mind. But as my eyes raked over her body, taking in the cuts and bruises marring her beautiful face, and the arm in the sling, I forced myself to continue.

"I'm sorry you got hurt because of me, I wish I could take away all of your pain, and I promise you, I will do whatever it takes to bring Angel back. And when I do," I cut off, the words lodging in my throat and refusing to come out. Taking another deep breath, I tried to find the strength within me to remain resolute. "I'll get you and Angel out of here. I'll get you new identities and find a place for you in Europe where you and Angel can live your lives in peace and safety. From now on, you'll never have to see me again. But I swear to you, baby, I'll make sure no one hurts either of you ever again."

Before I could second guess myself, I stood from my chair and leaned over her, brushing my lips over her forehead as light as a feather. "I love you, Star. I will always love you."

Tip-toeing out of the room, I closed the door softly and headed towards my own bedroom, ignoring the pained sobs that broke out from behind the door.

Chapter 4

Riley

The next week passed agonizingly slow, and with every day that passed, the gaping wound in my heart grew deeper.

Daylight hours were almost bearable.

Almost.

Between the doctor's visits, intense physio, and spending time with Miles learning about the search for Danny and Angel, I just about made it through the day, mostly ignoring the unbearable pain I now carried in my heart.

But the nights were pure torture.

When I had no one else to talk to, and my thoughts consumed me, I felt like I was descending into insanity. I missed Angel more than I could express, and as soon as the lights went out, my imagination went into overdrive with all the things that might have happened to her.

Was she alive?

Was she hurt?

What psychological damage would being kidnapped have on her?

Every night the question spun around in my head until I was curled into a ball, sobbing my heart out and willing sleep to come, just so I could get some rest.

As if that wasn't bad enough, every so often my brain would kindly remind me of Kai's visit to my room, and my already broken heart would break all over again.

Kai loved me.

I tried my best to ignore the warmth that spread through me when he uttered those words. The same warmth that spread through me anytime my brain chose to repeat them, but despite trying to ignore it, I couldn't help but find the smallest bit of comfort in knowing that Kai loved me.

Once again, I was thrust into a roller coaster of emotions, warring with myself over whether I thought I loved Kai back or if I truly hated him.

Deep down, I knew what the answer was, I just didn't want to acknowledge it because how could I love a monster?

Because that's what he was, he was a cruel murderer who had dragged me into his life of mayhem for his own selfish gain, and as a result, the only reason for my existence had been stolen away from me.

At least, that's what I told myself every time his words popped into my head. An internal battle would follow, where the need to find him and tell him how I felt fought against the logic to stay as far away from him as possible and focus on getting Angel out of Hollows Bay.

Logic always won.

But then the same process repeated the next night.

And the night after that.

And the night after that.

It was nothing but pure torture, and because of the lack of sleep I was getting, I ended up looking like a walking and talking zombie.

True to his word, Kai stayed well away from me to the point I wasn't even sure he was still staying under the same roof. While part of me was glad I hadn't seen him, the other part *desperately* craved him. I never thought I would reach a point where I missed Kai Wolfe, but I did.

I missed his scent wrapping around me when he was close.

I missed feeling his hands on my body.

I missed the way he would look at me with such fierce possessiveness.

But it wasn't just the physical side I missed. I missed talking to him. Once the reality of the car crash and Angel's abduction sank in, I had a million and one questions. Whether it was out of sheer stubbornness or not trusting myself to be around the man, I refused to seek him out.

Instead, I hounded Miles to tell me everything, and eventually, he recounted the events of the day Danny decided to fuck Kai over. As he filled in the blanks, I slowly regained my memory.

Parts of it anyway.

I remembered Danny telling me Kai had ordered him to take me to a safe house. I remembered being in the car when Miles phoned him and accused him of being in contact with Detective Anderson. And I remembered Miles accusing Danny of betraying Kai, and Danny protesting his innocence.

Miles told me they initially thought Jane was involved but he was sure she wasn't. I agreed with him, there was no way the timid woman would ever work against Kai. I'd asked Miles what happened to Jane, and he told me that after Kai interrogated her, he let her go. At least someone was able to get on with their life.

Much to his reluctance, Miles told me what happened when he and Kai arrived at the crash. As he was speaking, a flashback took hold and I felt like I was back in the moment when the truck hit the car. I remembered the all-consuming fear that riddled my body when Danny pulled Angel from the wreck and dragged her away.

I cried all day and all night after remembering that part, and I had never wanted to feel Kai wrapped around me so badly as much as I did then.

When Miles told me Kai had teams of men scoping the city every day looking for Danny, I decided I'd had enough of sitting around helplessly and wanted to go on one of the missions. Obviously, that was never going to happen. Even if I hadn't been recovering from my injuries, there was no way on god's green earth Kai would let me go.

That's when Miles dropped the bombshell that I couldn't leave the penthouse even if I wanted to. I had a big red target painted on my back thanks to an anonymous asshole who had put an ad on the dark web to kidnap me for a reward of a million dollars.

Miles didn't know who had put the ad on the dark web, it was untraceable. I'd asked Miles how the dark web worked, and he'd bored me to tears about the ins and outs. Something to do with onions. Or was it leeks? Either way, it made no sense, not that it mattered. By the time Miles tried to find the ad after the crash, it had been removed.

Still, Kai was taking no chances, and until Detective Anderson had been located, I wasn't leaving the penthouse, and no way I was being left alone.

After that, I didn't grumble about being confined to the penthouse, besides, where was I going to go? Not at least until Angel was found, then we'd be hot footing it as far from Hollows Bay as I could get us.

The good thing about being confined to the house was that my physical injuries were getting better from all the sitting around I was doing. Aside from the ache in my muscles, the cuts started healing, and ugly yellow marks mottled my skin as the bruises disappeared. It wasn't the look I was aiming for but at least I was on the mend.

The constant headache finally disappeared, and although it was just over a week since the crash, Dr. Harris was pleased with how my arm was doing, and agreed I no longer needed to wear the stupid sling, so long as I didn't overdo it.

Given that I wasn't going anywhere until Angel was home, I wasn't about to start swinging around a pole again in order to feed her, so there was no protesting on my part. Plus I was glad to be rid of the damn thing, it made showering very difficult.

Dr. Harris let slip that Kai was paying a small fortune for me to have daily intense physio sessions with a respected physiotherapist called Jenny Sinclair. Jenny was a no-nonsense ballbuster, but she was what I needed to get my arm moving quickly.

She was a tall woman who towered over me, making her seem quite intimidating, but once I got to know her, she was actually really kind, albeit strict about making sure I stuck to my recovery plan.

Jenny came every day, and we spent several hours in the gym going over exercises to help get my shoulder moving. Most days when she left, I wanted nothing more than to curse her out for the ache left behind in my shoulder, but when I started seeing results in a short space of time, I was glad she was being as strict as she was.

Jenny was usually chatty, she always started the session bitching about how she was practically strip searched anytime she came to the apartment. I felt bad for her, but I won't lie and say I wasn't a little relieved to know just how seriously Kai was taking my safety.

About a week into my sessions, Jenny arrived in the afternoon and I immediately knew something was off. She was scared of her own shadow, jumping at every little noise. By the time the session was almost over, she was a nervous wreck. She constantly glanced at the door like she was expecting Satan himself to come bursting through it and demand she spend all of eternity as his bride.

"Are you okay?" I asked her tentatively. Not that it was any of my business if she wasn't, but she was putting me on edge, and my own nerves weren't fully intact right now.

She couldn't meet my eye, instead once again looking over at the door. "I'm fine."

Not convinced, but not wanting to pry, I carried on with the exercise. She was making me lift dumbbells above my head and hold them for ten seconds before I could bring my arms down again. It hurt like an absolute bitch. Figuring I should focus on the exercise rather than on something she clearly didn't want to talk about, I lifted the weight again.

Jenny watched, although from the corner of my eye, I could see she wasn't *actually* watching me. Her eyes were glazed over, and I wouldn't have been surprised if she didn't know where in the world she was right then.

When I started the second reps of the exercise, Jenny snapped out of the weird trance she was in and glanced down at her watch before letting out the biggest sigh.

"Carry on, I need to go to the bathroom," she said, but not really *to* me. She didn't give me a chance to reply before she spun on her heel and took determined strides over to where the adjoining bathroom was. I watched her go, my brows pulled into confusion at what the hell was going on with her, but as it turned out, I didn't have to wait long to find out.

A few minutes later, Jenny came out of the bathroom, her face as white as Casper the ghost. I gaped at her as she walked closer towards me, and it took my brain a few seconds to process that she was clutching a phone in her hand. Ordinarily, the sight of a phone wouldn't have sent chills down my spine, but with the way she had been acting all afternoon, the sight terrified me.

"I'm...I'm so sorry, I didn't have a choice," Jenny said when I gave her a questioning look. Her voice shook and tears welled in her emerald eyes. With a trembling hand, she held the phone out to me. I stared at the thing for a long second, seeing it more as a bomb about to detonate rather than an innocuous looking phone. "Please, Riley," she begged, breaking my stare from the phone as the first tear slid down her flushed cheek.

Dread pooled in the pit of my stomach. My brain yelled at me not to take it, that nothing good could come of talking to whoever was on the other end of the line. But my stomach told me to take it and tell whoever was on the other end to go fuck themselves and remind them of the big bad wolf that was after them.

My stomach eventually won. With my own hands shaking, I reached out and took the phone from Jenny, her whole body sagging with relief now that she had passed the ticking time bomb onto someone else.

I didn't speak when I took the phone, just held it up to my ear and waited.

"Is she there?" a familiar voice growled, almost making me drop the phone in shock.

No.

No, I couldn't be right.

Right?

"Jenny, where the fuck is Riley? I don't have long," the voice growled again, proving that I was indeed right. Red mist clouded my vision as anger swept through me like a tidal wave. My hand crushed the phone to my ear as my brain tried to compose words.

"You fucking bastard," I gritted out through clenched teeth. "Where the fuck is my sister?!" My words came out in a furious yell that echoed around the silent gym, my sudden outburst startling Jenny who took a step away from me as she watched the scene unfold with a horror-struck look on her face.

"Riley, I need you to listen to me," Danny rushed out.

The audacity of this man, honestly.

First, he betrays his boss. Secondly, he kidnaps my sister, and now he has the cheek to tell me *I* have to listen to *him*.

Un-fucking-real.

"No, I haven't got to listen to you. Tell me where the fuck my sister is!" My wrath got the better of me, and a frustrated sob left my lips as angry tears filled my eyes.

"I was set up, Riley! I didn't have a choice but to take her!" Danny roared back.

My chest tightened. It felt like an invisible hand had wrapped around my throat and was squeezing the air out of my lungs, making it impossible to breathe.

"You're full of shit, Danny. I swear to god if you don't tell me where Angel is, I will march my ass straight to Kai and give him the phone right this second," I screeched in frustration. I knew damn well my plan was flawed, Danny would hang up the phone before I had a chance to find Kai, that was if he was even somewhere in the apartment.

"Please, Riley. Just give me one minute to explain everything. If you don't believe me, you can go straight to Kai and tell him all about this call, but please give me one damn minute."

I heard the plea in his voice and once again, my brain and gut fought for dominance, with my head saying to go straight to Kai, and my gut saying to hear him out. My eyes locked on Jenny, who by now had tears streaming down her face, but was watching with rapt attention.

Staring at her, comprehension dawned. She had said she didn't have a choice. I'd bet my last fucking dollar that Danny had found a way to blackmail her into helping him, and if Kai ever found out she had been instrumental in Danny making contact with me, it would be Goodnight Vienna for her.

Fuck sake.

"One. Minute," I said, doing my best to channel Kai's deadly calmness when shit was going down. I kept my eyes fixed on Jenny, silently letting her know she was the sole reason I was giving the asshole a chance to explain.

She received my message loud and clear, mouthing a, *'thank you,'* before walking to the other side of the room and crouching down against the wall.

"Thank you, Riles," Danny sighed, drawing my attention back to the phone.

"Don't fucking call me that. Where's Angel?" I hissed back, the anger flaring again at his use of my abbreviated name, something he always called me with fondness before all this shit happened.

"She's safe, I promise you. She had some cuts and bruises from the crash, but they're healing fine. She misses you, but she understands why I had to take her."

The invisible hand squeezing my throat moved down until it had a tight grip on my heart, and my knees buckled. I fell to the ground, thankfully landing on a padded mat as relief swamped me.

She was alive.

There was so much sincerity in Danny's voice that I couldn't help but believe him. I accepted he had pulled the wool over everyone's eyes, and there was every chance he was feeding me a ton of bullshit, but there was *something* in the way he spoke that convinced me he was telling the truth. It was like old times, when he'd spoken about Angel with nothing but fondness for her.

The tears I had been holding back slowly trickled down my face as I curled my knees up to my body and wrapped the hand that wasn't holding the phone around them.

"Can I see her, can you send a picture or something?" It came out more like a choked whisper, full of desperation. But I was desperate, more than anything, I just wanted to make sure she was okay with my own eyes.

"I can't, I'm on a burner phone that doesn't take photos or videos. But I promise you Riles, she's safe. And driving me crazy for that matter," he chuckled, his words mixed with a whole heap of adoration, and I couldn't stop the little twitch of a smile tugging at my lips. Even his use of my nickname didn't bother me this time.

"Can you at least tell me where she is?"

There was a pregnant pause before he finally answered. "Not yet. Not until I can find the evidence I need to prove I was set up."

His words were the reminder I needed to relight the fire under my skin that had begun to recede at knowing Angel was okay. I needed to remember that he had betrayed Kai and stolen my sister away for reasons only known to him. But before I could respond, he continued.

"Hendrix set me up."

As if I had stuck my fingers into an electric socket, a memory flashed through my head. One I hadn't remembered until now, until the mention of Hendrix's name from Danny's mouth.

Something doesn't feel quite right, would Kai really pack me off to a safe house without talking to me first? I mean, I know I haven't spoken to him for the past few days but surely he would talk to me first. I grab for Angel's hand, hoping to find some comfort without scaring her, but the perceptive little bugger knows something is up if the little squeeze of my hand she gives is anything to go by.

The elevator doors slide open and we follow Danny towards the parked cars. Frank appears from an office that I hadn't ever seen before, he usually waits by the cars when he chauffeurs us somewhere.

"Everything okay?" Frank asks Danny and I hear the hint of suspicion in his voice.

"All good Franky boy, we're headed out," Danny tells him in return. He opens the car and starts loading our bags into the trunk.

"Where are you going?" Frank asks, curious about the sudden journey, and that only makes me feel even more anxious about what the hell is happening.

"Riley's being moved to a safe house. Kai's orders."

I breathe a sigh of relief knowing Angel wasn't able to read Danny's lips as his back is turned. I really don't want her to know we are going to a safe house, it might scare her.

"Kai said that?" Frank says with raised eyebrows. He clearly didn't know about this little trip which doesn't help to allay the butterflies in my tummy. Danny waves us to the car, indicating we should get in. I drop Angel's hand and flick my hand telling her to get in first, and then I start climbing in next to her. Just before the door shuts, I hear Danny's reply.

"Yeah man, what's the problem? I got a call from Hendrix like twenty minutes ago saying Kai wanted Riley moved to the safe house pronto. Give him a call if you don't fucking believe me."

Holy shit.

"Hendrix told you Kai had given the order." The words came out slowly as the memory played again in my head, the pieces of the puzzle slotting into place.

"Yeah," Danny laughed, but there was no humor this time. "I should have known Kai never would have moved you to a safe house without taking you there personally and making sure you were on board with it. I fucking fell for it hook, line, and sinker.

"The last few days leading up to that day, I caught Hendrix having secret phone calls, and he was acting all sneaky and shit. I didn't think anything of it, just assumed he was working on something he didn't want Kai to know about straight away, but when Miles called and said the phone found at Anderson's house only had one number in it, and it was mine, the penny dropped. I think he sent those messages from a burner phone to make it look like *I* sent the messages. He knows I hate texting and always shorten my words, and he copied it to make it look like it was me who was talking to the bent cop or something like that. I'm not sure yet, tech isn't my strong point."

Oh. My. Fucking. God.

Another memory flashed in my mind, one from well before the crash. It was the night I had struggled to sleep and went to get some milk. Hendrix had been sitting at the kitchen counter, and I'd heard him on the phone. He'd said, *'It'll be done, Boss.'* I'd assumed he was talking to Kai, but what if he wasn't? What if he'd been plotting something all along?

"We have to tell Kai!" I shrieked, making Jenny, who was still crying in the corner, flinch.

"We can't Riles, he'll never believe you. Not without hard proof. Look at the evidence, a phone with messages allegedly between me and Anderson, the timing of the crash, and me taking Angel, it all points to me, so unless there is something to prove otherwise, the second Kai sees me, he'll put a bullet in my head without giving me a chance to explain."

He was right. Fuck, it did look bad. Kai believed he'd been fooled by Danny once, and everything *did* point to him betraying Kai. Kai was stubborn at the best of times, there was no way he would listen to a word Danny had to say without irrefutable proof.

"Doesn't explain why you took Angel," I said, remembering how Danny had dragged her away.

"I was going to come back for you, but I had to get her somewhere safe. Riles, you were the target, do you think for one second those fuckers who were there for you would have thought twice about shooting her."

I squeezed my eyes closed as pain tore through my chest and images of Angel bleeding to death in my arms came unbidden into my mind.

Danny was right again. Here I was thinking Danny had taken Angel for his own sick game when really, he had been protecting her.

"I was going to come back for you, I promise. The second I had her somewhere safe, I was going to come back, but when Kai and Miles got there, I knew Miles would have told Kai what he thought had happened, Kai would have killed me on the spot."

What a fucking mess. Hendrix had a lot to answer for.

Nervous energy zapped through my body, and I suddenly had the need to move. I stood from the mat before beginning to pace up and down the length of the gym trying to make sense of everything.

"Why can't you let Angel go now, Danny? Just find a way to bring her back to me," my voice cracked in desperation. I *needed* to hold my sister, needed to see her with my own eyes.

"I can't Riles," he said, sighing heavily. "She's my insurance policy until Kai gets the proof he needs to see who the real traitor is."

Fury like I had never felt before hit me like a lightning bolt, and any sympathy I was beginning to feel for Danny vanished into thin air.

"Your insurance policy?" I shrieked, unable to control the volume of my voice. "That's my fucking sister you're talking about, Danny. She's a little girl, not something that can be bartered with, you asshole!"

"Riley, I know you are mad, and believe me, I hate myself for what I've done to you and Angel. If there was any other way, I would have taken it, and I'll spend the rest of my days making it up to both of you. I promise you though, I won't let anything happen to her."

The regret and sincerity in his tone made me close my mouth. Shouting at him wouldn't bring me any closer to getting her back. There would be a time when I could kick Danny's ass for using Angel as his 'insurance policy,' but right now, we needed to figure out a way to find proof that Hendrix was the one Kai needed to destroy.

"What do we do then? How do we find the evidence?"

"Not we," Danny said. "You. I can't come within a mile of the city without it getting back to Kai one way or another. You're going to need to find the evidence without my help."

"How?!" I exclaimed, not knowing where the hell I would start. Who did he think I was, *Sherlock Fucking Holmes?* Jesus, I barely knew how to work a phone or a computer, did he think I was suddenly going to gain some all-seeing power overnight?

"You need to get Miles on board. He'll know what to do, but Kai can't know, Riley, not yet," Danny replied firmly, and in response, I slapped a palm against my forehead, cursing that this was my life.

How on earth was I going to convince Miles that not only was Danny innocent, but to go against his boss to find the evidence to prove his other friend was the one who had been disloyal all along?

Funnily enough, my head started pounding.

"Danny. This is insane, Miles will never-" I started to protest but he cut me off.

"You have to try, Riley, he's the only one we can trust, and he knows what he is doing with all the tech stuff, he'll find what we need, you just need to get him on board."

"Fucking hell," I sighed, crestfallen at the mammoth task laid out in front of me. What an absolute shambles my life had become. Why couldn't I have just been happy swinging around my pole, shaking my booty for dirty old men, and making enough money to put bread and water in front of Angel?

Oh yeah, I was trying to make her life better.

Kinda fucked that up.

"There's one more thing," Danny murmured.

"Of course there is," I replied sarcastically. Because, *of course* there was going to be another little plot twist to this ridiculous tale of woe.

"Kai's got Jane locked up in the basement. She hasn't got anything to do with this, Hendrix dragged her into this shit to make it easier to convince Kai of my involvement."

What. The. Actual. Fuck?

"No," I whispered in disbelief. "Miles told me Kai let Jane go."

"He lied. Ironic, huh?"

He could say that again. My stomach twisted with disgust followed by a pang of sympathy for the woman, it had been well over a week since the ambush, had she been Kai's prisoner all this time?

"How do you know she's in the basement?"

"I don't for sure," Danny replied sadly. "But Kai will want her close by in case I try to break her out. He'll have someone watching her around the clock as well."

I pinched the bridge of my nose, trying to relieve some of the building tension in my head. "This keeps getting better and better," I mumbled, almost to myself.

"Riley, she won't survive Kai's treatment, she's not like us."

"Us?" I hissed, offended that Danny had categorized me in the same bracket as him.

"Yeah, Riles, we're fighters. We do what the fuck we need to do to survive, but Jane, she doesn't have that in her. I need you to find her and get her out of there," he said matter of factly.

My mouth dropped open at his request. Like I could just walk into a cell that was being guarded twenty-four-seven, no doubt by some scary ass bastard who had a scary ass gun, and walk her out of there without anyone running to Kai and blabbing on me.

It was on the tip of my tongue to tell Danny to get fucked, and that I would use Jane as *my* insurance policy in exchange for getting Angel back, but even as I thought it, I knew I couldn't use the poor woman for my own gain. She was innocent in all this, just like Angel.

Once again, I squeezed my eyes shut, hoping that when I opened them, Angel and I would be back in our shitty apartment, and this was all a bad dream. Of course, when I opened my eyes, I was still in the gym, still clutching the phone, and Danny was waiting for me to reply.

And then, for the first time in a week, and at the worst possible moment, my brain had one of its amazing brain to mouth malfunctions. I should have said, *'No freaking way am I doing that!'* Instead, my mouth opened and what came out was, "I'll see what I can do."

Fuck my life.

I was way, *way,* out of my depth, and it looked as if things were only going to get worse from here on out.

Chapter 5

Kai

"I want a progress report. Why the fuck haven't we found the cunt yet?" I snarled at Miles as I walked into the kitchen to find him sitting at the breakfast bar staring at his laptop. Hendrix stood behind him, leaning against the counter and a fresh cup of coffee in his hand.

To say I was frustrated with the lack of progress we had made to find Danny would be an understatement. Wherever he was, he was doing a damn good job at not sticking his ugly fucking face out from the rock he'd crawled under.

It had been a whole week since Riley had regained consciousness, a whole one hundred and sixty eight hours with no sign of the bastard. Seven full days of watching Riley from a distance while she tried to survive her own personal nightmare and not being able to do a damn thing to help her.

I ached to hold her in my arms, and every night I fought my own demons to stop myself from going to her room to make sure she was okay.

Especially after one night when she had been inconsolable and I was genuinely concerned for her mental state. Miles told me the next day she had regained some of her memory, including the one where Danny dragged Angel away from her. I watched her from the camera in her room, watching as she bawled her goddamn heart out, and all I wanted to do was go to her.

Instead, I got blind stinking drunk and passed out.

My head was a fucking mess. I wasn't sleeping, barely eating, and not giving a fuck that my businesses were falling apart. All I wanted was Riley, but she made it clear how she felt about me, and as much as it killed me, I had to respect that she didn't want anything to do with me anymore.

Even if there were times when part of me still wanted to burst into her room and tell her she was never leaving me.

The only thing that had my full attention was the search for Danny. In my head, I thought if I found him and returned Angel back to Riley safe and in one piece, then maybe, *just maybe,* she might decide she didn't really want to leave at all.

I'd been beasting Hendrix and Miles, making them work all hours around the clock doing what they could to locate Danny. The pair of them were as shattered as I was, the heavy bags under both their eyes were a telltale sign of how exhausted they both were.

When Miles wasn't keeping Riley company, something I only trusted him with as Riley wasn't a fan of Hendrix, he was working day and night, monitoring different databases that might give an indication of where Danny was hiding. He also spent hours reading through the documents on Detective Anderson's background in the hope that *something* would give us a lead to where he or Danny could be.

Hendrix had not only been following up potential leads, but had also been dealing with a number of business deals because I wasn't in the right frame of mind. He had always had my back, but he was proving his capability to step up to be my second in command more and more.

"No word from any of my sources," Hendrix spoke first, sounding as resigned as I felt. "We've searched his room again on the off chance we missed something the first time we turned it over. We've searched the apartment he rents out on Main Street, we've even searched the foster homes he grew up in, nothing." He grimaced into his coffee, withering from the glare I gave him.

"What about Jane? Anyone in her family who might be helping him?" I knew what the answer would be, but I didn't want a single stone left unturned.

"Jane's house and her mom's old house have been searched and perimeter alarms set should he decide to try and hide out there, but so far, nothing. Danny is using the same fucking vanishing trick that Anderson has been using all this time." He gripped his mug so tight that it was a good job he put it down on the side before it cracked. "Kai, he's not in Hollows Bay, he probably hasn't been since the day of the ambush. He could be anywhere in the world right now, it's like looking for a fucking needle in a very large haystack," Hendrix grumbled.

He was right. We'd been focusing our attention on Hollows Bay because Danny had no connection to anywhere else in the world. He was born and bred in Hollows Bay and he always said he would never leave. But what choice did he have now he was a wanted man, and *everyone* knew he was wanted.

"I have a theory about where he could be, but I don't think you'll like it," Miles said, finally tearing his gaze away from his computer screen. He was tense, his shoulders hunched, and his expression was one of caution.

"What part of any of this do I like?" I huffed, pouring my own mug of coffee before taking a stool opposite Miles and sitting down. "Let's hear it then."

"Right," Miles closed the lid of his laptop and took a deep breath. "I've gone through all the files Isaac sent over to us regarding John Anderson. Isaac told you he went into the care system when his mum died and he bounced around care homes until he was nine?" he paused, awaiting confirmation that I already knew this. I nodded.

"Well, if we think Danny is working with Anderson then there has to be a link between them, right?"

"Get to the point, Miles," I snapped, beginning to lose my patience at his rambling.

"Sorry," he said sheepishly before continuing. "We've known Danny most of our lives, so I figured the link between him and Anderson could have been when Danny was in foster homes. I dug through his records and identified all the care homes he used to live in."

"Let me guess, he was in one with Anderson," Hendrix chimed in.

"No," Miles smirked, he always enjoyed proving us wrong. "Danny spent all his time in different care homes, but all of them were somewhere in Hollows Bay, While he was in one particular care home in East Bay, another kid moved in, by the name of Michael Tucker."

The name rang a bell, but I couldn't figure out who he was.

"Is that meant to mean something?" Hendrix asked, clearly on the same page as me.

Miles sighed. "Yes, it's meant to mean something," he replied, exasperated. "Don't you remember when Isaac was briefing you on the research he'd done on Anderson's background? He said he'd found his family who died, and most of their personal records had been deleted, to the point where it wasn't possible to identify names of other kids they'd fostered or adopted?"

The penny dropped. Isaac *had* said that, but there was one name of a kid still held on the record.

Michael Tucker.

"Holy shit," I said. I mean, it was a bit of a tenuous link, but it was still a link, more than what we had before now.

"That's not all, and this is the bit you're not going to like," Miles said. I waited patiently, trying not to snap his head off to tell me what I needed to know. "Before Anderson was adopted by the Brown family and moved to Florida, one of the care homes he lived in was in Forest Point."

Instantly, tension filled the air.

"Fuck," Hendrix growled.

"Told you you wouldn't like it," Miles mumbled.

He wasn't fucking wrong.

Forest Point was a massive no go area. When my great-grandfather had been running Hollows Bay, he had waged a war on Forest Point, the city across the border in another state and was run by the Bianchi family.

My great-grandfather had been an arrogant man and thought he could take on the Italian Mafia. He was wrong of course, and the fallout had been spectacular, resulting in my great-grandfather losing his life. Once my grandfather took his father's place, he talked the head of the Bianchi family into agreeing to a peace treaty.

Both parties agreed that neither the Wolfe family, nor their associates would set foot in Forest Point, and because my great-grandfather had started the dispute, my grandfather had to pay a fee of ten million dollars. The final agreement was that for as long as the Wolfe family ruled Hollows Bay, we would continuously pay the Bianchis 5% from the sale of our drugs and weapons.

In exchange for the Bianchi family agreeing to the treaty, they vowed never to seek retribution against us. The treaty passed from my grandfather to my father, and then on to me. I vowed that for as long as I had Hollows Bay under my control, I would never break the agreement. The Bianchis had a lot of power behind them, and it wasn't a battle worth fighting unless they forced my hand.

If Miles' theory was right, that Danny knew Anderson through a shared connection with Michael Tucker, and Anderson had connections to Forest Point, there could be a chance that he and Danny were hiding out there. If that was the case, and if the Bianchis got wind that one of my men was on their territory, there would be the biggest shitstorm landing at my door. Bigger than anything I was dealing with right now.

The three of us were silent for a few minutes. The information spun around in my head as I tried to come up with another plausible explanation, when deep down, I knew there wasn't going to be one. It would make sense as to why we hadn't been able to track down Danny or Anderson.

"What do you know about this kid, Michael Tucker?" Although, if he had been in a care home with Danny, he wasn't a kid now.

"I'm still trying to find him, there are a lot of Michael Tuckers in the world, and whoever erased the family records did a good job at making sure Tucker would be hard to find," Miles replied. "I think Isaac was right though, his whole *someone leaving you breadcrumbs* theory makes a lot of sense right about now."

"It's just a theory though, right? It's a bit of a long shot," Hendrix said, but his words held no conviction.

"Yep, it's a theory." Miles yawned and then stood up, his bones cracked when he stretched. "I need to crash for a few hours before my brain starts shutting down."

"It's good work, Miles, get some rest," I called to his retreating back as he left the kitchen, wishing I could go to my own room and sleep, but knowing full well all the new information would only add to the thoughts that already kept me awake.

"What do you think?" Hendrix asked when Miles' footsteps had disappeared down the hallway.

"It's a good theory." I paused, thinking about it again. "Actually, it's a damn good theory."

"Yeah, it is," Hendrix agreed reluctantly.

We both fell silent. My brain raced with all sorts of possibilities about what the fuck my next steps were going to be. If Danny was laying low in Forest Point, even if someone told me exactly where he was, I couldn't go waltzing into the city without causing World War Three. I reached for my coffee and took a mouthful, almost spitting it back out when I realized it had gone cold.

Fuck sake.

I stood, intending to pour myself a fresh one when really, I could have done with a whiskey right about now.

"What are you thinking, Boss?" Hendrix questioned after another few minutes of silence passed.

"I don't fucking know," I growled. "This is a fucking nightmare." Abandoning the idea of coffee, I slammed my mug down on the side. "We're missing something. Even if Danny has some kind of connection to a kid he met in a care home years ago, why the fuck would Anderson want to bring me down? I mean, why kill Theo? What does Danny stand to gain from all of this? We're missing pieces of the jigsaw."

"Maybe the Bianchis are behind all of this," Hendrix suggested. I'd be lying if I said the thought hadn't crossed my mind, but I didn't believe it.

"They don't stand to gain anything, why risk losing the 5% they get from us for doing fuck all? Besides, since the treaty, our numbers have grown to equal theirs, in fact, we probably have more numbers on our side. It's not a risk Georgio Bianchi would take."

Georgio was the current head of the Bianchi family, he had been in power when my father had been, and was rumored to be a ruthless fucker, more so than me, especially after his wife had been murdered leaving his twins motherless.

I rubbed my hand against the stubble growing on my cheeks as I thought. I fucking hated having stubble but I hadn't bothered to shave, something I'd rectify soon. Leaning back against the counter, I crossed one leg over the other and stared at Hendrix, hoping he might have some answers, 'cos I sure as shit didn't have any. But he stared down at the floor, the cogs in his head turning as much as they were in mine.

"I agree, we are missing something. What it is though, I have no fucking clue." He sighed and stood. "But I can at least start somewhere. I've got a few sources with links to Forest Point that might be able to help out with locating Danny if he is there."

The fact he had sources in Forest Point wasn't news to me, he had sources in most places across the US. Hendrix was a resourceful man, it was one of the reasons why I kept him close, he had a way of getting information that no one else could get. I just hoped he was able to get something on Danny before the Bianchis found out that one of my men might be in their territory.

Hendrix pulled his phone out of his pocket and tapped away at it, no doubt already arranging to meet one of his contacts. He gave me a curt nod and then turned to walk out, but I stopped him before he got too far.

"Hendrix. Before you go." He stopped and turned back to face me, a questioning brow raised. I took several steps over to where he was waiting by the door, stopping short in front of him. "Look, you know it's been hard since Theo died for me to think about promoting anyone to be my second in command."

My voice suddenly turned thick with emotion, like it always did when I spoke about my brother. It seemed there were only two things in my life that could penetrate my blackened soul and make me feel real emotion.

My brother, and my Star.

"Yeah, course." Hendrix shrugged, trying to remain casual, but the grimace on his face said otherwise. He was another one that didn't like to show any emotion when it came to Theo but also failed to mask it.

"Over the last week, you've proved your loyalty to me. You've stepped up when I've been distracted and have handled all the business when I haven't been able to. If you hadn't done that, I don't know what the fuck would have happened to my city."

Hendrix gave me a gentle slap on the arm. "Just doing my job, Kai." He almost seemed embarrassed. In fairness, it wasn't like I ever dished out praise.

Threats, yes. But not praise.

I hesitated over the next words. Not because I didn't want to say them, but because once they were out, I would be replacing Theo, and that was hard to accept. Still, if anyone was deserving of a promotion, it was Hendrix. "I want you to be my 2IC."

Hendrix gaped at me for a long second, looking as though he hadn't heard me correctly. "You...you want me to be your second in command?" he eventually said with a dry voice, his eyes narrowed in confusion.

"I do. Like I said, you've proved your loyalty, and I couldn't run this organization without you. So yes, I want you to be my second. Do you accept?"

He was quiet for a minute and I gave him time to consider. It was a huge step up, I didn't have an heir so if anything happened to me, Hendrix would take my position. But not only that, he would be responsible for so many more decisions, decisions which could cost money and lives. It was a massive responsibility I was asking him to take on, so it was only right he had time to consider it.

"Kai, I'd be honored. Fuck, yeah I accept." He beamed at me and I instantly felt a little weight lift from my shoulders. Running not just a city, but gangs, arms dealing, and trying to manage a number of legitimate businesses was a heavy burden, and one I was grateful I could now share with Hendrix. I reached out my hand and he took it, shaking it firmly and confirming his acceptance.

"I can't tell you how much this means to me, Kai, I won't let you down," Hendrix said enthusiastically.

"I know you won't because if you do you will pay with your life." My tone was deadly serious because I was being *deadly* serious. If Hendrix fucked up, he would pay with blood and he needed to be aware of that. He grimaced and his face paled, but he gave a small nod of his head, acknowledging what was at stake.

When his phone beeped, I dropped his hand so he could read the text. "I think I've got a lead already. I'll tie in with you later." He turned and headed out of the door before I could reply, disappearing from my view, and it was only moments later when I heard the ding of the elevator.

I was about to head back to my room to throw on a suit and head into the city when the most beautiful sight I had ever seen appeared in the doorway. My mouth dropped open in surprise at seeing Riley standing there looking back at me with her gorgeous doe eyes.

She looked good.

Better than good compared to the last time I saw her. Her arm was no longer in the sling, and the cuts and bruises that had marred her soft skin had started to heal.

"Hi," she said shyly, giving me a little wave of her hand. The sound of her voice was like music to my ears. I ran my eyes over her body, not really believing she was there. She was barefoot and had baggy jogging bottoms on, but on her top half, she wore a plain vest with no bra underneath. Her nipples poked through the thin material and the sight went straight to my cock.

"Hi," I replied, trying to keep any hint of hope out of my voice. Hope was a very dangerous thing.

Riley took a tentative step into the kitchen. She looked up from under her long lashes and my fingers twitched with the need to reach out and touch her. To drag her against my body, and feel her pressed against me. Her scent of strawberries and sunscreen invaded my senses, and as I stared down into her gorgeous chocolate brown eyes, her mouth curled into the tiniest smile.

"I didn't think anyone would be up yet-"

"I can go if you want?" I interrupted, desperately hoping like a fucking idiot that she would grant me permission to stay in the kitchen of my own home.

"No," she said quickly, her eyes darting around the room nervously. "No, it's fine. It would be nice to have some company."

It took everything in me to refrain from fist-bumping the air like a pathetic teenager who'd just been invited to prom by the head cheerleader.

She gave me a small, but genuine smile, and for the first time since she told me to get out of her room all those days ago, my heart started beating again.

Chapter 6

Riley

What in the ever living fuck was I going to do?

That was the question that churned around in my head the minute Danny hung up on me, and remained churning in my head until the following morning. Once again, sleep eluded me until eventually, I dragged my exhausted ass out of bed to watch the sun rise over the city.

I wish I could say I had a plan.

The way I saw it, I had three options.

Option one. Tell Kai everything and hope like hell he would believe me when telling him Danny was innocent, and *Hendrix* was the one he should be after. But this was Kai, the most stubborn, pig-headed man on the planet. Deep down, I knew Danny was right, the only way Kai would believe Danny was innocent was if he had undeniable proof put under his nose.

Which I didn't have.

Yet.

Option two. Do nothing. Pretend the call didn't happen and live in pretend blissful ignorance that everything was as it should be. But I dismissed that option straight away. There was no way I could leave Jane rotting in a cell or watch Kai get fooled again and again by Hendrix. Not to mention that if I did nothing, I was basically condemning an innocent man to death.

So that left option three. Somehow I had to get Miles on my side, find *irrefutable* proof Hendrix was the one to betray Kai, free Jane, and hope Danny was true to his word that Angel would be looked after while I was on my one-woman mission to save the world.

Easy, right?

Resting my head against the cool window, I sighed heavily, feeling the weight of the world on my shoulders. As if my brain wasn't pickled enough by the current situation, I was also having to pick through my complicated feelings for Kai, the man who consumed my every waking thought.

Even before my call with Danny, some of my anger had faded, and it was only out of sheer stubbornness that I stopped myself from going to find him. It was simple. *I missed him.* Kai might have been a monster, infecting my life with his poison, but it was too late now, his poison was running through my veins and there was no cure for it.

The last few days of not seeing him had been torturous, and I was beyond desperate to lay my eyes on him, to smell his familiar scent, and to feel his hands on me again.

I cared for him. In fact, I *more* than cared for him. But niggling away in the back of my mind was the constant reminder that Angel was caught up in his mess. Not to mention *I'd* been injured because of his mess. What would have happened to her if I hadn't made it out of the crash alive?

It was a question I couldn't bear to think about, so no matter how strongly I felt for Kai, Angel had to be my priority. I couldn't allow myself to be distracted from my ultimate goal: get her back and get the hell out of dodge.

Only when I was far away from Kai Wolfe would I figure out a way to remove him from under my skin and out of my heart.

But the only way Angel was going to return to me in one piece was if I did what Danny had asked me to do, and in order to do that, I needed a freaking miracle.

But I had to try something.

The more I thought about everything, the angrier I became at Hendrix and the sheer audacity at thinking he could betray Kai, frame Danny, and get away with it.

Nope, I *couldn't* let him get away with it.

I should have felt bad when I realized I was condoning Kai killing a man, but didn't Hendrix deserve everything that was coming to him? Didn't he deserve to be the one strung up and tortured until he was begging for the sweet relief of death?

Sheesh, I think I had been spending too much time with Kai.

The image of Hendrix's smug face flashed in my mind and that was just the image I needed for a wave of determination to crest through me.

Hendrix was going to get what was coming to him.

With my newfound determination, I made my way to the bathroom to get ready for the day, something resembling a plan beginning to form in my head.

The first thing I needed to do was make amends with Kai and figure out a way to get him to tell me that Jane was locked up. I couldn't admit to knowing, after all, Miles told me Kai let her go. If I let slip that I knew she was in the clink, he'd smell a rat, and my plan would be foiled before it even got started.

I wasn't going to be able to bust her out, but if I could at least assess the situation around the guards, I could come up with an idea of what the fuck I was going to do.

But seeing as the last time I'd seen Kai, I told him I hated him and I never wanted to think about him again, I couldn't saunter up to him and say,

'Hey, I know we haven't talked in a week, but I was thinking about Jane, I wonder how she is.' No, I had to get him to believe I had calmed down after some time apart and get him to trust me again.

Ultimately, I needed to play him.

Without getting my heart stomped on in the process.

It would be all too easy to allow my true feelings for Kai to grow even deeper and I couldn't afford for that to happen. But I knew how Kai felt about me, and I was going to have to use that to my full advantage if I wanted to get anywhere.

A short while later, dressed in sweatpants and a vest, I quietly padded barefoot through the apartment, intending to loiter in the lounge and wait for Kai to make an appearance.

I wasn't expecting anyone to be awake so I was almost caught off balance when I heard voices coming from the kitchen. Dread pooled in my stomach as I recognized the voice I really hadn't wanted to hear.

Hendrix.

I hadn't seen him since before the ambush, he'd avoided me and I hadn't given him a second thought. Even before all this, I hadn't been his biggest fan. It sounded like he was about to leave, and I was *so* not prepared to face him just yet.

I darted to the side and hid in the shadows, much like I'd done when I got out of bed in the middle of the night and found him talking on the phone to someone he called 'Boss'. Knowing what I knew now, I wondered if that had been Kai he was talking to, or if he had been working with someone else then.

Listening to their conversation, what I heard next made me feel downright sick to my stomach.

Kai was asking him to be his second in command.

No, no, no, no, no.

Fuck, what was Kai doing?

Oh, that's right, he didn't know what a lying, cheating fuckwit he had working for him.

I barely managed to restrain myself from barging in and shouting at the top of my lungs when I remembered what was at stake. As frustrating as it was, I had to get this right, and slow and steady would definitely be the right way.

A few minutes later, Hendrix waltzed out of the kitchen, smiling like the cat that got the damn cream. He was so engrossed in his phone that he didn't see me glaring daggers at him from my hiding place. If looks could kill, that man would have been dead within an instant from the glare I was giving him.

I waited until the elevator dinged and took a deep breath, preparing myself to face the man who haunted my every waking thought.

Stepping through the doorway of the kitchen, Kai looked up when my movement caught his attention. His eyes widened in surprise like he couldn't quite believe I was standing there.

He looked delicious, the stubble that had graced his face the last time I'd seen him had grown thicker, not quite a beard, but not far off. It made him look all the more scary.

And hot.

Really fucking hot.

Butterflies sprang to life in my belly at memories of what it felt like to have his hands on my body, to feel his mouth on mine, his tongue licking my nipples.... It dawned on me just how damn hard it was going to be being around him and not give in to the intense feelings I had for him.

I cleared my throat and gave my head a quick shake as if I could banish the memories, but the images lingered in the back of my mind.

"Hi," I eventually plucked up the courage to say after what seemed like an eternity of the two of us gawking at each other. Like a complete idiot, I gave a little wave with my hand and then immediately felt my cheeks blush at how stupid that must have made me look.

"Hi," he replied. His eyes roamed my body and landed on my braless tits hidden under my vest.

I'd purposely left my bra off as a backup plan to get his attention on the off chance he told me to go away. There was no way he'd want me walking around the house with my nipples poking through the thin material, and right then, thanks to the memories that had been playing in my head, they were rock hard.

I resisted the smile twitching at my lips when Kai noticeably swallowed before his eyes found mine again, the desire blazing like an inferno in his dark orbs.

"I didn't think anyone would be up yet-" I started but Kai interrupted.

"I can go if you want."

"No," I cringed internally when I realized how eager I sounded. "No, it's fine. It would be nice to have some company."

For a moment Kai looked unsure, a look I had never seen on him before, and against my will, my heart softened. I hated seeing my strong, powerful monster unsure of himself. I wanted him back to who he was when I first met him.

"Have a seat and I'll make you some breakfast," Kai said, indicating to the table.

I couldn't help the chuckle breaking free. "You're going to make me breakfast?" Skepticism laced my voice as my lips tugged up into a bigger smile, and in that instant, the tense atmosphere between us eased. Even Kai cracked a smile, his shoulders relaxing, and damn, I'd forgotten how beautiful he was when he smiled. It was a shame it was a rare occasion.

"I'll have you know I can cook a few things." There was a hint of amusement in his tone, and for a second it would have been easy to forget everything else, it was just him and me, alone and enjoying each other's company. But as if to remind me that things were not what they once were, my shoulder twinged, sending a pain shooting down my arm.

Tearing my gaze away from Kai, I walked to the table, ignoring his heated glare on me as I crossed the room.

We were silent for a while as Kai made his way around the kitchen grabbing various items. He whisked a bunch of ingredients together before throwing the mixture in a pan and making an omelet. It only took a few minutes before he put a plate down in front of me, along with a steaming mug of coffee goodness.

"Thank you," I muttered, desperately trying to ignore the blasted butterflies fluttering wildly in my belly while I watched him move around the kitchen. His broad, solid muscles flexing under his t-shirt as he whisked, his firm ass cladded in jeans....holy hell, I was in so much trouble when I realized my panties had dampened.

Kai didn't say anything but slid into the seat next to me. I had suddenly lost my appetite but not wanting to be rude and turn my nose up at the effort he had made, I took a small bite of the eggs, surprise filling me when my mouth watered at how good his omelet tasted.

"This is really good," I said as I shoveled another forkful in. From the corner of my eye, I caught Kai looking smug. He drank his coffee in silence, letting me enjoy my breakfast, but I could feel him watching me in that intense way he had, and fuck me, I had missed that.

"How's your arm?" he asked when I put the fork down. His eyes burned into the side of me so I twisted in his direction, finally allowing myself to look at him. He was close enough that I could see the gold flecks in his black eyes.

"It's good actually, Jenny has been doing a great job." I instantly regretted mentioning her name and I worried for a moment if I looked guilty, but Kai didn't seem to notice, he nodded his head and gave me a tight smile.

"That's good to hear. Although she won't be able to come here for a few days, she had to fly to New York yesterday as her mum was taken ill."

I gaped at Kai as panic began to bubble up. Did he know what she had done? Had he hurt her? Or had she told him a lie to get the hell away from here?

"Oh," I replied, hoping like hell I sounded just the right amount of disappointed and not at all suspicious.

"Doc says you won't need much more physio anyway," Kai said casually, unaware of my internal crisis. I took a sip of my coffee to give myself a chance to compose my features.

"I think he is right, it really does feel much better." As if to prove my point, I rolled my shoulder around, ignoring the twinge of pain that shot through my body. "I'll be twirling around the pole again in no time."

That, apparently, was the wrong thing to say. Kai's eyes grew darker and a growl rumbled in his chest.

"Not that I'll be dancing any time soon," I quickly added. It seemed to appease him so I took the opportunity to change the subject to more pressing matters. Kai didn't need to know that I would probably be dancing a hell of a lot sooner than either he or I wanted, it was the only talent I had to fall back on once I got Angel away from here.

The thought lay heavy in my gut.

"Any news on Danny?" I asked tentatively, crossing my fingers under the table in hopes the answer would be no. At the mention of Danny's name, Kai's jaw clenched, and in the blink of an eye, the stone-cold killer I knew him to be was sitting in front of me.

"I've got my men working around the clock trying to find him but nothing yet."

I let my shoulders slump in relief but Kai must have thought it was out of frustration as he spoke again, only this time, some of the softness was back. "I'll find him, Riley, Angel too. He can't stay hidden forever, and I made a promise that I will get her back for you."

He fixed his dark gaze on me and there was so much emotion swirling around. In such a short space of time, I had come to learn to read Kai and all his crazy emotions, and although he was seething, I couldn't avoid seeing the pain in his eyes.

He was scared.

Scared of what, I didn't know. Maybe losing his status as the King of the city, or maybe something else, like losing me. Or maybe that was wishful thinking on my part. Whatever it was, I hated seeing it on him. He was supposed to be a big, scary, brooding asshole, but to see this look on him, this pity, it almost broke me.

It was on the tip of my tongue to tell him everything and hope like hell he would listen. Without thinking, I reached out and took his hand in mine. The second our hands touched, a bolt of electricity zapped up my arm. Kai's eyes darted to where we were connected before coming back to mine, and as if out of habit, my gaze fell on his mouth.

At that moment, everything fell away. All the bullshit and drama vanished, we were just two people who were crazy about each other, and no matter what adversities were thrown at us, we would get through them because we had each other.

"Kai," I started, dragging my attention back to his eyes and suddenly intent to take the risk and tell him everything. Only, I was interrupted by the biggest asshole on the planet walking back into the room.

"Oh, sorry to interrupt," Hendrix said, sounding anything but sorry. He came to a stop in the doorway when he saw Kai and I sitting at the table and looked from us, to our connected hands and back again. A look of disdain flashed across his face before he composed himself. "Riley, it's good to see you up and about. How are you feeling?"

Visions of me launching out of my seat and throttling him swam in my mind. I withdrew my hand from Kai's and hid it under the table where it clenched into a fist.

I wasn't a violent person, but Hendrix was bringing out the worst in me. Never in my life had I wished for someone to self-combust on the spot, yet here I was wishing death on this man. In fact, not only was I wishing death on him, but I was envisioning being the one to snuff out his life.

"I'm okay, thank you." I tried to keep composed instead of letting the violent thoughts consume me. I needed to get out of here before I said something stupid. Or worse, *did* something stupid, like find a way to embed a kitchen knife into Hendrix's heart.

"I'm sorry to interrupt, Boss, but I have some news," Hendrix said, dismissing me from the conversation and making it quite clear he didn't give one iota about my wellbeing.

Kai snapped into business mode, sitting up taller and squaring his shoulders. "What is it?"

"I should go." I started to get up, suddenly very self-conscious and feeling rather silly that I wasn't wearing a bra. I was fine with Kai seeing the goods, but Hendrix, not so much. Before I could stand, Kai's big hand landed on my thigh and held me firmly in place.

"Go on," Kai said expectantly at Hendrix who gave me a quick look, but must have decided that I was allowed to hear whatever it was he had to say. That was good of him.

The asshole.

"I thought you ought to know, the new Chief of Police for Hollows Bay has just been announced."

"Who?" Kai rumbled, far more interested in this news than I was. I didn't think it would matter who took the top role in the police department, it would only be a matter of time before they were Kai's pet.

"He's not local to the area, in fact, he isn't even from this state. Cop called Max Thorne, spent all his time in Florida."

There was a pregnant pause between the two of them as they seemed to have a silent conversation, Kai's brows furrowed in thought.

"That can't be a coincidence," Kai said.

"I thought that too," Hendrix replied. "Especially as his name was never in the running for consideration, in fact, the job had practically been given to the Deputy Chief."

"Get Miles to start digging, I want to know every single thing about this Max Thorne, including any dirt I can use to get him in my pocket," Kai instructed as he took his hand off my thigh and dug into his pocket to pull out his phone.

"On it," Hendrix chirped, spinning on his heel and striding out of the kitchen with an air of arrogance. His back would have made a perfect target for a knife to land.

Urgh.

"I'm sorry, Riley, but I need to get to work on this," Kai said regretfully.

"Of course, I'll leave you to it."

This time Kai didn't stop me as I rose from my seat, and a pang of disappointment filled me as I started walking away. I didn't want to admit it, but I'd enjoyed being in Kai's company again.

I almost made it out of the kitchen before Kai's voice stopped me in my tracks.

"Riley," he called. I turned to face him, surprised to see he was smirking at me. "Do me a favor?"

"What's that?" I asked, raising a questioning brow.

"Put a bra on."

His heated eyes dropped to my chest where my nipples were still poking through the cotton material. I resisted the smile when I saw Kai's tongue run along his bottom lip and he swallowed.

"Sure."

I turned and walked out of the kitchen with a little bit more sway in my hips, knowing full well his eyes were on my ass.

Point to me.

Chapter 7

Riley

After my breakfast with Kai, I went back to my room feeling even more like the weight of the world was on my shoulders. It felt good being with Kai again, *too fucking good*, and I dreaded to think how hard it was going to be to leave him when the time came.

And that's when I had to acknowledge it.

I loved him.

I could deny it all I liked when I hadn't seen him all week, but half an hour in his presence, and a warm, contented feeling had settled so deep in my bones that I couldn't ignore it any longer.

I had stupidly fallen head over heels in love with the baddest man in the city, and it was only going to end in heartache for us both.

Needing a distraction from my predicament, I spent the morning watching tv, but when hours passed and I had no clue of the nonsense shows I'd been staring at, I decided I needed to find something else to occupy my mind.

Jacqueline brought me a sandwich at lunchtime and informed me that Kai and Hendrix had gone out, but Miles was in the apartment if I needed anything. A heavy sense of apprehension settled over me- it was now or never. The longer I waited to speak to Miles and convince him of Danny's innocence, the longer that cretin, Hendrix, had to fool Kai. And who knew what the hell his long-term plan was.

What if he wanted to kill Kai and take his place now he had been promoted to 2IC? Maybe that was his plan all along.

Like having a rocket shoved up my ass with that thought, I jumped off the sofa and went in search of Miles.

I found him in the gym, pounding the treadmill as he ran at a ridiculously fast pace. He gave me a nod in acknowledgment but didn't break his stride. Seriously, how he did not fly off the back of it with the speed he was going at, I would never know.

His long legs carried him easily though, and not wanting to disturb him, I went over to the weights bench to start the exercises Jenny had instructed me to do.

Heavy bass music thumped around the gym, and as I started lifting the dumbbells, I watched Miles run, debating how to broach the subject. Sweat poured down his back, soaking the vest top and shorts he was wearing, his muscular back flexing every time his feet hit the belt.

Miles was more athletic when compared to Kai, Hendrix, and Danny. Don't get me wrong, he had muscles for days, but he wasn't as bulky as the other three, and seeing him running now, it was clear he was more of an athlete than a weights' monkey.

I'd grown closer to Miles this past week seeing as aside from Jacqueline, Jenny, and Dr. Harris, he was the only other person I had spoken to. I had known Miles was Kai and Theo's cousin, but Miles had opened up a little about his friendship with Theo. They had been born only a few weeks apart so had practically grown up as brothers.

Miles did not have a good word to say about his father, Brian. Much like Kai's dad, Brian was a complete bastard and had bullied Miles for being smaller in build than his cousins, and for being a geek.

I wasn't in the least bit surprised when Miles told me he got sick of his dad's bullying ways and put a bullet through his brain. In fact, if I ever needed more proof that I had spent far too much time with a bunch of killers, this was it. I had been glad Miles had killed his old man.

Miles had been blessed with the good looks that ran in the Wolfe family. I'd asked Miles if he had a girlfriend, and his response had been that he didn't have time to commit to one person, he was too busy hacking into databases and invading people's personal lives.

He'd been more than willing to tell me he had a number of favorite girls at Sapphire who fulfilled any needs he had, which I really didn't need to know.

When I first met Miles, I hadn't really known what to make of him, it had taken time for him to learn to trust me before he relaxed and opened up to me. After getting to know him better, much like Danny, I came to see him as a brother figure, and like anyone I considered family, I wanted to protect him. Protect him from the giant asshole, otherwise known as Hendrix.

After about twenty minutes of Miles sprinting and me attempting to pump weights with my achy shoulder, Miles slowed down to a walk and regained his breath. He guzzled down about a gallon of water before finally coming to a stop and getting off the treadmill. Wiping away the sweat that had soaked his face and neck, he came over to where I was working out and sat on the weight bench next to me. He fiddled with his phone and a second later the music in the gym stopped.

"How's the shoulder doing?" he asked, watching as I lifted the weight above my head and held it for a few seconds. I was pleased it was getting easier to lift the weight, even if it was only light.

"Getting there," I replied. "Sure it won't be long til I'm champion of the world's strongest woman competition."

Miles snorted and rolled his eyes. He laid down on the bench and lifted the bar above him, his huge biceps bulging.

Damn show off.

"Heard you had breakfast with Kai," he said after pumping the weight a couple of times. The mention of Kai's name made my heart rate spike, I was so fucked for that man. I looked over at Miles to find him watching me with a conspiratorial grin on his face.

Miles had been very vocal these last few days in telling me how much Kai had changed since meeting me, and that Kai would be devastated if I left. I'd shut the conversation down several times, not willing to hear what Miles had to say on the topic and not sure my heart could have handled the thought of devastating Kai. It was easier to ignore it than hear what he had to say.

But with the smirk on his face now, it was clear he thought he'd been right all along, that I would eventually come around and forgive Kai.

If only it was that easy.

"It was just breakfast, Miles," I replied, trying to play it down. It was hard enough keeping my own emotions in check. I didn't need Miles to start getting ideas that Kai and I would be back on track, he would just be another one left disappointed when I inevitably left.

"Sure, sure," he replied before resuming his weightlifting.

As Miles carried on with his reps, nerves swam in my belly. Now was my chance to talk to him about Danny, but I didn't have one iota on how to start the conversation, or how Miles would react. Much like Kai, if I blabbed that Danny had been in contact and was declaring his innocence, Miles wouldn't listen. He'd march his ass straight to Kai and everything would go to shit even more than it already was.

No, I couldn't just tell him Hendrix had framed Danny. I needed to start small. Plant a seed of doubt in his head and stand back to let it grow.

Finishing with my weights, I started stretching my arms, waiting patiently for Miles to finish, all the while, nerves getting bigger in the pit of my stomach. When he finished and sat up, he gave me an expectant look, almost as though he knew I had something on my mind.

"What's up?" he asked, confirming my suspicion.

I sighed. Here goes.

"Guess I've been doing a lot of thinking about things these past few days. I just can't wrap my head around Danny betraying Kai. It doesn't make much sense to me."

I waited with bated breath. Miles' face contorted into a murderous scowl, pretty much like anyone else's did whenever Danny's name was mentioned. He rose from the bench and for a second, I thought he was going to storm off. Thankfully, he didn't.

"I never thought he would be capable either, Riley, but just goes to show, you don't always know someone the way you thought you did."

Okay, so that wasn't the worst response. If he thought Danny wasn't capable then maybe there was a slim chance I could plant that seed of doubt.

"I guess so. I dunno, Miles, I just don't get it. What would Danny stand to gain by betraying Kai? His whole life had been dedicated to the Wolfes."

Miles sighed, his shoulders slumping as he came to stand in front of me. "I know you liked Danny, Riley. Fuck, he was our brother. I don't know what he stood to gain, but there is no denying the evidence."

"But what if you were wrong?" I bit out in frustration, not meaning for it to be as harsh as it came out. I knew Miles wouldn't take too kindly to me questioning his mad tech skills, and sure enough, his eyes narrowed as he glared at me.

"Technology doesn't lie, Riley," he ground out, bitterness lacing his tone. "I went through every one of the messages between Danny and

Anderson myself. There's no doubt Danny was the one who had been feeding him information."

"But-"

"And let's not forget where the phone was, who else could have given it to Jane? Danny was fucking her, he had plenty of opportunity to plant the phone on her."

My shoulder sagged in disappointment. He wasn't getting it.

Miles placed a sweaty hand on my good shoulder and gave me a soft smile. "Sorry, Riley, I didn't mean to snap. I'm as pissed off about it all as you are. It's fucking gutting Danny could do this to any of us, but to drag Angel into it as well, it's bullshit. And when Kai gets his hands on Danny, he will pay for the misery he has caused us all."

I don't know if it was the mention of Kai hurting Danny that made me snap. Maybe it was hearing the defeat in Miles' voice, or maybe I had reached the end of my tether with the whole damn situation, but either way, words roared out before I could stop them.

"Danny isn't the one who betrayed Kai. Hendrix fucking set him up!" I yelled. My words echoed around the gym and I wanted to take them back as soon as they were out. So much for planting a seed, I'd just dropped a fucking oak tree.

Miles snarled angrily at me, his nostrils flaring. "What the fuck are you talking about?"

His wrath scared me, I'd never been on the end of Miles' venomous stare. It rivaled the one Kai dished out, showing he was a true Wolfe. There was no taking the words back now, they were out there, and now was crunch time. I could either play them down and make out it was just a theory, or I could tell the truth.

I settled for somewhere in the middle.

"I think Hendrix set Danny up. I had a memory come to me yesterday of before the crash when Danny had taken me and Angel from the apartment. He told Frank that Hendrix had phoned him and told him Kai had ordered him to take me and Angel to a safe house."

"So? That doesn't mean anything, Riley. Danny must have lied to Frank, he would have said anything to get you out of there," Miles snapped, getting angrier by the second. He puffed his chest out, somehow he'd grown in size in the last few seconds and was now towering menacingly over me.

To be fair, he did have a point. Danny *could* have lied to Frank but now the memory was clear in my mind, I knew without doubt, he wasn't lying.

"Miles, you weren't there," I said softly, trying to defuse the bomb standing in front of me. He was more like Kai than I had ever realized. "When you phoned Danny and accused him of being a traitor, Danny was as surprised as I was. And he didn't take Angel from the car to kidnap her, he took her to put her somewhere safe, he knew those men wouldn't have killed me, but wouldn't have given a damn about killing her. He was protecting her."

"How do you know that, Riley?" he growled, taking a step closer to me. I looked away, unable to hold the glint of betrayal in his eyes. "Riley, I swear to god, you need to start talking."

Shit.

It was now or never, and seeing as never wasn't an option...

"I spoke to Danny," I whispered, squeezing my eyes closed and holding my breath as I waited for the bomb to detonate. When it didn't go off, I tentatively cracked open an eye to find Miles watching me carefully.

"How?" he snarled.

"It doesn't matter-"

"It does fucking matter!" His voice boomed around the gym, making me flinch. "If you know where Danny is, you need to fucking tell us!"

"I don't know where he is," I replied holding my hands up and trying to hold on to the slither of courage that was rapidly declining. This was going horribly wrong, by the end of the day, I was going to be hauled in front of Kai and no doubt tortured until I told him everything I knew. "Miles, please. Just hear me out."

He paused for a moment, glaring daggers at me until eventually, he folded his arms across his broad chest and stared at me expectantly. Taking a breath, I was about to open my mouth when a thought occurred to me.

If Miles was a hundred percent sure Danny had been working with Kai's enemy, then why wasn't he on the phone this very instant telling Kai I was a traitorous little bitch? Did that mean he had a tiny slither of doubt? I didn't know. But if there was the slightest chance there was, I needed to turn that slither into a gaping hole.

"Look, I don't know Hendrix that well, but his behavior has always been a little strange toward me," I started as Miles continued to glare. "I heard him on the phone one night, before the crash, before Anderson grabbed me at the charity ball. I'd got out of bed to get some milk and Hendrix was in the kitchen on the phone. Whoever he was talking to was stressing him out, he kept tugging on his hair, and he was saying things like, 'It's not that easy,' and, 'It'll be done.' And then whoever he was talking to, he called them 'Boss.'"

"Fuck sake, Riley, that doesn't mean anything. He was probably talking to Kai," Miles hissed.

"I thought the same thing too, but the way he spoke, Miles, it didn't sound like the way he spoke to Kai."

Miles didn't reply, instead, a muscle ticked in his jaw as he clenched his teeth. I took his silence as permission to carry on. Biting the bullet, I decided to lay all my cards out.

"Think about it, Miles. Hendrix could have been working for someone else. You said yourself that all the messages to Anderson was information Danny had been privy to, but surely if he was privy to it, then so was Hendrix? And the three of you can come and go from Kai's apartment as you see fit, Hendrix could have easily taken the opportunity to sneak into Jane's room and plant the phone. And then on the day of the ambush, Hendrix phones Danny to tell him to get me and Angel out of the house, knowing full well what was lying in store."

Miles dropped his arms and took a deep breath, cogs whirring in his head. The fact he hadn't jumped down my throat and told me I was wrong gave me a small token of hope.

And then, as if a lightbulb went off in his head, Miles' brows rose.

"Fuck," he whispered and ran a hand down his sweaty vest, another trait similar to Kai. "Fuck," he said again, only this time there was pure venom behind it.

"What?" I asked, confused by his sudden change.

"I couldn't figure it out, but that would make sense."

"Miles, what couldn't you figure out?" I asked, having completely lost what he was talking about.

"No one could get hold of Kai. When I found the burner phone on Jane, I tried ringing Kai again and again to tell him. Fuck, Frank even tried calling him but it kept ringing and ringing, and Kai never ignores his phone."

"Okay...."

"There was no logical explanation, I fucking checked his phone while you were being looked over by the doctor, it was working fine after the crash."

"Miles, you're not making much sense," I said, a headache growing behind my eyes from where my brain was using far too much energy to try and figure out what the hell he was going on about.

"Someone must have used a jammer to block the signal to Kai's phone. To do that you have to be close to the phone you are trying to block, like within about twenty meters. I ruled it out because the only way Kai's phone could have been blocked was if someone near him was controlling the jammer," Miles said as the pieces slowly started fitting together in my head. "Hendrix was in the car with him."

Oh shit.

"Fuck!" Miles roared. He stormed over to the pile of weights and picked up a dumbbell before launching it at the huge wall mirror, the thing shattered into a million pieces, making me jump back when glass sprayed everywhere.

For a few minutes, the only sound in the gym was the pounding of my heart and Miles' labored breathing. Neither of us spoke as the reality of the situation set in. A mixture of emotions raged through me, anger mainly, but also vindication. Vindication for Danny.

"We have to tell Kai," Miles said suddenly, turning to face me. His cheeks were bright red, his fists clenched, and his nostrils flaring.

"We can't."

"Of course we fucking can." He stomped back to me, standing mere inches away and towering over me again. "Riley, Kai is being led down a fucking garden path by Hendrix every day. Fuck sake, Kai's just made him his second in command! Do you know what that means?" When I shook my head, he continued with his rant. "It means if something happens to Kai, Hendrix steps up and takes over Hollows Bay. Fuck, if whoever Hendrix is working with is helping him to end Kai, it won't be long until they strike again. If we don't fucking do something now, who knows what will happen next time they strike."

"Miles, you and I know Kai will never just take our word for it. He believed you before because you had the phone with those messages. Hendrix has gotten this far fooling everyone, he's been one step ahead the whole time. What if Hendrix has a plan in place to hurt Kai if Kai confronts him? Kai needs a plan before he takes action against Hendrix, and you know full damn well the only way we will be able to convince Kai that Hendrix is behind all of this is if we have hard evidence."

He paused, seemingly taking in my words before letting out a frustrated roar.

"Fuck, you're right," Miles finally said in resignation, and for the first time since Danny called me, I felt a smidgen of relief. I'd have someone in my corner. "Fine. We get the evidence we need and we present it to Kai, but we need to move fast, Riley, like *really* fucking fast, and we can't let Hendrix be alone with Kai again."

"What do you propose we do?" I asked because I didn't know about Miles, but I was stumped for ideas.

"I need to get back to my place but I've got some ideas. In the meantime, you need to keep Kai away from Hendrix."

"How do you suggest I do that?" I asked, but it was pointless. Miles was already heading out of the gym, lost in his thoughts. The door slammed behind him, leaving me staring at my distorted reflection in the shattered mirror.

So much for having someone in my corner.

Chapter 8

Kai

Instead of focusing on my upcoming meeting with the new Chief of Police, Max Thorne, my mind kept drifting to breakfast with Riley. It was impossible to ignore the tiny pang of hope that had awoken and taken up residence in my chest. Maybe she wouldn't want to leave after all.

I stared blankly at my phone, the words in Miles' report not making any sense when all I could think about was how her voice had sounded after almost a week of not hearing it, her soft, velvet tone was like music to my ears. Or how her beautiful chocolate eyes filled with lust and desire when she watched me make her breakfast. She thought I didn't know she was watching me under her lashes, but Riley should have known by now, I knew everything about her.

Like I knew she purposely didn't wear a bra. The little minx knew I'd fucking hate her walking around the apartment with her pert tits on display, and the second I saw her mouth-watering nipples puckered against her vest, it dawned on me that she had gone without a bra to get my attention.

It fucking worked.

It took everything I had in me not to storm over to her, rip her vest down, and latch on to those sweet buds.

"Anything in there?" Hendrix asked, nodding to my phone and dragging me from my thoughts, which was a good thing given the way my cock was twitching at the thought of sucking Riley's nipples.

Even though Miles had been desperate for some sleep, the second news broke about Max Thorne being made Chief of Police, Miles started his research. He'd spent the morning pouring over his computers, pulling as much information together about the man as he could find. In the meantime, I reached out to my contacts within the force to get a meeting set up with Thorne.

I didn't like that he was an anomaly. The job should have gone to Graham Shaw, in fact, it was a given. Graham had been the deputy when Victor had been Chief, and after Victor met his demise at my hands, Graham had been temporarily promoted to Chief, the job was all but his while the paperwork was formalized.

It helped that Graham was already in my pocket. I didn't have dirt on him like I did with Victor, but Graham had been born and raised in Hollows Bay, and had seen the power the Wolfe name held. From the day he joined the force, he made his loyalty to my father very clear, and when I took over, he vowed his loyalty to me. Over the years, he'd proved invaluable with the information he provided.

It would have made my life a hell of a lot easier had he been made Chief, so the fact Max Thorne had materialized, seemingly out of nowhere, had me on edge. Not to mention he came from Florida, the place where Anderson joined the police academy. That was too much of a coincidence for my liking.

"Not a huge amount," I replied to Hendrix's question as I slowly scrolled through the report Miles had sent over before he'd gone for his daily workout. "Miles will need a bit more time to get the full background on him, but from his police records, looks like he joined the force at twenty and worked his way up the ranks quickly. To be fair to him, he's done well getting this job at his age, he's not even a month older than me."

In fact, the more I thought about it, the more I wondered if that should be admired, it was almost unheard of for someone to achieve the rank of Chief of Police at the age of thirty-five. Looking through the information Miles had found, it was clear Thorne had a perfect career. He'd received medals and awards for all the work he had done, clearing up gangs and reducing the crime rate.

One thing was crystal fucking clear. Thorne was going to be a pain in my ass.

The drive to Hollows Bay Police HQ took a little over forty-five minutes thanks to the never ending traffic. Hendrix was driving, allowing me to make some calls and reply to messages when I wasn't distracted by thoughts of my Star. Finding Graham Shaw's contact details, I pulled up his number, and he answered after the second ring.

"Thought I'd be hearing from you," he grumbled as a way of greeting.

"What do you know?" I asked, cutting to the chase. He wasn't someone I would class as an associate so there was no point in small talk.

"I only found out this morning," he sighed. "The paperwork for my promotion was practically stamped, so when the Mayor called me into his office this morning, I thought it was to approve the position, not fucking tell me someone else had been appointed."

The anger in his voice was undeniable, not that I blamed him. He'd worked hard to climb up the ranks, only to have it pulled from under his feet. His words added more questions to my already long list though, it looked like I'd be having a chat with the Mayor at some point too.

"What do you know about this new guy, Max Thorne?" His name tasted like acid on my tongue, I hadn't even met the guy yet and already I was fucking suspicious.

"First time I met him was about an hour ago, strolled into the station like he owned the god-damn place and started barking orders at me like I was his personal errands' bitch," Graham sneered. "I tell you, Mr. Wolfe, if he carries on like this, I'll be handing in my resignation before the week is out."

"Don't do anything rash. Something doesn't add up with his new appointment," I admitted, earning a confused look from Hendrix who could only hear my half of the conversation.

"You're telling me," Graham retorted.

"I'll be in touch." I hung up on him before he had a chance to respond.

The rest of the journey was spent with me filling Hendrix in on what Graham had said. Before long, Hendrix was pulling up outside HBPD headquarters and the two of us made our way inside.

"Mr. Wolfe, how can I help?" The front desk Sergeant purred when I approached her. She fluttered her lashes at me and flashed me a sly grin.

"I'm here to see Chief Thorne," I growled back and gave her my best scowl, letting her know I was *not* fucking interested. Even if I didn't have my Star waiting for me back home, I'd never fuck a cop.

The woman squeaked and quickly disappeared into the back office.

Hendrix chuckled behind me at her reaction. "Still as charming as ever," he snickered.

The desk Sergeant returned with a sheepish look before summoning us through the door and leading us through to the heart of the station. Hendrix and I followed as cops went about their day. Some nodded my way in acknowledgment, some scowled, and others were completely oblivious to us passing through.

As we passed the deputy's office, I glanced inside and caught the eye of Graham, who was sitting with his head in his hands, his cheeks red with fury. I nodded at him, hoping like fuck I would be able to have some sway in sorting this mess out and getting him promoted like he should have been in the first place.

What in the ever living fuck had the Mayor been thinking?

He would be next on my list to visit when I was done with Thorne. But as it turned out, I was saved a trip to his office.

The desk Sergeant knocked on the door and when a deep voice called, 'Come in,' she opened the door before scurrying away. Hendrix and I stepped inside to find Mayor Trevor Wilson standing next to the new Chief of Police.

Max Thorne stared with his dark eyes as Hendrix and I spread ourselves in the office. He was an ugly fucker, his nose had clearly been broken several times over the years and had been left at a disjointed angle, his thin lips were pressed into a scowl, filled with contempt. His light brown hair was receding around his hairline, and he had started to go bald on top.

Max wasn't quite as tall as me, but he was a large man. From the way his police uniform clung to him, it was clear he had a lot of muscle, no doubt from years of a grueling fitness regime.

"Mr. Wolfe, it's a pleasure to meet you," Thorne said, his tone full of disdain, indicating he was anything but pleased. He held out his hand for me to shake.

"Chief Thorne, congratulations on the promotion," I said stoically while gripping his hand. His grip in return was as firm as mine, a power play on both our parts. "I have to say, it came as a surprise, Deputy Shaw has been doing a fine job keeping Hollows Bay in check since the death of Victor."

I cast a side eye over to Mayor Wilson who was standing in the corner unable to meet my eye, and shifting awkwardly on his feet. I'd had a number of dealings over the years with the Mayor, and he had only ever been too happy with the Wolfe family running the city. What we said went, and he never contested it. I'd given my approval for Graham to be promoted so the fact that Max Thorne was wearing the Chief's uniform was unsettling, to say the least.

"Yes, well, the Mayor and other government figures decided it was time for a changeup in Hollows Bay," Thorne said smugly.

"That so," I growled, glaring at Wilson who looked nervously at Thorne before meeting my gaze.

"Mr. Wolfe," Wilson started, immediately wilting under my scowl. "The FBI have taken an interest in Hollows Bay of late as it was identified as one of the worst cities for gang culture. The powers that be decided a new chief would be a good starting place to tidy the city up." He stumbled over his words and rubbed his hands together.

That was bullshit if ever I heard it. There were cities in the US that were far more gang riddled than Hollows Bay: Los Angeles, Detroit, and New York to name a few. Wilson was talking shit and we all fucking knew it, so what in the hell was going on?

"That's right, I've been brought in to clear the streets up, and I intend to do just that," Thorne said, looking far too self fucking satisfied. "And from what I understand, you seem to be of the belief that you are above the law, so let me tell you this. I'm coming for you, *Kai*, I'm going to make your life a living hell while I take everything from you, and I mean *everything*. And there isn't a single thing you can do to stop me."

He grinned maniacally. The words he spewed were filled with venom, and they hit me hard. This wasn't business, this wasn't a one-man fucking band thinking he was a superhero and saving the city.

This was personal.

I glowered at the man for a few seconds, wondering who the fuck he thought he was. He stared back at me, grinning as if he thought I had been threatened by his words.

I wasn't.

Throwing my head back, I let out a loud laugh that reverberated around the room. Then, as quick as a flash, I pulled my gun from its holster and aimed it directly at Thorne, all traces of humor gone. From the corner of my eye, I saw Hendrix had done the same, only his gun was pointed at the Mayor.

"Let me tell you this, Thorne, this is *my* city. I own this place and the people in it, so it's in your best interest if you fuck off back to whatever rock you crawled out of before *I* come for you. And I won't stop at destroying you, I will destroy *everything* that's dear to you."

The smile on his face grew as his eyes turned wild. In the blink of an eye, he'd gone from composed to crazy. I wasn't scared of anyone, but the look of mania that consumed him was enough to make me question his sanity, and insane people could be fucking scary with how unpredictable they were.

"Oh, Kai, we are going to have so much fun. By all means, shoot me," he said, glancing at the nozzle of my gun, daring me to pull the trigger. "But the FBI are expecting my first report this afternoon, and if anything happens to me or to the good Mayor here, I have their assurances that you will be rotting in a cell by the end of the day."

His threat didn't bother me. I had contacts who had a way in with the bureau, and I had measures in place for situations like this should the Feds ever come sniffing. It wasn't like I hadn't spent the odd night in a cell when they'd shown an interest before, but I had a shit hot legal team, and I paid them a fuck ton of money to get me out of trouble.

No, his threat didn't bother me until he said the next words that turned my blood to ice.

"And if you are locked up, what happens to sweet little Riley? There will be no one to protect her from the monsters that lurk on street corners."

"You motherfuck-"

"Kai," Hendrix growled in my ear, snapping me out of the murderous haze that descended and stopping my finger from squeezing the trigger. "Keep it together, brother, let's get the fuck out of here and regroup."

It took a moment for his words to sink in, for the haze to clear enough for me to regain control. Burning rage pumped through my veins as Thorne smirked when I lowered my gun. I wanted nothing more than to empty the chamber into his heart, but if he was right, if the Feds were going to come after me, I couldn't leave Riley unprotected. If I emptied the chamber, the only way I'd get her and me away before they came for me would be to run, and I wasn't fucking running away from my city.

There was more to this than just Thorne trying to make a name for himself by ridding Hollows Bay of gangs. His arrival here at a time when everything was going to shit was more than a coincidence. How he slotted into the puzzle though, I had no fucking idea.

Hendrix was right, the best thing I could do was get the fuck out of here and bide my time. If I acted without thinking, who knew what kind of repercussions it would cause.

"I'll be seeing you, Thorne," I snarled.

A look of triumph crossed his face as he watched me re-holster my gun, resisting the urge to fire one bullet straight through the cunt's head.

"Before you go, Wolfe," Thorne said, coming to stand the other side of his desk. "There's someone I'd like you to meet. Needless to say, the protection of the FBI stretches to him too."

The door to his office opened and I turned to see who he was talking about. My fists clenched, and my lips curled into a snarl when the ghost of a man I'd spent months looking for walked in.

"Kai, meet my new deputy, John Anderson."

Chapter 9

Riley

My afternoon of fretting was interrupted by a loud roar, followed by glass smashing. Curiosity got the better of me, and I ventured out of my room to see what the disturbance was. I reached the lounge to find smashed glass on the floor, and Hendrix and Miles both staring helplessly as Kai stormed away from them, his retreating figure emitting wave after wave of rage.

"Is he okay?" I asked, wondering what in the hell had happened to rattle him this much.

"No, he's not," Hendrix replied gruffly, still staring down the hallway where Kai had disappeared to. He quickly turned his gaze on me, heated eyes trailing over my body. "Be a good girl, Riley, go back to your room."

Patronizing asshole.

My hands twitched with the need to pound his ugly face in. Who the fuck did he think he was speaking to me like that?

Gah, I fucking detested the man!

I was about to open my mouth to tell him to go to hell when Miles grabbed my attention.

"Riley, I'll come and see you later." He subtly indicated to Hendrix with a slight nod of his head, which thankfully, Hendrix didn't see because he was too busy staring at my tits. I swear the man was getting creepier every time I was unfortunate enough to be in his company.

I took a breath and reminded myself that I needed to act cool, like I didn't know the truth about Hendrix's betrayal. I needed to take a leaf out of Miles' book. To look at him, you'd never know he was quietly simmering under the surface at being in the presence of a traitorous asshole.

Giving Hendrix a scowl, I went back to my room, all manners of thought racing through my brain wondering what the fuck had happened now. The bad news was never ending.

An eternity passed before Miles came to my room and told me everything about Kai's meeting with Max Thorne. When he finished, I had no words to say, my mind was blown. In one respect, at least Kai knew where to find John now, not that he could do anything about it without the FBI instantly jumping on his ass.

Long after Miles left me, and night had fallen outside, I found myself wide awake trying to put the jigsaw pieces together. But it was no good, all I could think about was Kai. John Anderson had something to do with Theo's death, for Kai to have to stand there and not get the retribution he so desperately needed must have been hell on earth. No wonder he'd stormed around the house smashing shit up.

But I also knew Kai well enough to know he was scared, even if the stubborn bastard refused to admit it. He'd be scared his city would be taken from him, and he'd be scared something would happen to me if the Feds did come for him. And damn, all I wanted to do was comfort him. Before I had time to stop myself, I was out of bed and on the hunt for Kai.

Seeing as it was early hours of the morning, I checked his room first thinking maybe he would have tried to get some sleep, but he wasn't there. Next, I checked his office, but there was still no sign. I walked around the apartment trying to find him, and just as I was about to give up hope and assume he'd gone out for the night, I found him on the roof terrace, leaning over the balcony and staring out over the city.

His city.

I'd only been up on the roof terrace a few times, but never at night.

I had to admit, it was *beautiful*. A huge infinity pool lit up with blue lights dominated the area, several cabana sunbeds stood around the pool, and lavender and yellow flowers with tiny twinkling lights embedded into them adorned the area. I understood why Kai had come up here, it was calm and peaceful, the perfect place to clear your head.

I don't know why, but it took all my courage to say, "Hi." Despite everything that had happened between us, Kai still made me nervous, and I could practically feel the tension vibrating off him.

He turned to look at me, his eyes roaming over the loose-fitting pajama shorts and vest I had on. I really needed to wear more clothes around him, it wasn't fair taunting him like this. He swallowed down a gulp of whiskey before turning back to look out on his city.

"Hi," he eventually replied. I hated hearing the defeat in his voice, it sent a sharp pain directly to my heart. The overwhelming need to console him consumed me, and before I knew it, I was taking tentative steps toward him, a moth drawn to a red-hot flame.

The view was magnificent. As I crept closer, the whole city was lit up before me. For a moment, I could feel the power, feel what it would be like to rule over a city like this. It was bizarre, never before had I understood the concept of a man owning the city, yet standing here, looking out, I completely understood it.

I didn't get too close to Kai. From the way his whole body tensed, it was clear he was a time bomb waiting to go off, and I didn't want to be too near when that happened.

"I can go if you want?" I asked, breaking the awkward silence that had descended around us.

Without looking at me, Kai rested his now empty glass on the ledge. "Come here, Riley," Kai ordered.

His gruff tone sent a shot of desire straight to my core, one I tried my damn hardest to ignore. From the minute I met Kai, there was always something about his deep voice that sent shivers of lust through me, and even though I knew I needed to keep my walls up around my fragile heart, I could already feel them starting to crumble. How could they not when the man I loved smashed through them with a wrecking ball?

Trepidation filled me, but it didn't stop me from moving closer. As I did, Kai grabbed my hips and pulled me in front of him, my back to his front. His arms came down either side of me, caging me in, and as much as I was stuck with him surrounding me, his alluring scent invading my nostrils, I wouldn't have wanted to be anywhere else.

He took a deep breath, his nose nestling in my hair as he inhaled sharply, sending tingles down my spine. Somewhere in the back of my mind, an alarm bell started ringing, warning me danger was approaching, but honestly? I didn't give a damn. Tomorrow, I would. But right now, Kai needed this.

"You see that house, right on the edge of the city?" he murmured softly in my ear as he pointed to a house in the distance. It was an enormous structure nestled in the forest that surrounded one side of West Bay. There were a few lights on within the house but a lot of the windows remained dark.

"I see it."

"That's where I grew up," Kai said, surprising me with that little nugget of information. If I'd learned anything about Kai, it was that he didn't like to talk about his upbringing.

"Oh," I replied feebly. The house was a far cry from where I had grown up. Even when my parents were alive, we'd lived in a modest three-bed semi.

Kai moved a step closer so my back was now flush with his chest. His hands fell from the balcony to my hips, and as he pressed against me, his hard length rested against my pajama clad ass.

"See the window at the top of the house, to the right?" I nodded in response. "That used to be my bedroom. I lost count the amount of times I used to stand at the window looking over the city, knowing one day, I would rule over it."

He paused as I stared hard at the room he had indicated. It was stupid really, it was obviously too far to see into the room, but my head filled with images of a little Kai, no older than five or six, standing at the window and looking out upon his family's legacy. I'd never seen a picture of Kai as a child, but I conjured up a vision of a serious looking boy with dark hair and dark assessing eyes.

A little king in the making.

"I had such visions for Hollows Bay," he went on. I kept my mouth shut, sensing he wanted to get things off his chest. Instead, I rested my head back against his chest, relaxing against him, and listened to the words that fell from his mouth. "My father, he was a ruthless bastard. He ruled with an iron fist, he didn't give a shit what any of his friends or associates had to say, what he wanted, he got. But the power went to his head, he had grand ideas to take over other cities but in trying, he made so many enemies."

His voice was distant as he recalled the memories. He shifted behind me but his grasp on my hips grew firmer. He hated talking about his father, the man had been a bully and had made life hell for Kai, Theo, and their mom. Wanting to offer him a shred of encouragement, I moved my hands and placed them on top of his where they held me, lacing my fingers with his.

"When I took over from my father, and Theo took the place of my 2IC, we had to work so fucking hard to undo the damage he caused. It took us years, but we were finally making progress. Don't get me wrong, we were still ruthless, and we were still fucking criminals, but we started doing good. We did things my father never did, invested in a number of legal businesses, started contributing towards charities. Theo and I, we never wanted more than Hollows Bay, and that's why it worked. We put our focus into one city and earned the respect of people."

This was the most Kai had ever spoken about the way he ruled the city. It was fascinating. I never knew Kai had to undo the damage his father had done, nor that he had spent time investing in businesses, I'd always assumed they'd been handed to him when he took over.

I understood then. In his own way, Kai cared for the city and the people in it. Which begged the question, what was going to happen if the new Chief of Police was true to his word?

"Miles told me about the meeting with Max Thorne," I murmured when he was silent again. Kai hummed in response. "What happens now?" I asked tentatively, certain the answer wouldn't be anything good.

Kai sighed, and yet again, his grip on my hips tightened. "We go to war."

My stomach roiled at his words, and in an instant, I was torn. Torn between wanting to get Angel back and getting the hell out of Hollows Bay before the chaos truly began, while the other part of me wanted to stay and fight for Kai.

With Kai.

He dropped his head and pressed his lips to the bare skin where my shoulder curved into my neck. His warm breath skated over the sensitive spot as his tongue darted out to lick the area he had just kissed.

I should have stopped him. I knew full damn well him kissing me like that would lead to a point of no return, but the feel of his mouth on my skin sent tingles all over my body, and holy hell, did I like how that felt. I squeezed my eyes closed, the burning need for him to kiss me like that *everywhere* consumed me

"You know what the funny thing is, Riley?" He paused and waited until I responded. Words escaped me, my mind too focused on the feel of his touch. Instead, I shook my head. "I only ever wanted Hollows Bay, but now, I'd give it all up in a heartbeat if it meant I got to keep you."

Holy moly.

As if the walls around my heart weren't already crumbling, his admittance sent a bulldozer crashing through them, destroying anything that was left. There was so much sincerity and vulnerability in his voice that I couldn't stop myself from turning around to face him, needing to look at him.

The second I did, my lips were on his, taking us both by surprise. My body acted on autopilot, my hands flew to his neck and pulled him in closer, deepening the kiss. There was no resistance from him, his hands pulled my hips closer so my core pressed against his cock, and *damn*, did I want him inside me so much right then.

The alarm bells that had been ringing now sounded like an annoying fog horn, telling me to stop, that I couldn't carry this on because all I was doing was giving Kai false hope. But as his tongue slid into my mouth and danced with mine, eliciting a groan from me, I shut the alarm down. There would be consequences, but at that moment, I didn't have a single fuck to give.

Kai's hands moved from my hips to my thighs and he lifted me easily into his arms. My legs wrapped around his waist, my damp pussy grinding against his hard cock. He walked us over to one of the cabanas, never breaking the kiss while his tongue toyed slowly with mine as he nipped my bottom lip gently.

We had never kissed this way before, Kai usually kissed with a raw, gritty need. But now, he kissed me like I was the most precious thing in the world to him, like I was a delicate butterfly that would break if he was too rough with me. I liked it when Kai was rough, but this was a whole new experience, and I was so fucking down for it. My entire body tingled with desire, and as Kai laid me down on the cabana, my pussy pulsed with the need to be filled.

"Fuck, Star, you have no fucking idea how much I need you," Kai whispered, desperation in his voice. His hand stroked up my body and stopped on my breast where he cupped it firmly in his big palm. His words should have been my cue to stop, to tell him this couldn't happen, but I was too far fucking gone.

I wanted Kai.

Even if it could only be just one more night.

"Kai, I need you too. Just once more," I moaned, but he cut me off by plunging his tongue into my mouth again. I feared he hadn't heard me say it could only happen once, or if he had heard me, he would ignore me.

But then, he reached down between us and undid the buttons on his jeans, his cock springing free. Sliding my pajama bottoms aside, Kai thrust inside me hard, making us both groan in unison.

"Just once," he hissed as he pulled out and thrust back inside me again. My pussy clenched around his shaft as he grabbed my hips and hitched them higher. I wrapped my legs around his broad frame allowing him to drive deeper, hitting that sweet spot inside Kai was *oh so good* at finding.

His mouth moved to my throat where he pebbled it with tiny kisses all the way to my jaw, and then back to my lips again, before his tongue slid inside my mouth and twirled against mine. His hands roamed everywhere, cupping my breasts and running over every curve, almost as though he was committing the shape of my body to memory, knowing he'd never get to touch it again after tonight.

When I was close to coming, he slowed his movements to excruciatingly slow thrusts, taking his time to bring us to climax. Neither one of us wanted this to end if it really was going to be the last time, and even if I could have rewound the clock and stopped this from happening, to stop the inevitable heartbreak this would lead to, I wouldn't have.

Kai moved his hand above me where he cupped the top of my head. In doing so, his body moved lower to me, pinning me to the bed as his head buried into the crook of my neck, his cock driving in deeper. My orgasm was building, and as much as I didn't want this to end, I desperately needed my release.

As Kai continued to slowly thrust into me, it occurred to me that he wasn't fucking me. He was making love to me. He was taking his time to show me how much he needed me, how much he loved me, and the realization made tears well in my eyes.

With a final few thrusts, Kai sent me over the edge, and as my orgasm crashed through me, and my pussy throbbed around his length, the tears spilled from my eyes. He grunted as he found his own release, spilling his load deep inside me.

For a long moment, neither of us moved, neither of us said anything. We lay there, his cock still buried inside me, his face still nestled against my neck, both accepting this was our last time being together like this.

Chapter 10

Kai

I carried an exhausted Riley back to her room after several hours of us lying wrapped around each other on the cabana. Neither of us said anything, but what was there to say? She made it clear this would be the last time we would be together, and I wasn't going to beg her to change her mind.

If I'd been a stronger man, I would have stopped it before it got as far as my dick plunging into her tight cunt, but for her, I was weak.

Lying there with her in my arms, the peace I felt when only she was near descended, calming the storm that forever seemed to be brewing within me. For the first time in days, I could hear myself think.

I'd been putting off making arrangements for Riley and Angel to start a new life outside of Hollows Bay after my talk with Kimmy, but holding her, I finally accepted that I couldn't hold off any longer.

She was my goddamn weakness, and she always would be.

And that made her a sitting duck.

She'd never leave without Angel, but as soon as I got her sister back, I would let Riley go. The realization that any day now could be my last day with her was like a heavy weight settling deep in my bones.

She didn't stir when I laid her down on her bed, and I was so fucking tempted to climb in next to her and enjoy more time with her in my arms, but for once, I decided not to be a selfish prick. I didn't want to take advantage of her gift of giving me one last time with her. Besides, if she showed any sign of regret for spending one last time with me, I was likely to cut out my own heart.

I left her slumbering, but instead of going to get some sleep myself, I headed to my office and started reaching out to my contacts across Europe. I had a trusted associate who was in charge of a bunch of mercenaries across the world. His company, Apollo, was well respected because the men he had working for him were the best in the business, they'd never lost a target they were protecting.

I couldn't keep Riley, but I could damn well make sure she and Angel would be safe, far, far away from Hollows Bay.

And me.

Within a few hours, I had the best forger money could buy making new ID's for her and Angel, and a safe house in the South of France with round-the-clock protection on standby. Knowing Riley would be protected for the rest of her life gave me the clear head I needed to focus on my next challenge: destroying Max Thorne and John Anderson.

As the sun rose, I called Miles and Hendrix for a meeting to issue their tasks for the day. Miles was to carry on delving into the background of Thorne. I wanted as much information on him as possible, after all, knowledge was power.

As for Hendrix, my new second in command and I were going to pay the Mayor a little visit. I may not have been able to kill the man, but I could certainly put the fear of the devil in him.

Before we left, I headed for a shower and reluctantly washed the scent of Riley off me before changing into a suit. Fifteen minutes later, I found Miles and Hendrix waiting for me by the elevator, Miles wearing a scowl on his face as he glared at Hendrix, who was none the wiser as his eyes were glued to his phone. When Miles saw me, in a blink of an eye, the scowl disappeared.

Odd.

"You good to go?" I asked Hendrix, pulling his attention away from whatever he was reading.

"Ready when you are," he replied, pocketing his phone and pressing his thumb on the pad next to the elevator, making the doors open. Just as I was about to take a step inside, I was stopped in my tracks by the sweetest sound, the sound that hit me in the chest every time she opened her fuckable mouth.

"Kai," Riley called softly. I turned to face her, and instantly, my temper rose, my mouth twisting into a snarl.

My beautiful girl was standing in the hallway wearing the skimpiest fucking negligee known to man. The silky black dress barely contained her luscious tits, and the thing was so damn short that another inch higher and her delicious pussy would be on full display. The delicious pussy I was suddenly desperate to bury myself in.

What the fuck was she thinking?

My cock stirred as I took her in, and behind me, Hendrix audibly gulped. The sound made my anger flare to life at the fact she was allowing my men to see her like this.

To see what was mine.

It took all my effort to not turn around and pluck Hendrix's eyeballs out. Miles' too, for that matter.

Narrowing my eyes on my Star, who was about thirty seconds away from being put over my knee and spanked, and not for pleasure, I took a step toward her. She watched me like a hawk, fully fucking aware of the effect she was having on me.

"What do you need, Riley?" I growled, doing my best to keep my voice level and ignore the way my cock was pressing painfully against my zipper.

Her eyes flashed apprehensively over my shoulder to where Miles stood before meeting mine again. She swallowed nervously.

"You."

The one word went straight to my heart. The promise of so much more than, *'just once more,'* hung between us, and despite everything I told myself all morning about letting her go, I couldn't help the firework of hope that exploded in my chest.

"Hendrix," I snapped without taking my eyes off her, my mind running wild with all the things I was about to do to her. "Take Miles with you."

My visit to the Mayor could wait, in fact, everything else could fucking wait.

But she couldn't.

There were murmurs of agreement behind me, followed by feet shuffling and the closing of the elevator door, leaving Riley and me alone. Her chest rose and fell quickly as her pulse thudded heavily in her delicate neck, and when she sucked in her bottom lip and bit it, I fucking snapped.

Storming over to her, I lifted her easily, tossing her over my shoulder like I had done on previous occasions, and knowing how much she hated it. Sure enough, as soon as I started marching her ass to my bedroom, she squealed, cursing my name and attempting to wriggle out of my grasp. With my free hand, I slapped her ass hard before shoving two fingers into her pussy, finding her soaking. Her cursing turned to something else entirely.

Almost kicking my door off its hinges and slamming it shut behind me, I marched to the bed and threw Riley down, her pretty little cunt peeking out from underneath the negligee. She bounced on the bed but before she had time to move, I pounced on her, pinning her to the bed and gripping her chin roughly.

"What the fuck do you think you are playing at, Star? Showing off what belongs to me to my men?" My lips skated over hers, her warm breath hitting me as she shuddered, making my already throbbing cock throb harder. Fuck, I was likely to come in my pants if I didn't calm the hell down.

Her brows pulled together in worry, and rightly so, she should have been worried. The thought of anyone getting to see her like I did drove me fucking crazy. In fact, it made me *murderous*.

"I wanted you to want me again," she whispered, uncertainty lacing her voice.

Christ, did she think I didn't want her? *She* was the one who had stopped us from being together after the ambush, *she* was the one who said we could only be together just once more. Fuck, I loved this girl, there would *never* be a time when I didn't want her. Hearing the uncertainty in her voice began to soften the anger pumping through me.

"Baby, I always want you. Never doubt that for a single second, Star, I'll always want you, and only you." Unable to resist any longer, I slammed my mouth down on hers, eager to taste her again. She immediately opened her mouth for me, and as my tongue twirled with hers, my hand found her slit.

She gasped when I ran a finger over her clit before plunging two fingers deep inside of her. Riley's hips started grinding against my hand, and it would have been so easy to give her the pleasure she was seeking, but my beautiful Star was forgetting something.

For showing off what was mine, she needed to be punished.

Breaking our kiss, I stared down at her with a malevolent grin on my face, her brow raised in curiosity.

"Star," I said, resting my forehead against hers and staring into her molten chocolate lust-filled eyes. "You were a naughty girl, showing off that beautiful pussy that belongs to me. You should have known there would be consequences."

"Kai-" she started, but I cut her off. As soon as her mouth opened, I pulled my fingers from her pussy and shoved them in her mouth, silencing her.

"Suck, baby." She faltered for a moment but when the rumblings of a growl started in the back of my throat, she knew better than to disobey. Her plump lips wrapped around my fingers and she sucked hard, tasting herself on me. The feeling of her warm mouth on me was *incredible*, and suddenly, her lips wrapped around my fingers wasn't enough. I needed them around my aching cock.

Pulling my fingers from her mouth, my hands found the hem of the negligee, and with a hard yank, the material ripped apart, baring her gorgeous toned body to me. I'd never get enough of looking at Riley naked, she was fucking exquisite.

Not wasting any time, I pulled myself up and ripped my tie off, quickly followed by my suit jacket. Not bothering to undo the buttons of my shirt, I ripped it off, sending the buttons scattering everywhere. My pants and boxer briefs were the next to come off, and within seconds, I knelt above Riley, naked and with my cock standing proud.

Desire pooled in Riley's eyes as she gazed up at my body. Picking up the tie I'd just taken off, I grabbed her wrists, pressed them together, and wound the tie around, making it tight so she couldn't free her hands.

She didn't say anything, just stared wide-eyed as I bound her hands together. When she met my gaze again, I saw how fucking excited she was at being tied up.

I yanked her, pulling her forward so she had no choice but to fall on her front with the tip of my cock mere inches from her face, her arms pinned underneath her. Threading my fingers roughly through the back of her hair, I bought her mouth the rest of the way forward.

Knowing exactly what I wanted, Riley opened her mouth, and the second she did, I thrust my cock to the back of her throat, making her gag.

She tried to pull away, but I gripped her hair harder, holding her in place as I fucked her throat. Tears sprung in her eyes, and drool trickled down her chin, her groans turning into mewls of need.

I was relentless as I drove my cock further and further down the back of her throat, tingles shooting up my spine as the need to come grew stronger.

I had so much planned for my Star, but I couldn't hold back any longer, her hot mouth was too damn good, and as I thrust again, I couldn't stop myself from coming down the back of her throat.

"Fuck!" I panted, as ropes of come shot from my tip. "That's it, baby, swallow me down."

She made incomprehensible noises, but my beautiful Star obeyed my order and drank up everything I gave her, looking up at me from under her lashes.

Fuck, she was perfect.

Pushing her back, Riley fell back against the bed, her legs spread, and her slick pussy ready to be filled. It was the most beautiful sight I'd ever seen. Her cheeks were flush, her pupils blown, and saliva mixed with my come dribbled down her chin.

Even though I'd just blown my load, my cock twitched and she eyed it hungrily. I was desperate to bury myself deep in her pussy, but I was more desperate to taste her.

"Turn over, face down on the bed, ass in the air," I demanded, my voice low and husky. She gave me a sly smile but did as I ordered, turning around and leaning forward to expose herself to me.

I lost the ability to speak.

To even fucking breathe.

I was *mesmerized* by the vision in front of me. Her pink pussy glistened with wetness, her puckered hole on display, there for the taking.

Fucking hell.

I leaned forward, ready to taste her delicious cunt for the first time in weeks. She exhaled a shaky breath as my tongue licked her from clit to asshole and back again. I'd forgotten how good she tasted and I needed more. I latched onto her slick bud and I sucked hard, almost making her come instantly as my cock grew hard again.

"Fuck, Kai!" she cried, burying her head in the crook of her arm as her other hand fisted the sheets. I smirked, satisfied with how quick I could make my girl moan for me. I licked her length again, her hips bucking as she grinded against my face, but I paused when I got to her tight hole.

"Ever been fucked here, Star?" I prodded the puckered hole with a finger, enough for my fingertip to press inside. She gasped and her whole body tensed.

"No," she said, her lips trembling. The one word filled me with so much fucking joy. Her ass was mine to claim.

"Good," I growled, a delighted smile taking over my face. "This ass belongs to me, Star. I'm the only one who will ever be here, understand?" I prodded again, only this time, it went further than my fingertip.

"Yes," she whined as her ass clenched around my finger. Fuck, I needed her to be clenching around my cock.

Withdrawing my hand, I left her where she was so I could open a drawer in the table next to my bed. Riley's curious eyes followed me until they landed on the bottle of lube I pulled out. She pulled herself up, holding herself up on her arms, her pert tits swaying as she moved.

"Kai....I don't know...." she said hesitantly, her eyes darting from the bottle in my hand and back to me, her cheeks flushed pink. "I'm scared it'll hurt."

I cupped her cheek, stroking my thumb over her soft skin. "Riley, baby." I leaned in close and placed a delicate kiss on her nose before looking her dead in the eye. "This is your punishment for flaunting yourself, of course it's going to hurt."

Her breath hitched and her face turned ashen. This time I placed a chaste kiss on her lips before whispering, "but I'm also going to make it feel so fucking good for you."

My poor Star, I could understand why she would think I would hurt her, after all, my favorite way of punishing people was to hurt them. But I could never hurt her, she was far too precious to me.

When she gave me a small nod, I moved behind her again and dropped the lube on the bed next to us. I wouldn't be needing it yet. She lay back on her front again, ass up in the air, and I didn't waste any time diving into her wet heat. My tongue stroked her bud before I nipped at it with my teeth. Riley squirmed, groaning my name and within seconds she was riding my face again, soaking me with her juices.

I thrust two fingers into her pussy, driving into her so they were knuckles deep. She shuddered as I fucked her with my hand, and sucked and nibbled at her clit. I withdrew my fingers, trailing her wetness up to her puckered hole and slipping a finger in. With the help of her juices, it slipped in easily, and with my tongue still lapping at her clit, it was all she needed to push her over the edge.

"Kai!" she cried as she exploded all over my face. I drank up everything she had to offer, relishing in how goddamn delicious she tasted. Her body shook with tremors from her orgasm, and as she panted, my cock throbbed painfully with the need to fill her.

Grabbing her hips, I thrust deep inside, her pussy gripping me tightly as she recovered from her orgasm.

"Fuck, Riley, I'll never get enough of this perfect cunt," I hissed as I pounded into her. She groaned underneath me, powerless to move as her body prepared to take her straight into her next orgasm. Slowing my movements enough to grab the bottle of lube, her body stilled when she heard me open the cap and pour the liquid over her tight hole. My cock twitched inside her as I smeared the lube over her hole, pressing one finger inside. Her body tensed as I slid my finger in further than it had ever been.

"Relax, baby, or it'll hurt more," I instructed. She didn't immediately loosen up, so I gave her a few seconds to accommodate having my finger in her ass. When she finally unclenched, I moved, thrusting my cock deep inside of her again. Fuck, she felt so fucking good, I was so desperate to empty my balls in her, but there was no way I was going to miss this opportunity to claim her ass.

When her hips started grinding in time with mine, and I knew she was nearing another climax, I pushed a second finger into her ass, joining the first one and stretching her.

"Kai....it's too much....I can't," she whined, but the way she was clenching around my cock and fingers told me otherwise.

"You can, Riley, and you will," I rumbled, once again slowing my thrusting down. I didn't want her to come yet, I wanted us to find our release together. Besides, the more I brought her to the edge to then deny her would make her climax harder when I eventually let her come.

I moved my fingers inside her, scissoring them and stretching her tight hole. The way she was gripping them, and with her cunt squeezing my cock, it took so much fucking effort to not spill into her.

"Baby, you look so fucking magnificent with my cock in your pussy and my fingers in your ass," I hissed, looking down at where we were joined together, and knowing I'd remember this image until the day I died.

"Kai, please! I can't take much more," she moaned, her pussy and her ass clenching again.

I couldn't wait anymore. Pulling both my cock and fingers out at the same time, Riley moaned at the loss of contact. She really was such a wanton little minx.

Grabbing the lube, I soaked my dick with it, even though it was coated in Riley's juices, and then I positioned the tip at the entrance to her puckered hole.

"Kai," she squealed as I pushed forward. "Kai, you're too big."

"You're fine, baby, you can do this." I eased in gently, her ass stretching to accommodate me. "I promise you, I'm going to make you feel so good, just relax for me."

She listened to me, unclenching and letting me slide in, inch by painful inch. She cried out when I was almost balls deep, her words incoherent.

"I'm so fucking proud of you, baby, you're doing so well," I coaxed, and the way she clenched around me told me my words had spurred her on. I gave her a few seconds to adjust before sliding out, not all the way, but enough to thrust slowly back in.

And then I did it again.

And again.

Riley's pained cries soon turned into cries of need, and as I picked up my pace, I reached around to find her clit, rubbing it in time to my thrusting.

"Kai, oh fuck, I'm going to come," she cried. I was so fucking glad because I wasn't sure how much longer I could hold on.

I thrust again, harder this time, and with a final rub of her clit, she came, her whole body tensing before a violent shudder ran through her entire body. Her fingers gripped the sheets, her toes curled as she yelled my name over and over again. It was enough to set off my own orgasm. I pulled out of her ass just in time to shoot ropes of come all over her back and ass.

I barely had the strength to hold myself up, I'd never come so hard before in my life. Collapsing next to her, I undid the tie and grabbed her, pulling her into my arms, and not giving a fuck that her back was covered in my come. We both lay panting as we recovered, until after a few minutes passed and Riley moved so she could look at me.

Her hair was all mussed up, a sated look on her face. She gave me a coy smile before she chuckled.

"If that was my punishment, I think I need to be a bad girl again."

I couldn't have agreed more.

Chapter 11

Riley

I woke the following morning to find myself pinned under the weight of Kai's heavy arm, his hard body curled around me as he slept peacefully. Probably for the first time in weeks if the black bags under his eyes were anything to go by.

I didn't want to disturb him, it was still dark outside and he looked so content as he slumbered on, he deserved to rest. Without waking him, I moved onto my side so I could get a good look at his face. He'd shaved the beard he had started sporting in the past few days, but overnight the smatterings of dark stubble had grown over his cheeks and across his prominent jawline. His black lashes rested on his sharp cheekbones. Even in sleep, Kai was quite possibly the most magnificent man I'd ever laid my eyes on.

Staring at him, guilt set in. I'd meant what I said when he made love to me on the cabana, that it was only going to be just once more between us.

What I hadn't expected was a frantic Miles to burst into my room telling me Kai and Hendrix were planning on leaving for the day, before demanding I intervene. When I'd asked Miles exactly *how* he expected me to do that, he gave me a knowing look and told me he was sure I would find a way. I didn't particularly appreciate the sarcasm that laced his voice.

I quickly showered, all the while wracking my brains as to how I could make Kai stay with me for the day, ignoring the obvious.

I just needed to offer him me.

But I didn't want to give Kai false hope. As I scrubbed away the memory of him from the night before, I tried to think of other solutions, but with time drastically running out, I accepted the only option I had. It meant I'd be manipulating Kai, something that sat heavy in my heart, but what choice did I have?

I had to offer more than a simple fuck if I wanted to completely distract him, so I raided my closet for the skimpiest negligee I could find. Kai would hate me walking around in it, especially if the others saw me, but I knew he'd never be able to resist. I hated the thought that Kai would think I was giving him the promise of more, and if he ever discovered it was a ruse, he'd be devastated, yet I held my head high as I walked out of my room in lingerie that barely contained my assets.

I still had every intention of leaving as soon as Angel was home, but the only way to get her back was for Miles to find the proof we needed. Ultimately, an alive and pissed off Kai was better than a dead Kai, and seeing as no one knew what Hendrix's end game was, it was best to keep Kai as far away from him as possible.

The downside of giving myself to Kai once again was that my feelings only grew for him. I gave myself to him in ways I'd never imagined giving myself to anyone. The walls he'd already knocked down were well and truly smashed to smithereens after a day of him worshiping me, and me submitting to him.

After that first insanely intense session in the morning, the rest of the day was spent with Kai pouncing on me at any given moment and fucking my brains out. He fucked me over the kitchen counter after eating my pussy like a starved man. I rode him hard on the sofa when we tried to watch a film in the lounge, and then when Hendrix had called and told Kai he was needed elsewhere, I distracted Kai by sucking his cock and letting him come down my throat.

In the moments when Kai wasn't having his wicked way with me, I silently wished for Miles to hurry up and find evidence of Danny's innocence because there was no way my pussy could take the pounding Kai had given it for another day.

The man was insatiable, but as it turned out, so was I.

When night fell, Kai once again made slow passionate love to me, whispering in my ear that he loved me and couldn't live without me. I wanted so badly to echo the words, because I did love Kai. I loved every single thing about him, even the darkness, but if I said those words to him, there was no way either of us were getting out of this unscathed. It was a cowardly thing to do, and I knew I was kidding myself, but if I kept those words in, maybe neither of us would break as much as we seemed destined to.

Exhausted and sated, we both fell asleep in each other's arms.

As I lay there watching him breathe, my heart split down the middle. Tears welled in my eyes at the thought of leaving him, and when it eventually became too overwhelming to lie next to him, I gently slid his arm off me and got out of bed. If I stayed for another minute, I was likely to wake him up and pounce on him, or declare my undying love, neither of which was an option.

I needed to get out of here and away from him *asap* because with every minute I spent with him, my resolve to leave weakened that little bit more.

I snuck into the bathroom and freshened up when a thought occurred to me. While Kai was dead to the world, now was my opportunity to sneak into the basement and see if I could talk to Jane.

Miles had run out of the gym before I'd had a chance to talk to him about whether he could get word to her that we were trying to help her, and who knew when he would have time to see her when he was busy trying to find the proof that would bring Hendrix down.

Even if there was no chance I could spring her out of her cell, I could at least let her know Miles and I were trying.

I poked my head out of the door to find Kai in the same position I'd left him in, small little snores emitting from the back of his throat. I dressed in a t-shirt and joggers belonging to Kai, and with one final look to ensure he was still asleep, I crept out of his room.

The apartment was deathly silent, but the sun was only beginning to rise, so it wasn't a surprise Jacqueline or any of the other staff weren't here. Despite the emptiness, I tiptoed to the elevator and pressed my thumb against the pad, praying like crazy that Kai hadn't taken my prints off the system.

He hadn't.

As the elevator glided smoothly to the basement, it gave me enough time to come up with a plan to get past the guards. Trepidation filled my belly when the doors slid open, and immediately my gaze landed on two armed men at the end of the corridor.

As I stepped out, memories of the last time I was in this corridor filled my mind. Kai's torture room was just along from where the armed men stood, and upon seeing them, distant echoes of my screams begging Kai not to kill Toby filled my head.

Shaking the mental images away, I held my head high and marched towards the guards, trying to portray confidence that I *absolutely* did not feel.

They watched me intently as I approached, and as I did, I recognized one of them from the night I went to Kai's club. I thought his name was Jacob, or something similar.

The pair of them were terrifying. Like all of Kai's men, the two of them were lumps of solid muscle, and definitely not men to be messed with. There was zero chance that if either of them decided to pick me up and throw my ass back in the elevator I'd be able to do anything about it. Still, I held my nerve, refusing to let their intimidating glares stop me from my goal.

"Good Morning. I'd like to go in there, please," I said as confidently as I could, pointing to the door behind them.

"Why do you need to go in there?" The one I thought was Jacob growled, folding his arms across his chest, which for some reason made him seem all the bigger.

Still refusing to be intimidated, I popped my hip to one side and placed a hand on it. "Because I want to see Jane," I replied curtly. It should have been fucking obvious. Seriously, did he think I wanted to go in there for shits and giggles?

Please.

"And what makes you think we are going to let you in, sweetheart?" the other meathead interjected, puffing his chest up to intimidate me more.

The two of them were beginning to piss me off. Okay, so I wasn't expecting them to bow down and open the door, but I didn't like the way they were trying to scare me, even if I was shitting my pants.

By now, the fear in my gut had spread throughout my entire body, and I was doing everything I could not to let my hands shake. But there was no way I was going to let these assholes see that they were getting to me.

Narrowing my eyes, I held firm on meathead. "Because I have Kai's permission," I lied, crossing my fingers behind my back hoping they would take the bait. I smirked at the pair of goons, daring them to challenge me when really I was praying like mad they couldn't see the lie I was sure I was wearing on my face.

"That so, yeah?" Meathead said, challenging me.

"Yeah, that is so," I huffed as though he was keeping me from an important date. "Call Kai if you don't believe me."

I raised an eyebrow expectantly, silently hoping to whatever god was out there that their phones would suddenly stop working or they wouldn't have a signal down here. If they spoke to Kai, I would be rumbled and I'd have one heck of a job explaining myself. There was no way I'd be able to seduce my way out of this if Kai caught me.

Meathead narrowed his eyes menacingly at me, and I prepared myself to spin on my heel and run as fast as I could back down the hallway. That was until Jacob pressed his thumb against the pad and pulled the door open, stepping aside to let me in.

"We don't need to disturb Mr. Wolfe. Take as long as you need, Riley," he said. I'll admit his sudden change in demeanor somewhat surprised me, but wasn't there a saying about looking a gift horse in the mouth?

"Uh...thanks," I said before taking a hesitant step into the cell.

The first thing that hit me was how dark the cell was. There were no windows, and the light from the only bulb in the room was pathetic at best. The second thing that hit me was the smell. It was the smell of staleness and unwashed things, the kind of smell that gets into your hair and pores, and makes you wash four times before it's gone.

"Riley?" a timid voice called out. It took me a hot second to realize the sound had come from the corner of the room. Spinning around, my brows rose in shock when I found the form of a tiny woman sitting on a cot bed.

Jane Timpson had always been a petite woman, certainly not a formidable woman. Now? She looked like a child. Lack of sunlight had made her skin sallow. Lack of exercise had made her muscles practically disappear.

Lack of human contact had broken her.

I stared at her for a moment, unable to comprehend that this was the same woman who had looked after Angel. A spike of anger at Kai rolled through me. He had done this to her. She was innocent, and yet here she was, locked up like a goddamn animal.

But a little voice in the back of my head reminded me Kai was only doing what he thought was right, when in fact, my anger should be aimed at the real culprit, Hendrix. Either way, it didn't matter who was to blame, she shouldn't be locked up here.

Closing the cell door behind me, I crept towards Jane who watched me cautiously, and a sickening feeling came over me. Did she think I was here to hurt her?

Christ on a cracker.

I held my hands up to show her I meant no harm, and as I crept toward the tiny woman, my eyes landed on a flash of red from the corner of the room. *A camera.*

"Jane, I'm not here to hurt you," I said as I approached her. She must have heard the sincerity in my voice as her wary eyes softened. I lowered my hands in relief.

"Are you okay? When Miles came to see me, he said you'd been in a car crash?" The look of concern on her face broke my heart. Despite her rotting away in a cell, she was worried about me. Jane was too good of a woman to be caught up in this shit.

"I'm okay, few cuts and bruises, and a dislocated shoulder, but I'm doing okay now," I replied, swallowing down the guilt that while I was upstairs getting the best medical attention Kai's money could buy, she was down here languishing in a cell. "Are you okay?"

Tears sprung in her eyes prompting me to take the final few steps towards her.

"Jane, I'm so sorry you got caught up in all of this," I said as I sat next to her and grabbed her hand. The tears slid down her pretty face, and that was all it took for me to reach out and hug her. She clung to me for dear life, and my eyes flashed to the door wondering how the hell I could get her past those fucking guards and out of here. The simple truth was I couldn't. Not without Kai knowing, and there was no way he was going to let her stroll out of here.

She pulled back to look at me, her cheeks stained with tears and dirt. "Riley, what the hell is going on?"

I was about to tell her everything when the flash of a red light caught my attention again.

Shit.

If Kai had access to that camera, which I would've bet my bottom dollar he did, he'd hear everything I had to say, and that couldn't happen, not yet.

But Kai had hired Jane to help Angel. My *Deaf* sister. And Kai didn't have the foggiest clue how to sign.

'I have to be quick, Kai doesn't know I'm here,' I signed to Jane, taking her by surprise when I started signing. Her eyes flashed to the camera before coming back to me and she nodded, understanding why I was signing.

'It's too long to explain, but Danny has Angel, she's okay, and Miles is trying to find a way to clear Danny's name,' I explained as quickly as I could. Relief clouded her eyes when she realized what I was saying, that Danny was innocent.

'Do you know where he is?' she signed back.

'No, but as soon as Miles gets what we need, we can clear his name and get them both back, and when I do I'm getting Angel out of here.'

'Take me with you,' Jane replied without hesitation and giving me big doe eyes.

'I will, I promise I'll get you out of here,' I signed back, trying to convey how serious I was.

More tears slid down her face. Danny was right when he said Jane wasn't like us. It was a miracle she'd lasted as long as she had in this cell.

It was clear from the orderly state of the cell that Jane had made no effort to get out of there, she'd sat and taken the punishment. If the shoe had been on the other foot, I would have fought tooth and nail to get the fuck out.

If it meant digging my way out of the cell, then so be it. If it meant seducing my guards, then so be it. Even if it meant certain death, I would have done it, because it beat being locked up waiting for a slow death to come to me.

I nodded. *'I promise you, I'm going to get you out of here. Just hold tight, it won't be much longer.'*

She threw her arms around me and I hugged her back, trying to ignore the odor that came from her. It wasn't her fault she stunk, and hopefully, it really wouldn't be long until she was out of this hell hole.

"I need to go," I said, reverting back to speaking. I stood and made my way back to the door, and before I yanked it open, I took one last look at Jane, who, for the first time since I walked into this blasted cell, had a glimmer of hope written on her face.

Stepping outside the cell and closing the door behind me, I ignored Jacob and Meathead and kept my head down as I walked back to the elevator.

I knew there was every chance they would tell Kai about my visit. Hell, there was every chance he'd see the camera footage of my little trip to the cell I probably shouldn't know about, but just to be able to give Jane the reassurance that I was going to get her out was enough to make me think the risk was worth it.

I jabbed the pad and the door slid open, reassuring me that Kai hadn't risen yet. Ignoring the glare of the goons as the door closed, the tension in my body eased when the elevator moved, and when I reached the penthouse, I breathed a sigh of relief.

I made my way through the silent penthouse, thanking my lucky stars that I hadn't been caught when I rounded the corner and ran head first into a solid, muscular body.

Chapter 12

Kai

The clicking of the door woke me from a deep sleep, my body so in tune to listen for threats even when I was asleep. I reached for Riley, but the instant I realized she wasn't next to me, the calmness that had seeped into my bones over the last twenty-four hours began to fade. It was a peace only Riley could bring, and although I figured she'd probably gone to get a drink, I wanted her back desperately.

I closed my eyes again, telling myself to chill the fuck out, and that she would be back any minute, when my phone beeped with a notification from the bedside table.

I had a number of security apps on my phone that indicated practically every movement around the apartment block. If someone drove into the garage, I'd be notified. If someone unlocked the main front doors, I'd be notified. The damn alert went off more times than I cared for on any given day, but most of the time, I didn't pay it any notice.

The notification was alerting me to someone calling the elevator. It was too early for anyone to be coming to my apartment, even Jacqueline had orders not to be here before 6 am unless it was life and death, so for once, the ding drew my attention. I was instantly on alert in case it was Miles or Hendrix coming with important news. Imagine my surprise when I opened the app to find *Riley* had been the one to call the elevator.

Where the fuck was she going?

Panic spread through me like fire. Was she running? She couldn't leave the apartment, she had a fucking target painted on her back, surely she realized the danger she was in if she ventured outside without any protection. Or was she just desperate to get away from me?

I leaped out of bed, grabbing my clothes, intent on getting to her ass as quickly as possible when the alert went off again notifying me that she had selected the button to take her to the basement.

My blood turned to ice in an instant.

What. The. Fuck.

There was only one reason Riley would be going to the basement, but there was a problem with that. Riley shouldn't know Jane was there, Miles was under explicit instruction not to tell her Jane was locked up. Aside from Miles, Hendrix, and the men who guarded Jane's cell, no one else knew she was there. Either Miles had let the cat out of the bag or someone else had told her, and I didn't like the connotations that thought held.

Quickly bringing up Jacob's number knowing he had been on guard duty overnight, the phone rang once before it connected.

"Boss," Jacob said, fully alert and ready for instruction.

"Riley's on her way down. See what she wants, but if she asks to go in and see Jane, let her. Do not tell her we've spoken," I rushed out, knowing it wouldn't take long for the elevator to take her to the basement.

"Yes, Boss," Jacob replied.

I hung up and threw some clothes on before marching to my office and loading up my computer. Pulling up the footage from the camera in Jane's cell and turning the volume up, I settled in my chair in time to see Riley enter.

The calming peace completely vanished. In its place, rage took over. My whole body vibrated with the need to punch something as I watched Riley sit next to Jane and apologize to her for being my prisoner. Betrayal laid heavy on my heart from the realization that the one person I trusted more than anything in the world had been keeping things from me.

How the fuck did Riley know Jane was in the cell?

Of course, Miles *could* have told her despite my instruction not to, but I knew Miles well enough to know that if he had told her, intentionally or accidentally, he would have told me. I hadn't given Hendrix the opportunity to speak to Riley since the ambush as I knew she didn't like him, and I didn't want her to be uncomfortable. There was only one other person who would have an inkling that I had Jane locked up in the basement.

Danny.

But surely he couldn't have made contact with Riley without me finding out? And why would she want to help Danny when he had her sister? Something wasn't adding up, but the more thoughts circled in my head, the more I fucking knew she had been keeping things from me.

The iron walls I had let down around my heart when Riley entered my life sprung back firmly into place. My hands clenched with the need to wrap them around her delicate throat and squeeze the truth out of her.

My fear was only compounded when on the screen, Riley looked directly at the camera in the cell before turning back to Jane and continuing their conversation in sign language.

Whether she knew I'd be watching right now or not, it didn't matter. Riley was telling Jane something she didn't want me to know, and that feeling of betrayal deepened until I could no longer watch my deceitful girl on screen.

It took a lot of fucking strength to not throw my laptop across the room and smash my office up. Standing from my desk, I took several deep breaths to calm the fury bubbling away under my skin. I never thought I would hurt Riley, but then I never thought she would lie to me.

Movement on the screen caught my attention as Riley walked away from Jane and out of the cell. Within seconds, my phone alerted me again to the fact she had called the elevator. It took me all of ten seconds to decide what my next course of action would be.

Doing my best to school my features so she wouldn't be able to notice the rage simmering underneath my skin, I left my office and made my way down the hallway, ready to intercept her.

"Oof!" Riley said as she rounded the corner and smacked straight into my chest. I grabbed her hips to steady her, guilt written all over my pretty little Star's face. "Kai, I didn't see you."

I pulled her closer to me. "Where did you go, baby? I woke up and you were gone," I replied softly. My voice nearly cracked at the devastation tearing me apart inside. It was almost fucking impossible to act like nothing had happened, that I didn't know she was hiding something from me. Having my hands on her again, I wanted nothing more than to carry her back to our bed and forget all about this.

I'd been ignorant yesterday when I'd spent the day fucking her senseless, I'd purposely not let myself think past that one day, and all I wanted to do was the same now, take her back to bed, fuck her into oblivion, and forget everything.

She couldn't quite meet my eye, and that only added to the already gaping wound in my chest.

"Oh, I went to get some water," she replied, tugging a strand of hair behind her ear. Even if I hadn't seen the footage, I would have known she was lying, she was a terrible liar.

But by lying to me, she had just sealed her fate.

I leaned forward and placed a little kiss on the tip of her nose, and in return she gave me a shy smile, plunging the imaginary knife she was wielding deeper into my heart. I smiled back at her, giving her a smile filled with affection, luring her into a false sense of security, but knowing full well Riley was about to feel the full force of my wrath.

"Come with me, I want to show you something." I didn't give her any choice in the matter, dropping my hands from her hips, I grabbed her hand and led her down the hallway to my office.

She didn't resist. Whether she knew she was on her way to face the monster who lived inside me, or if she thought I was taking her back to bed, I didn't care. Either way, she followed, her soft hand clasped in my big one as she padded silently behind me.

When we reached my office, I pulled her through the door, closing it behind us, and led her to the desk. I turned to look at her, expecting to see confusion on her face, but instead, I was met with a look of fear.

Fear at the realization she'd been caught out.

"Kai..." she started hesitantly, but I wasn't giving her a chance to talk. Not yet.

"Quiet, Star," I rumbled and she fell silent in an instant, dropping her gaze to the floor like she was a naughty, little schoolgirl.

Sitting in my chair, I pulled her into my lap, wrapping one arm around her waist, and holding her tightly against me so she had no chance of moving. Her luscious scent enveloped me, and despite the wrath I was feeling, it calmed me. Even now, when she was the source of my fury, she was still the only one who could bring quiet to the storm inside.

With my free hand, I reached my laptop and hit a few buttons, and within seconds the footage of her talking to Jane sprung to life. She squirmed on my lap, her fuckable ass writhing against my cock which was growing harder with every passing second, only it wouldn't be getting the reprieve it so badly needed.

Riley's breath quickened as the audible conversation between her and Jane died out, replaced by their signing. Her pulse thudded in her neck as she tried to rise from my lap, but I pulled her closer to me, tightening the grasp around her waist to the point of pain.

"Kai, you're hurting me," she winced and again tried to stand.

Never in my life had I felt guilty for hurting someone, but fuck, right then I did. Knowing I was physically hurting her tore me apart inside, but I couldn't stop, couldn't see past the betrayal playing out in front of me.

I grabbed her chin and held her in place making her look at the screen.

"Hurting as much as you've hurt me with your lies, Riley?" I sneered in her ear, the tenuous thread holding my control in place about to snap.

In true Riley bravery, something I had always admired about her, she yanked her chin out of my grasp and fought her way against my arm, scratching me with her nails so she could turn to face me. When she squirmed enough to twist around, her cheeks were red, and her nostrils flared. She had the fucking audacity to be angry at me. In any other situation, I'd find it endearing. *Cute.* But not now, not when I was so fucking murderous.

"It's not what you think," she replied tersely. Her attitude was the final blow, the control I'd been struggling to hang onto snapped as the rage boiled over and exploded out of me like an erupting volcano.

Leaping out of my seat, I grabbed Riley's arms, gripping her hard enough to leave bruises on her soft skin. It shouldn't have bothered me that I was hurting her, but it did. It really fucking did. The only time I ever wanted to leave my marks on Riley was when I was biting or sucking her while my cock was buried deep in her cunt.

She was so petite, hardly weighing anything. As I jumped out of my seat with her in my arms, I backed her up against the wall, her brows raised in surprise at my sudden outburst. Riley had seen my vicious streak on a number of occasions, she'd been at the receiving end several times. But nowhere near as bad as now. Now, I was the wolf unleashed.

I pinned her against the wall and held her with my hand holding her jaw, her feet barely touching the floor. If it had been anyone else, my hand would be wrapped around their neck, and they'd be fighting to get air, but I couldn't bring myself to choke Riley.

If I ever needed more proof that she was my weakness, this was it.

Her tiny hands flew to my shirt as she tried pushing me away, but there was no way she was strong enough to move me. I was an immovable object right now.

"Get your hands off me, Kai," she squeaked. Finally, fear reflected in her chocolate orbs at the realization that not even she was safe from my murderous tendencies.

"You better start talking, Riley, 'cos right now it's looking to me like you've been lying your cute little ass off right to my face, and you know I don't tolerate liars. How the fuck did you know Jane was in the basement?" I growled. My face was so close to hers that our noses were almost touching.

"I...Miles told me," she said, avoiding eye contact, and once again blatantly lying to my face. I bared my teeth, snarling. My patience was wearing thin, and the more she lied, the more I knew she was hiding something significant.

"Don't fucking lie to me," I hissed, slamming her back against the wall, knocking the wind out of her. I hated what I was doing to her, yet I was powerless to stop myself. Rage had consumed me and I was no longer in control of my actions. "Start talking, Riley, don't make the mistake of thinking I won't hurt you because I love you. You may be my weakness, but I will do whatever I need to fucking do to get the truth out of you," I hissed, holding her eye to let her know just how fucking serious I was. With every lie she told, the iron cage around my heart squeezed harder, reminding me how stupid I was for letting her in in the first place.

I saw the moment when defeat set in, when she accepted she had no choice but to tell me the truth. Her shoulders slumped, her fingers stopped tearing at my shirt, and tears sprung in her eyes.

"I spoke to Danny," she admitted quietly, so quiet it was almost a whisper, but every single word sounded like a fog horn ringing in my head, along with a white-hot poker stabbing me directly in the heart.

"What?" I rumbled in disbelief. As much as it had been one of my theories, hearing her admit to it was too much to accept.

"Kai, you need to listen to me. It's not what you think-"

I slammed her against the wall again, making her wince in pain. This time I did not feel fucking guilty for hurting her, in fact, I wanted to inflict more pain on her. Pain in retaliation for breaking my goddamn heart.

"I'll tell you what I think, shall I?" I snarled. "I think you've been playing me, Riley. I think you've been a sneaky little cunt behind my back. But why?" Anger swirled in the pit of my stomach, warring with the love I had for this girl.

I couldn't understand why she would be helping Danny.

And then the penny dropped.

Something had been going on between them. Something more than just a friendship had developed between them. The second the thought landed in my head, images of them together ran wild until they consumed me.

"Have you been fucking him, Riley? Is that it? You've been playing me when all along you were giving him your pussy too?" I roared, spittle flying in her face.

Her eyes widened briefly at the accusation before they narrowed on me, filling once again with her own anger.

"Hendrix is the one who betrayed you, not Danny!" she bellowed, her voice reverberating off every surface in the room.

Her words hit like a tsunami, hitting every single nerve in my body.

"You're fucking lying again," I replied through gritted teeth, and once again, I slammed her against the wall.

How *dare* she try to pin Danny's deceit on Hendrix, was this her angle? Blame Hendrix to cover up her own deceit?

My head swam with images of her and Danny together, times when I'd seen them laughing and messing around, times when I thought they were bonding as friends, *as family.* Had I really been so blind by my feelings towards her that I hadn't seen what was going on right under my nose?

In the back of my head, a tiny voice told me I was being stupid, that Riley loved me, and maybe I should give credence to her words because she was the only person who would tell me the truth. But the voice was drowned out by the angry fog. I couldn't think straight, all I could see was the girl in front of me and her betrayal.

"How fucking dare you, Riley. How dare you fucking lie to me," I snarled as huge tears slid down her cheeks.

Somewhere in the background of my office, I was aware of a door being kicked open and banging loudly against the wall, but I was too focused on Riley to see who had disturbed us. I didn't give a fuck who it was anyway, all I cared about was the girl I had pinned against the wall and the lies spilling from her devious mouth.

"Kai," a deep voice said, a familiar voice that managed to penetrate the haze. "She's not lying, and I can prove it."

Chapter 13

Riley

There had been times in my life when I thought I was going to die.

When I was seven, my parents took me to a fair and let me go on a roller coaster when I was clearly too small for it. As the carriage sped around the track, I clung on for dear life, terrified I was going to fly out of my seat and plummet to my death.

When I was eighteen, just after Joe died, and Angel and I moved into our new apartment, I'd come home from the shops to find a junkie blocking the stairwell. He was having a bad trip and accused me of being a serial killer clown. He was convinced I'd come to kill him, so he thought he'd get in there first. He pulled out a knife and took a swing, but thankfully, he was so off his face, all he managed to do was face-plant on the concrete stairs and knock himself out.

And of course, there was the night I was followed home from the club by the guy who grabbed me in the alleyway. I'd thought I was going to die then, that was until Kai snapped his neck.

I never once thought I'd die at the hands of Kai. There had been times since he bulldozed his way into my life when he had terrified the hell out of me, but I never thought he would hurt me. That changed the moment he pinned me against the wall.

He wasn't the man I loved in that moment, he was the cold, brutal killer who didn't give a fuck who he was hurting. I'd never seen his eyes as black as they were when he pressed his face so close to mine, snarling and baring his teeth, his entire body vibrating with fury.

There was no getting through to him, especially after he got the idea into his thick head that I had been fucking Danny behind his back. I saw the moment the thought materialized in his head, his hand had twitched around my jaw with the need to lower it to my throat and squeeze the life out of me.

Despite Kai being who he was, he had his own insecurities, and losing me to one of his men was one of them. I had no choice but to tell him the truth, that Hendrix was the one to betray Kai, but the instant the words were out, I regretted it, realizing I was only adding fuel to the growing fire behind his eyes.

"How fucking dare you, Riley, how dare you fucking lie to me," he snarled in my face. The tears I'd been desperately holding back overflowed, not at the realization that Kai would be the one to end my life, but with sadness that I would die with him thinking I had betrayed him.

Taking a shuddering breath, I prepared myself to feel his full wrath when the door slammed open and a furious looking Miles stood there, wide-eyed at the sight before him.

"Kai," he barked, grabbing Kai's attention as the murderous intent in his eyes cleared infinitesimally. "She's not lying, and I can prove it."

Kai froze.

I froze.

The room stilled as we waited for the words to sink in. Finally, after what seemed like forever, Kai released me and turned to face Miles. I took the opportunity to move the fuck away from him, breathing a small sigh of relief that Miles had burst in when he had.

"What the fuck are you talking about, Miles?" Kai growled menacingly, his eyes narrowing on his cousin. The cogs were whirling in his head, he was putting two and two together and coming to the realization that Miles had been in on my secret.

"Riley is telling the truth, Kai. Hendrix is the one who betrayed you, not Danny." Miles took a tentative step forward, treading carefully to not rile the beast any further. "Kai, I will explain everything," Miles said, his tone changing from one of fury to one of panic. "But we need to get on the road, I think....I think," he paused as his eyes flashed nervously to me before settling back on Kai. "I think Hendrix knows where Angel is and he's going to get her."

My heart leaped into my throat as my own panic flared to life.

"What?" I cried, my heart pounding wildly in my chest.

No. No.

No.

"No one is going anywhere until you explain to me what the fuck is going on!" Kai roared, slamming his hands down on the desk and causing an almighty bang that made me jump out of my damn skin.

"We don't have time, Kai. I can explain on the way," Miles said, turning towards the door, but before he could reach it, Kai moved.

For someone as big as Kai, he could sure move fast when he needed to. This time, Miles was the target of his anger. Kai shoved him violently but he didn't fall back. He grabbed Kai by the shirt, surprising me with his strength.

Miles wasn't as strong as Kai, but he wasn't afraid to stand his ground with him. Unsurprisingly, Kai didn't stand back and allow Miles to manhandle him, he grabbed Miles right back and the two of them went nose to nose.

I barely saw them though, my vision blurred as images of Hendrix hurting Angel consumed me. My heart raced so damn fast, I thought I was having a heart attack. We didn't have time for their bullshit, we needed to find her, and fast.

"Get your fucking head out of your ass, Kai!" Miles boomed, shaking Kai. "Hendrix is on his way to kidnap Angel, and do you think for one second, he won't hurt her? Huh? That girl over there," he pointed at me, "the girl you fucking love is about to be left devastated unless we act now. Either come with me or don't, but I'm going, 'cos I'm not about to stand back and let that little girl come to harm, she's our fucking family."

I'm not sure if it was Miles' words that hit Kai hard, or the choked sob I let out at Miles' declaration that he was going on a one-man mission to save Angel. Either way, he let go of Miles' shirt and looked over at me, devastation and guilt etched all over his face. He stared for a few seconds, blinking away the rage, before turning back to Miles, decision made.

"Explain on the way," he said, devoid of any emotions. The two of them started to head towards the door and I sprung to life, following behind them.

"We'll take the Audi," Kai said, back in full business mode. His earlier fury focused elsewhere, at least for now. "And I'll call some of the men in for backup."

"I think we need to do this on our own, Kai, we need to clean house, and until we know if anyone else is working with Hendrix, we need to work alone," Miles replied stoically.

It was amazing how emotionless the pair of them could be when my whole world was imploding. I followed behind them, not paying a huge amount of attention to their conversation as they continued to talk about what weapons they might need. I didn't really care. All I could think about was getting to Angel before it was too late.

We reached the elevator, and as the doors opened, I stepped forward to follow Miles and Kai in, but Kai blocked my way.

"Where the fuck do you think you are going?" he snapped.

"I'm coming with you," I fired back as if it was obvious. Because it *should* have been fucking obvious. There was no way I was going to sit here alone and wait for him to bring Angel to me.

"Like fuck you are," he hissed. "It's going to be dangerous, Riley, you could get fucking killed."

"That didn't seem to bother you a few minutes ago when you had your hand wrapped around my throat. Or is it only *you* who gets the honor of killing me?" I retorted venomously. A flash of guilt crossed his face, but I didn't care. I was hurting. Hurting from his actions, hurting from fear of something happening to Angel.

Before Kai could reply, Miles interrupted. "We don't have time for this now, Kai. She needs to come with us, it's not safe to leave her here alone. This could be another decoy to get us out of the house so they can send someone else to grab her."

Kai opened his mouth to respond but closed it again, staring intently at me. "Fucking Christ!" he roared before turning his angry gaze on me, pointing a finger in my face. "You come with us but you do as you're goddamn told, Riley, I'm not fucking about."

He stepped aside and indicated for me to get into the elevator.

The irony was not lost on me. Kai had been minutes away from choking the life out of me but now he wanted me to listen to him so he could keep me safe. But wasn't life about picking your battles? And ultimately, I'd won. He was letting me come, and right now all that mattered was getting to Angel.

The three of us stood silently as the elevator descended, the tension palpable. I tried not to get my hopes up, there was so much that could go wrong, so much at stake. Miles hadn't even said if he knew where Angel was, just that Hendrix did. But *if* he did know where she was, and *if* we got there before Hendrix, I'd get my sister back, and how could I not get my hopes up about that?

"You said, 'they,' who did you mean?" Kai asked, breaking the silence. I turned to look at him, but his gaze was fixed on Miles.

"What?" Miles asked, confused as I was at Kai's question.

"You said this might be a decoy, so *they* could come for Riley. If Hendrix is going to get Angel, who could be coming here for Riley? Anderson?"

The elevator doors slid open and the three of us stepped out. It was the first time I'd been to the parking level since Danny had taken me and Angel a couple of weeks ago. I half expected Frank to be waiting like he always was whenever Kai and I went out in the car, standing with the door open for us to get in.

But Frank was dead, he'd been killed in the shootout following the ambush. Reality hit home at just how dangerous this situation was. Maybe I should have stayed behind. But as an image of Angel's terrified face flashed through my mind, I knew there was no way I'd stay put.

As we approached the row of cars, Miles pulled a set of keys out and unlocked a black SUV, before chucking the keys to Kai who headed towards the driver's side.

Before he opened the door, Miles stopped and turned to Kai.

"Max Thorne. Hendrix is working for Thorne."

Chapter 14

Kai

Pressing my foot down hard on the gas, the tires squealed as I pulled out of the garage.

"Where am I going?" I asked Miles, grinding my teeth at the realization he hadn't actually told me where he thought Hendrix was headed.

"East Bay. I'm tracking him now, he's got about ten minutes ahead of us though, we need to make up some ground," Miles replied, staring at the tablet he held on his lap. A quick glance at the screen showed a map and a tiny red dot moving across Hollows Bay. Riley was in the back, gripping the door handle for dear life when I yanked the wheel to steer the car towards the freeway. Thankfully, it was still early and traffic was light.

"Start explaining," I barked, flicking my eyes to Riley in the rearview mirror. She stared daggers back at me, hatred oozing from her. I couldn't blame her, I'd been mere seconds away from throttling her. Now the angry haze had cleared, I felt nothing but guilt at my actions. How could I have ever thought she would lie to me?

Between the two of them, they told me everything. How Hendrix had called Danny and told him I'd ordered him to take Riley to a safe house, how Miles believed my phone signal had been jammed, something that could only be done by someone close to me. Riley, her own guilt etched all over her face, explained about the call she had from Danny.

My knuckles whitened from where I gripped the steering wheel so tight as words spilled from their mouths. I wasn't sure if I was angrier at the pair of them for keeping things from me, or at Hendrix for everything he had done.

How had I been so fucking blind?

Maybe if I hadn't been so intent on getting Riley to fall for me, I would have seen what was going on under my nose.

"After Riley told me of her suspicions, things started making sense. He'd been acting off, sneaking away to make phone calls or disappearing for hours to allegedly meet one of his informants," Miles said.

Now that I thought about it, there were days where he was gone for hours at a time but I'd just assumed he was taking care of my business. My jaw clenched in frustration at how damn stupid I had been.

"Anyway, I figured the only way I'd get the proof I needed was directly from the horse's mouth. You know our phones are encrypted so I couldn't hack his calls or messages, I knew I'd have to plant a listening device on him somehow. Thanks to you, I had the perfect opportunity yesterday when you sent me with him to see the Mayor."

Miles paused to tap at the screen, and my eyes flashed to Riley, but she looked away, guilt written all over her face when the realization hit as to why she had been so keen for me to stay home and spend the day fucking her.

Fuck, that hurt.

Had any of it been for real? Or had it all been a ruse so Miles could do what he needed to do? I clenched my jaw harder, despising the thought that everything we experienced the day before had been nothing but lies.

Unaware of the bomb he'd just dropped, Miles carried on as if he hadn't stopped to do whatever it was he was doing with the screen.

"After we saw the Mayor, which by the way, was a complete waste of fucking time, we went to the snooker hall on Mead Street as Hendrix said he was owed some money. There were a couple of guys looking for trouble, and I saw my opportunity. You know Hendrix only ever takes his watch off to fight, right?"

I nodded. Hendrix was obsessed with his smartwatch, having paid a small fortune for it. It was an ongoing joke between us, he took better care of the watch than any woman he'd ever had in his life, and that meant taking it off when he was about to fight or kill, he refused to get a drop of blood on it.

"I wound the guys up when Hendrix went to the toilet, telling them he had been chatting shit behind their back," Miles continued, smirking. "Hendrix was only too happy to teach them a lesson, and of course, he took his watch off and gave it to me for safekeeping. He played right into my hands, Kai. He was so distracted kicking the guys' asses that he didn't see me take a picture of the back of it where the serial number is recorded. Our phones might be encrypted, but his watch isn't. Once I had the serial number, I hacked it and installed a program that allows me to listen into his calls and track his location." He waved the tablet to indicate his point.

I'd said it before, and I'd probably say it again a million times in the future. Miles was a fucking genius.

By the time Miles had filled me in, we'd hit the freeway. I pushed the SUV, reaching speeds of 120 mph, passing by trucks and other cars in a blink of an eye.

"I'm guessing you heard something relevant this morning?" I asked, swerving last minute to miss a fucking idiot who decided to switch lanes without indicating.

"The alert went off at the crack of dawn, Hendrix took a call. He didn't acknowledge who it was but he said he'd just heard from his informant that he knew where Angel was, said she was holed up in East Bay, and he was about to head out. The last thing he said before he hung up was, 'Have Max call me,' hence why I think he's working for Thorne."

"You don't think it's a ruse? Any chance he might have gotten wind that you'd hacked his watch?" I asked skeptically. Apparently, Hendrix had been one step ahead of us of late, there was every chance he was leading us into a trap.

"No, he was too excited, Kai. You should have heard him, it was like fucking Christmas had arrived early."

"Fucking hell," I sighed heavily. What a fucking morning it had been and the sun was barely up.

Tension filled the car as the three of us fell silent. Thoughts circled my head, not just about what was happening right then, but with *everything*. Hendrix knew everything about my businesses, I'd asked him to be my second in command for fuck sake, he knew every little detail of how I ran my organization, locations of warehouses, details of important contacts. And why? Why the fuck had he done this? Why had he framed Danny?

My hands trembled with the need to break something. Not just break it, but destroy it into fucking pieces. So much of this could have been avoided if Riley came to me when she got that fucking call from Danny. She should have said something at the first inkling that Hendrix was up to something.

"You should have come to me," I said in a low voice, trying to keep my anger in check. I met Riley's angry gaze in the mirror, her eyes narrowed on me.

"Would you have believed me?" she snapped. The honest answer was, *probably not*.

Before I could answer, a shrill alarm sounded from Miles' tablet, making the three of us jump.

"What the fuck is that?" I huffed, my heart pounding furiously.

"Incoming call to Hendrix's phone," Miles replied, tapping away at the screen. "Everyone shut up."

"Boss," Hendrix answered, his chipper voice filling the car.

"John said you have news for me?" The undeniable voice of Max Thorne replied, confirming Miles was right, Hendrix was working for Max. And if he was referencing John speaking to Hendrix earlier, then no doubt he was referring to our new Deputy Chief, John Anderson.

Thunder roared in my ears as my pulse sped up. I was craving blood. I would rip all three of their throats out when I caught up with them.

"I certainly do," Hendrix continued, oblivious to us listening in. "Remember the redheaded whore John took a shine to?"

Blaze.

My eyes flashed to Riley, her brows raised in comprehension.

"How could I forget," Thorne huffed.

"Yeah, well, she finally came good on some intel. Told ya she was worth keeping alive."

"That fucking bitch!" Riley shrieked from behind me.

I should have killed that fucking whore when I had the chance, I never should have let Riley convince me to let her go. Yet more evidence of her power over my decision making. I glared at her, silently telling her to shut the fuck up so we could hear.

"And what exactly did Blaze have to say?" Thorne replied, confirming we were talking about the same girl.

"You'll like this, Boss, she gave up the location of the brat. Danny stashed her with the old whore who owns the nightclub Riley used to work for, Diana Brooks. I'm on my way to her house now."

"No," Riley cried, her eyes instantly filled with tears.

"Fuck," Miles whispered, echoing my thoughts.

"Good, good. About time we moved this forward after that fuck up with the ambush," Thorne said, sounding thoroughly fucking pleased with himself. "Well, get the girl, Hendrix. The sooner we can use her as bait to lure Riley, the sooner we get Kai where we need him."

I wasn't just going to rip their throats out. I was going to take my time tearing every single one of their organs from their bodies, I was going to make their deaths slow and excruciatingly painful.

"Good, if I have to listen to him fucking Riley for much longer, I think I may slit my own throat," Hendrix growled.

My knuckles gripped the wheel even tighter. Hendrix would be wishing he had the opportunity to slice his own throat by the time I was through with him.

"Don't be a drama queen," Thorne chuckled. "As soon as we are done with Kai, Riley is yours, and you can spend the rest of your days fucking that girl until your heart is content."

"Over my dead fucking body," I snarled, my lips curling in disgust.

Once again, I met Riley's eye in the mirror. Despite trying not to let it show, there was no denying the fear in her eyes. I wanted to console her. Pull the damn car over and wrap her up in my arms to remind her that she was safe, that I'd never let anything happen to her, but there wasn't time.

"I'll be seeing you soon, Boss," Hendrix replied before the line went dead.

Before Miles or Riley had a chance to say anything, I pulled my phone out of my pocket and found my contact list. Pressing the call button, the phone rang and after several rings, a worried voice answered.

"Mr. Wolfe, what...errr....what can I do for you?" Diana said nervously.

"Where's my sister, you bitch!" Riley roared from the back, angry tears streaming down her face as she leaned forward to get closer to the phone for Diana to hear her fury.

"Riley," I barked, silencing her again. I knew she was emotional, but we didn't have time for it. When the dust was settled, I'd make sure she had an opportunity to deal with Diana however she saw fit, but right now we needed to focus. "We don't have long, Diana. Where are you?"

"I...I'm at the club. Don't have time for what?"

"Hendrix is coming for Angel, where is she?" I yanked the wheel, coming off the freeway to take the junction to East Bay, the car rounded the corner fast, almost tipping onto two wheels.

"I don't...Hendrix....what's going on?" Diana asked, confused.

"Just tell me where Angel is, Diana, for fuck sake!" I roared.

"She's here....she's here with me," Diana said.

"Christ," Riley muttered, rubbing her hand down her face.

What the fuck was Diana thinking of taking a child to a fucking strip club? I'd worry about that later, right now, I had more important things to think about.

"Hendrix thinks you are at home," I replied, looking over at Miles who held up the tablet. From the map on the screen, the little tracker was heading in the direction of Diana's house. Although she didn't live a million miles from the club so he could divert at any time.

"I had to come in early to do a stock take," she said, answering the question as to why they were at the club so early. At least she hadn't left Angel at home alone.

"We're on our way, but Hendrix is ahead of us. Get Angel and hide somewhere in the club. We'll be there as soon as we can." I hung up and gritted my teeth as I floored the gas again. I didn't like how far away we were from the center of East Bay, it wouldn't take long for Hendrix to find Diana wasn't at home, and it wouldn't take a genius to figure out where she was.

The car sped through the slums of East Bay, the dive where I barely spent any time but had a large percentage of employees here. Despite needing to concentrate on the road ahead, my eyes kept drifting to the mirror to check on Riley. The tears had now dried but the scowl on her face deepend every time I looked.

I fully intended on locking her in the car when we arrived at the club for her own safety, but there was no way she was going to take that lying down. She was in full protective sister mode.

"He's arrived at Diana's," Miles said. I glanced over to see the dot had stopped on the map.

"Fuck!" I swung the car too wide around a corner and almost hit a garbage truck. Turning the wheel quickly, I managed to avoid it but I clipped my side mirror knocking it clean off.

The ringing of my phone echoed around the car, an unknown number flashing up on the dashboard computer. I debated about answering it, not really giving a fuck who it was, but if there was any indication Hendrix or Thorne knew we were on their tail, I wanted to know.

"What?" I snapped.

There was a short pause before a familiar voice said, "Diana just phoned, I'm on the way to the club."

A lump of rare emotion clogged my throat at hearing Danny's voice. The second his tone hit my ears, realization dawned on me at how fucking stupid I'd been. The Wolfe family had been Danny's whole life, how could I have ever believed he was the one to betray me?

"We're a few minutes out," I replied, swallowing down the lump.

"He's on the move again," Miles said. "He'll go to the club."

"Yeah, well, that fucker best be prepared for fucking war after the carnage he has caused," Danny hissed. "I'll meet you there."

"Wait," I said, stopping him from hanging up. But I couldn't find the words, they just wouldn't come. I needed to apologize, fucking hell, I should have been groveling at his feet, not expecting him to go to war next to me. Before I could get the words out, Danny put me out of my misery.

"You did what you needed to do, Kai, I would have done the same," Danny said softly. Jesus, the pair of us were turning into a pair of emotional pussies. "I'll kick your ass later, Boss. Let's just get Angel out of that shit hole."

"Amen, brother," I replied.

The streets were getting busier as the slums started waking up. When we were mere minutes away, Miles pulled his gun out and reloaded the chamber. He started doing the same with a second gun but stopped to look back at the tablet.

"Fuck, he's at the club!"

Ignoring the panic on Star's face, I took the final few bends, the club coming into view in the distance. As we approached, Miles scanned the area, assessing for any threat. It sounded like Hendrix had come on his own, but we knew better than to take any chances.

When we both confirmed the coast was clear, I pulled the car into the parking lot, the tires screeching to a halt. I jumped out, and as Riley was about to open the rear door, I shoved it closed, pushing her back inside and locking the door.

Understanding dawned on her tear-streaked face. "Kai, let me out you fucking bastard!" She slammed her tiny hands on the window but I wasn't worried about it breaking, the car was practically bomb-proof. Even if Hendrix had backup, they wouldn't be able to get her out.

Without giving her another look, Miles and I took off toward the back of the club, ready to face my newest enemy.

Chapter 15

Kai

The club was silent. Too silent, especially seeing as we knew Hendrix was here.

Miles and I had come in through the back exit, which given how the door was hanging off its hinges, was likely to be the same way Hendrix had entered. I'd only been to the club once which was once more than Miles, so neither of us was familiar with the layout. We were going in blind.

The corridor leading from the back door into the club was lit up from the sunlight spilling in, but as soon as the door closed, darkness descended around us. I very much doubted Diana would have turned all the lights out, it was a distraction technique, another sign that Hendrix had been here. I fucking hoped he was still here and we weren't too late.

My question as to whether Hendrix was still here was quickly answered. A piercing scream filled the air, followed by two gunshots, instantly silencing the scream. In the dark, I looked at Miles and could just make out the expression on his face from the dim emergency light that was on above another door, an expression that mirrored my own.

Without needing to see proof, we knew Diana was dead.

Now it really would be a race to get to Angel first.

Miles pressed himself to one side of the corridor as I did the same on the other side. Slowly we crept along the corridor, guns raised and on high alert. We passed several doors and took turns to open them, checking each room, only to be met with mops and brooms, but not one sign of Angel. There were a million and one hiding places the little girl could have hidden in, she was tiny, like Riley, she could have easily fitted into a number of hiding places.

Adrenaline flooded my body. Usually, I thrived on situations like this, would even go so far as saying I fucking enjoyed the hunt. But now, I wanted to be anywhere else but here. I wasn't a coward, far fucking from it, but if something happened to Angel, Riley would be devastated. I promised her I'd get her sister back, and even if it meant giving up my life to make it happen, I was going to see that promise through.

The corridor reached the end and joined with another one that opened up into somewhere I recognized. This was the corridor with four small rooms where the dancers took their clients for a private dance. Memories flooded my head as I opened the door to the room where Riley had first danced for me.

It was strange to think that I had only met her a matter of weeks ago, so much had happened in a short space of time, it felt like she had been in my life forever. I couldn't imagine my life without Riley, but I dismissed the thought as soon as it formed. I knew without a shadow of a doubt, after today, Riley would be out of my life.

It was for the best for both our sakes. I was poison to her, she was a beautiful distraction to me.

We cleared another two rooms, silently indicating to each other that no one was here. There was one room left to clear and then we'd need to enter the main stage area. It was a huge area and would be where we were most exposed, but if we were exposed, so was Hendrix.

Nudging open the final door with my foot, I raised my gun and entered. In the darkness of the room, lit only by the faint glow from the emergency light, was the lifeless body of Diana.

Her eyes were open, unseeing as they stared at the ceiling. Her chest was coated in blood from a bullet wound, but that wasn't what killed her. Between her eyes was another bullet wound. Blood, bone, and brain matter splattered across the sofa where she had fallen. Aside from the danger Riley would have been in, I was fucking glad she wasn't here to witness the sight.

Miles and I shared a grimace, but being the cold bastards we were, we crept out of the room, putting the body of Riley's former boss to the back of our minds. Edging our way to the door that would open into the main stage, I braced myself for what was about to come.

Pushing the door open, several things happened at once. The lights to the club came on, lighting up the entire room. Gunshots rang out from different directions forcing Miles and me to duck for cover behind the bar that ran the length of the club. Rows and rows of bottles smashed behind us, soaking us in smashed glass and alcohol.

"Fuck, we're surrounded," Miles hissed, trying to protect his head from the glass raining down on him.

"We need to wait them out," I shouted back.

I'd grown up handling guns, I knew what different guns sounded like, and I'd lay money on them being Glock 19s. Whoever was firing at us would have to break at some point to reload. It would give us an opportunity to figure out where they were shooting from, even if we couldn't take any of them out straight away, but right now, any fucking intel would be helpful.

Bottles continued to smash for a few more seconds, but as predicted the rounds began to die down. Preparing to stick my head above the parapet, I cocked my gun, Miles doing the same.

"Kai! Now!" A voice boomed from across the other side of the room, a voice I would recognize anywhere. Miles and I jumped to our feet, my eyes landing immediately on the hulking figure of Danny who was standing on the stage, gun raised, and firing at balaclava clad men. A mixture of feelings coursed through me in an instant, relief at seeing Danny, fury at him for stashing Angel with Diana, and sheer rage at the assholes who thought they would win in a fight against us.

I didn't hesitate to join in the fight. I aimed at the first cunt who caught my attention and my shot hit him straight in the head. He went down as I turned to another figure who took a hit directly to the heart. Miles picked off another one from next to me, and Danny took out two as he leaped off the stage. One minute, the men were firing back at us, their shots going wide like the fucking amateurs they were. The next minute, the room began to quieten.

I jumped over the bar, slicing my hand open on broken glass, but the pain barely registered as I raised my gun and shot the final asshole at point-blank range. My heart thudded in my chest as I surveyed the carnage in the room, my eyes landing on Danny who was watching me carefully, his gun semi-raised as though he didn't fully trust me. It was a fair assessment given I had issued a number of threats against his life in the last two weeks.

"You good?" I asked him, raking my eyes over his form to make sure he wasn't hurt. He'd lost weight since I last saw him, his hair had grown longer, shaggier, and he sported a thick beard. Questions sprung to mind about where he'd been hiding but now wasn't the time.

"I'm good, brother," he replied, relief flooding his eyes. He lowered his gun. "I'll never say this again, but I've fucking missed you two."

Despite the situation, despite that we still had no fucking clue where Hendrix or Angel was, I couldn't help the smirk tugging at my lips.

"Good to see you too," I replied. He gave me a smile back, his own version at least which always made him look more menacing with the scar that marred his face.

"Looks like they were Stags," Miles said, distracting Danny and me from the weird staring contest we'd entered. For as long as I had known Danny, we'd never shared emotions, we didn't do fucking hugs and telling each other how we felt, yet in the seconds that passed, we both said so much without saying anything at all.

I tore my gaze away from him. When this was done, we'd talk. I'd fucking find the words to apologize to him, and I'd make things right between us, but right now we needed to focus on the problem at hand.

Staring at the body Miles rolled over, my eyes landed on the very thing that gave the dead body away. Tattooed on his neck was a large stag, the same tattoo that every member of the Huntsville Stags had as a sign of membership.

I joined the dots. Hendrix was here with the Stags, he was working for Max Thorne, did that mean Thorne was the silent partner behind the Stags? Could Hendrix be the silent partner, and he'd been deceiving me for longer than I imagined possible?

Before I could give it too much thought, a noise from the corner of the room grabbed all three of our attention. We turned, raising our guns simultaneously and aiming at where the noise came from.

Everything happened quickly in the minutes that followed, and it felt like I was watching the scene unfold from out of my body, powerless to stop any of it from happening.

The door closest to Danny flew open, and a tiny figure sprinted through. If I didn't know better, I would have said Riley had managed to get out of the car, the little girl looked so much like her big sister. Her cute face was contorted into sheer terror as behind her, two balaclava clad men chased her.

Danny sprang to life, grabbing Angel and wrapping his huge body around her as Miles and I fired shots at the men chasing her. The two of them fired their own weapons, their bullets going astray before our bullets hit their targets. They were dead before they hit the ground, but as they fell, three more shots were fired from the other side of the room.

Shouts and roars of anger mixed with the echoing gunshots rang around the club. I spun in the direction the shots had come from, catching the retreating figure of Hendrix running away like a fucking coward.

Miles and I began to take off in the direction he had gone, only to be stopped in our tracks by the hulking figure of Danny crashing to the floor, and a pained cry from Angel who was crushed underneath him. My raging blood turned to ice as dread pooled in my gut.

"Kai," Danny choked out, managing to pull himself up to free Angel, tears streaked the little girl's face as she clung to Danny.

Time stood still at that moment, the moment when my vision narrowed on the three wounds on Danny's back that were pissing blood. I knew what had happened, *knew* Hendrix's bullets had embedded into Danny's back, but I didn't want to acknowledge it. My feet twitched with the need to go after Hendrix, but my goddamn heart pulled me in the other direction.

Miles and I sprinted over to where Danny had collapsed, Angel's terrified eyes landing on me as she clung harder to Danny. She'd met Miles before, but I hoped like fuck she'd know I meant her no harm.

Why the *fuck* hadn't I bothered with her before?

Relief flooded me when Danny shifted, his giant hand reached out to Angel, getting her attention. He grunted in pain as he pointed to me and made an *'okay'* shape with his thumb and pointer finger. Riley always said Angel was a smart kid, and even now, with carnage and death around her, she knew what Danny was saying. She looked from him to me and gave me a small nod of understanding, before moving back, letting Miles and I move in.

"I need to see how bad it is," Miles said, his voice shaking as he ripped Danny's shirt up. By now the material was soaked through with his blood, and within seconds, Miles' hands were also covered in blood. Danny winced from the pain and I grabbed his hand, moving so I was kneeling next to his head, his sorrowful eyes landing on me.

"I've got you, brother," I said, squeezing his hand and doing my fucking best to not let the fear show. I looked at Miles who met my eyes and gave a small shake of his head. My gaze dropped to Danny's back, there was too much blood, even if we got him out of here, he'd never fucking make it to the hospital.

Tears pricked my eyes. I never fucking cried, but then I'd never let myself feel before. I prided myself on being a ruthless, cold bastard, but in recent weeks, since meeting Star, I'd changed. Somewhere along the line, she'd changed me, and the walls around my heart had collapsed, allowing me to feel everything.

Did that make me weak?

Maybe, but I wasn't sure I cared. Not right then, at least.

"Am I going to make it?" Danny groaned, but resignation filled his voice. He fucking knew he was going to die.

The first tear slid from my eye.

"You're going to be fine, brother." I squeezed his hand again.

He chuckled, but there was no humor to it. His eyes briefly closed before they opened and landed on me again.

"You're a shit liar, Kai." The effort of speaking brought on a coughing fit, bright red blood spluttering from his mouth. "I'm sorry for everything," he said, his words growing faint.

"Don't you dare fucking apologize," I growled, anger bubbling up. Not at Danny though, anger at myself. Anger at how I was such an obnoxious prick that no one felt they could tell me the truth. "If anyone needs to apologize, it's me. I'm so fucking sorry, Danny. I should never have doubted your loyalty. Forgive me, brother."

More tears slid down my cheeks, and from the corner of my eye, I saw Miles wipe his own tears before standing up and storming out of the room.

Danny squeezed my hand, it was fucking laughable. Here he was dying, and yet he was reassuring me. "There's nothing to forgive, Kai. I fucking love you, man." His eyes filled with his own tears as his breath became labored. "Do me a favor though, Kai."

"What's that?" I replied, my voice cracking.

"Look after Riley and Angel. They're too good for this world, too pure." He coughed again, more blood spilling from his mouth. "Promise me. Promise me you'll take care of them."

Wiping the tears from my face, I gently wiped some of the blood away from his mouth. There was too much to get rid of all of it, but for some reason, I needed to try and clear some.

Grief makes us do strange things.

Movement from next to me caught my eye as Angel tentatively crept forward and sat next to Danny, placing her little hand on top of where my hand was holding his.

I stared at her innocent face, tear stained and fearful, but she was so much like her sister, so fucking brave when she needed to be.

"I promise you, brother," I said, holding it together enough to get my words out. "I promise you, I will keep our girls safe."

He didn't reply.

After all, the dead didn't speak.

Chapter 16

Riley

"Fucking bastard!" I kicked the back door for the hundredth time, frustrated tears streaming down my face at my futile attempts to get out of the car. I was going to kill Kai when I got out of here, I was going to murder him with my own hands. In fact, I hoped Hendrix got to him first.

I regretted the thought as soon as it formed. I didn't mean it, of course I didn't want Hendrix to kill Kai, but how *dare* he lock me in here and run off to play the hero.

Giving up on my attempt to break free, I collapsed on the back seat, lying down to stare at the roof. All manners of thought circled my head.

What if we were too late and Hendrix took Angel?

What if something happened to Kai?

Why was this taking so damn long?

I don't know how long I lay there, alternating between cursing Kai, and praying he was okay when a noise caught my attention from outside. I bolted upright, only to immediately duck down again when Hendrix came flying out of the club, phone raised to his ear and gun in hand.

He was too far for me to hear what he was shouting, but boy, did he look mad. He was fixated on getting the hell out of here, without even looking around, he jumped straight into a parked car and sped out of the parking lot.

I waited expectantly, my gaze fixed on the door he'd come from. Surely if he left, Kai or Miles, or even Danny would be right behind him. But minutes passed without a sign from anyone. Thoughts ran rampant in my mind again, had Hendrix killed them all?

Damn Kai for locking me in this fucking vehicle.

I was about to launch another attack on the back window to try and break it when the most beautiful sight I'd ever seen emerged from the club. In an instant, all my anger and frustration disappeared, replaced by the most overwhelming relief I had ever felt.

Air in my lungs whooshed out as Kai marched determinedly out of Club Sin with Angel held tightly in his strong embrace. Her arms clutched to his neck, legs wrapped around his waist, and her head buried in the crook of his neck.

My two worlds had finally collided.

A choked sob escaped when relief turned to panic and fear. The two people I loved the most were covered in blood.

My body acted on instinct, desperate to get to them. I slammed my fists against the solid glass as I screamed bloody murder to be let out of the car. The pain in my knuckles barely registered, all I could think of was getting to them.

Seeing my panic, Kai reached into his pocket with one hand and pulled out the keys, keeping the other firmly wrapped around Angel. The second the doors clicked open, I leaped out and sprinted over, ripping Angel out of Kai's arms. Blind panic consumed me as I ran my hands over every inch of her, trying to find the source of the blood.

"Where are you hurt, baby girl?" I screamed over and over, not comprehending that she couldn't see my face to lip-read because I was holding her too close to me.

"It's not her blood, Riley. She's not hurt," Kai rumbled from next to me.

My head whipped to him. If Angel wasn't bleeding then the blood must be his. My worried eyes raked up and down him, searching for the wound. I didn't dare to take my hands off Angel. Now that I had her back, I doubted I'd ever let her go again.

"It's not mine either," Kai said softly, despite a snarl forming on his lips. "It's Danny's. He's dead."

I gaped up at him, mouth wide as the words repeated in my head. My heart squeezed painfully in my chest like someone had clamped it in a vise as words lodged in my throat.

"I need to make some calls to get this mess sorted. Get in the car and we'll go home soon," Kai said stoically, back to his emotionless self.

How the fuck he could tell me Danny was dead and then go about making calls as if this was business was beyond me. I bit my tongue to stop myself from calling him a cold-hearted bastard and focused instead on getting Angel in the car.

I don't know how much time passed as Kai made his calls, or who he was even on the phone to, it didn't matter. I had my world back. As Kai paced around outside, I sat in the back of the car with Angel on my lap, trying to coax her into a signed conversation, but she looked as numb as I felt.

'You okay?' I asked, even though I knew she was *far* from okay.

She'd just spent the last two weeks away from the only person she had been with her entire life, and given how much blood coated her hair, skin, and clothes, I guessed she'd either witnessed Danny dying, or at the very least, found his dead body.

Of course she wasn't fucking okay.

But my brave girl nodded, not a single tear in sight. She'd lost some of the weight she had gained when she had been well fed at Kai's, and heavy bags lay under her eyes. I clutched her in a hug, needing to feel her pressed against me.

Eventually, she pulled back, enough to free her hands. *'Can we go home now?'*

'Soon,' I signed back, giving her a small kiss on her forehead.

I peeked out the windshield, hoping to find Kai and indicate that we needed to get out of here, but I was taken aback to see Miles had appeared. The two of them were locked in a heated argument, glaring and snarling at each other. Miles waved his hands angrily, and Kai's fists clenched by his side.

As if he could feel me watching, Kai turned to look at me through the window, his angry eyes softening when they locked on Angel huddled in my lap. He turned back to Miles and said something, prompting Miles to turn and look in our direction. He visibly swallowed, guilt creeping across his face before he turned back to Kai, nodded his head once, and walked off in the direction of Club Sin.

Kai stared at his retreating figure before he clambered into the driver's seat, started the ignition, and floored it out of the parking lot so quickly that my former place of work disappeared behind a cloud of dust.

Tension radiated from him the entire way home. I clung to Angel, and as we left East Bay to get back on the freeway, she gave into exhaustion and drifted off to sleep.

I didn't really want to know the ins and outs of what went on in the club, but I also knew I couldn't bury my head in the sand. Like ripping off a band-aid, I asked Kai to tell me exactly what happened.

I heard him talk, heard the words echo around the car, but I didn't take in what he was saying except for the odd word. Numbness seeped deep in my bones which only penetrated further the more Kai explained what had happened.

Diana's dead.

Danny protected Angel as Hendrix fired his gun.

Hendrix killed Danny.

Hendrix got away.

He finished by telling me that the argument I'd witnessed between him and Miles outside the club was because Miles wanted to hunt down Hendrix right then and put a bullet in his brain. If it hadn't been for the sleeping girl in my arms and the need to get her the fuck away from all the violence, I would have agreed with Miles.

By the time we reached the apartment block, Kai had run out of words, and I had lost the ability to speak or even think straight.

Reluctantly, I woke Angel and allowed Kai to lead us to Angel's room. I gripped her hand as we made our way through the penthouse, reminding myself that she was really here. I was devastated that Danny was dead, and as much as I understood the reason for him taking Angel away from me, there would always be a little part that would hate him for it.

Kai opened the door to Angel's room and let us in before turning to leave without saying another word.

That was the last I saw of him for the rest of the day.

Hours passed. Morning turned to afternoon, afternoon to evening. I stayed with Angel the entire time, refusing to let her out of my sight from fear that she would vanish. Even when Angel showered, I refused to leave the bathroom. But she shoved me out, reminding me she was nearly a teenager, and was more than capable of washing herself without my help, before slamming the door behind her.

I couldn't help but smile at her attitude, despite everything she'd been through in the last few weeks, my Angel was still there, and as she became reacquainted with her space, the light in her eyes slowly crept back.

Her attitude didn't stop me from sitting with my back against the door though, listening for the faintest sign that she was not okay. As I waited, it occurred to me this was probably going to be the last night we would spend in the penthouse.

Home.

That's what Angel had called it back in the parking lot. Kai too for that matter. Once upon a time, Kai's penthouse had felt like a glamorous prison I couldn't wait to get out of, counting down the days until our agreement would come to an end. But somehow, it had become home, and not because of its grandeur, but because it felt safe.

Even before Hendrix turned out to be a sniveling traitor, for the first time in years, it had been somewhere Angel and I could relax and not worry about someone bursting through a flimsy door, or passing crackheads on the stairs every time we left the apartment.

It wasn't just that though, it was the people too. Miles and Danny, Jacqueline, and the other staff. And Kai. They were home too.

But on the other side of the walls, danger lurked, and the only way to be free of the danger was to get as far away from here as possible.

The sickening feeling of this being our last night lodged deep in my belly and stayed put as evening turned into night. After Jacqueline brought us food, and Angel scoffed the lot, she finally opened up and told me everything about her time with Danny and Diana.

After the crash, they spent the night in a car Danny boosted, communicating by typing messages to each other on his phone. The following morning, he took her to Diana's and begged her to look after Angel so he could figure things out without having to worry about Angel. She never knew where Danny stayed, but every few days he'd come back to make sure everything was okay.

Angel had communicated with Diana by writing notes to each other, and apparently, Diana even started learning some signs. She didn't go to work during the time Angel stayed with her, Danny had made Diana swear to never take Angel there.

As much as Angel never went to the club before today, for reasons only known to Diana, she thought it was a brilliant idea to tell Angel all about the club, and that I had worked there. The little brat found it hilarious that I spent my nights dancing around a pole for sleazy old men. Despite the somberness of our reunion, she tripped over her own feet pretending to spin around a pole, and the two of us collapsed on the bed in fits of laughter.

Her laughter quickly died when she explained what happened earlier.

She shouldn't have been there, Diana wasn't going to take her, but one of the girls who was meant to do the stocktake had let Diana down at the last minute. Diana had no choice but to take Angel. I didn't dwell too much on the fact that had Diana left Angel alone at her house, Hendrix would have got her.

Angel saw the panic on Diana's face when Diana took a call, presumably the call from Kai to say Hendrix was after her. Diana dragged Angel into a dressing room, hiding her in the wardrobe and making her promise to stay there. But when two men with guns entered, she panicked and ran. It was only because she caught them off guard that she had been able to get a head start on them. It was damn fucking lucky she ran towards the stage where Danny was.

The poor girl cried her eyes out when she told me about Danny's death, her hands shook so much that she had to repeat signs several times. She sobbed and sobbed, and all I could do was hold her and let her get it out as my own heart shattered. Eventually, the sobs quietened down until she fell asleep, wrapped up in my arms.

If only sleep would come as easily for me.

I lay there for hours, not moving a muscle for fear of disturbing her. Of course, my mind wandered to Kai, and how he was coping. I knew he'd be denying himself the time to grieve for Danny, and although I was still angry with him for what happened in his office, I ached with the need to see him. I wanted nothing more than for him to climb on the bed next to me and hold me while I held Angel.

But he didn't come.

Maybe it was for the best.

Eventually, I dozed off but something woke me. I wasn't in the least bit surprised to find Kai sitting in a chair watching us, lit only by the soft glow of a lamp that stood on the bedside table. His long fingers curled around a half-empty bottle of whiskey and his eyes were bloodshot. If I didn't know better, I would have said they were bloodshot from crying as opposed to the alcohol.

He stared at me in the intense way he usually did, like he was seconds away from devouring me. Only this time, there was no lust, just defeat. Acceptance of the moment neither of us wanted to come.

Under his dark gaze, I couldn't find any words to say, so I stayed quiet and waited for him to speak first. He took a swig of the whiskey, grimacing as he swallowed it.

"How's she doing?" He nodded towards the sleeping form of Angel as if he needed to clarify who he meant.

"She seems okay for now. But who knows what tomorrow will bring, or the day after that."

It was something that had played on my mind as she fell asleep.

What impact would there be on her with everything she had been through? Not just recently, but even before Kai came into our lives. Losing our parents, running away, living on the street. It would all take its toll.

"She's a strong kid. Besides, she's got you to get her through it," Kai whispered, his gaze falling to my sister and settling there.

He was right, she would have me. The question was, would I be enough?

I stared at Kai, my heart cracking down the middle at the broken look on his face. He'd lost so much today, and no matter how much neither of us wanted to accept it, he was going to lose more.

He took another gulp of the whiskey before his sorrowful eyes met mine. "Riley, I...earlier," he paused to run a hand down his shirt. "I shouldn't have reacted that way, I never should have believed you would have intentionally deceived me, and I shouldn't have grabbed you the way I did." He tore his eyes away, unable to look at me any longer.

"It's okay," I said softly. I may have hated the way he acted, but I understood his actions. It was the way Kai dealt with most things, fists first, questions later, and that was something that would never change, nor would I want it to change. Loving someone was accepting all of them, even the dark parts.

His dark eyes snapped back to mine. "No, it's not fucking okay," he hissed. "I'll never forgive myself for hurting you."

I didn't reply. There was nothing more that could be said about it, and though I knew he'd never forgive himself, it wouldn't change the outcome. I had Angel back, Hendrix had been exposed for what he really was, and now we both had to find a way of moving forward.

A deathly silence fell over us as Kai stared thoughtfully at Angel, but when a determined look crossed his face, the heartbreaking reality sunk in as I watched him watching my sister.

He'd come to say goodbye.

A lump clogged my throat and my eyes started to burn, but I wouldn't let my tears fall. I couldn't, they wouldn't do any good. They wouldn't change the inevitable.

He took another swig of his whiskey before standing from the chair, towering over me. "Miles is going to take you and Angel to a private airfield on the outskirts of Hollows Bay," he said matter of factly. "Jane wants to go with you."

"Jane?" I asked, brows raising in surprise as a sliver of guilt crept in when I realized I hadn't given her a second thought since leaving her cell earlier.

Christ, how was that only this morning? So much had happened.

He sighed. "Her mom died last week. She has nothing left here. Giving her a new life is the least I can do for the shit I put her through," he replied, sounding remorseful, something I'd never heard from Kai before.

"Okay." Poor Jane. I didn't know what else to say, but if she wanted to come with us, I wasn't going to stop her.

He bobbed his head several times as if the truth had hit him too.

"You'll all have new identities, and I've arranged for you to go to a safe house in the South of France, you'll be met by a team of mercenaries who will keep you safe, they are some of the best in the world."

"Do you trust them?" I asked, worried that we could be walking straight into another trap.

"Not everyone who works for me is a criminal, Riley. There are some good people out there."

I gave him a small smile in response and an awkward pause passed between us until Kai shook his head, continuing to speak in his business, no nonsense tone. "You'll stay at the safe house for a few days and then the team will move you on," he paused, squeezing his eyes shut before saying, "I won't know the location of where you'll be moved to."

Didn't that feel like an arrow going straight through my heart? I couldn't form the words to reply, so I said nothing, swallowing the huge lump in my throat instead.

Giving me one final look, Kai turned toward the door, and like a rocket had just been shoved up my ass, I gently moved Angel to the side and jumped off the bed.

Surely that wasn't his goodbye.

"Kai, wait."

He turned, and finally, *finally,* the heartbreak played on his face.

"Riley, don't."

I opened my mouth to give him a piece of my mind if he thought he could leave without a proper goodbye, not after everything we'd been through. But the look of despair he wore on his handsome face silenced me and I snapped my mouth shut.

"Don't think for one second there isn't any part of me that wants to shut this fucking door with you and Angel locked inside and keep you here forever." He glanced at Angel, before looking back at me. "But the pair of you deserve better than that. You both deserve a life without constantly looking over your shoulder and worrying about the danger I'd inevitably put you in. The last thing I said to Danny before he died was a promise to keep you both safe, and I intend to do that."

The tears I'd been holding back welled again, and the first tear slid down my cheek as I stared into his dark eyes. His eyes tracked it, and stepping forward, he used his thumb to swipe it away, the brush of his pad leaving a wake of fire that only Kai could elicit.

"I can't say goodbye to you," he whispered as he cupped my cheek. "It's too fucking hard. But what I will say is, thank you. Thank you for coming into my life and changing me. Even if I only got to keep you for a little while, it was the best goddamn time of my life. I should be sorry for what

I've put you and Angel through, but I'm not, not in the slightest. And the worst part is, I'd put you through it all over again if it meant I got to have these last few weeks again with you."

His voice cracked, stopping him from saying any more, and as the tears flowed, he leaned forward and placed a delicate kiss on my forehead. I squeezed my eyes closed to prevent a sob from breaking free.

Pulling away, he took one last look at Angel behind me before giving me a small smile that would stay with me forever.

And then he walked out of the room, and out of my life.

Chapter 17

Kai

I watched her go. From the privacy of my office, I watched the camera feed from the parking level as Miles loaded Jane, Angel, and my reason for living in the car with all their belongings.

I must have been a masochist. Must have enjoyed the torturous feeling of having my heart ripped from my chest and stabbed a thousand times with a needle because I couldn't turn away from the screen.

For the briefest of seconds, Riley hesitated to get in the car. Despite myself, I allowed images of her running back and into my arms to play in my head. But she closed her eyes and took a deep breath, and when they opened again, a new determination was written all over her face. She slid in next to Angel, and Miles closed the door behind her.

My hand tightened around the whiskey bottle I'd been nursing through the night, squeezing it so tight it was a miracle the glass didn't crack. The alcohol wasn't enough to dull the pain in my chest which intensified a million times more when the car came to life.

Miles maneuvered towards the exit, quickly swamped by three black SUV's filled with Apollo mercenaries who had arrived during the night. They were armed to the nines and tasked with getting Riley safely to the safe house. There was no way I was taking any chances of another ambush.

When the car left the garage, I jumped from my chair, standing to look out the mammoth windows that surrounded my office. Unable to look away from the convoy emerging onto the street, I took a long swig from the bottle to stop myself from picking up the phone and demanding Miles turn the fucking car around.

The whiskey burned as I swallowed, but the pain in my throat was a blissful relief from the pain in my heart. I took another gulp, desperately needing the liquor to numb everything I was feeling.

I kept my eyes fixed on the car as it made its way through the city, my black heart splintering as the distance grew between us. I'd never known anguish like this, a pain so deep that it settled into the marrow of my bones. Yet, if there was a way to travel back in time and prevent the moment when our worlds collided, I wouldn't have gone. Even with the knowledge of the heartache that awaited.

I wondered if Riley was thinking about me at that very moment.

Was she twitching with the need to feel my skin one last time? Was she aching with the desire to feel my lips pressed against hers just once more?

Because I damn sure was.

As the car took the final turn before disappearing completely out of sight, I lifted the bottle to my mouth again. Only this time I didn't take a swig, I chugged it down, hoping like fucking crazy the alcohol would hit my veins imminently and give me the peace I was craving.

I'd instructed Miles to go with them to the South of France to make sure they arrived safely, and Riley had everything she and Angel would need. I didn't acknowledge the tiny part that knew I had sent Miles with her in case she changed her mind and came back to me.

With Miles' absence, I decided I'd give myself twenty-four hours. I had problems to take care of, Hendrix, Thorne, even that cunt Blaze would be dealt with. But they'd have to wait for now. For once in my life I was going to do the one thing I'd denied myself for as long as I could remember.

I was going to grieve.

Not for Danny. Not for Theo, and certainly not for that asshole, Hendrix, he could rot in hell for all I cared. No, I was going to let myself grieve for the one person who was still alive but had left a gaping hole in my life, one that would *never* be filled again.

Twenty-four hours, that's all I would allow myself. Let me have my fucking pity party, and then I'd move on.

As if it would be that easy.

It was a good thing Riley was gone, she wouldn't be here to distract me from making decisions. I wouldn't be constantly worrying if she was safe. I'd be able to refocus, and put plans in place, plans I'd already formulated in the short time since I'd learned Hendrix was the real traitor.

At least, that's what I tried to tell myself.

The liquor finally kicked in as I stared at the quiet streets, hoping like fuck the car would reappear, and Riley would come back to me. But of course, it didn't.

A pleasant buzz worked its way through my body. But with it, came exhaustion.

I'd been awake for a solid twenty-six hours, having stayed awake through the night to put plans in motion. To affirm loyalties to me, and the Wolfe name. To get the word out that Hendrix was a wanted man, and anyone who brought him to me alive would be rewarded handsomely, and anyone found working with him would suffer a fate worse than death.

I'd been flooded with support, people declaring their allegiances to me, and it had kept my mind busy, distracting me from acknowledging the reality that within a matter of hours, Riley would be out of my life for good.

I stumbled from my office, the whiskey swimming through my veins. My vision blurred as I stumbled through the deathly silent penthouse. A place that had become home, not just somewhere I lived. But without the people who had become my family, once again, my home had become an empty vessel, a place to get my head down.

Reaching her room, nausea crept up my throat from the alcohol, the bottle near enough empty. I swallowed the bile and opened the door to her room, instantly hit with the scent of strawberries and sunscreen. It was a smell I'd never get enough of, but one I'd have to forget.

My Star.

The room felt empty without her. All of her clothes, shoes, and makeup had been packed and loaded into the car. I didn't know if Riley had wanted to take it with her, but I insisted, ordering Jacqueline to pack up every last item. Even if Riley hadn't wanted to take it, it would have been thrown away or given to charity, I didn't want constant reminders of what I once had.

Stumbling to the bed, I kicked my shoes off and undid a couple of buttons on my shirt before falling face down onto her bed and taking a huge inhale of Riley's scent, knowing that as soon as the sheets were changed, I'd have nothing left of her.

I passed out soon after that.

I woke with a start hours later, the overwhelming need to vomit rushing through me. I hadn't been sick from alcohol since I was a teenager, and I'd long since forgotten how vile the sensation was.

Disorientated, I sat up and took a moment for my bleary eyes to focus. The second I realized I was in her room, the nausea became too much. I jumped from the bed, making it to the bathroom just in time to chuck my fucking guts up.

I wish I could say I was ashamed I'd drunk so much I'd been sick, but I didn't have it in me to care.

Exhausted, mentally and physically, I dragged my sorry ass back to bed when there was nothing more to come up before falling back to sleep. My dreams were anything but peaceful, they were consumed with a gorgeous brunette who always disappeared before I could reach out and hold her.

And just like that, my twenty-four hours of grieving were over.

The following morning, my head thumped like someone had taken a sledgehammer to it. As I came to, the scent of Riley invaded my senses once again, and as much as I wanted to stay put and wallow in self-pity, I had to get out of there if I had any chance of moving on.

Begrudgingly, I dragged my ass out of her room, taking one last look at the empty space before I closed the door, vowing to never step foot in there again.

Movement from the corner of my eye caught my attention, and I turned to see Jacqueline watching me in surprise as I emerged from Riley's room. Normally, Jacqueline wouldn't dare to look my way, she'd keep her head bowed if she had cause to speak to me. But now she was watching me with pity in her eyes, and a sad smile on her face.

"I need you to clean this room," I said stoically, wanting to give the impression that I was indifferent to the room being cleaned when really, I was fighting the need to lock the room and leave it *exactly* as it was, a makeshift shrine to Riley. "I don't want any trace of her left in there."

"Of course, Mr. Wolfe," she replied sadly, her eyes watering. Evidently, I wasn't the only one already feeling Riley's loss.

I spent the next few hours making calls, and ensuring plans were in motion but of course, my mind kept wandering. There was nowhere in the penthouse that didn't spark a memory involving Riley.

My office, the place where I first tasted her delectable pussy. The kitchen where I fucked her over the island. Every fucking room I went in held reminders I couldn't escape.

Not just sexual experiences either, but other moments too, her laughing as Danny tried to teach her pool, her taking the piss out of Miles when he talked to her about geek shit, her eating every meal with me.

It drove me fucking crazy, no matter how hard I tried to put her out of my mind, I couldn't. I was beginning to regret asking Miles to go with her, if he'd stayed, we could have started dealing with the issues together, and I'd have him to keep me distracted.

As the sun started setting, I couldn't take any more.

Claustrophobia set in, to the point it was hard to breathe. I needed to get out of the fucking penthouse and escape the goddamn memories. Not just memories of Riley either, but memories of Danny too.

Grabbing my keys and a bottle of whiskey, I headed down to the garage and jumped into my SUV, burning rubber as I floored it out of there.

I didn't have a destination in mind initially. I just wanted to get away from home, but before I knew it, I was pulling off the freeway and heading into the heart of East Bay. It was hard to think that I had taken this same journey not less than forty-eight hours previously, yet so much had changed.

Danny was gone.

Riley was gone.

Hendrix....he was gone too. I hadn't thought a lot about him, other than thoughts of vengeance, but alone in the car, taking the same route I had when the truth came out, that's when it hit me.

I'd known Hendrix my entire life. His father was my father's second in command, and I'd just promoted him to *my* 2IC. He wasn't just a colleague, he was the closest thing I had to a fucking best friend, and this is how he repaid years of friendship. And for what? What the fuck did he stand to gain from betraying me? And why the hell had he framed Danny in the process? One way or another, I'd get the answers I needed, I was damn sure of it.

My jaw clenched in anger as my mind churned with questions, my knuckles gripping the steering wheel until they turned white. As I made my way through the slums, and without conscious thought, I found myself parking up outside Carter House, the tower block where Riley had lived before I crashed into her life.

I'd never been to Carter House before, I'd only read about how bad it was from the report Isaac compiled when I first asked him to find everything he could on Riley.

Carter House was one of the worst tower blocks in East Bay. Rent was dirt cheap but that was because the studio apartments were tiny, yet most of them had at least four or five people cramped inside. Riley's was one of the few apartments that had electricity, no doubt because she worked her cute ass off to keep the place going for Angel's sake.

Before I could think about it, the car was parked, and I was making my way up to the twelfth floor where Riley's old apartment was. The smell of piss and crack assaulted my nostrils, making me hold back a gag, and offensive graffiti covered every single wall leading up the stairs.

It was a dump, and if anything good was to come of Riley leaving for Europe, it was that she would *never* have to live in a place like this again. Not that she knew it yet, but I'd given her access to enough money to ensure she and Angel would have the life they both deserved.

Reaching the twelfth floor, I made my way to apartment 1204, the place where Riley and Angel had spent the last few years of their lives. It was laughable, I'd left my apartment to get away from memories of her, yet here

I was, in a place that held all her belongings and memories from a time before.

I can't say I was the least bit surprised to find the lock had been smashed off the door, and it was now standing ajar. Places like this were notorious for squatters, so it wouldn't be a surprise at all if her apartment had been taken over. Nudging the door open with my foot, it swung open easily, and I stepped inside.

The apartment was filthy. I didn't think for one second Riley would live like this which only added to my suspicion that squatters had taken over in the time she had been living with me. If I had been hoping for any scent of Riley still being here, I was sadly mistaken.

The entire place stank of crack and stale cigarettes. Empty takeaway containers were scattered across the room, mixed with empty liquor bottles. Piles of clothes were dumped everywhere, and used needles and burnt foil littered the floor.

Tentatively stepping into the living area and bracing myself for a junkie to attack, I was stopped in my tracks by the sight of flaming red hair spread out on the thread-bare sofa belonging to none other than the woman who was on my shit list.

Correction, my *death* list.

Blaze, of all people, was passed out on the sofa, a tourniquet tightened around her upper arm which was hanging down limply to the floor, her fingers almost touching a needle that had been dropped.

A snarl curled on my lips as anger roared to life at the sight of her. Not just because she was the one who snitched on Angel's whereabouts, but at the audacity she had for squatting at Riley's. It made sense though, all the time Riley was living with me, there was no use for her apartment, and no need for anyone to keep tabs on it.

"Well, well, well," I growled, loud enough to wake the sleeping ugly, but she slumbered on. The last time I had seen Blaze, she'd been going cold turkey having spent a week locked up in the basement of my warehouse. But from her sallow skin and gaunt face, it didn't take a genius to work out she'd hit the drugs again, no doubt drugs supplied by Hendrix in exchange for information.

A plan formed in my mind. Blaze would pay for snitching. After everything Riley had done for her, she repaid her by giving up the location of Angel, and for that, she would pay with her life.

I didn't want to touch her, but I also didn't want to lose an opportunity when one had fallen into my hands. It seemed like fate was on my side today when I spontaneously decided to drive to Riley's apartment.

Jabbing a finger into Blaze's collarbone, the whore didn't stir. When I did it a second time, and there was still no movement, I grabbed her arm and yanked her so her unconscious body fell to the floor with a thud. Still, no movement which made my life easier.

Ripping the tourniquet off, I grabbed her arms, and pulled her up, throwing her roughly over my shoulder. Her body lolled as I marched out of the apartment, not in the slightest bit careful to avoid bouncing her head off the wall. Not one person bothered to challenge me as I popped the trunk, and threw her unceremoniously in, and yet she still didn't wake.

Flooring it out of East Bay, I made my way to the warehouse where I had once kept Blaze as my prisoner, stopping along the way to pick up a few supplies. By the time I arrived, calmness had descended on me knowing I was getting justice for Riley. Angel too, for that matter.

"Wha...what's going on," Blaze murmured, as I lifted her from the car once we reached the warehouse. She fucking stunk, as soon as I was done with her, I'd be stripping out of these clothes and throwing them away, there was no salvaging them from her stench.

"The devil has come for you, Blaze," I rumbled menacingly. Despite the heroin swimming in her veins, recognition kicked in. Blaze started squirming in my arms, trying her best to pull free, but I was the immovable object here to seal her fate.

"No, no, no, Mr. Wolfe, you don't understand, let me down." Panic laced her voice as she started kicking, but her attempts to break free were futile.

"Save it," I roared, slamming the door behind us. It would be the last time Blaze ever saw the light of day.

She continued to plead for freedom as I carried her down the stairs, back to the same room she had been held before. Only this time when we reached the room, I didn't tie her to the chair. Instead, I threw her on the floor, making her wince in pain. She righted herself and scrambled to the corner of the room, cowering like the pathetic whore she was.

"Mr. Wolfe, I didn't have a choice," she cried. I didn't want to hear it, there was nothing she could say to redeem herself. I'd let her go once before, but there was no way in hell she would be leaving this room now unless it was in a body bag.

"There's always a choice, Blaze. Looks like you chose the wrong one," I replied absentmindedly as I laid out the items I had purchased on our drive over here, a needle, a tourniquet, and a shit load of fentanyl.

Fentanyl wasn't a product I sold. I prided myself on selling only the purest gear on the market. I didn't like it being sold on my streets, it brought too much attention from law enforcement agencies. As soon as I made my purchase from a dealer, I messaged Ernie, the head of my gang, The Shadows, and told him to clean his act up. I wouldn't tolerate that shit being peddled on my streets, even if it had done me a favor now.

Turning back to find Blaze watching me with fearful wide eyes, I walked over to where she cowered in the corner, her eyes growing wider the closer

I got. Really, she need not have feared, I wasn't going to hurt her. At least not in the way she thought.

"Where is he?" I asked, not needing to elaborate on who I was talking about.

"I don't know, he would just come to the apartment every few days to check on me and see if I had the information he wanted," Blaze replied, staring at me with fearful eyes. She knew straight away that I was referring to Hendrix.

I'd quickly come to learn that Blaze was only loyal to one person, and that was herself. She would have happily given over the information if she knew it, and I wasn't going to waste any more time in this room with her than was necessary.

"Why did you do it?" I asked, curiosity getting the better of me as to why she would treat Riley in such a way when Riley had helped her in the past. Had it been just for the drugs?

She paused for a moment, choosing her words. "Because I wanted to hurt her," she replied callously.

Her answer was like a punch to the gut. My knuckles clenched as I ground my molars. The plan I had for Blaze suddenly didn't seem like punishment enough. She needed to suffer, I needed to *watch* her suffer. My hands twitched with the need to wrap them around her throat and squeeze the life out of her, but for some reason, I didn't. Instead, I crouched so I was eye to eye with her. She pressed herself further into the corner as I glared at her.

"What did she ever do to you?"

Blaze met my eye with tears in her own. Her arms were wrapped around her knees and her whole body shook. Not from fear now, but from the need to get her greedy mitts on the goods I had laid out on the table.

"Because she is such a fucking goody two shoes," she hissed, venom in her voice despite her predicament. "Everyone fucking loves Riley, even though she thinks she is so much better than us. Just 'cos she doesn't take her underwear off, or let customers come down her throat," she sneered, making my lips curl into a snarl at the thought of Riley sucking anyone else's cock but mine. Blaze chuckled humorlessly. "Look, she's even brought the wolf to his knees."

I didn't want to listen to another word she had to say. Nor did I have anything else to say to her. The time had come to deal with Blaze once and for all.

Standing back up, I rolled my sleeves up to my elbows, and fear once again filled her eyes.

"Mr. Wolfe, please don't kill me. I can still help. Hendrix will reach out again, I can feed you information from him," she begged pathetically.

I couldn't help but chuckle. The stupid whore thought I would trust her enough to become my informant. Christ, I wouldn't have pissed on Blaze if she was on fire, that's how little time I had for her.

Reaching the door, I turned back to face her. "I'm not going to kill you Blaze, you're going to do that all by yourself." Her brows rose in question, and deciding not to drag this out any longer, I put her out of her misery.

"When this door closes," I indicated to the solid metal door behind me that could only be opened by my fingerprints, "You won't see me again, in fact, you won't see anyone. It won't be like last time with someone watching you twenty-four hours a day, bringing you food and water until that shit you inject is out of your system."

I walked back towards her, towering over her as she looked up at me with a pitiful expression on her drug-addled face. She had no one but herself to blame for the mess she was in.

"Count yourself lucky, Blaze, I could make this a very painful death for you. But I'm giving you a choice. You can thank the girl you hate so much for the fact that I'm not going to be spending the next few hours making you bleed slowly to death."

I should have been hell-bent on making Blaze pay for her sins with blood. Should have spent the rest of the day making her scream in agony as I peeled layer after layer of skin from her body. But deep down, I knew Riley wouldn't want Blaze to suffer. Even if Blaze had hurt Riley, she still wouldn't want the whore to suffer.

And that was exactly why it was best Riley was out of my life.

"What, erm, what do you mean?" Blaze asked, her voice shaking with nerves.

"It's not rocket science, Blaze. When I walk out this door, that will be it, you'll be left here alone. No one will come, no one will rescue you. How long you suffer is up to you, you can drag your death out by slowly starving to death, or...." I trailed off, and let my eyes wander over to the table where the equipment sat. "Or you can end it all quickly."

Blaze followed my gaze and let out a sharp gasp when the penny dropped. Personally, if I was left with such a choice, I'd rather OD than slowly starve to death.

There was enough fentanyl on the table to take down a small elephant, it really would be a quick ending for Blaze when she finally made the decision to overdose. How long she waited to make that decision though, well, that was up to her.

A deathly silence filled the room as I walked back to the door.

"Make good choices, Blaze," I chuckled as I stepped out of the cell, Blaze's sob echoing as I slammed the door behind me, sealing her in for all eternity.

Without an ounce of guilt, I got back in my car and sped away from the warehouse, not giving Blaze another thought.

I didn't want to go back to the penthouse only to be plagued by more memories of Riley. I thought about going to Sapphire and crashing in my office, but again, memories of fucking Riley there sprung to life.

There was only one place I could go where there would be no reminders of her, but it would mean facing ghosts of my past. A place I hadn't been since I buried Theo on the land at the rear of the family house. I'd rather face the ghost of my past than deal with the crushing weight in my heart every time I got a whiff of Riley's scent.

Decision made, I fired a message to Thomas, the butler who kept the Wolfe family home running in case there were times, like now, when I needed somewhere to crash. I told him I would be staying the night and he needed to vacate. I also messaged Miles, telling him where I was so that when he got back from France, he knew where to find me.

I made it in next to no time to the house I grew up in, the house that held nothing but bad memories. But I'd take them over the memories of Riley any day.

Abandoning my car in the driveway, I grabbed the whiskey bottle I brought from the penthouse, and marched straight through the mansion, ignoring the images that wanted to overwhelm me the second I stepped inside.

Heading straight to my old bedroom, I stripped off my ruined clothes and ditched them in the trash, before changing into a pair of gray sweatpants I'd left behind after my last visit.

The rest of the evening was spent in a whiskey haze, doing my fucking best to ignore thoughts of Riley, of Theo and Danny, of my parents, until eventually I passed out on my bed.

Dreams were once again filled with visions of my Star smiling at me, only this time she was laying next to me. In an instant, my hand was on her hip, needing to feel that she was real. She leaned forward to place a kiss on my lips. The dream was so damn vivid that I could practically taste her, and even though I knew I was dreaming, I squeezed her hip harder.

"Kai," she breathed against my lips. If I never woke up, I'd die a happy man here in her memory.

But the whiskey pulled me back into darkness, and Riley was no longer there with me.

When I woke the following morning, my head thankfully wasn't thumping as hard as it had the day before. It took a few seconds before comprehension of where I was dawned on me, I hadn't woken up in this bedroom for years.

Sitting up in bed, I was hit with the familiar smell of sunscreen and strawberries which I knew couldn't be fucking possible because Riley had never stepped foot in this house.

I sighed heavily in resignation, accepting that I would never escape the memory of the girl I once had.

Chapter 18

Riley

I'd only ever been on a plane once. I was three years old, and my dad had received a Christmas bonus one year at work and had decided to take mom and me on a family holiday. I didn't remember it, but growing up, mom and dad had often joked about how much of a disaster it was. I'd been ill, and it had rained the entire time, meaning they spent the whole week in their hotel room with a screaming toddler.

Angel, who had never been anywhere *near* an airport, let alone inside a plane, had been in her element. Despite the majority of the time we were over the ocean, she spent the journey with her cute nose pressed against the thick glass window looking for whales and sharks, even though I told her we were far too high to see them.

The only time she tore her gaze away from the window was, unsurprisingly, when food was served, and as soon as she had gobbled it down, she went back to whale watching.

I wish I could have enjoyed the view as much as she was. Instead of relaxing and looking forward to our new life ahead of us, I was fucking miserable.

I missed Kai.

It hadn't even been a full day since I'd last seen him, yet I missed him like crazy. I spent the entire journey lost in thoughts, wondering what he was doing, if he was okay, if he was missing me as much as I was missing him.

Miles had tried several times to engage me in conversation, but he gave up when he only got one word answers. The twelve hour flight to a private airfield just outside of Cannes went by in a blink of an eye because I was so consumed with my thoughts of the man I had left behind.

I didn't want to get in the car back at the apartment, but when I saw Angel's little hands balled into fists and fear etched on her face as she sat waiting patiently, I knew we couldn't stay. I couldn't expose her to any more danger, and the longer we stayed in Kai's life, the more at risk she became.

No matter how much it hurt, Angel would always come first.

It didn't stop me from wanting desperately to return to him though. But if I was honest, it wasn't just Kai I wanted to go back for.

I wanted revenge.

I'd never really condoned violence. Don't get me wrong, I would have done whatever I needed to survive, but I never understood the level of violence Kai used. But over time, that changed.

Kai often said that I had changed him, but he had changed me too. He gave me a family, and like him, family meant everything to me. And now that one of my family members had been killed, I understood the need to make the person responsible bleed. I *ached* with the need to hurt Hendrix and Blaze, and every other asshole who had been involved in Danny and Diana's deaths, in plotting Angel's kidnap, in hurting Kai.

So yeah, I wanted to go home to him more than anything, but I also wanted to go home to be by his side in getting the vengeance that was rightfully ours.

With the time difference between the US and France, it was the early hours of the morning when we finally touched down. Miles ushered us from the plane into a waiting car, filled with more men from the security company Kai had organized to keep us safe.

Some of the team who had escorted us from Kai's apartment had traveled with us on the plane. Once upon a time, I would have thought the protection was overkill, but now I'd had firsthand experience of losing something dear to me, I was damn glad Kai had taken the measure to hire them and keep Angel safe.

Once again, Angel spent the entire journey from the airport with her nose pressed against the window, watching the passing scenery flash by even though it was too dark to see.

Even Jane, who had spent most of the plane ride asleep, no doubt catching up on weeks' worth of sleep, was glued to the window. The pair of them were oblivious to the numbness I was feeling the further the distance between Kai and me grew.

Miles knew though. He watched me carefully, at times with pity in his eyes, and several times he'd open his mouth to say something, but would think better of it and shut his mouth again.

The bright lights of the airport were soon left in our wake as the road we were on ascended into the hills. The roads became darker without street lamps lighting up the way, but it didn't faze the guy driving, he knew the roads like the back of his hand. The further into the hills and mountains we traveled, the fewer cars we passed, until eventually, we were the only ones on the road.

After nearly an hour and half of driving, the convoy turned onto a dirt track that led to a two-story farmhouse surrounded by nothing but land. Miles started explaining that almost every inch of the land was covered by cameras. There were guards who patrolled the perimeter every thirty minutes, and no one could come or go without one of the security team knowing about it.

I knew Miles was trying to reassure me that Angel would be safe, and I was glad such measures were in place for her sake. But for me, it sounded like hell.

As much as there were times Kai kept me locked away, it had never felt like a prison. Yet the more Miles explained about how restricted our movement would be, the more I felt like I was being thrown in a cell and the key tossed away.

The next couple of hours passed in a blur. We were met at the house by the head of security, a burly ex-SAS soldier who introduced himself as Tank, who then introduced several members of the security team on the night shift. He explained that the team rotated on a twelve hour shift and I'd meet the day team in the morning.

Tank offered to show us around the house, but when Angel tugged my hand and signed that she wanted to sleep, I asked him to show us to our rooms and the tour could wait. Obliging, Tank led us through the huge house, taking the stairs to where our bedrooms were.

Jane was in the first room. Saying goodnight, she disappeared inside, letting out an enormous yawn. Tank showed Angel and me to our rooms, and while we had separate rooms, I was glad to see they were adjoining, with an internal door between the two.

Leaving us to it, Tank disappeared. Despite Angel wanting to get straight into bed, I made her brush her teeth before tucking her in for the night. Her head barely hit the pillow before she was out like a light.

Hoping I would be able to fall asleep as quickly, I made my way to my own room, leaving the adjoining door open a crack in case Angel woke up and needed me. I cleaned my own teeth and changed into my pajamas before slipping into bed and willing sleep to come.

Of course, the second I closed my eyes, there was only one person I could think of.

Dark eyes with flecks of gold haunted my mind.

The sound of his voice echoed in my ears.

After I had twisted and turned for the umpteenth time, I kicked the covers off and got out of bed giving up on the hope of sleep. Crossing the room, I was about to throw open the balcony door to get some fresh air when a figure caught my attention.

The light from the house lit Miles up as he walked across the dark garden before coming to a stop at a fence. I guessed he was having as much trouble sleeping as I was, and figuring it was pointless lying in bed wide awake, I set off to join him.

The cool night air hit me as I stepped outside, eliciting goosebumps on my skin. The dewy grass soaked my sneaker-clad feet as I walked to where Miles was.

A flick of a lighter flame surprised me, I never knew Miles smoked. Expecting to smell cigarettes from the puff of smoke Miles blew out, I was even more surprised when the sweet smell of marijuana hit me.

I'd know the smell of marijuana anywhere, it used to be rife in the apartment block Angel and I lived in. Quite often I'd have to open the windows to air the apartment out from where so many of the other residents smoked it, filling the air vents with the stench. It was almost impossible to get away from it.

I'd only smoked it once in my life though, it was the night after I gave my virginity to Toby. We'd snuck off the following night intent on having sex again, only Toby bought some weed with him and we ended up getting too high to be able to do anything but laugh.

"Didn't know you smoked weed," I said to Miles as I stepped up next to him on the fence he was leaning over, my voice echoing in the still night.

Aside from Miles and I, there wasn't a soul to be seen. The guards were out there somewhere, but seeing as every one of them was dressed in black, it was unlikely I'd be able to see where they were anyway.

"I don't make a habit of it, just sometimes I need my brain to shut off, you know?" Miles replied.

Boy, did I know. I'd give anything to switch my brain off from thoughts of Kai right now.

Seeing me look longingly at the joint, Miles handed it to me with a knowing look in his eye. I didn't think twice about accepting it or not. I was exhausted, I needed sleep, and if a little bit of weed helped to turn *my* brain off for a few hours then that was fine by me.

Taking it from him, I took a long drag and nearly coughed up a lung. Fucking hell, whatever brand of weed this was, it was damn potent.

Miles and I were silent for a few minutes as we stared into the night, passing the joint between us. It didn't take long for my muscles to start relaxing, and a calming feeling washed over me. Enjoying the comfortable silence, I tipped my head back to look up.

The dark sky was filled with millions of twinkling stars, there wasn't a cloud in sight, and the full moon shone down brightly. It was a beautiful sight, and I couldn't help but wonder if Kai was looking at the moon from the other side of the world, seeing what I was seeing.

"Do you know how he is?" The words slipped unbidden from my mouth before I had a chance to stop them, breaking the ambient silence that had fallen between us.

Miles sighed heavily and took the joint from me, taking a long drag and holding it before letting out a huge puff of smoke. "He's passed out on your bed."

Christ on a cracker.

The words hit me like a punch to the gut and guilt washed through me. The weed wasn't strong enough to numb my feelings completely. I'd never been one for drugs, not after seeing what they did to my mom, but right then, I wondered if Miles had any other goodies that would make me forget about Kai, if only for a few hours.

"How do you know that?" I asked, unable to help myself.

"Jacqueline contacted me to say she was worried about him, said he'd drunk a bottle of whiskey and then disappeared. She was worried he'd gone out somewhere."

Miles handed the joint back to me and I gratefully took it. My lungs burned as I inhaled, and blood rushed to my head, but it was a buzz I needed to get through this conversation.

"How do you know he passed out in my room?" Images of Kai spread across my bed filled my head, and I could imagine myself lying next to him with his heavy arm pinning me to his body, just like he always did whenever I slept next to him.

"There's a camera in your room, it didn't take a genius to work out he would have headed there," Miles replied casually as if it was perfectly acceptable to drop a bomb of a camera planted in your room somewhere.

I didn't have it in me to get angry, or even *care* about the camera. In fact, it didn't surprise me. Kai was obsessed with me, the man had no problem whatsoever with invading my privacy before I had even really met him, so of course he'd have no problem invading it further when I lived with him.

Ask me again tomorrow if it bothered me, it may have been a different answer, but right there and then, I didn't care.

"Can I see?" I asked, because, yeah, I was a glutton for punishment. Miles paused for a second but then pulled his phone out. He tapped a few buttons, and in exchange for the joint, he handed me his phone.

My heart cracked straight down the middle. Kai was face down on my bed, one hand stretched across to my side, and his fist gripped the sheets tightly. It was as if he had reached out for me, only to find I wasn't there. His other hand was down by his side, clutching an empty whiskey bottle, and worry grew in the pit of my stomach.

Kai didn't drink himself to the point of passing out. He was always controlled, never allowing himself to be in a position of vulnerability, but there he was, oblivious to everything. Anything could have happened to him and he wouldn't be sober enough to even be aware of it, let alone deal with it.

Because I had left him.

Unable to look anymore, I handed the phone back to Miles. "Is he going to be okay?" I asked in a whisper.

Pocketing his phone, Miles took another drag of the joint which was nearly down to the butt. He handed it to me to finish and stepped down from the fence. "Honestly, Riley? I don't know. I've never seen him like this, not even when Theo died. I used to think Kai was unbreakable, more than a force to be reckoned with, but that was before….." He trailed off, but he didn't need to finish the sentence, I knew he was going to say, *'Before you came along.'*

I didn't know what to say in reply, instead, I took the final pull on the joint, taking a second to enjoy the last heady rush the weed gave me. Miles reached out and put a reassuring hand on my shoulder, before giving it a gentle squeeze.

"Get some sleep." With that, he walked away, leaving me to replay the images of Kai on my bed over and over again as his words rattled around my brain.

A combination of exhaustion and marijuana made me sleep. I was rudely awoken a few hours later by an over-excited Angel jumping on my bed, and demanding we went to explore the house. The little bugger barely gave me ten minutes to shower and get dressed before she was pulling me out of my room, and down the stairs. The only thing that distracted her from her mission to explore the house was the delicious smell of bacon and pancakes wafting from the kitchen.

Once breakfast was done, Tank instructed one of the security guards, Mark, to give Angel, Jane, and me a tour of the house. Miles, who looked as though he hadn't had any sleep at all, joined us as we went from room to room.

The house was pretty spectacular. It had everything we would need to keep us occupied for months- a huge library, a games room, a gym, indoor and outdoor pools, tennis courts, a cinema room including a popcorn machine, which of course made Angel's eyes light up, and finally, a state of the art panic room should we ever need it.

It was a shame we wouldn't be staying longer than a few days, but Miles was insistent we would be moved on, and when we got to the next place, wherever in the world that would be, we would stay there for a few days before we were moved on again.

Miles said we'd easily be moved on six or seven times before we eventually settled. Apparently, it was another layer of protection to water down our location should Max or Hendrix, or anyone else for that matter, somehow get wind we were being helped by the security company, Apollo.

By the time we arrived at the location we would be living, there would only be one man who knew who we really were and where we came from, and that was the head of the company, a man who would die before he gave up the location of any of his client's whereabouts, or so Mark said.

I didn't ask the question that was on the tip of my tongue the whole time Miles was explaining.

Would Kai know where we were?

After the tour had finished, Angel wanted to play in the garden. It was probably the first time in history my sister wanted to be in the fresh air instead of being cooped up playing computer games, so I certainly wasn't going to say no.

Mark and Miles left us in the garden, Miles saying he had a few bits to sort before he'd be getting on the plane back to Hollows Bay in the next couple of hours. I had started to relax a little, but at the thought of Miles heading back without me, my muscles instantly tensed.

Jane stayed with us, and we spent the next hour playing frisbee in the huge garden, which unsurprisingly, I was terrible at. Despite my ability to twirl around a pole and know where to move my hands and feet to at the right time, I was awful at hand-to-eye coordination.

The scenery surrounding us was stunning. The house was in the middle of nowhere, shrouded by acres and acres of fields. In the distance, forests of thick green trees stretched for miles, and aside from the hustle and bustle from within the house, the only other noise to be heard was the chirping of birds.

It was a beautiful location, and under different circumstances, it would be a great place to relax from the hassle of life.

'*I need to stop,*' I signed to Angel when the frisbee hit me yet again in the kneecaps. The sun was shining, and I'd opted to put some shorts on, a decision I was now regretting.

Sweat was beginning to form on my forehead, and I could feel the sun tanning my skin. Knowing it was only going to be a matter of time before I, and Angel for that matter, started burning, I called her over so we could sit in the shade of the trees.

"I need to get back into shape," Jane panted as she collapsed next to Angel, lying down on her back as she took big deep breaths. She had some color back in her cheeks, and I hoped she wouldn't be left too traumatized by her time in the cell. Maybe once Miles left, she would be able to relax.

"Guess you'll have all the time in the world now," I replied nonchalantly, staring off into the distance as thoughts of Kai tried creeping in once again.

I'd done my best all morning to keep memories of him at bay and not allow Miles' words from the night before to repeat in my mind, but I was failing miserably. From the minute I opened my eyes, images of him were there, hovering in the distance. No matter how much I tried to shake them, Kai was still there, lingering in the back of my mind.

Angel tapped my hand, pulling my attention from the gentle swaying of the trees in the distance.

'When will we be going back home to Kai?' she signed. It was the first time she'd mentioned him since he had carried her out of Club Sin.

When she spelled his name on her fingers, my heart dropped into my stomach.

'We're not,' I signed back, trying to keep the pain off my face, not wanting her to know just how much acknowledging the truth of that statement hurt.

'When will we see him again?' she replied, her brow raised in question.

A lump of emotion clogged my throat as I replied, *'We won't see him again. We're never going back to Hollows Bay.'*

Angel jumped to her feet, taking me by surprise, even Jane sat up to see what the commotion was about. I looked up at Angel, using a hand to shield my eyes from the glare of the sun behind her. Confusion filled me when Angel stared back at me with a look of anger and worry on her face.

'You have to go back to him! You can't leave him,' she signed so quickly I thought I'd misunderstood what she had said.

I looked to Jane to see if she had any idea what Angel was on about, but she looked just as confused as I did.

'What are you talking about?' I signed back slowly. Angel looked from me to Jane, and then back to me again, her shoulders slumped as the anger on her face replaced with a look of fear.

'He won't survive without you.'

I gaped up at my sister, my heart now doing somersaults and my pulse racing faster than a speeding train. I'd always known Angel was an intuitive little girl, but I did my best to shield her from the reality of our life. There was no way she would have known the heartbreak I was going through.

Or maybe I wasn't as good at protecting her from the truth as I thought.

Grabbing her hand, I pulled her down so she was sitting in front of me. 'Kai will be just fine, you don't need to worry about him,' I replied, wondering why on earth she thought Kai wouldn't be okay. I didn't have to wonder for too long.

'Danny made me promise that when I went home, I wouldn't let you leave Kai. He said Kai wouldn't know how to go on without you.'

Fuck sake.

What in the hell was Danny thinking when he made a twelve year old girl promise something like that?

'Danny should never have made you promise that,' I signed back, furious at Danny, even though he was dead. But Angel jumped to her feet again, determination etched all over her cute face.

'But he did, and I promised because I've seen how you've changed since we went to live with Kai. He makes you happy, and since the minute we left Hollows Bay, you've been miserable. For so long all you did was work and look after me, but he gave you something else to live for. You need to go back to him for you as much as for him.'

Didn't I always say she was a perceptive little bugger?

Tears pricked at my eyes as I stared back at her. She reached out and cupped my face, giving me a soft smile. At that moment, I wasn't looking at my younger sister, I was looking at a girl who was years older than her actual age.

'I can't leave you,' I signed to her, needing her to understand why I couldn't just hop on a plane and go back to Kai, as much as I *really* fucking wanted to.

She lowered herself back to the grass so we were at eye level and the first tear slid down my cheek as my sister signed her reply.

'You've always put me first. I always knew you worked at that strip club, you thought I didn't, but I did. I knew you did it to give me somewhere to live.'

Christ, how the fuck did she know that?

I raised my hands to reply, but she cut me off. My little sister shut me up. Despite the seriousness of the conversation, I couldn't help but smirk. It was time for me to accept that Angel was no longer my little girl.

'You are the best big sister I could have ever asked for, but it's time you put you first for once. I'm safe here, but Kai needs you now. Besides, Danny was my friend, and he died protecting me. Kai is going to kill the man who murdered Danny, and he should, that man deserves to die the most painful of deaths. But Kai won't be able to do it without you by his side. That's why Danny made me promise that you wouldn't leave him, because he knew Kai couldn't do it without you.'

The tears flowed freely down my cheeks now. A sniffle from my side made me turn my head, only to find Jane staring at Angel with her own tears streaming down her cheeks.

I swiped the tears away and pulled Angel in for a cuddle. She came willingly into my arms and we both sat for a few minutes, the two of us wrapped in each other's arms.

It didn't matter what she said, I couldn't leave her. She was my life, Kai was just a temporary distraction. But deep down, I knew that wasn't true.

Kai meant as much to me as Angel did. I hated that it felt like I had to choose between them.

"Riley," Jane said softly, pulling my attention away from Angel. "For what it's worth, I think Angel is right. I'll never forgive Kai for the way he treated me these last few weeks, but I understand why he did it." She leaned forward and grabbed my hand, a pleading look in her eye. "I loved Danny. In the few short weeks we had together, I fell in love with him, and I trusted him, and he said on a number of occasions that if you ever left, Kai wouldn't be able to go on." She paused to take a deep breath before summoning the courage to say her final words. "So, for what it's worth, I think you should go back to Kai because that man will undoubtedly get the retribution that is owed for Danny's death, but I don't think he could do it without you."

Angel once again cupped my cheek, pulling my attention back to her. *'I love you, Riley, and when Kai makes Hollows Bay safe again, I can come home, but he can only do that with your badass back with him.'*

I snorted at her. I was definitely not a badass, but I'd be lying if I said it didn't give me the warm fuzzies that she thought I was. I pulled her in again for a cuddle and held her there while thoughts rampaged through my mind.

It seemed I had a very important decision to make.

Chapter 19

Riley

Kai's childhood home loomed in the darkness like a solid fortress watching over the city.

The whole way back to Hollow's Bay, I'd been a bag of excited nerves, desperate to see Kai. A twelve hour flight felt like twelve fucking years, every single second passing excruciatingly slow.

The entire time I questioned how Kai would take my return. I hoped like mad he would be over the damn moon, but I'd be lying if there wasn't a little part of me that was worried. Especially when Miles had been skeptical about me returning with him, claiming it would be safer for me to return once the shit with Max Thorne had been dealt with. But once my mind had been made up, I was determined to be on the plane home with him.

Miles stopped the car outside the huge mansion but made no move to get out, not even shutting off the engine.

"You coming in?" I asked, brows raised in question.

"Nope." He turned to look at me, a smirk playing on his lips. "I've got better things to be doing than spending the day listening to you pair fuck each other's brains out."

Despite my cheeks heating in embarrassment, 'cos quite frankly, Miles was right, that's exactly what would happen, I let out a chuckle.

"Code to the front door is 16247," Miles said, leaning forward to peer out of the windshield to see the house. "There aren't many lights on so I reckon he'll be in his old room. Go through the front door, take the set of stairs on the left, follow the hallway to the last door on the right."

Still smirking, my mind running wild with all the things I hoped Kai would do to me once we were reunited, I hopped out of the car, grabbing the small bag I had packed before leaving France. As I rounded the car, Miles wound down his window.

"Tell Kai to call me when he's done busting my balls for bringing you back." And with that, he sped off, leaving a cloud of dust in his wake, and leaving me all alone to face the big bad wolf.

Entering the code, I crept into the house. I could instantly tell the foyer was *huge,* but it was too dark to make out any features. On either side of the foyer was a set of marble staircases leading up to the next level. Why the Wolfes felt they needed two sets of stairs to take them up a flight, I did not know.

I followed Miles' directions, taking the staircase on the left up to the first floor. A dim light from a crystal chandelier lit the hallway which was lined with a royal red carpet that ran the length of the floor. I followed the hallway, not paying much attention to the doors I passed, focused on getting to the one I hoped Kai was behind.

As I neared the end of the hallway, I stopped outside the last door on the right, it was open just a crack, light from within spilling out into the hallway.

Excited nerves filled my belly, the kind I used to get before I would go on stage to perform. I always looked forward to doing my routines, but I was always nervous in case it went wrong and I made a complete tit of myself. But I was being stupid, I didn't think I needed to worry about Kai's reaction.

At least, I hoped I didn't.

I stood silently for a minute, not even allowing myself to breathe as I listened intently for the slightest sound to indicate Kai was in the room, and debating about how I should let him know I was here.

Should I knock?

Should I call out?

Should I push the door open and say, *'Ta-dah! Guess who's back!'*

Fuck, what if he thought I was an intruder and shot me?

I was just about to call his name when soft snores drifted from inside. I sighed in relief, gently nudging the door open with my foot and keeping my hands up in a placating manner, just in case he woke up and grabbed his gun.

My heart beat wildly as I stepped inside. The sight of my gorgeous man asleep on the bed made my belly start doing fucking somersaults.

He was lying on his side, facing the door with one muscular arm tucked under the pillow, and the other reaching across to the other side of the bed, much like he had been when I had seen him on the camera. His kissable lips were parted, allowing soft breaths to escape, and his brows were furrowed. Even in sleep, he couldn't escape his demons.

I glanced around the room, quickly spotting the half-empty bottle of whiskey on the side and my heart broke. Kai rarely drank, let alone got shit-faced two nights running. I knew him well enough to know that he'd drink his way to oblivion rather than confront his emotions, and I damn well hated that I was the cause of his pain.

At least it was only half a bottle this time.

Unable to resist touching him any longer, I was on the bed next to him before I had a chance to think about it. The second I lay next to him, Kai's hand reached further across the bed and landed on my hip. It was almost as if we were two magnets that couldn't help but attract each other.

He mumbled my name, his soft lips almost unmoving. The need to feel them against mine consumed me. I didn't want to disturb him, but I couldn't wait another minute. Leaning forward, I tentatively brushed my lips against his, and with the faintest touch, I felt like I was home again. I knew at that very moment I had made the right decision to come back to him.

I pressed my lips firmer against his, needing to feel more, needing him to wake up and see me, but the only movement that came from him was his hand tightening on my hip.

"Kai," I breathed against his mouth, hoping like hell he would wake up and ravish me. But he slept on, the power of whiskey running through his veins. I pulled away, disappointed that I would have to wait.

Time crawled by. I stayed right where I was, lying next to him, and waiting patiently for any indications that he might be waking up. Hours, minutes, seconds ticked by as I watched his chest rise and fall, his lashes fluttering against his cheeks as he carried on dreaming, his hand occasionally twitching against my hip.

And still, he didn't stir.

The morning light crept in, bathing the room in a hue of red and orange. Giving into the need for the toilet, I reluctantly rolled off the bed and opened a door that led from the room, thankful that it took me into the ensuite. I took care of business and washed my hands, taking a minute to splash some water on my face.

I was exhausted. I hadn't slept on the plane, I was too buzzed about seeing Kai. The cold water was refreshing on my skin and helped to wake me up, and although there were heavy bags under my eyes, I couldn't help but notice I looked brighter than when I was in France.

Angel was right. I was miserable when I left Kai, and even though he was clueless I was back, I was already a million times happier. Don't get me wrong, I'd miss Angel, of course I would. For so long she was my sole reason to survive, but now I had another reason. Knowing she was well protected and living the life of luxury helped me to accept that maybe, just maybe, it was *my* time to be happy.

Besides, Jane had been more than happy to look after Angel, she said it would give her a purpose after her mom had died, and Angel loved Jane. It would do her good to spend time with a figure who was a better influence than me.

Miles left a burner phone with Jane so we had a way of staying in contact, it wasn't like I wouldn't get to speak to the brat again, and as soon as the shit with Max was dealt with, I had every intention of bringing her home.

Sounds from the bedroom caught my attention, and my gaze snapped to the bathroom door. Butterflies danced in my belly, and for a second I stared at the door, waiting to see if he would come in. When the door didn't open though, I took a deep breath and steeled myself for what was to come next.

As I opened the door, I found Kai standing in the middle of the room, bare-chested with his glorious tattoos on display, and mid-stretch. His solid abs flexed as he reached up to the ceiling, but the second his gaze fell on me, he froze in place, his eyes wide as if he'd seen a ghost.

"Hi," I said sheepishly, not at all prepared for the flash of anger that crossed his face. His arms dropped to his side as his gaze darkened.

"What the fuck are you doing here?" he rumbled, venom in his voice. My blood turned to ice, the nervous excitement vanishing, replaced by dread.

"I came back," I replied meekly, trying to sound confident, but failing miserably.

A growl rumbled from his chest as his gaze grew darker, if that was even possible. Clearly, I'd been fucking delusional for thinking Kai and I would have a happy reunion.

"Where's Miles?" he barked, throwing me off course. Before I had time to answer, he stormed out of the room. "Miles!" he roared angrily.

I sighed but followed him. This really wasn't going the way I'd hoped. "Miles!"

"He's not here," I snapped, my temper beginning to fray at his reaction. "He wanted us to have some time alone."

"That cunt has got some fucking questions to answer!" Kai roared as he pulled his phone from the gray joggers he was wearing. I had to avert my eyes from the shape of his cock pressed against the fabric. Scowling at the phone, he mashed buttons, cursing to himself.

Seriously, I had not expected this reaction. Yes, I thought he'd be shocked, but I thought more than anything he'd be pleased. The man claimed to love me for crying out loud, surely you were pleased to see the woman you claimed to love, right?

"Fucking prick!" he bellowed as he yanked the phone from his ear when Miles didn't answer. "I'll ring his fucking neck for doing this!"

That was it.

My temper snapped.

I marched over to him, forgetting momentarily who I was dealing with.

"What the fuck is wrong with you? I came back! I came back for you!" I screamed in his face, unable to control the rage building in me at his petulant behavior.

"You shouldn't have fucking bothered," he snarled back, his black eyes wild with rage.

Urgh, why did that hurt so much?

Before I could retaliate, he stepped forward, a menacing glint in his eye. His chest brushed against mine as he towered over me.

"You have no fucking idea how hard these last two days have been, Riley. No fucking idea." His voice was low and deadly, the kind he used when he was about to strike. But all that did was make the anger in my veins flare even more. Did he think the last two days had been a walk in the park for me?

"You left me, Riley. You walked out of my life without looking back, and I grieved. I fucking grieved for you. I came to terms with never seeing you again and I moved on."

A little voice in the back of my head said he was lying, that he wouldn't get over me just like that. But he had a damn good poker face because the way he was glaring at me, hate written all over his features, told me it really had only taken him all of two days to move on.

Well, fuck him.

"Is that all it took, Kai?" I jabbed him hard in his solid chest, poking the beast and riling him up. "Because I'll tell you something now, you gigantic asshole, leaving you was the hardest decision I ever had to make, and I knew, I fucking *knew* as soon as I got in that car, it was the wrong decision." I jabbed him again, my voice rising with rage as angry tears stabbed the back of my eyes. "I've left my sister to come back to you because I fucking love you, but you know what, you're right, I shouldn't have fucking bothered!"

I spun on my heel, ignoring the way his mouth fell open when I dropped the L bomb. It was the first time I'd said it to him. Sure, he'd said it to me before, but I'd never uttered those three little words back because it would have hurt too much when I had to leave.

I shouldn't have come back. I forgot what an insufferable fucking asshole he was. I didn't know how I was going to get back to France, but once I did, I was staying put. Fuck him. Fuck Kai Wolfe to hell. Steam bellowed from my ears as I stormed down the hallway, wanting to put as much space between me and him as quickly as possible.

I didn't get far. Kai grabbed my arm, spun me around, and pressed me against the wall, his hips pinning me in place as one hand grabbed my throat, a position I'd been in once before with Kai. Only now, I didn't fear for my life. My sanity, yes, especially with the hungry look in his eyes that said he was about to eat me whole. Not to mention the growing bulge pressed against my core.

"Say that again," he growled, his face mere inches from mine.

"Fuck you," I hissed back, ignoring the growing dampness in my panties.

"Say. It. Again," he spat through gritted teeth.

I don't know whether it was out of sheer stubbornness or damn pride, but either way, I refused to say the words again. Kai didn't deserve to hear me confess my love for him when he was being a Grade-A douchebag.

Instead of saying what he wanted to hear, I prised his fingers away from my neck. "Let me go."

To my surprise, he allowed me to remove his hand but I knew full fucking well that if Kai didn't want me to go, I wouldn't be going anywhere. I pushed him away, making him step back. Once again, I started to storm away from him, done with his shit.

This time, he didn't just grab my arm and pin me against the wall. Oh no, he used his favorite dickhead move that he seemed to use far too fucking often on me. He grabbed me, tossed me over his shoulder, and marched straight into his room. I didn't bother protesting, I knew from experience it wouldn't get me anywhere.

"If you think you're leaving me again, Star, you've got another thing coming." He tossed me on the bed, and before I had time to sit up and make my escape, he was on me, ripping my leggings right off, along with my panties, leaving me bare and exposed.

And of course, wanting.

Always fucking wanting when it came to Kai.

"Don't fucking touch me!" I hissed, but of course, he ignored me.

With one hand keeping me pinned, he yanked down his sweatpants, his hard cock springing free. He roughly grabbed my legs and pulled them apart before positioning himself between my thighs. My cries of protest fell on deaf ears, and with one brutal thrust, he was inside of me.

I cursed at the intrusion. Not because it hurt, nope, I was dripping wet and ready for him, but cursed because he felt so damn good.

Kai slammed his mouth down on mine. I wanted to resist, I really did, but my body had other ideas. My mouth opened, letting his tongue slide in to dance with mine. My teeth found his plump lip, and wanting him to know I was pissed at him, I bit down hard. The metallic tang of blood filled my mouth, but the sadistic bastard, who had now started thrusting deeply inside of me, only chuckled darkly.

"You think I'm bothered about you biting me, baby?" Blood trickled from his lip and onto his chin. "You can bite me all you like. I'll happily bleed for you, Star, especially when my blood is mixing with yours, making us one."

Christ.

He was going to be the death of me, and what a fucking wonderful way to go.

Kai thrust harder, hitting that sweet spot perfectly while his hand moved to where we were connected and he started rubbing my clit. It didn't take long before my curses turned into cries of pleasure and demands for more as I reached the point of no return.

And then the bastard stopped moving and took his hand away.

"Fuck, Kai, don't stop," I mewled, hating myself for wanting to beg him to continue. He held himself above me but lowered his head so our noses were practically touching. He thrust back in but at a deliberately slow pace, torturing me and making me whine again.

"Please, Kai, I need to come."

"Say it," he growled, a smug satisfaction on his face. The bastard knew he was edging me, and I wasn't strong enough to resist him.

"Fuck you," I replied, but there was no heat in it this time.

He pulled out slowly again, but this time, he slammed back in hard, pushing me that little bit closer to the edge.

"I can do this all day, Riley," he said, with a sick grin twisted on his bloodied lips. "Say. It."

I couldn't hold it in any longer. "Fuck! I love you, Kai. I fucking love you, you stubborn asshole!"

A beautiful smile took over his face, one that smashed through the remaining anger and sent a wave of warmth through me.

"You know I'm never letting you go now, Star. This is it, you and me, forever." His thrusts resumed at a quicker pace, the two of us needing to find our release together. "If you ever think about leaving me again, Riley, I swear to all that is holy, I will end you, and then I will end myself and follow you into the afterlife, because without you, I can't go on."

His words were a knife to the chest, his pain hitting me like a freight train. Tears filled my eyes and slid down my cheeks from his words and the overwhelming need to come so fucking badly.

Kai licked the tears that escaped, his tongue leaving a trail of heat wherever he touched. He moved a hand between us and found my clit again, and with two strokes, and his length buried deep inside me, I was so fucking close to the edge. Just one more thrust and I would go over.

As Kai slammed into me a final time, sending me into a blissful climax, he growled two little words in my ear as he emptied his load, sending me barreling straight into a second orgasm.

"Marry me."

Chapter 20

Kai

I'd never given marriage much thought. Sure, I knew I wanted to spend the rest of my life with Riley, but I'd been so focused on getting her to fall for me that I hadn't stopped to consider what our future actually looked like.

But the second she screamed those three words at me, I was hit with a lightning bolt of images of what our future could be. Her walking down the aisle in a wedding dress, her becoming my wife, *my queen,* and one day, carrying my child.

My heir.

It wasn't a question. I wasn't proposing to her and giving her a choice, I was telling her. *Commanding* her to marry me. Riley cried out as her orgasm crashed through her, but she didn't give any indication she had heard me.

Once I emptied every last drop of come inside her, I didn't immediately move. Instead, I hovered over her, my cock twitching in its favorite place. I placed little kisses on her cheeks, over her cute nose, her plump lips, and down to her delicate throat while she regained her breath.

I couldn't believe she was here. She was real and not some figment of my imagination. When she came out of the bathroom earlier, I thought I was still dreaming, and then when the realization hit that she was really there,

I was fucking *furious*. Not because I wasn't ecstatic to see her, but because I was scared.

There she was, telling me she had come back, and all I could think about was how much it hurt to see her walk away from me, how *easy* it had been for her to get in the car and let Miles take her away.

I told her I'd moved on, but that couldn't have been further from the truth. The agony I'd experienced over the last two days had grown deeper with every passing second until it had become unbearable, a weight I just couldn't shoulder. If she changed her mind and left again, I knew damn well I wouldn't be able to survive the pain a second time.

So I did what I always fucking did when I was backed into a corner.

I lashed out, hurting her with words and pushing her away. Until she said she loved me, and then the penny dropped.

She chose me.

She chose me over Angel, and even if it meant leading her to danger and accepting the life I led, she made the decision on her own to come home to me. There was no way I was *ever* going to let her go again. I had to make her mine, once and for all, and the only way of doing that was by putting a ring on her finger and giving her my name.

She giggled underneath me as my hand slid up her top and my thumb brushed across her nipple, the sound hitting me square in the cock. Reluctantly, I pulled out of her, otherwise, it wouldn't have been long before I was pounding her again, but before that could happen, I wanted her to acknowledge what I said.

Kissing her lips, relishing in her taste, I rolled onto my back, pulling her with me so she cuddled into my side. I lifted her chin gently so her chocolate orbs met mine, and I smirked at the sated look she wore on her face. My girl was always placid after she'd had a good fucking.

"Say it again," I demanded, needing to hear her say it one more time when she wasn't angry or I was balls deep inside her.

She smiled, and fuck me, did it make my heart pound hard against my rib cage. "I love you, Kai Wolfe. Even if sometimes you are the most infuriating man on the planet."

I didn't deserve to hear those words from her sweet mouth, but I'd take them. I always said I was a selfish prick. I leaned down and planted a light kiss on her lips, making her sigh happily.

"You never answered my question." Not that it was a question of course, even if she said 'no,' she'd still be my wife. I would just have to find a way to convince her.

Her body tensed against mine, and the contented smile she had been wearing only moments ago faded.

"You're not serious."

I rolled her onto her back again and pinned her to the bed with my body, my thighs separating hers.

"Deadly serious," I replied, my voice stern so she knew just how fucking serious I was.

"Kai, we can't get married, we've known each other for less than two months. You're crazy," she chuckled, her eyes rolling.

I was crazy.

Crazy about her becoming my wife.

Crazy about spending the rest of my life with her.

Running my thumb across her bottom lip, I stared down into her beautiful eyes that had a way of seeing through all my bullshit and bravado, right through to my soul.

"From the minute I saw you, Star, I knew I wanted to spend the rest of my life with you. If I had it my way, you would have been wearing my ring from the very first night you danced for me."

Her heart started pounding madly against my chest as any trace of joking disappeared. She finally realized I wasn't playing a game. Her lips parted, ready to protest no doubt, but I silenced her by putting a finger across her lips. Her eyes narrowed in a flash of anger, reminding me of how feisty my girl could be. It was one of the many things I loved about her, she was always ready to challenge me.

"Riley, baby, you came back to me. You had the choice to walk away, but the second you decided to come back, you devoted yourself to me and a future together, whether you knew it or not."

My cock hardened again, and when I rubbed against her dripping center, she purred like a fucking cat. I slammed my mouth against hers, kissing her hard and showing just how fucking much I loved her. She groaned and writhed under me, trying her damndest to find friction against my cock even though she had orgasmed only moments ago.

I pulled away from her, her eyes filled with lust. "You will be my wife, whether it's today, tomorrow, or five fucking years' time, you will be Riley Wolfe."

I slipped inside her with a powerful thrust, her pussy gripping my cock tightly and eliciting moans from both of us. I grabbed her thigh and pulled it up, driving my hard length further into its favorite place.

"So, baby," I whispered in her ear, "do us both a favor, don't fight me on this because I promise you, it's fucking happening."

She didn't reply. Mainly because I didn't give her a chance. I fucked her into oblivion, my name on her lips as she came. She didn't need to answer me though, I saw it in her eyes.

Acceptance.

After another two rounds of me pounding Riley's sweet cunt, she fell asleep, exhaustion finally taking over. I watched her for a few minutes, my beautiful Star who I never wanted to live without. Now the idea was in my head, it was all I could think about, it consumed me to my very core.

I didn't want to wait any longer, and why should I? I had the money, power, and contacts to make it happen today. While Riley hadn't quite said yes, I meant what I said to her. It didn't matter if we said 'I do' today, tomorrow, or in five years' time, it was going to happen, so why wait?

Besides, with the war that Max Thorne was intent on starting, who knew what was around the corner. He'd been quiet since Hendrix ran with his tail between his legs, no doubt to take Thorne's side, but his lack of action made me nervous. It was only a matter of time before he struck again, so now was the time to give Riley the ultimate protection.

The Wolfe name held a lot of power and respect, not just in Hollows Bay, but across the States. The second Riley took my name, everyone would know she belonged to me, and not just some whore I was screwing. She would get the protection that any Wolfe had.

As if that was the final push I needed, I snuck out of bed, leaving my future wife sleeping soundly. Heading straight to my office which, once upon a time, was my father's office, I pulled my phone out to make some calls.

The first call was to my contact who owned Apollo. I needed to keep my girl safe, no matter the cost, and until I had cleaned the mess up, and made sure that everyone who worked for me was loyal to me, I was going to do whatever I needed to protect her.

Within a few minutes, it was agreed that a team of mercenaries would be at the house within the hour, and at my disposal as I saw fit. I owed my contact massively for the resources he was sending my way.

With that taken care of, I called Miles.

"Am I forgiven for bringing her home?" Miles asked cautiously as a way of greeting. "Or do I need to change my name and get the hell out of Hollows Bay?"

"You're safe. For now at least," I replied, letting him hear the amusement in my voice. After all, how could I be mad at him for bringing home my reason for living?

"Great, I'll put the fake passport away for now. What do you know?"

"I'm getting married," I said casually, as if dropping that bomb was an everyday occurrence.

A short pause greeted me before Miles spoke. "Does Riley know?"

"Of course she fucking knows," I barked. But Miles had a point, he knew me well enough to know that even if she had said no, it didn't mean a wedding wouldn't take place.

"Well, shit," he said, pride lacing his voice. "Congratulations. When's the big day?"

"Tonight."

Another pause. I could practically hear the cogs whirling in Miles' brain through the phone. "Again, does Riley know?"

It was my turn to pause, and when I didn't answer, he sighed.

"Fuck, Kai, what are you going to do, tell her you're taking her on a date when really you are taking her to the altar?"

See, Miles really did know me too well.

"Christ," he said, taking my silence as confirmation. "Fine, what do you need me to do?" The resignation in his tone said it all. There was no point trying to get me to change my mind once I had made a decision.

"Pick Jacqueline up and take her to Carmen's bridal shop on Grosvenor Avenue so she can pick out a dress for Riley-"

"Shouldn't Riley pick out her own wedding dress?" he interrupted, even though he fucking knew how much I hated to be cut off mid-sentence.

"Riley doesn't care about that sort of shit, she'll wear whatever Jacqueline picks out. Trust me, I know my girl."

Miles kinda had a point, women spent most of their childhood dreaming about their special day. But I knew Riley, she probably never considered meeting a guy, let alone walking down the aisle. And my Star was not one for a big affair, she would want something simple and small.

"You really are fucked in the head over that girl, aren't you?" Miles said with a chuckle, although I could hear the affection in his voice. Who'd have thought me of all people would be losing their head over a girl?

"Yeah," I replied with a smile on my face, not bothering to deny how far gone I was for her.

"What else?" Miles asked, snapping my attention back on him as it wandered to my sleeping beauty upstairs.

"I'll deal with Colin Andrews, this will be a nice opportunity for him to clear his debt."

Colin Andrews was a council official, and yet another pompous prick who was living *way* above his means. Tempted by the bright lights of the casino, Colin had amassed quite a large debt to me thanks to his roulette addiction. Luckily for him, he also happened to be a celebrant, having performed weddings in Hollows Bay for the past ten years.

"And where exactly do you plan on doing this?" Miles queried. It was a good question, and one I hadn't thought about having been too carried away with the images of Riley walking down the aisle in a white dress.

"Good question. It needs to be somewhere low-key. I don't want to give Thorne an opportunity to ambush us when we're distracted," I replied, my mind churning with where we could go where the rumor mill wouldn't instantly go into overdrive. It would be risky enough making sure Colin didn't speak, but I'm sure with some extra cash lining his pockets, he would keep his mouth shut.

"How about the house?" Miles suggested, which seemed like a fucking obvious suggestion once he had said it. "I mean, you're already there, I can collect Colin once Jacqueline is done in the city and be with you in a few hours."

That would work.

"Do it," I instructed. "And pick up some flowers and shit as well."

Miles burst out laughing. "Aren't you Mr. fucking romantic?"

"Fuck off. This might not be the wedding Riley had in mind, but I'll make it the best damn night of her life."

"Sure you will, stud," Miles retorted, testing my patience. Although I had to admit, I hadn't heard him sound this light-hearted since before Theo died. Nothing like a good wedding to cheer everyone up.

"Alright, enough," I said, not having it in me to scold him for his mocking. "Get Jacqueline and get moving, I want to be putting that ring on her finger by the time the sun sets."

"Need me to pick up some rings as well?"

A smile graced my face as an idea popped into my head. "It's sorted."

I hung up and looked at the grandfather clock that stood in the corner of the office, counting down the hours until Star would officially be mine.

Chapter 21

Riley

I woke several hours later, my body aching but *oh so deliciously*. I'd been dreaming about Kai, and even though I'd just woken up, I was ready for him to fuck me again.

Kai really had turned me into a sex maniac.

I stretched across the bed with a smile on my face, only to be disappointed when I found it was empty.

"Kai?" I called, sitting up and looking around the room.

"Oh, Ms. Bennett, you're awake," Jacqueline said, surprising me as she came bustling out of the ensuite.

Her eyes briefly flashed to my chest, her cheeks reddening as she looked away. I'd forgotten that Kai had yanked my top off and spent what felt like an eternity teasing me by nipping and sucking all over my boobs.

"Shit, sorry," I squeaked, quickly pulling the covers up as my own cheeks heated. "Wait, Jacqueline, what are you doing here? Where's Kai?" I added in an afterthought. Now I was fully awake, confusion set in as to why the hell Jacqueline was in Kai's family home.

"Mr. Wolfe is getting ready. I'm here to help you," she replied politely before crossing the room to a table and fiddling with something I couldn't see.

"Ready for what?" I mumbled, feeling like I was missing something.

Kai hadn't said anything about us going out tonight. Was it even safe for us to go out?

"For the wedding." Jacqueline turned to face me, a bright smile on her face. It was the first time I'd seen the woman show any kind of emotion, she was always so stoic.

"Whose wedding?" I replied, my brows furrowed.

"Well, yours, of course!" she replied, exasperated.

"I'm not get-" I froze mid-yawn as my eyes landed on a large dress bag hanging up behind Jacqueline.

What. The. Actual. Fuck?

"Jacqueline. Please tell me that's not what I think it is." I glared at the dress bag as though it was personally responsible for the way my heart was thudding against my rib cage.

Jacqueline looked from me, to the bag, and then back at me again, the smile disappearing to be replaced with a look of caution.

"Erm, well," she stuttered, confirming my fears.

"Son-of-a-bitch!"

I threw back the covers, not giving a hoot that I was butt naked. Jacqueline very kindly averted her eyes as I stomped around the room, picking up my discarded clothes and throwing them on, all the while muttering to myself about how I was going to kill Kai.

I was serious. I was going to murder the big lummox with my bare hands.

Honestly, who the hell did he think he was?

He'd only proposed mere hours ago, and if I remembered correctly, I hadn't actually given him an answer.

Urgh!

He really was going to be the death of me.

As I threw on my shirt, I ignored the little voice in the back of my head *screaming* with delight that Kai wanted to marry me right now. I didn't want to acknowledge it because it was sheer craziness. I couldn't marry someone I'd only known for a matter of weeks, it was insane!

I had every intention of telling Kai that it was not happening, not today, not tomorrow, not for the fucking foreseeable.

Ignoring that my shirt was not only on inside out but also back to front, I stormed over to the door, ready to find Kai and give him a piece of my mind for once again being an insufferable controlling bastard, when a soft voice stopped me.

"Riley," Jacqueline called. I don't think I'd ever heard her use my first name before, she always referred to me as Ms. Bennett. For that reason alone, I found myself turning to face her, finding her with a pleading look on her face as she rubbed her hands together.

"It's not my place to say this, but I'm going to say it anyway, and hope that you forgive me and don't have me fired." She took a step closer, swallowing nervously.

I wasn't sure I wanted to hear what she had to say, yet my feet were glued to the floor, my eyes wide and fixed on her.

"It's my job to stay quiet and remain unseen, but in doing so I see a lot. I've known Mr. Wolfe since he was a young boy, and I've never seen him as happy as he has been these past few weeks. He's changed, since you came to be in his life, he never smiled before, but now he does. Mr. Wolfe was brought up to be a ruthless man, but you've brought out another side to him."

I wanted to plug my fingers in my ears and refuse to listen, because with every word Jacqueline was saying, my anger was receding and my stupid heart was fluttering wildly, lapping up the compliments that I'd been the one to change Kai.

Stupid, stupid heart.

"Mr. Wolfe loves you, and I can honestly say he has never loved anyone as fiercely as he loves you. I know this wedding might be a surprise to you now, Riley, but if you decide to go through with it, I would bet every cent I have to my name that Mr. Wolfe will spend the rest of his life loving you, protecting you, and making sure you are happy, and that's not a life to be sniffed at."

Fucking hell.

Jacqueline spoke with so much passion that her words hit me right in the chest, my anger now completely gone, and all that was left was affection for the man I loved.

I stared at her, a war raging between my head and my heart. Seeing my resolve hanging by a fucking thread, Jacqueline played her final card.

"Riley, when you left for France, I've never seen Mr. Wolfe in the state he was in, he was devastated. I think every single one of his enemies could have strolled right on through the apartment if they had chosen to, and I don't think he would have cared whether he lived or died. I didn't think he would survive without you by his side."

Echoing Angel's words, my resolve shattered, my heart winning the battle. Letting out a sigh, I closed my eyes and counted to ten.

Marrying Kai wouldn't be so terrible, right?

After all, he loved me and I loved him. Did it matter that I'd only known him for a short period of time? Every second I'd been away from him had been pure torture believing I would never see him again, and now we had been reunited, I couldn't bear the thought of not having him in my life. So why wouldn't I make a commitment to him? Sure, it was quick and unconventional, but didn't that sum up our entire relationship?

When I opened my eyes again, a sense of clarity washed over me.

Jacqueline was staring at me, waiting for me to turn around and march my ass out of this room to confront Kai, so when I dropped my hand from the handle and took a step away from the door, the bright smile returned to her face.

"Guess I'm getting married then," I said quietly, excitement firing to life in my belly.

Several hours later, I was dressed in the most gorgeous mermaid wedding dress I'd ever seen.

The entire dress was made of the finest silk, and it fit my curves perfectly. Thin straps held the soft material against my chest which tied up at the back of my neck in a bow. The tails from the bow trailed down, brushing over my bare back. The skirt was snug against my hips but flared out the lower the material went until it pooled into a small train behind me.

Jacqueline had picked out a beautiful pair of white and silver peep-toe high heels which gave me just the right height so I wouldn't trip over the front of the dress. I didn't think I could have picked out a more perfect dress for myself, Jacqueline had nailed it.

To finish off, she had selected a diamante hair slide that sat just above my ear, pinning a section of hair off my face. I sat patiently as Jacqueline styled my hair into loose curls that fell around my shoulders, trying to engage her in conversation. But after her speech earlier, the most I had *ever* heard her say in one go, she had reverted to her quiet self.

Finally, she applied a very light layer of makeup and beamed proudly as I stared at my reflection in the mirror. I couldn't quite believe it was my reflection staring back. Never in a million years had I imagined myself getting married, hell I'd never even thought I'd meet someone given my job was to twirl semi-naked around a pole. Not to mention I had *some* baggage in the form of Angel.

But here I was, the blushing bride.

I felt like a princess from a *Disney* film, only I wasn't marrying a prince. I was about to marry a king with a somewhat broken moral compass who was more often than not the villain in our weird story, and yet I wouldn't have changed it. Everything that had happened had led us to this point, and why on earth would I change that?

Jacquline led me through the house, my heels clacking loudly against the marble stairs as we descended, butterflies flapping wildly in my belly. The hallway seemed to go on forever, and from the sneak peek I had of each room, they all looked huge. Eventually, the hallway led to a sun room at the back of the house.

Dusk had fallen outside, but the terrace was lit up by a canopy lined with thousands of twinkling lights. In the distance, at the end of the terrace and under an archway covered in flowers, stood Kai.

He was dressed in a black tux, the sight of him stole my breath away. I'd seen him in a tux before, but I'd forgotten how damn hot he looked in one. He was engrossed in conversation with Miles, who was also wearing a black tux, and another male who I'd never seen stood with them, looking equally terrified as he was curious.

"Here," Jacqueline said, tearing my gaze away from Kai. She handed me a bouquet of pink and red roses, the fragrant smell instantly hitting me. How Kai had managed to arrange this in a few short hours was beyond me, but I had to admit, he did well.

There was only one thing missing from the wedding, well, two actually. I wished Angel and Danny were here to see this. At least one day, hopefully in the not too distant future, I'd get to tell Angel all about it.

"Thank you, Jacqueline. For everything."

She gave me another one of her bright smiles and then surprised the shit out of me by reaching out and cupping my cheek.

"You look absolutely stunning, Ms. Bennett. I wish you and Mr. Wolfe a lifetime of happiness." With that, she opened the door and stepped outside.

I watched her walk down the path, catching Kai's attention as she reached him and Miles. Although I couldn't see her face as she had her back to me, she must have said something to Kai as his eyes snapped to where I was waiting. Even with the distance between us, I could feel his heated eyes burning over every inch of my skin.

As our eyes met, something strange happened.

The butterflies stopped fluttering, my heart stopped racing, and the nerves disappeared.

As I stared at the man who would soon become my husband, I suddenly couldn't wait to walk down the aisle and be by his side. It was the first time since his proposal that I knew, from the bottom of my heart, that I wanted to be his wife, that I wanted to spend eternity with him.

Not waiting a minute longer, I opened the door and stepped out into the cool evening air.

The intensity in his dark eyes grew as he watched me walk towards him, his eyes never leaving mine. The path leading to him was rocky, and with the stupidly high heels I had on, I had to walk slowly to avoid tripping over and busting my ankle, but that gave me time to take everything in.

Soft classical music played from somewhere in the distance, the arch that Kai stood under had the same red and pink roses decorated around it. Both Kai and Miles had red roses in their buttonholes, and Jacqueline was standing on the other side of the man, who I assumed was there to marry us.

All eyes were on me as I made my way to them.

When I reached Kai, he was momentarily speechless. He held out his hand for me, and as soon as I took it, he pulled me into his hard body, his arms immediately wrapping around my waist. I was pretty sure he was breaking some kind of wedding etiquette, but I didn't have it in me to care. Kai was never one to play by the rules.

"You look exquisite, Star," he whispered in my ear, the world around us forgotten.

"You don't look too bad yourself," I replied, earning a rare shy grin.

He pulled away from me but still held my hand. "For a minute, I thought there was a chance I'd be marching down the aisle with you over my shoulder, kicking and screaming," he smirked.

"For a minute, you almost would have. You can thank Jacqueline for convincing me otherwise," I replied, looking over at Jacqueline and giving her a grateful smile.

Kai looked over his shoulder to where she stood, bowing his head in thanks. She responded by giving him a smile, filled with fondness, and I hoped that maybe, after we were married, Jacqueline would be seen as more than just the maid.

"Are you ready to begin Mr. Wolfe?" the man standing in front of us said. He was a short man, in his mid-fifties, and had a kind face.

"Fuck, yes," Kai replied confidently, making me giggle.

The ceremony was quick. The man, who introduced himself as the celebrant, Colin, read through legal bits, giving an opportunity for anyone to declare why Kai and I shouldn't be married.

I knew he had to say it, but it was laughable, as if Miles or Jacqueline would stop the service. Kai would have had their heads on a platter before they finished their declaration.

Kai and I held hands as we called upon Miles and Jacqueline to bear witness to our marriage. Neither of us could tear our eyes away from the other. My heart beat madly, not from nerves but from excitement of knowing I would be spending the rest of my life loving this crazy man who drove me insane, but who I couldn't live without.

When the time came to exchange rings and say our vows, Kai surprised me with a beautiful ring. It was a platinum band, with a solid square diamond nestled on top, it was simple, yet stunning. His ring was a plain black titanium band, and as I placed it on his ring finger, I promised to love him until death parts us.

In a blink of an eye, the ceremony was over and Kai and I signed the register, followed swiftly by Miles and Jacqueline as our witnesses. Once that was done, Kai and I took our places back at the makeshift altar with Colin.

"Kai and Riley, you have made your declarations as required by law and in front of your witnesses. It is my pleasure to now announce you as husband and wife," Colin said, looking between Kai and me and smiling affectionately at us. "Kai, you may now kiss your bride."

Chapter 22

Riley

It didn't matter that we had an audience. Kai kissed me like I was his lifeline, as though he couldn't breathe without a part of him touching me.

I kissed him back with just as much hunger because that was *exactly* how I felt.

"I think that's our cue to go," Miles chuckled from somewhere in the distance as Kai gripped my waist and pulled me closer to him, his hardened length pressing against the silky smooth dress.

I'd had to go panty-less, otherwise, I would have had major VPL issues, but now I was regretting my decision. The soft material was pressed against my bare pussy which was already throbbing thanks to the way Kai was devouring me.

I was vaguely aware of retreating footsteps and the soft music still playing in the background. When the beat changed to a song I recognized, Kai pulled his mouth away from me before staring down with adoration in his eyes, and a loving smile on his face.

"This song always makes me think of you," he whispered against my lips.

"I wouldn't have guessed you were a Rhianna fan," I chuckled, surprised at his admission. Although it didn't sound like Rhianna was singing this version of *'Love on the Brain,'* it was an acoustic version, sung beautifully by a woman with a lilting voice.

"It was the song that played the first time I ever saw you dance," he replied, shocking the shit out of me.

"You remembered that?" I asked curiously.

"I remember everything about you, Riley, every second I've ever spent with you will live with me until I take my last breath."

A warm, fuzzy feeling flooded me. I'd never felt so loved in all my life, nor did I think I could love my husband any more than I did right then. For such a scary bastard, he was also charming and soft, and I loved that he only showed this side to me.

"Dance with me," he murmured in my ear as he pulled my hips against his and started swaying gently.

I wrapped my arms around the back of his neck and for the rest of the song, Kai and I stared into each other's eyes, wrapped in our own bubble of love.

Right then, nothing else mattered. Not the impending war with Max, not the betrayal committed by Hendrix, only us, lost in each other and our love.

As the song came to an end, Kai placed a tender kiss on the tip of my nose and then surprised me again when he spoke.

"I wish my mom had been alive to meet you, Star." Kai never spoke of his mom. Hell, he barely spoke about any of his family. Aside from knowing she had passed away when he was thirteen, I knew nothing else about her.

"Do you think she would have liked me?" I asked apprehensively. Even though she wasn't alive, it was important to me to know she would have approved of her son's choice of wife.

"Baby, she would have loved you," he said, kissing my nose again. "That's her ring, you know?"

My brows rose in surprise as I pulled my hand away to examine the ring on my finger, falling in love with it even more at the knowledge that it once belonged to his mom.

"What about your ring, was that your father's?"

His eyes darkened, and I instantly wanted to take the words back, I knew Kai didn't have a very good relationship with his dad.

"No, it was Theo's." Kai copied my action of looking at his ring. The darkness in his eyes faded, replaced with fondness as he stared at the black band. "Actually, it was my grandfather's, but he gave it to Theo. I debated about burying it with him but something told me Theo would have wanted me to keep it safe."

Kai disappeared into a memory, his eyes glazing over. I didn't want to pull him away from it, he had never grieved for Theo, never allowed himself to think of his brother unless it was in his quest to find the person who killed him. So when moments like this happened, rare as they were, he needed to have it.

As if remembering I was there, Kai shook his head, dismissing the memory. "He's buried here, in fact, all the Wolfes are."

"They are?" I stupidly looked around expectantly, as if a bunch of graves would somehow magically appear in front of us. Kai softly nudged my chin back to look at him.

"There's a graveyard on the land at the far end of the house. I'll take you there at some point. But right now, I don't want to think about the dead, I want to enjoy living in this moment with my wife."

Wife.

Holy hell.

I was married, and to Kai Wolfe of all men. Hearing him call me his wife made it all seem real.

Before I could reply, his mouth was on me again, his tongue brushing against my lips, seeking entrance. When I opened my mouth, and his tongue entwined with mine, a contented sigh left me. I never wanted this night to end.

We kissed for a few minutes with as much passion as we had immediately after Kai had been granted permission to kiss his bride, the throbbing in my pussy bursting to life again.

"I think I need to fuck you now, Mrs. Wolfe."

A sly, seductive smile spread over my face. That sounded like a marvelous fucking idea to me. "I best be a good wife then and let my husband ravish me."

His eyes darkened again, only this time for an entirely different reason.

Kai scooped me up in his arms, making me giggle as he carried me through the house, stopping briefly in the kitchen as we passed through so I could grab the champagne chilling in a bucket, and two flutes that had been left on the side.

There was no sign of Miles, Jacqueline, or Colin as Kai carried me up the stairs and to his old bedroom. Nerves filled my belly, which was ridiculous, it wasn't like Kai and I had never had sex before, yet my heart pounded furiously with the knowledge that we were about to consummate our marriage.

When we reached his room, Kai placed me on my feet before taking the champagne bucket and flutes and setting them aside. He pulled the thick curtains, plunging us into darkness before flicking a switch, and turning the light on to a soft glow.

Who knew my husband could be so romantic?

Ditching his tuxedo jacket and bow tie, he popped the cork from the champagne bottle, managing to not spill a drop, something I'd never achieved in the few times I'd tended the bar in Club Sin, somehow I'd always end up covered in bubbly.

He poured the champagne into the two flutes before handing one to me. "To our future," he said, holding his glass up to toast.

The simple statement held so much promise, and as I tapped my glass against his and drank, his eyes never left mine.

The champagne was delicious but one mouthful was enough for me. I wanted to taste something more delectable.

Namely, my husband.

Evidently having the same thought as me, Kai took my glass and put both of them on the side. Stepping in front of me, he grabbed my hips.

"Turn around," he commanded. I obeyed instantly, turning to give him my back.

His hard length pressed against my ass as he placed delicate kisses across my shoulder, working his way up to my neck, before nipping at the sensitive spot below my earlobe. He took his time, teasing me into a frenzy. I don't think I had ever been so desperate to feel Kai inside me.

Excruciatingly slow, Kai pulled one of the tails hanging down my back, the bow holding my top up falling apart. As he let go, the silky material slipped down my front caressing my nipples as it fell to my waist.

Kai's mouth latched onto my neck, his teeth scraping my skin before biting down hard and leaving his mark on me. When a gasp erupted from me, he licked the spot he had just bitten, soothing the sting. He had claimed me with a ring on my fingers, and now he was branding me with his mark.

His hands came up to cup my breasts, and as his thumbs brushed over my rock-hard nipples, my breath quickened and my pussy throbbed, aching to be filled by the only man who could sate me.

My head fell back against Kai's solid chest, my neck opening up to him. He didn't hesitate, his mouth moved over every inch of skin he could reach from the position we stood, branding me wherever he touched.

Come tomorrow, I would be covered in his mark but I was so fucking down with that. I wanted the world to know that I belonged to Kai Wolfe.

Kai's hand moved to the zipper on my dress. Again, he took his sweet time undoing it, and when he did, I wiggled my hips as he helped me shimmy out of it, the material pooling at my feet when it fell to the floor, leaving me naked with the exception of my heels.

He chuckled from behind me. "It was a good job I didn't know you were bare under that dress when you walked down the aisle, Star. I never would have made it through the ceremony without hitching your dress up and eating your delectable cunt."

I snorted. "Oh, husband, you have such a way with words."

"Only for you, wife." He spun me around, keeping his grip on my hips so I didn't fall. "Now undress me."

His heated eyes landed on my taut nipples, and he licked his lips in anticipation. A wicked grin toyed at my lips. He'd taken his time undressing me, knowing full fucking well I was getting more and more worked up.

Payback was a bitch.

Running a finger down the front of his shirt, I trailed it down until it ran over the bulge in his pants. His cock was straining against the material, and as I cupped my hand against his length, his chest rumbled in frustration. I bit my cheek to stop myself from laughing.

I removed his cufflinks first before starting with the top button of his shirt. Slowly, *very slowly,* I undid the buttons, allowing my fingers to brush over his skin. He watched me like a hawk, every little movement I made, he followed, waiting for the moment to strike, and oh, how happy I was to be his prey.

"Star, you're testing my patience," he growled when I took too long undoing the last button.

"What's the rush? We have the rest of our lives," I said in a sultry voice, looking up at him from under my lashes.

His reaction was exactly what I wanted. His hand whipped out, wrapping around my throat and squeezing playfully.

"I've told you once before, don't play games with me, you won't like it when you lose."

They were the words he'd muttered the first time he fucked me in his office, backing up his earlier comment that he did indeed remember every second we had spent together.

"Seems I haven't learned my lesson," I whispered, leaning forward to lick his lips. His pupils dilated and the next thing I knew I was on my back on the bed.

Kai stood at the base, staring down at me like a wild animal, his shirt hanging open to show his impressive chest which was heaving as he struggled to regain control, his dark eyes filled with lust.

"Allow me to show you what happens when you think you can play games." He grabbed my ankles, tugging me hard so I slid down the bed, my ass almost falling off the end. Dropping to his knees, Kai threw my legs over his shoulders before diving face-first into my soaking pussy.

He wasn't gentle. His teeth clamped down on my engorged clit, sending shockwaves through my body.

"Kai, fuck," I hissed, somewhere between pain and pleasure. My hips rolled against his face, seeking more of what he had to give, but he stilled me by placing one of his big hands on my belly and holding me down.

"Maybe this will remind you what happens next time you think about teasing me with what's mine, Star," he mumbled against my slit, before shoving three thick fingers roughly inside me as his tongue and teeth toyed with my clit, making me cry out.

Kai was ruthless as he ate my pussy, his three fingers fucking me hard. I would feel his presence every time I moved tomorrow but I wouldn't have had it any other way.

As I drew nearer to my climax, Kai pulled his fingers out and moved his mouth away from where I desperately needed him. He looked up at me from between my thighs, a wicked smile on his glistening lips and his eyes filled with mirth.

"Kai, what the fuck?" I panted angrily. I was so fucking close to coming, but the gorgeous bastard smirked up at me.

"Let me know when you've learned your lesson, baby," he said smugly before diving right back in.

Three times. Three fucking times he drew me closer to the edge, only to stop and wait for my impending orgasm to rescind before starting again. Each time he did, he gave me a smug smile that only made me want to throat-punch him.

It was at the start of the fourth time that I broke. Keeping one hand flat on my belly and putting pressure on my pelvis, his lips latched onto my clit as a finger found its way into my ass, and I couldn't take it any longer.

"Kai, please!" I cried. "I'm sorry!"

"What are you sorry for, Star?" His words were muffled where his face was still buried between my legs, his finger thrusting slowly in and out of my tight hole.

"I'm sorry for teasing you!" I swallowed my pride for the sake of finding my release. "I won't do it again!"

The bastard laughed, the vibration hitting me in the core and pushing me ever closer to the edge.

I wondered if it was too late to annul the marriage.

"Who does this pretty cunt belong to?" Kai growled as he pulled his finger from my ass and thrust two fingers into my pussy.

"You!" I whined like a whore in a whore house.

"Don't ever forget that, Star. You, your cunt, every delectable part of you belongs to me."

I answered with a scream as he finally let me come. My orgasm crashed through me, the intensity so extreme that my breath caught in my throat as my pussy flooded with my warm release.

Kai didn't give me time to recover. At some point while fucking me with his mouth, he'd removed his shirt. Now, he stood and shoved his pants down, his thick cock springing free. He hitched my legs over his shoulder, lifting my ass off the bed and slamming his cock straight into my dripping core.

"Fuck, I'm going to fuck this pretty pussy every day for the rest of our lives," Kai groaned, thrusting hard and fast into me as he gripped my legs.

From the angle he held me, I could barely move, helpless with no choice but to lay there and take everything he had to give me. Our moans reverberated around the room, mixed with the sound of skin slapping against skin.

When my orgasm started to build again, Kai pulled out and dropped my legs from his shoulders. Instead, he grabbed my hand and yanked me up. He spun to sit on the bed and twisted me around before pulling me into his lap, my back to his chest. As I sank down, impaling myself on his length, his mouth latched onto my neck, and he sucked, giving me more of his mark.

"Fuck yourself on my cock, baby. Make yourself come," he said, tugging my hair and making my head fall back before he slammed his mouth on mine, letting me taste my release on his lips.

Kai gripped my hips and started moving me at the pace he wanted me to go at, and once I'd found my rhythm, his hands moved up, his fingers tweaking my sensitive nipples which sent sparks of desire straight to my core.

I bounced on Kai's lap, my climax just beyond reach. Kai's fingers tugged at both nipples and with a final suck on my neck, my orgasm ripped through me.

"Kai!" I screamed as my pussy clamped down around his shaft, pushing him over the edge to join me in finding our release, his hot seed filling me.

As we regained our breath, Kai kissed my shoulder before whispering in my ear, "I fucking love you, Star, forever and always."

Chapter 23

Kai

Riley and I didn't leave our room for the next day, the world outside be damned.

I alternated from making love to my wife, to fucking her roughly, claiming every inch of her again and again. It was only ever going to be a matter of time before our bubble was shattered, but until that happened, we were determined to make the most of our time alone.

I woke the following morning to her delectable mouth around my hard cock, once again sucking me dry.

Damn girl was insatiable, not that I was complaining.

"Fuck, Riley. If I wake up every morning to my cock in your mouth, I'll die a very happy man," I hissed as her tongue ran over the swollen head.

She flashed me a sultry smile before taking me fully into her mouth, the tip reaching the back of her throat. It wasn't enough though. I wanted to bury myself so deep in her perfect pussy that we wouldn't be able to tell where I ended and she began.

"Ride me, wife," I ordered, grabbing her arms and pulling her up my body. She came willingly, spreading her legs and impaling herself on my length, gasping as she sank down.

"Baby, do you have any idea how fucking gorgeous you look when you are bouncing on my cock?" I rumbled, but I had no clue whether she heard me. Her head was thrown back, her eyes closed as she moaned in ecstasy.

That was until we were interrupted when the door flew open, crashing against the wall with an almighty bang.

Instinct kicked in.

With the exception of the days when I had been comatose through alcohol after Riley left, I was always alert, always waiting for a threat to attack. It was the nature of the life I led, I had enemies all across the globe, and they could strike at any time.

Even before assessing who had barged in, I threw Riley on her back, grabbed the gun that I kept strapped to the bed behind my pillow, and moved in front of her, aiming the gun at the fucker who had dared to disturb us.

"Kai, you're not going to believe this!" Miles panted, out of breath from where he must have sprinted up the stairs. I'd forgotten he was in the house, lost in my little Riley bubble.

From behind me, Riley peered over my shoulder, her bare tits and pussy covered by my body. She cursed when she saw who it was, adjusting the sheets to cover up my now flaccid cock.

What a way to kill a boner.

"What the fuck, Miles?" I roared, cocking the gun.

Cousin be damned, unless he had a good reason for bursting in here while I was fucking my wife, he was a dead man.

As if seeing us for the first time, Miles turned to find my gun on him and a furious look on my face.

"Shit! Sorry!" His hand flew to cover his eyes as if that would erase the fact he got a glimpse of my naked wife riding me.

"I swear to god, Miles, this better be life or death or I'm going to fire a round into each of your kneecaps."

Riley chuckled over my shoulder, the sound calming me fractionally, enough for me to lower my gun.

"Kai, I'm sorry, I didn't think. But this is bad. Really bad." He dropped his hand and cracked one eye open, making sure it was safe to look.

It was never safe to look when my wife was naked.

A growl rumbled in my chest, only calming when Riley placed a hand on my shoulder.

"Miles, I think you need to stop procrastinating and tell him what's going on. He's practically vibrating with anger over here, and I can't see that ending well for you," Riley said, amusement lacing her tone.

"Right," he said, his hands going to his hair and tugging like he always did when he was frustrated. "It's Thorne, he's made his move."

That got my attention.

"What's he done?" I snarled, my anger moving from Miles to the fucking thorn in my side. Riley's hand tensed against my shoulder.

Miles' hands fell from his hair and onto his hips. "He raided all your businesses this morning and ordered closures against them. Plus he's issued arrest warrants for both you and me."

Riley gasped from behind me.

"What are the arrest warrants for?" I asked curiously.

"For the murder of Danny," Miles said before taking a step forward with a pleading look on his face. "But Kai, that's the least of our worries. Didn't you hear what else I said, he's raided all your businesses and ordered them to be closed."

"Yeah I heard you," I replied with a shrug.

"Why are you so calm about this?" Miles said, eyeing me suspiciously.

"Because I knew Thorne was going to do this."

"You knew?" Riley piped up, surprised.

"I didn't know *exactly*, I guessed that's what he would do. It's what I would have done. So I put contingencies in place," I replied calmly, shrugging.

Seriously, just because I'd been pining over Riley leaving my ass, did Miles think I was sitting back and wallowing in my own self-pity? I mean, I did, at least for the first day, but before I found myself in East Bay and stumbling across Blaze, I was busy putting plans in place. Plans for as many eventualities I could think of.

"What contingencies?" Miles asked, his voice going up an octave.

"I tell you what, Miles, give me an hour and we'll talk."

I'd had enough, I had unfinished business with my wife. There was nothing I could do right this second about my businesses being closed, and if I reacted without thinking things through, I'd be playing straight into Thorne's hands.

Nope, the best thing to do was let the dust settle before I took action.

Riley's hand slipped down my back and wrapped around my waist.

"An hour, hey? Think you can last that long, stud?" she said loud enough for Miles to hear, before dipping her tongue in my ear.

My cock was hard in an instant.

"Better make that two hours, Miles," I growled at her challenge.

"Christ," Miles said, rubbing a hand over his brow in frustration. "The city is falling apart, and you two are acting like a couple of fucking horny teenagers."

Miles had barely left the room before I pounced on Riley.

It was closer to three hours later when we emerged from the shower together. What can I say, my wife had a fucking glorious body that I couldn't help but worship.

"Why don't you go explore the house while I talk to Miles?" I said to Riley as we dressed, the mood somber as we both crashed back to reality.

"I'd rather come with you and hear what he has to say. Aren't you worried about the arrest warrant?"

"No. And you aren't coming with me, this is my shit to deal with, I'm not dragging you into it any more than I already have. Go enjoy your afternoon," I replied, trying not to snap at her, but my mood had rapidly deteriorated. I was going to murder Thorne with my bare hands for ruining my happy bubble with Riley.

"Oh, okay," Riley said, far too happily, which would have raised my suspicion had I not been lost in thoughts of how I was going to skin Max fucking Thorne alive.

She threw her top on and marched her cute ass to where I was standing by the dresser. Taking her wedding ring off and slamming it on the side, she glowered at me.

"Guess you can have this back then," she hissed angrily.

I don't know if I was more pissed at her tone, or the fact she had taken her ring off. She turned on her heel, storming toward the door, but of course I was never going to let her walk away from me. Especially without her ring on.

I grabbed her arm, spun her, around and slammed her against the wall. "What the fuck do you think you are doing?" I snarled in her face, only to be met with her own snarl right back at me.

"Taking your ring off until it gets into your thick head that when I married you, it meant your shit became my shit, just like my shit became yours," she barked. "We're a team now, Kai, we share our troubles and we work through them together!"

And then she poked me in the chest.

I glared at my girl, my brave, feisty girl who had no problem standing up to me, and I hoped she never changed.

She had a point. I would do anything to help resolve any problem she had. If it meant slaying every one of her enemies and bringing their heads on a platter to her, I would. If it meant burning down the city of Hollows Bay so she never had to be reminded of the shithole that was her life before she met me, I would. We were a team, and that meant letting her share the burden of some of my problems.

Besides, now she was my wife, if anything happened to me, she would be left with a whole lot of responsibilities. I had every faith that Riley would be strong enough to deal with them, should the worst happen, but bringing her in on my problems now would only make her stronger.

Sighing, I took a step back. Her brows rose in surprise, no doubt at my lack of fight. Gently, I grabbed her hand and placed her ring back where it belonged.

"You're right baby, we are a team. I just didn't want to drag you into my trouble anymore."

"If it meant being by your side, I'd happily let you drag me into the deepest pits of hell." She smiled her beautiful smile and the last of my anger faded. I fucking loved this girl, more than life itself.

"Just do me a favor?" I said, kissing the tip of her nose. "Don't ever take your ring off again."

She heard the warning in my tone, and a sly grin spread across her face. "Maybe you ought to teach me another lesson."

It was another hour before we finally left the room.

Miles was pacing the length of the lounge when we found him, his eyes darting to Riley's hand in mine. If he was surprised to see her with me, he didn't say anything.

"Thank fucking god," he said. "I've been going out of my mind down here."

"Why? There isn't anything we can do about the businesses being closed." I sat down on the sofa, pulling Riley down next to me.

"Kai, seriously! How can you be so calm about this? He's closed every single one of your businesses. That's millions of dollars going down the drain," Miles exclaimed.

"I'm aware," I snapped, getting tired of his hysterics. "And I assure you, it will only be a temporary measure until we figure out who Thorne is, and what he wants."

Miles glared at me, before sighing and falling into the armchair opposite us.

"There's something else," he said, leaning forward.

"What?"

"The police raided the penthouse this morning with their arrest warrants, I think they've taken Jacqueline."

"What?" Riley sat up, alarmed.

"Yeah. I assume they've taken her to the police station but I haven't been able to get any news," Miles replied.

"Kai, we can't just leave her in the police station," Riley said, grabbing my arm. This was exactly why I didn't want her getting involved.

I put my arm around her, not knowing how to comfort her. Truth was, as much as Jacqueline had been in my life for a long time, she wasn't family. And that meant she was collateral damage.

"We'll figure something out, she's a tough old bag." I shared a look with Miles, he also knew we wouldn't give Jacqueline too much more thought, she wasn't the priority right now.

"Something doesn't add up, Kai," Miles said, changing the topic before Riley could demand we did something immediately about Jacqueline. "As soon as they checked the penthouse, and we weren't there, why didn't they come here? Hendrix knows every single one of our locations, including this house. So why haven't we been raided yet?"

"Because he's playing a game with me," I replied, confident that Max Thorne was toying with me. But for what reason, I didn't know.

"You think they'll raid here soon?" Riley asked. "Maybe we should hide somewhere else."

"Wolfes don't hide, Star," I growled, moving my arm from behind her back to put on her knee as if to hold her in place. "We don't run, and we don't hide. If Thorne wants to raid this place, let him. But I suspect he hasn't because he knows he'll be bringing the war to my door, rather than holding the battle on his ground."

She was about to reply, when my phone rang, cutting her off.

"Wolfe," I snapped as I answered it.

"Sir, Ericson here, I'm the head of the team stationed outside," a deep voice rumbled. My eyes snapped to Miles, my body instantly tensing.

The team outside knew to only contact me if there was a security risk. Miles knew straight away something was wrong, his hand moved to behind him where he kept his gun.

"Sir, I'm sorry to disturb you, but there's something you need to see out here," Ericson said. "We've scoped the perimeter, it's safe to come out," he added as if I was fucking scared to leave the house.

"I'm coming," I replied, hanging up. "That was the team outside, he said there was something I needed to see."

Miles stood, and Riley quickly followed suit. It was on the tip of my tongue to tell her she wasn't coming but she was already giving me her look that said I'd have an argument on my hands if I dared stop her.

Besides, it was safer for her to come with us, as much as I trusted the men outside, I wouldn't risk leaving her in the house alone.

Taking her hand, I led her outside, Miles walking on my other side as we passed the huge fountain that stood in the front courtyard. The winding path led us through the long front garden, the three of us silent, filled with anticipation about what we were going to find.

As we neared the end of the driveway which led to the road, a man dressed in black combat gear started walking up to meet us.

"Mr. Wolfe, Jack Ericson," he said, offering his hand with a grim expression on his face.

"What's going on?" I asked, shaking his hand.

His eyes darted to Riley before coming back to me, an unspoken question reflected there. He was asking for permission to tell me what had happened with her standing next to me, and I instantly respected him for it. I gave him a nod, letting him know he was free to speak openly.

"About thirty seconds before my call to you, a van sped by. It stopped just short of the property, and a body was thrown from it before it took off again. There were no registration plates, or identifying marks on the van but I have one of my guys reviewing camera footage to see if we can identify the driver."

"Fucking hell," Miles muttered, echoing my thoughts.

Riley's hand tensed in mine but that was the only sign she showed of being affected by the news.

"Show me the body," I ordered Jack. He nodded once and turned to walk back towards the road, the three of us following behind.

A group of men wearing the same black combat gear surrounded a lump on the floor but cleared as we approached.

"Christ," Miles said as we reached the body. My jaw clenched as recognition dawned on me.

The front of his body was soaked in red where his throat had been slit, his eyes wide open but unseeing.

"Who is it?" Riley asked, her voice quiet. I looked down at her to find her staring at the dead body, her face pale.

Wrapping an arm around her, I pulled her into my chest, wanting to protect her from the sight before us.

"Isaac, my private investigator," I told her.

"Sir, there was something attached to his body, a letter addressed to you," one of the guards said. He handed over a plastic wallet that was soaked in blood but had protected whatever was inside.

Dropping my arm from Riley, I took the wallet and opened it, pulling out the envelope inside. On the front in scruffy handwriting were the words,

Wolfe- *I believe you have been looking for this.*

Not waiting a second longer, I tore open the envelope and pulled out the contents, two pieces of paper.

The first was the deed poll indicating a change of name from Michael Tucker to Max Thorne.

The second piece of paper was the results of a DNA test confirming that Michael Tucker, a boy who had been born just shy of a month before me was the biological son of Christopher Wolfe.

My father.

Chapter 24

Riley

The three of us walked back to the house in stunned silence.

Kai has a brother.

Max Thorne is Kai's brother.

The shock hadn't sunk in for me, so I could only imagine how Kai was feeling. When we reached the house, Miles muttered something about needing to get in front of his computer to see if the bullshit was true before scuttling off, leaving Kai and me staring at his retreating figure.

I turned to look at Kai, unsure what the hell to say or do next. I mean, it's not every day your husband finds out he has a brother, and a brother who wants to ruin your life at that.

Kai was staring absentmindedly at the door Miles had just walked through, a million emotions etched on his face.

"Are you okay?" I asked, and then internally cringed for asking such a dumbass question. Of course he wasn't alright, duh.

"I don't really know," he replied, raw vulnerability in his voice. I hated hearing him like that, he was usually so confident and sure of himself. Hell, if he had been furious it would have been easier to handle, but as he was now, I didn't know whether he wanted comfort or for me to leave him the fuck alone.

Taking a tentative step forward, and putting on my big girl panties, I wrapped my arms around his body, placing my head on his chest. His heart thumped against his rib cage. I sighed in relief when his arms came up to hold me tighter to him.

"What do you need?" I asked when a few minutes passed and he didn't speak.

"I just need some time to process all of this. It's a fucking mess," he replied, pulling away from me. In the space of a few minutes, Kai looked like he had aged by ten years.

"Do you want me to leave you alone?"

He exhaled heavily, running a hand through his hair. "No," he said before brushing his thumb against my cheek. "If it was anyone else asking me that, I'd tell them to fuck off and leave me alone. But no, I need you, Riley."

For the rest of the day, Kai barely spoke. He alternated from staring off into the distance, to clenching his fists and glaring at random objects, ready to smash the house up, to pacing the room like he was trying to wear a hole in the carpet.

At one point, I suggested leaving his family home, but as Kai reminded me, Max Thorne, *his brother*, had taken control over all of Kai's assets, and aside from leaving the city, there was nowhere else to go.

Besides, not even a chemical bomb would make Kai leave Hollows Bay.

I didn't push him to talk about how he was feeling. I'd learned to tread carefully when it came to Kai's feelings about his family. Aside from telling me how he felt about me which seemed to come easy to him, he wasn't so good at expressing his emotions in other areas of his life. The last thing I wanted was to push him and rile him up more than he already was.

As evening drew closer, I made Kai dinner from the food Thomas, the butler dropped in but he didn't touch it. In fact, neither did me or Miles.

Miles was too busy squirreling away with research on the internet, and the worry I had for Kai, coupled with the roller coaster of events the past few days had brought on a migraine. The thought of food turned my stomach.

It was getting dark outside when Kai lifted me out of the armchair I was snuggled in, sat down, and positioned me on his lap. He still didn't speak, just held me close to his body. With the pounding in my head, and the comfort of Kai's safe arms, exhaustion finally took over and I fell asleep.

I woke hours later to find I was in Kai's bedroom, alone in the bed. At some point he'd carried me up here, taken my sneakers off, and draped a cover over me, and I had been none the wiser.

The first thing I noticed when I woke, aside from being alone, was a light breeze drifting in from the open balcony doors. The second thing I noticed was, I felt like shit. My head was pounding, my throat was sore, and I was full of snot.

Fucking great.

Despite a light sheen of sweat covering my skin, I was freezing. I dragged my aching ass out of bed, wrapping the cover around me and covering up the thin vest and leggings I was wearing.

Crossing to the other side of the room to close the door, I paused when I saw Kai sitting on the balcony, staring out across his city, an unreadable expression on his face.

"Hey," I croaked, my voice scratchy and sore. Kai's head snapped to where I was in the doorway, his brows creasing as he took in the cover wrapped around me.

"You okay?"

"Yeah, I'm fine," I replied, playing down the fact of just how rough I felt. Kai had enough to worry about.

"You don't sound fine." He stood and took two steps to where I was. Reaching up, he put a hand on my forehead, frowning when he pulled his hand away.

"Baby, you're boiling. What's wrong?" His voice was full of concern.

So much for not worrying him more.

"I think I may have a little fever coming, I'll be fine after a good night's sleep, I'm sure."

He didn't look convinced, so before he could fret too much, I took his hand and gave it a gentle squeeze.

"How are you doing?" I asked, ignoring the goosebumps erupting all over my skin from the chilly breeze.

Kai didn't miss anything though, especially when it came to me. He promptly picked me up and carried me back into the room, pausing to close the doors behind him. He laid me down on the bed before lying down next to me, and pulled me into his arms, still wrapped in the cover.

"Do you need any medication?" he asked. It was sweet, even with his own issues, Kai was still making sure I was okay.

"Honestly, Kai, I'm fine. I'm probably just a bit run down, it's been a mad few days." I don't think I'd properly recovered from the jet lag from flying to France and back in the space of forty-eight hours, followed by the emotional roller coaster of the wedding. Not to mention the latest antics by Max. "Now stop avoiding the question. How are you doing?"

His lips brushed the top of my head as his arms wrapped around me tighter. "I feel like a fucking idiot. I always knew my father was a cunt who cheated on my mother time and time again, he was never discreet about it. I never considered for one second he would be stupid enough to knock someone else up."

"Is there any chance the DNA results could be fake? Maybe he isn't related to you at all, and he's somehow managed to forge the results?" I asked hopefully.

"I wondered the same thing. But Miles has found proof that it's true."

"He has?" My voice went up an octave, making my throat hurt.

He kissed my forehead again. "Miles hacked the forensic company's database that conducted the DNA test. It's the original file, it hasn't been tampered with or altered. The test was carried out twenty years ago when Thorne was fifteen. The results are real."

Christ.

Questions churned in my head which only made the pounding worse. There was so much I wanted to ask Kai, but I didn't know where to start. But the man had a sixth sense when it came to me. He rolled me off his chest and propped himself up with one arm so he could look down at me.

"I know you have questions, Star. Believe me, I have a shit load of them myself, but you need to get some rest. Nothing will have changed by the morning, so sleep, we can talk tomorrow."

I didn't have it in me to argue.

When I woke in the morning, I felt worse than I had in the middle of the night. Kai was lying next to me, watching me sleep as he often did, the weirdo. But it seemed to bring him comfort, and I had to admit that I secretly liked waking up to find him watching me. It felt like he had been protecting me when I was at my most vulnerable.

When he asked how I was feeling, and I told him I was still feeling rough, he ordered me to stay in bed while he scurried off. He returned a short while later with two Tylenol, a glass of water, and some chicken soup. I couldn't face the soup, but once I swallowed down the tablets, I fell back to sleep again.

I don't know how many hours passed before I was gently shaken awake. I opened my eyes to find Kai sitting next to me, a worried expression on his face. He was dressed in a smart suit and the bulges underneath his jacket told me he had his guns holstered under it. I sat up, instantly alert despite the pounding in my head.

"What's happened?" I asked urgently, my eyes darting around the room expecting to see the grim reaper standing in the corner.

"Ssh, baby. Don't panic," Kai cooed, grabbing my hand and stroking his thumb over my knuckle. "How are you feeling?"

"I...I don't know, what's going on? Why have you got your guns strapped to you?"

Kai grimaced. "I was hoping you wouldn't see that," he replied. He should have known better, I saw everything about him, the same way he saw everything about me. "We got a tip on where Jacqueline is being held, me and Miles are going to follow it up."

"Where is she?" My heart raced. Fuck, I hoped she was okay.

"I'll tell you everything later, right now I need to get you to the panic room."

"Panic room?" I asked, confused. My brain was sluggish thanks to the darn fever. Why the hell would I need to go into a panic room?

"Yeah, there's one in the basement of this place. I don't like the idea of leaving you alone, but it's too dangerous to take you even if you were feeling better," Kai said, standing.

"Is that necessary? Isn't the house surrounded by the security team?"

"It is, but half of them are coming with me and Miles, and I'm not taking any chances with your safety. Not with Thorne and Hendrix out there somewhere. The panic room is impenetrable, there's no way anyone will be able to get in," Kai replied.

I opened my mouth to protest, but Kai stopped me before I could get any words out. "Riley, this is non-negotiable. I hate having to leave you alone but it's the only way I will leave this house to try and get Jacqueline."

Meaning, if I wanted Kai to find her, I had no choice but to get my ass in the panic room.

I gave him a small nod of acceptance. I wasn't thrilled about going into a panic room, I knew it was a means to keep me safe, but I didn't relish the idea of being locked in a room. Still, if it meant getting Jacqueline out of harm's way, I'd do it.

Allowing Kai to scoop me into his arms, he carried me through the house and to a door I'd never seen before. Like always, Kai pressed his thumb against the fingerprint pad that was on the outside of the door, and the door clicked open. He carried me down a set of stairs until we reached another door.

"See that camera?" Kai indicated with his head to a camera that was hanging above the door.

"Yeah."

"Inside, there is a monitor, you'll be able to see if anyone is out here."

Again, using his thumb on the pad to open the door, he walked in.

The room wasn't what I was expecting. To be honest, I didn't really know what to expect, it's not like I had ever been in a panic room before.

It was bigger than I thought it would be, the main area consisting of a large, comfy looking three-piece suite, an armchair, an enormous flat-screen television, and a desk with a computer screen.

Kai set me down on my feet and walked over to the computer. He clicked a few buttons and then paused while it loaded.

"Kitchen is over there," he said, pointing to an arch that led to a row of cupboards. "There's plenty of food if you get hungry, there's everything you need to make dinner-"

"Firstly," I interrupted, receiving a glare from Kai which I ignored.

"How long do you plan on leaving me in here for? And secondly, no offense but I can't imagine the food in there is very fresh, it's not like anyone lives here."

Leaving the computer, Kai walked over to stand in front of me and reached up to brush his thumb down my cheek. "I'll only be gone a few hours. And part of Thomas' job is to make sure this place is stocked in case there is an emergency."

"Oh," I replied sheepishly.

"Bathroom is over there," he said, pointing to a closed door. "And bedroom is over there." He pointed to a door behind me which was open enough that I could see the bed in the room.

"Come here, I want to show you something." Kai took my hand and led me to the desk. He clicked a few buttons on the screen and the image changed to show the hallway outside.

"This will show you who is outside," Kai said. He then pointed to a little microphone sitting on the top of the monitor. "This button here," he pointed to a button on the keyboard that had a little microphone symbol, "will allow you to speak to whoever is outside."

"Can they speak back?" I asked, impressed by the technology.

"Yeah, there's a microphone outside. And here," Kai pointed to another button, this time it was a red button on the wall next to the monitor, and underneath were the words 'Door Release.'

"Let me guess, that opens the door?" I smirked.

"Yeah, smart-ass, that opens the door. It's the only way the door can be opened once I step outside. Once the door closes, and you are in here, not even I can open the door again."

"Good to know, you know, in case you ever piss me off and I want to get away from your stubborn ass for a bit."

For the first time all day, Kai cracked a smile. "You must be feeling better if you are giving me shit, baby." He placed a delicate kiss on my nose before turning serious again. "Promise me you won't open that door for anyone but me? Not even Miles?"

"I promise," I replied because that was an easy promise to make.

Or at least, I thought it was.

Chapter 25

Riley

Kai showed me the telephone that was on the wall near the kitchen. He explained that it could only make calls, no one could ring in. To make a call, I'd have to input a code before dialing whoever I wanted to ring.

It seemed pointless to me. The panic room was stocked to get me through a long cold winter, plus it was impenetrable, so why would I need to call anyone? Still, he scribbled down the code followed by the number for one of the guards who was remaining outside, just in case I needed anything.

He then showed me a button on the outside of the room that would ring inside to let me know he was back. Basically, a panic room doorbell. After making me promise for a second time that I wouldn't open the door for anyone but him, he reluctantly left me.

The second the door closed, anxiety flooded my body. Not just at the thought of being locked in the panic room, albeit, I wasn't *exactly* locked in, I could open the damn door whenever I needed to, but anxiety about Kai heading off to god knows where to find Jacqueline.

I knew Kai could look after himself. Both Miles and Danny had previously bitched about how good a shot Kai was and that they envied his aim.

He also worked out in his boxing ring almost every day, so again, he could look after himself in a fight.

Did that stop thoughts about him coming to some kind of harm though?

No, of course it fucking didn't.

After all, it didn't make Danny invincible.

Still, after Kai left, I made myself comfy on the sofa, put the tv on, and tried to watch a film to distract myself from thoughts about Kai getting hurt.

About an hour after Kai left, I was finally beginning to relax, so much that my eyelids were drooping. The pounding in my head had eased, but my body ached, and another little nap was on the cards.

That was until a loud *beeeeeeeep* echoed around the room, scaring the living shit out of me. I was lying down on the sofa, but at the noise, I bolted upright, my heart pounding as adrenaline coursed through me.

When the penny dropped that it was the doorbell, I slowly got up, my legs shaking as I made my way over to the computer. Kai hadn't been gone long, I didn't know if that was a good or a bad thing.

On one hand, it might have been a quick snatch and grab to get Jacqueline out of whatever hellhole she was in. On the other hand, he might have been too late. The thought weighed heavy on my shoulders as I walked over to the screen.

It didn't occur to me for one second that someone other than Kai would be standing on the other side of the door.

Kai had told me about the security team who were positioned around the house. I'd met some of the others from the team when I'd gone to France with Angel, I knew how scary they were and how seriously they took protecting their client. The only way someone could have gotten past them was if they had taken down every single one of the men outside.

So it was no wonder my jaw hit the floor and my blood turned to ice when on the monitor stood the last person on earth I expected to see.

He reached out and pressed a button on the wall, and as I watched him open his mouth to speak, his voice echoed through the monitor.

"Riley, I know you're in there," Hendrix sang. His voice alone sent a chill down my spine, not to mention the gun he was holding in one hand.

Hendrix's bright blue eyes stared up at the camera, an evil smile gracing his face.

I think Kai's influence must have rubbed off on me. I wasn't a violent person, yet staring at Hendrix, my hands twitched with the need to wrap them around his throat and squeeze the life out of him.

I'd felt the same when we discovered Blaze had been the one to give up Angel's location. There hadn't been even the smallest part of me that had felt guilty for her when Kai, in between fucking me, filled me in on how she came to meet her fate.

It was a shame Kai hadn't left me with a gun because in all honesty, I wouldn't have had a single regret about opening the door and blasting his head off.

"Come on, *Star*, I know you are in there," he repeated, making me even madder for using the name that only Kai called me.

My eyes flashed to the phone hanging on the wall, and I raced over to it. Yanking it off the cradle, my heart sank when I held it to my ear only to be met with the deafening sound of silence. There was no dial tone, and when I mashed the code into the buttons with shaky fingers, nothing happened.

Fuck! Why the hell wasn't it working?

Fear trickled through me until I took a breath and reminded myself that Hendrix couldn't get in unless I opened the door. And that was *never* going to happen.

"Riley, you little bitch, you better fucking answer me," Hendrix hissed. Fear turned to anger as I marched back over to the screen to find him glaring daggers up at the camera. "I'm going to give you ten seconds to acknowledge me!"

I should have kept my mouth shut, but the rational part of my brain had switched off for the day. My finger slammed down on the button Kai showed me that would allow me to talk to him.

"Or what?" I barked, my throat croaky.

I instantly regretted it. His mouth turned from a snarl to a menacing grin as he beamed up at the camera.

"There you are, I've missed you, my little whore," Hendrix said.

My little whore?

Fuck, if only Kai could hear him claim that I was *his* little whore, he'd be ten feet under by now.

"How did you get in?" I asked, ignoring the letchy tone of his voice.

"All in good time. Why don't you come out here and we can get reacquainted?" He leaned against the wall, casually folding his arms across his chest.

"Hmm, let's think about that for a second. How about, get fucked you lying, backstabbing, piece of shit!"

A flash of anger crossed his face, and his hands dropped to his side. A sliver of fear crept up my spine as his hand tightened around the gun. But it was gone in an instant, replaced again by his evil smile.

"I had a feeling you would say that, so I brought something along that might help to change your mind."

My stomach plummeted.

I watched, numb and helpless, as a man I had never seen before walked onto the screen dragging someone I knew well with him.

Jacqueline.

They'd roughed her up. Her usually neat bun was a mess, blood trailed down one side of her face, and she had bruises under both tear-filled eyes. Her mouth was covered with silver tape, and the man held her with his arm wrapped around her throat, the barrel of the gun pressed against the side of her head.

"Jacqueline," I whispered to the empty room as my knees buckled. I grabbed the table to stop myself from collapsing.

"Now can I convince you to come out?" Hendrix said, stepping away from the wall to once again stand under the camera. A smug smirk played on his lips, and at that very moment, I wished for him to suffer the most painful death possible.

Hopefully at Kai's hands.

I didn't know what the fuck to do. Of course, my first instinct was to go out there, but the repercussions of that decision were far too reaching. I knew what it meant for Jacqueline though, and I wasn't sure I could live with that on my conscience.

"Riley, princess, have you ever seen the mess it makes when someone has their brains blown out?" Hendrix said, amusement thick in his voice, the sick bastard. "I assure you, it's a right fucking mess. And the smell, *Christ*, all that brain matter, and blood...."

It was a good job I had an empty stomach because the mental image his words created was enough to make me puke. It was damn impossible to ignore the whimper that came from Jacqueline, and her eyes screwed closed. I couldn't look at the screen any longer, I turned away as tears welled and slid down my face.

Jacqueline was more than a maid. She had looked after Kai from when he was a kid. She'd looked after me the minute I was carried into his penthouse. If I didn't go out there, her head would be splattered over the walls in a matter of seconds, but if I went out there, I'd be used as bait to lure Kai.

And my loyalty was to Kai.

I silently sent up a prayer, hoping Kai would be back soon and would come down to get me to find his nemesis standing there.

It was wishful thinking, but I didn't want to consider the reality.

"Open this fucking door, Riley!" Hendrix suddenly bellowed. My eyes flashed to the screen in time to see him strike the butt of his gun against Jacqueline's thigh. Behind the tape, she let out a pained scream as her leg collapsed. The only reason she didn't fall to the floor was because of the asshole holding her up.

A sob erupted from my throat, and I was about ten seconds away from hitting the door release button and going out there, but then Jacqueline looked at the camera. Despite the pain she must have been in, her eyes were hard, and she gave a subtle shake of her head, telling me not to come out.

My heart cracked. This brave woman was willing to sacrifice her life to keep me safe.

To keep Kai safe.

Despite the little voice in my head telling me to open the door, I reached out with a shaky hand and pressed the microphone button.

"Fuck. You," I growled at Hendrix. "I hope you enjoy the rest of your pathetic life because when Kai gets his hands on you, you are going to beg for the sweet release of death."

He glared at the camera before breaking out into the most chilling humorless laugh I'd ever heard. The sound made my stomach plummet even further.

"Oh, Riley. You're such a dumb bitch." His face twisted into a snarl, his veins prominent in his neck. "Do you really think this ends with Jacqueline? Let me tell you what happens unless you get that sweet little ass out here. I'll blow Jacqueline's brain out. And then I'll phone my man who is watching your friend at the club, Kendra, I think her name is, that right?"

My heart stopped.

I couldn't breathe, and my body shook violently. This time, I wasn't able to stop my legs from buckling. I collapsed on the floor in a heap, tears cascading down my cheeks as the voice of Hendrix floated around the room.

"She's a pretty girl. I've been watching her for a while now, her and that beautiful daughter of hers, Zara, right?" he said conversationally, as if he wasn't threatening the lives of a mother and her child. "It would be such a shame to see them suffer, so here's what I'm going to do. I'm going to give you one last chance to get your ass out here and save not only Jacqueline, but your friend Kendra and her little girl. What will it be, Riley?"

I couldn't think straight. The pounding in my head had come back tenfold. Huge tears fell like a waterfall as my heart shattered to pieces. But I didn't know if my tears were for the threats Hendrix had made, or for the fact I was about to break my promise to Kai.

I had no choice but to open the door.

Slowly, and on trembling legs, I got to my feet. My finger hovered over the microphone button for a second. But as I looked back at the screen to see Jacqueline with the gun pressed against her temple, an image fluttered into my head.

An image of a young baby being held, Kendra crying on the floor *begging* for me to help her daughter.

That image was what made me press the button.

"Will you let Jacqueline go if I come out?" I stuttered.

A delighted smile took over Hendrix's face while Jacqueline started screaming from behind the tape and shaking her head.

"I give you my word," Hendrix replied smugly.

It's funny, on the night Kai first offered me the deal, he said he was a man of his word, and the conviction in his voice made me believe him. But with Hendrix, I did not believe a word that came out of his slimy mouth.

But what choice did I have?

"I'll....I'll come out."

Numbness seeped into every pore in my body. Once again Hendrix had outsmarted Kai, and now we were playing straight into his and Max's hands. I hoped one day, Kai would understand why I had to break my promise to him.

As I was about to smash the release button, my eyes dropped to my wedding ring. Something in my head told me not to draw attention to the fact Kai and I were married, that whatever was about to happen would be a *million* times worse if Max and Hendrix found out I was now a Wolfe. Sliding the ring off my ring finger, I put it on the middle finger of my other hand.

My hands clenched into fists as I took a breath, my nails digging into the flesh. But the pain was welcomed, it was a distraction from the pain I had in my chest.

And then I hit the release button.

Pulling the door open, I was met with a beaming Hendrix, and although Jacqueline's mouth was covered with tape, it was hard to miss the disappointment in her eyes.

"Hello, Riley," Hendrix said. His eyes raked over my body like they had done on a number of previous occasions. Every time he did that made me want to bleach my skin.

He grabbed my arm, pulling me away from the door before I had a chance to change my mind. Spinning me around so my back was to his front, he wrapped an arm around my waist and pulled me tight against his body. Raising the gun, he pressed the barrel to the side of my head reflecting the way his sidekick held the gun to Jacqueline's.

Hendrix bent his head to the crook of my neck and inhaled deeply.

"Fuck, I forgot how good you smell," he crooned. His cock twitched against my ass making nausea churn in my belly. I wanted nothing more than to spin around and rip his appendage off.

"As much as I'd love for us to get reacquainted now, unfortunately, we have places we need to be. Besides, when I finally get my hands on you, I want to take my time. I want to enjoy every scream I pull from your lips," Hendrix whispered, and then he licked the spot under my ear.

I squeezed my eyes shut. The feel of his tongue felt like a knife stabbing me in my throat, and if it wasn't for the gun still held at Jacqueline's head, I would have thrown an elbow into his ribs. There was also the small issue of the gun being held at *my* head, although I knew Hendrix wouldn't use it, at least not to kill me.

He needed me alive.

Hendrix turned, dragging me with him, and at that moment the penny dropped as to how he had gotten into the house. Behind him, and out of view of the camera, a panel had been slid open, revealing a dimly lit passageway.

Hendrix pushed me forward, the concrete cold on my bare feet. He lowered the gun to the base of my spine as he ushered me along, walking so fucking close to me, his feet almost tripped me up. Behind us, the footsteps of Jacqueline and the man holding her followed.

"Bet Kai never told you about the history of this place," Hendrix said casually as we walked along the passageway that seemed to never end. "His great-grandfather, Theodore Wolfe, built this house when he first came to power, and then several years later, the Wolfe family went to war with an Italian family, the Bianchis. Theodore was terrified the Bianchis would attack the house so paid an absolute fortune for a panic room to be installed. A room so impenetrable that even if the house was set on fire, the panic room would survive."

Kai had only told me little snippets about his family, mainly about his mother and father. As much as I didn't want to give Hendrix any attention, and as much as I was trying to figure out a way to get me and Jacqueline out of this mess, I couldn't help but listen to what he was saying.

"He made sure to include a number of escape routes in case his enemies came knocking, and he had the bright idea of including a secret tunnel right next to the panic room. I'm sure you know the house has passed from generation to generation, but Kai being the stubborn ass that he is, refused to live here.

"You know, when we were kids, Kai and Theo thought they were fucking hilarious. They knew all the tunnels that would lead in and out of the house. They thought they were so smart, appearing randomly out of cupboards and shit. Used to drive me fucking crazy when they'd jump out and scare me. And then one day, I found a drawing in Theo's room. I wasn't looking for it. In fact, I was looking for his porn stash." He paused for a moment to chuckle at the memory. Up ahead, there was a sliver of light. Wherever this tunnel led to was drawing nearer. The question was, did I try to escape or did I just suck it up and hope like hell Kai would come to my rescue?

"Anyway, you'll never believe it, but Theo was fucking stupid enough to have a map of the house with all the tunnels. I'll never forget it, I was sixteen, and camera phones were all the rage, but the quality was shit. I took a photo, and then spent *weeks'* after trying to figure the map out. Reckon Kai thought I was going mad when I was constantly opening random wardrobe doors." He chuckled again, a sound I was quickly growing to despise.

Something in my brain told me to fight, to get out of his grasp and get away, but if I tried anything, it would only result in Jacqueline's brain being blown out.

Besides, we had walked a fair distance away from the house, and I had no clue where this passageway led. It would have been foolish to try and escape. The only thing I could do was hold on to a sliver of hope that Kai would return in the next few minutes or one of the security team would see what was going on.

Why the hell hadn't the damn phone been working? If I'd managed to get through to the security guard, none of this would be happening. And then it occurred to me. If Hendrix knew about the panic room, he would have known about the phone. I was no genius, but it didn't take one to figure out he'd probably done something to disable it.

We reached the door at the end of the passageway and Hendrix yanked it open. My feet faltered when my eyes darted around the room we'd entered, causing Hendrix to run into me.

"Oh, don't mind Thomas, Riley," Hendrix chortled, "He threatened me with a pistol he had hidden, and there was only one way that little situation was going to end." He waved his hand as if presenting the evidence.

The body of the butler was lying on the floor, his eyes open but unseeing. Blood soaked his body from the gaping hole in his neck. I didn't know Thomas but it didn't stop the guilt from flooding me.

"You're a fucking sick bastard," I hissed.

"I am indeed. And you'd do well to remember that, because when Max is done with you, he's promised I can have you, and you best believe I've got some *very* sick things planned for you, princess," Hendrix whispered in my ear.

I wished I could have remained stoic, I should have taken more lessons in the Kai Wolfe book of showing no emotions, but I was only a novice. My whole body shuddered in fear, which made Hendrix howl with laughter.

Hendrix pushed me forward again, jabbing the nozzle of the gun into my back. I side-stepped the body, but my bare toes landed in the pool of blood. I tore my eyes away, the sight of the sticky blood on my feet made my belly churn.

The lodge where Thomas had lived was only small, and it was a matter of seconds before we reached the front door. Hendrix dropped the gun from my back but grabbed hold of my waist, and once again pulled me back against his chest. He spun us around to face the other man who still held the gun to Jacqueline's head, her eyes filled with unshed tears.

"Now, Riley. I'm afraid I can't risk you trying to draw attention to yourself when we leave here," Hendrix hissed in my ear. "So what we are going to do is give you a little something to help you sleep."

"No!" I cried, panic flooding me at the thought of being completely unaware of what this fucker was doing to me and totally incapable of stopping it. I tried to pull out of his grasp, but he was too strong.

"Shh, shh, shh," Hendrix cooed, rubbing his hardening cock against my ass, which did nothing to stop the panic from rising. "Don't worry, princess, I'll take good care of you."

"Get your filthy hands off me, you fucking pig!" I yelled, but my words only earned me a chuckle from both Hendrix and the man holding Jacqueline.

Hendrix's hand lifted from where he was holding me, coming up to cover my mouth. I twisted my head to try and shake him off but as soon as he held the barrel of the gun to my head again, I stopped.

"I was going to do the decent thing and wait until you were out cold before I did this, but because you can't keep your mouth shut, I think I'll make you watch. Alex, do the honors," Hendrix sneered menacingly.

I didn't have time to understand what he was implying before the sound of the gunshot echoed around the small lodge, Jacqueline's brain splattered against the wall as her lifeless body fell to the floor.

Chapter 26

Kai

I surveyed the devastation around me. Bodies lay strewn over the pews that lined the derelict church. Stained glass windows had shattered thanks to stray bullets, and the smell of death hung in the air.

But there was no sign of Jacqueline.

Or Hendrix for that matter.

When the intel came through that Jacqueline was being held in a derelict church in East Bay, I didn't give it much credence. Did I really think Thorne was stupid enough to hold Jacqueline somewhere so obvious?

No, of course I fucking didn't.

But when the intel suggested Hendrix was the one holding her in the church, I wasn't going to ignore it.

The Apollo team were worth their weight in gold, and believe me, it was costing me the price of fucking *diamonds* to keep them employed. As soon as the intel came through, Jack and a team of his men headed to the outskirts of East Bay to deploy a drone that had a thermal imaging camera. The camera was capable of zooming into locations up to five miles away, and once the team confirmed heat sources inside the derelict church, I knew I had to go.

It wasn't ideal leaving Riley in the panic room, hell, if she had been feeling better, I would have taken her with me so I knew she was safe. But the panic room was impenetrable, and it was the best option I had.

Growing up, there'd been countless times when I'd been forced to lay low in the panic room. Not from a threat outside. No, the threat came from within. When my father was on a rampage, my mother would hide Theo and me in there, making us promise we wouldn't come out until she came to get us.

Sometimes she'd come for us a few hours later, sometimes it wouldn't be until the following day. It didn't matter when she came though, we would open the door to find her covered in bruises, having done a shitty job at trying to hide them with her makeup.

Theo and I vowed that when we were older, we would stop our father from hurting her, but we never had the opportunity. Cancer claimed her before we were big and strong enough to take on my father.

Since taking over Hollows Bay, I'd never had a need to use the room. But I always believed it was sensible to keep it in full working condition in case the need ever arose. I didn't run from my enemies, and I certainly didn't hide, but if I needed somewhere to regroup, the panic room was perfect.

Miles and I made our way to the RV point where Jack and his team were, and once we arrived, we formulated a plan to storm the church. From the heat sources detected by the thermal camera, there were at least fifteen people, all likely armed.

Within minutes, we attacked the church, but it quickly became apparent they were expecting us. Had someone tipped them off or were they just *that* alert to a potential threat? I didn't know.

Either way, they attacked back, managing to take out one of the guys from Jack's team.

It took us longer than expected to kill every single one of the assholes that had been guarding the nave, and while Jack and I searched the dead bodies, Miles and the remainder of the team searched the rest of the grounds.

I was not in the least bit surprised to find stag tattoos on each of the dead bodies.

"What do you want to do with the bodies, Mr. Wolfe?" Jack asked.

Blood stains marked his shirt, but he was an ex-military man. Shit like this didn't faze him.

"I'll get my cleaners in," I replied, searching the final body. None of the dead pricks had phones on them, making me lean more toward the theory they knew we would be coming at some point.

I was about to pull my phone out and call the team I used to clean up messes like this when a creek from the corner of the room drew mine and Jack's attention. Guns raised, we crept to the front of the nave to where the noise had come from.

Another creek indicated it had come from the abandoned lectern.

Jack and I rounded on it, and in one swift move, he whipped back the blood-spattered sheet while I aimed my gun at the *boy* curled into a ball in the small space. His entire body quivered at the sight of my gun pointed at him.

"P-p-please don't hurt me," he said, voice shaking and hands held up to show he had no weapon.

I grabbed an arm while Jack grabbed the other, and together we yanked him out, his hands still raised in defense from both guns trained on him.

He was only a young man, no older than sixteen, seventeen at a push. His age didn't matter though, the stag tattoo was still etched into the skin on his arm for all to see.

"I don't want to die, please Mr. Wolfe, I'll tell you everything you need to know."

Fuck me. First Toby, and now this little punk-ass bitch. The Stags really were a bunch of pussies. Carlos Rigby needed to toughen his men up so they didn't keep singing like birds at the sight of a gun.

"Where's Hendrix?" I growled, jabbing the barrel of the gun against the side of his head.

"He's....not here. He took the woman," the little snitch cried.

"Where did he take her?"

"I don't know."

Jack jabbed the barrel of his gun into the kid's ribs who squeezed his eyes closed and whispered a prayer for help under his breath. We may have been in a church, but he wouldn't be getting any help now.

"Are you sure you don't know? Or would a bullet in your lung help you remember?" Jack hissed.

I was beginning to like this guy.

"I don't know where he took her, I swear! But Hendrix knew you would be coming, he told us all to be on our guard for an attack," he sobbed.

I'd heard enough. He wasn't telling me anything helpful and I didn't care to waste my time any further. I glanced at Jack who saw my intention and stepped away before he could be covered with any more blood.

Thinking he was getting a reprieve, the kid lowered his hands just as I squeezed the trigger. His body fell to the floor with a resounding thud.

At that moment my phone rang. I pulled it out thinking it was Miles calling to give me a progress report on the rest of the search, so I didn't bother to check the caller ID.

"Tell me you have something," I growled into the phone.

"Oh, I have something alright. Something *very* precious of yours."

My blood froze.

My lungs constricted.

Fear sprung to life at the sound of Thorne's voice at the end of the line and the connotations of his words.

"Are you still there, brother? You've gone awfully quiet," he chuckled down the phone.

There had been few moments in my life where I had been paralyzed by fear so much that I couldn't say the words. But right then, it gripped me to the point where words were non-existent. My hand tightened around the phone, almost to the point of breaking it.

"I'll assume you are there, Kai, so let me show you *exactly* what I have."

A second later, my phone pinged again in my ear. I pulled it away and clicked on the video he sent through.

Never in my life had I felt as murderous as I did as I stared down at the video. Riley was tied to a chair, unconscious with her head lolling to one side. Behind her stood Hendrix, a malicious smile on his face as he towered over her. A roar left my throat as he reached over and cupped her breasts.

I was going to kill him.

I was going to take my time to peel every layer of skin *from* his body, break every single bone *in* his body before I finally ripped out his heart with my bare hands.

How the fuck had they got her?

She was supposed to be safe in the panic room, how the fuck had this happened?

Was one of Jack's men working with Max and Hendrix?

"You still there, Kai?" Thorne's voice came from the phone, pulling me from my stupor.

"You fucking bastard!" I roared like a wounded animal, catching Jack's attention who had been searching the body of the boy I had just killed. "Where is she?"

"She's safe. For now. Although your buddy Hendrix has been desperate to get his hands on her for a long time. He's got it *real* bad for her."

"I swear to fucking-"

"You can swear all you like, to whomever you like. This is *my* show, and I'll tell you where she is when I'm ready," Thorne said, wicked glee in his voice.

I closed my eyes to calm myself from turning into the bomb that was about to explode. I fucking hated that he was right, this *was* his show, and if I wanted to know where Riley was, I had to play his game. Much like I'd had to play his game from day fucking one.

"What's going on?" Miles said, appearing through a door, his brows raised in question. I yanked the phone away from my ear and put it on loudspeaker so Miles could hear.

"What do you want?" I hissed.

"I want what is owed to me," Thorne said venomously. Upon hearing Thorne's voice, Miles' face twisted into a sneer. "But for now, I'll settle with you coming to my location. And I mean, *just you*, Kai. If you turn up with any backup, Riley pays the price. If you try any heroics, Riley pays the price. If you turn up with so much as a fucking pen to use as a weapon, guess what? Your precious Star pays the price. Capishe?"

"Fuck!" Miles barked, storming to the other side of the church to smash up a pew.

Thorne chuckled down the line. "I'm guessing our cousin hasn't taken the news of Riley's capture too well. She really has you lot wrapped up in knots, I'm beginning to wonder if this girl has got a golden pussy."

"Where?" It was the only word I could get out. I was already marching towards the door, ready to agree to his terms. I didn't need a fucking weapon or any backup to take this motherfucker down.

"I want your word that you agree to my terms before I give you the location."

"I agree to your fucking terms," I snapped, kicking the dead body of a stag as I passed. "Now where is she?!"

"Excellent. Here's what's going to happen. You're going to get your ass out of the church and remove the tracker from your SUV, and then you're going to get on the freeway back to West Bay. I'll be in touch with where you need to go next. Better hurry though, Kai. I'm not sure how long Hendrix will be able to refrain from going to town on her sweet little ass."

With that, he hung up.

If it wasn't for the fact I needed my phone so the cunt could tell me where I needed to go, I would have launched it to the other side of the room.

"Kai!" Miles barked, sprinting through the nave to reach me as I exited the door into the bright light of the warm day. "What's the plan?"

"I go get my wife."

Reaching the driver's side, I knelt down on the road and looked under the car, the second I saw the little flashing light of the tracker, I grabbed it and ripped it free from its holder. When I stood back up, I launched it across the road before digging into my pocket for the key.

"You can't seriously be going there without a plan or backup?" Miles said, watching me with his mouth open in horror.

"That's exactly what I'm fucking doing, Miles," I replied, opening the door.

I'd never known Miles to go against anything I said. He was always on board with my plans, even if he didn't agree with them. He respected that whatever decision I made was because I was the boss.

But at that moment, he chose to ignore me.

Before I had time to slam the door closed, Miles jumped in the way and yanked the key from my hand.

"Kai-"

He didn't have time to get his words out before I had him pinned over the hood, my hand wrapped around his throat. Credit where it's due, he didn't panic, and he didn't try to prise my fingers off. He just glared back at me, the keys clasped tightly in his hand.

"Give me the fucking keys."

He shook his head.

I squeezed harder.

"Give me the fucking keys!"

I was vaguely aware that Jack and his team had gathered at the front of the church to watch the commotion, but I didn't have a single fuck to give that they were witnessing me losing my shit. I had one goal in mind and that was to get to my girl.

Miles' lips started turning blue, his eyes became hooded. The last thing I wanted was to kill my cousin but if he was the one thing stopping me from getting to Riley, then so be it.

His hand uncurled and the keys dropped. The second they did, I let him go, and he took several deep breaths. I grabbed the keys from the floor and got in the SUV, slamming the door behind me and glaring murder at him.

Wisely, he stepped away from the car, his hands rubbing his throat as I sped away, leaving Miles and the rest of the team in a cloud of dust.

Chapter 27

Riley

Holy fucking potatoes.

The damn head cold was getting worse. My head pounded, my body ached everywhere, and my hands were tied down.

Wait.

Why were my hands tied down?

Slowly, I opened my eyes. It took a few seconds for them to focus, and when they did, a cold shiver ran down my spine.

Hendrix was watching me from the chair he sat in, elbows resting on his knees, hands propping his head up. As soon as he realized I was awake, a malicious grin spread across his face, and a wild glint appeared in his eyes.

Fear hit me like a sledgehammer when it became abundantly clear why my hands felt like they were tied down. They had been cable-tied to the chair I was sitting in, and when I tugged against them, the plastic dug into my skin where they were tied so tight.

Light from the dying sun filtered in through several windows that surrounded the empty room we were in.

Where the fuck was I?

It looked like an empty room in a warehouse, similar to the warehouse Kai had kept Blaze in, only bigger, and it reeked of stale coffee. It wasn't anywhere I'd been before, and I didn't know if I was in West Bay or East

Bay, or even Hollows Bay for that matter, Hendrix could have taken me anywhere.

As my head thumped, memories filled my head of the last thing I remembered.

Jacqueline.

Jacqueline's brain blown out before a cloth was shoved over my mouth and everything went dark.

Jacqueline was dead.

I didn't have time to dwell on the fact because Hendrix opened his stupid mouth.

"You know you are fucking stunning when you are asleep, and not spewing shit from that delectable mouth," he said, his eyes raking up and down my body.

Another shiver ran through me. I had always hated the way he looked at me, it was like he couldn't decide whether he wanted to slit my throat or rip my clothes off and fuck me raw. I'd rather go with the slit throat than *ever* have his hands on me.

"Did you miss me, princess?"

"Look at my tail. It's wagging in delight," I deadpanned, my voice scratchy. I'd be damned if I was going to show this fucker an ounce of fear, even if my bones were trembling.

Hendrix snorted, the wild look in his eye turning maniacal. "Oh, Riley, I can't wait until Kai has been dealt with, and I get to fuck that attitude out of you."

At the mention of Kai, I looked around, or as much as I could seeing as I was tied to a chair, I couldn't exactly make my head spin around to see what was behind me. Was Kai here?

"He's on his way," Hendrix said, answering my unspoken question. "He was keen to get here as quickly as he could, even agreed to come here without any weapons or backup. He really does have it bad for you."

I should hope he had it bad for me, he married me after all. My eyes dropped to my tied hands, and I breathed a small sigh of relief when I saw my wedding ring was still on the finger I had moved it to.

Hendrix abruptly stood, pulling my attention away from my ring. My head spun with chaotic thoughts.

Should I try to get out of my restraints?

Should I wait until Kai got here?

Would he want me to try and escape or would he want me to stay put?

I tugged against the cable ties again and swiftly came to the realization that even if I thought I should try to escape, I was going nowhere.

The creepy fucker took several steps toward me, his eyes on mine the whole time, burning with fire. He disappeared behind me, and seconds later his hands were on my shoulders. The touch of him felt like I was being stabbed with a thousand needles pricking my skin.

"I remember the first time I saw you, Riley. It wasn't when Kai brought you home with him. You probably don't know that I saw you dancing in the club *months* before Kai ever laid eyes on you."

What?!

My jaw fell open. From behind me, the bastard chuckled and squeezed my shoulders, his rough fingers brushing the nape of my neck, leaving a trail of ice where he touched.

"Yep. I'd been ordered there by Max to get John. John had been sent to Hollows Bay to gather intel on Kai and Theo. Fuck knows how he ended up in East Bay, but the second he walked into Club Sin, the man became fixated on Blaze. I always said to Max that John was a liability. Still, had it not been for him going to Club Sin, I never would have been sent to get him, and then I never would have watched you dance."

His hands slid over my shoulders and down to my chest where he cupped both breasts and massaged them. When he let out a groan, I closed my eyes, shutting out the feel of him. I refused to give the sick fucker the pleasure of enjoying me asking him to stop. He wouldn't, so what was the point?

Blocking his touch from my mind was harder than I thought possible though, especially when his thumbs found my nipples, and he started rubbing them against each bud. They didn't respond to his touch, there was only one man my nipples got hard for, and it wasn't the prick standing behind me.

"I only went there once, but that was enough for you to crawl under my skin and nestle there. I promised myself when all this shit with Kai was done, and Max had taken over, I'd go back for you, so imagine my surprise when Kai showed us the surveillance photos Isaac took when Kai had him follow you," Hendrix hissed, pure venom in his voice when he said Kai's name.

His fingers joined the party at my nipples, and with his fingers and thumbs, he started tweaking them, trying to elicit some sort of reaction. I took a deep steadying breath, letting the fear I'd been feeling turn into anger, and picturing all the ways Kai was going to kill Hendrix, especially when he knew Hendrix had put his hands on me.

"Do you have any idea how fucking hard it was listening to Kai harp on about how he was going to make you his, how he'd never met anyone as beautiful as you. It was sickening because you were *mine*, not his."

His hands became rougher as the anger in his voice grew, and it wasn't long until he was pinching my nipples painfully hard. I wanted to yell at the top of my voice that I was never his, nor would I *ever* be his, but my voice caught in my throat, and the words wouldn't come.

"And then he came home with you. I'll never forget the look on your face when he opened the trunk, and there you were. You were like a caged lioness, her claws at the ready." He paused to chuckle and thankfully, *thankfully*, he released my nipples.

He walked around the chair to stand in front of me. I sneered in disgust at the sight of the bulge in his pants and turned away so I didn't have to look at it. I wanted nothing more than to rip his cock off.

"Look away all you like, Riley, but when this is over, you'll have no choice but to look at me. No choice but to open your legs, and let me do whatever the fuck I like to that sweet pussy." He reached out and grabbed my chin, twisting my head so I had to look at him. "After today, you belong to me, and I promise you, Riley, I'm going to make your life hell."

"Fuck you," I spat, unable to bite my tongue any longer. There was no way I'd be spreading my legs for him, he was fucking deluded.

Anyway, it didn't matter. Kai would be here soon, there was no way I'd be leaving here with Hendrix, I had full faith in my husband coming to my rescue.

"Believe me, princess, I intend to." He dropped my chin and walked back to his chair. He sat down and folded one leg over the other, leaning back casually with his arms on the armrests, and resumed his intense staring at me, his blue eyes blazing with desire.

When I couldn't take his heated eyes on me anymore, I blurted the question I'd been desperate to ask since the day I found out Hendrix was a lying asshole. "Why did you betray Kai?"

He smirked. "I was going to wait until he got here to answer that, but Max has got a lot of secrets to reveal first." He leaned forward and lowered his voice as if conspiring with me. "Between you and I, Max has got a bit of a temper on him and has even less patience than Kai. I doubt he'll be able to reveal *all* his secrets before his temper snaps and he kills Kai." He sat back, and again crossed his leg over the other. "So I'll tell you, it's quite simple. Kai was a fucking moron."

I glared back at him waiting for more, because that wasn't an answer.

He smiled that evil smile he had and rubbed his hands together.

"Kai's old man had the right idea, he wanted to expand wider than Hollows Bay. My father was Christopher Wolfe's 2IC, and they both had plans to take their control further. But when Christopher died, and Kai and Theo took over, they shut that idea down. They didn't see the need to go wider than Hollows Bay. It was such a stupid fucking decision.

"Kai sacked my father so Theo could take his place, and it devastated my father. My father was furious, he'd worked hard for Christopher, establishing connections in other cities, and making deals with important associates in other countries. All his hard work went down the drain in a blink of an eye, everything he'd worked towards his entire life. Gone."

Hendrix's face twisted into a scowl as he stood from the chair, stepping forward to tower over me, waves of anger rolling off him.

"Before he died," he continued. "I promised him I would make things right again. I spent years picking up from where he left off, trying to re-establish those connections, but Kai kept shutting them down. He wouldn't listen to me, wouldn't even consider that expanding our organization was for the best. He threatened that if I didn't stop talking about it, he'd banish me from Hollows Bay.

"But my efforts drew the attention of Max. He tracked me down almost a year ago and told me his story. He'll reveal all about that when Kai gets here, all you need to know for now is that Max has plans, brilliant plans that matched mine, and I agreed to work with him to ruin Kai."

I stared back at him with my jaw open.

Un-fucking-believable. This was the reason Hendrix had betrayed Kai? This was the reason Danny was dead? Why Jacqueline was dead? All because of Hendrix's greed?

That's what it boiled down to, greed. Being the 2IC to the King of Hollows Bay wasn't enough. It wasn't enough that Kai controlled the city and made millions of dollars each year through the businesses he owned. It wasn't enough that he paid Hendrix *incredibly* well, made sure he had everything he ever wanted, including Kai's friendship and loyalty. And this is how Hendrix repaid Kai, all because he wanted more.

I sincerely hoped Kai took his time when murdering this son-of-a-bitch.

I sneered at Hendrix and opened my mouth to tell him *exactly* what I thought of him when a loud bang from behind echoed around the room and stopped me.

Hendrix's evil eyes left mine and fixed on whoever had just come into the room, a wicked smile growing on his lips. Two sets of footsteps filled the space, drawing closer as Hendrix watched them. Trepidation grew in the pit of my stomach the closer the footsteps came, but I didn't have to wait long to find out who it was.

A man I'd never met before walked to stand in front of me. Although I'd never met him before, I knew who he was.

Max Thorne looked nothing like Kai, with the exception of the color of their eyes. Both Kai's and Max's eyes were as dark as the night sky, but where Kai's held nothing but love and adoration for me, Max's held nothing but malice.

He was dressed in a suit, a wannabe Kai in the making. But he didn't look anywhere near as intimidating or powerful as what my husband did. This guy, he really was a douchebag.

He was joined by someone I did know.

John Anderson joined them, and the three musketeers stood in a line facing me. John looked different from the last time I had seen him, the time when he had his hands around my throat and was squeezing the life out of me.

Now, the vacant expression on his face sent chills down my spine.

His brown eyes were empty of any emotion, his face was gaunt, and he'd lost weight. If I didn't know better, I'd say the man had been locked away for the last few weeks, deprived of food, water, and sunlight.

But that couldn't be right.

Right?

"Riley, I don't think we've met. I'm Max Thorne. Although I should start using my real name," he chuckled. "I'm *Michael Wolfe.*" He held his hand out as if for me to shake before pulling away with a smirk on his face. "Oops, my bad. Of course, I'm sure you understand the need to restrain you. Wouldn't want you trying to escape before Kai gets here and the fun can start."

I didn't reply. I wasn't going to give any of these assholes the satisfaction of riling me up. If they wanted to believe they'd walk out of here the victors, that was on them. I, on the other hand, was backing Kai.

"She's lost some of her usual attitude, Boss. Told you it wouldn't be long until I had her feisty ass under control."

"Fuck you," I spat. Okay, so maybe I wasn't quite in control of my mouth after all.

What can I say, Hendrix wound me the fuck up.

My words earned chuckles from both Hendrix and Max. John, however, stood staring vacantly at a spot behind me. Max noticed me looking at him and nudged his shoulder.

"Say hello to Riley, John," Max instructed as though he was speaking to a child.

"Hullo, Riley," John dutifully replied, his eyes still not meeting mine. Was he on drugs?

Something odd was going on here for sure, what though? I had no fucking clue.

"Kai pulled off the freeway a few minutes ago, he'll be here soon, and it looks like he has come alone. My sources reported Kai and Miles had a bit of a falling out, and Miles has headed home," Max said, turning to talk to Hendrix.

I hoped if Kai had come alone, he had a plan on how the fuck he was going to get us out of this.

"Watch him, Boss, he'll have something up his sleeve. I know him well, he'll have something planned," Hendrix replied.

I wanted to ring his neck for implying that he knew Kai well, I hated that it was true. He'd played Kai like a violin for the past year, and now he knew every single detail about how Kai worked, and no doubt had shared that with Max.

"He won't do anything to risk her safety," Max said confidently before turning to look at me again. "Before he gets here, there is one thing we need to take care of, although it pains me to have to do it."

He looked anything but pained.

Dread pooled in my belly, I didn't like the threat in his voice, and despite trying my damned hardest to not show how scared I was, I couldn't stop the tremble that started in my hands and made its way through my body.

"I'll make this part quick," Max said, his tone serious. "I want to make sure Kai is here before I tell you how I've spent the last twenty years planning the downfall of the Wolfe empire."

Twenty years?

What the hell?

I stared back at him, refusing to let him intimidate me, yet secretly sending out a prayer to whoever the fuck was out there that Kai moved his ass to get here.

Sharpish.

He smiled at me then, a real menacing smile before pulling out a gun from the back of his pants. Fear ran bone deep at the sight of it, and it took every ounce of courage I had in me to not react.

But he didn't point it at me like I expected. Instead, he turned and held the gun against John's head. Hendrix stepped back, but there was no reaction from John. The man stood staring into thin air, oblivious to the fact he had a gun pressed against his head.

Cogs whirled in my brain as I tried to understand just what in the fuckety-fuck was going on.

"I have to say, twenty years in the planning, I couldn't have done it without this man. It's such a shame he's become a liability."

And then he pulled the trigger.

Chapter 28

Riley

What in the ever-loving fuck was happening right now?

I think witnessing two people have their heads blown to smithereens in a short space of time short-circuited my own brain.

I stared at John's lifeless body, wondering what in the bloody fuck was going on. He was Max's deputy for crying out loud. Plus he'd been in on Max's little plot to bring the Wolfe family down, so why the hell was he now dead with his brains splattered everywhere? Including all over my leggings.

Yuk.

"I imagine you have some questions, Riley?" Max said casually as if he hadn't just blown his deputy's brains out.

"You could say that," I replied, dumbfounded by what I was witnessing.

Max chuckled before tucking the gun away in the back of his pants. "Well, there is a lot to reveal, but we'll have to wait for Kai to get here before I let you in on too many secrets, we wouldn't want the fun to start before he gets here.

"You mean, before Kai gets here and kills both you dumbasses." The words tumbled from my mouth before I had time to stop them, god bless my brain and mouth for not working together at a time like this.

I expected the slap to come, but I wasn't quite prepared for how much it hurt. Max's palm connected with my cheek making it feel like I had been stung by a hundred bees. My already pounding head whipped to the side when seconds later he roughly grabbed my chin and yanked it back to face him.

"Get that thought out of your head, you little whore, there will only be one Wolfe leaving here alive today, and it won't be Kai," Max snarled in my face, baring his teeth like a rabid dog.

I bit my tongue, hoping like fuck Kai would be here soon with the cavalry. Behind Max, Hendrix watched with a demented grin on his face.

Max dropped my chin and took a step back, taking several calming breaths. My cheek throbbed from his slap, only adding to the throbbing in my head.

"As I was saying, there is a lot to reveal when Kai gets here, but I don't mind filling you in on why I killed John, may as well talk about something to pass the time."

"I'm honored," I replied, tempting fate that I would be slapped again, but I couldn't keep my mouth shut around the Wolfe brothers. There was something about them that riled me up. At least with Kai, my punishment for sassing him usually ended up in multiple orgasms.

He glared at me, his eyes narrowing. and his nostrils flaring. "I haven't quite decided if you are as brave as you seem, or if it's an act."

I stared back at him. I'll hold my hands up and admit that I wasn't feeling brave at all, or at least, I would hold my hands up if they weren't tied down. But I refused to let this prick intimidate me. Max didn't know it, but I was now a Wolfe, and that meant I wouldn't cower and hide. No matter how scared I was on the inside.

"I guess we'll find out how brave you really are when Kai has been dealt with, Riley." He paused for a moment, his eyes sharp, like a hawk about to strike and capture a shrew. He clapped his hands together, the sound echoing around the empty warehouse. "But let's start with some details about John."

Max took several steps over to where John's body was, his face pulled into a disgusted scowl. "You probably already know John and I were fostered by the Brown family. They lived in Florida, and I was sent to live with them. John was already there when I arrived." He paused to look up at me and waited expectantly for me to respond.

I nodded once, remembering for the first time since Kai received the DNA results that Michael Tucker had been fostered by the Browns, and their other child was John. Meaning, John wasn't just Max's deputy, he was his foster brother too.

"Good. I have to say, Riley, I enjoyed leaving little clues for Miles to find, giving just enough that he couldn't figure things out until I was ready for Kai to know who I was. It was actually Isaac who found the last piece of the jigsaw, that's why I had to kill him. *I* wanted to be the one to reveal to Kai that we were brothers."

Jeez, this guy. He was something else. He really did like his theatrics.

"Anyway, when I moved in with the Browns, I quickly discovered John wasn't the full ticket, if you get my drift. He had a lot of issues, I won't go into details, Riley, but he had a bad childhood, kinda fucked him up.

"It played into my hands though, I was able to manipulate him to do whatever I wanted him to do, and for the past twenty years he has been my puppet, and I have been his master, pulling his strings to do my bidding." He paused and beamed at me, proud of himself for manipulating a man who, by the sounds of it, was vulnerable and had a lot of issues.

When I didn't reply, Max started pacing behind John's body, his hands behind his back. "I'll skip over the next twenty years, Riley, Kai needs to be here for that, so let's move forward to the night of the charity ball."

Despite my best attempt at feigning interest, I'd be lying if I said my attention wasn't piqued. After all, John tried to kidnap me on the night of the ball, so yeah, I was somewhat interested.

"I had a goal I was working towards, everything was carefully laid out. But John, well, he always believed he was my top dog, but when Hendrix came on the scene, he was pushed out, and John didn't like that. He was so desperate to prove himself, to prove he was better than Hendrix, that he went against my plan and tried to kidnap you. Obviously, it was a botched attempt, and if it hadn't been for my good friend, Hendrix here, well, my plan could have fallen before it even got off the ground."

My attention snapped to Hendrix who was practically preening like a peacock at the praise Max was throwing at him.

What a brown-nosing douchebag that man was.

"Fortunately, Hendrix spotted John lurking at the ball, and he knew he was up to something, but he couldn't deal with him because it would draw too much attention. So he got a message to me and alerted me to what was going on. It was a good job I wasn't too far away from the venue and intercepted John when he was chased off. Hendrix did a good job at staging shooting at my car, it was enough to convince that oaf, Danny, that Hendrix had made a good effort to stop John."

My mouth twitched into a snarl at the mention of Danny. Danny wasn't an oaf, he wasn't anything but a loyal, honorable man, unlike the asshole standing across the room from me, watching Max like he was a God.

"Of course, it helped I am somewhat of an exceptionally skilled hacker, if I don't mind saying so myself. Hendrix messaged the second you headed out for the restroom and John followed. It was easy to hack into the security system and loop the camera so it looked like the hallway you had walked down was empty. You know, John probably would have gotten away with you had he not been so fucking obvious when that waiter came scurrying out of the kitchen." He scowled at John's corpse while I sat there with my mouth hanging open, processing everything.

Stupid really, even though I knew Hendrix had been working behind Kai's back for a long time, hearing the ins and outs of his deceit made me damn furious. Kai had been nothing but a good friend to Hendrix, and this is how he repaid him.

"I was mad at him for that fuck up, Riley," Max said, dragging my attention back to him. "After that, his mental health continued to deteriorate, he kept going on and on about how Hendrix couldn't be trusted, and that he was the only one I could rely on. His incessant droning bored me to tears if I'm honest.

"I couldn't trust him to be out of my sight, so I locked him away. Kept him locked in a room for the next few weeks until I needed him again. I wheeled him out when my appointment as chief was made. You should have seen the look on Kai's face when I announced John as my deputy, it was priceless! Of course, Kai was so infuriated by our little meeting that he failed to see what a gibbering wreck John was, and he stormed out before John could do or say anything to give the game away."

Holy shit. This was like something right out of a movie. How was any of this even possible? But then, if you spent twenty years planning something, anything was possible.

"I locked him away again after that," Max went on, pulling me from my thoughts. "It was the safest option for everyone. I couldn't afford him taking any more risks and fucking things up. Sadly, being locked away didn't do much for his mental state, but at least he isn't suffering now."

Max paused and a deathly silence fell across the room as my eyes dropped to John. Despite the fact that he had tried to kidnap me, despite being involved in plotting Theo's death and Kai's downfall, I couldn't help but feel a pang of sympathy for the man. He'd spent his life believing that someone he trusted was his friend when all along he was just being manipulated.

"Tell her about The Stag, Boss," Hendrix piped up, earning a scathing look from me. "She had a soft spot for The Stag. You're going to love this, Riley."

Urgh.

Hate was not strong enough of a word to describe what I felt for Hendrix. If he had been on fire, I would have pissed on him, only so that I could cover him in even more accelerant and be the one to light the torch.

"Ah yes, The Stag," Max beamed, clapping his hands together again. "I hate to be the bearer of bad news, Riley, I really do. But Toby was as loyal to you as Hendrix was to Kai."

My hands whitened as I gripped the armrest, trying my damned hardest not to let any emotion show on my face, even though my heart was tearing in two.

How fucking stupid had I been to think Toby was the same boy I had met when I first arrived in Hollows Bay?

I should have listened to Kai all along. If I hadn't been so fucking stubborn, I wouldn't have spent three days mad at Kai, and he wouldn't have had to leave me with Danny on the day of the ambush. And if the ambush hadn't happened, everything that followed might not have happened, and maybe, just maybe, Danny would still be alive.

The thought was like an arrow to the heart.

I didn't want to hear anymore, and if my hands hadn't been tied down, I would have covered my ears so I didn't have to hear what else Max had to say. But of course, the asshole kept talking.

"You know, the second he heard your name, he didn't just tell the gang leaders, Carlos and Markus, that he knew you. Oh no, he *volunteered* to track you down and bring you in. I've never heard so much bragging from one person, Riley. He told everyone who'd listen how you and he had been friends, he even bragged about the time he fucked you. He was your first, right?"

Tears pricked the back of my eyes as regret and anger churned in my belly. I refused to cry, I'd wasted enough tears over Toby. He didn't deserve anything but my wrath. For the first time since Kai killed him, I was glad he was dead.

Max chuckled, the sound grating on me like nails down a chalkboard. "See, Toby thought by offering his services, he'd move up in the gang, but Carlos and Markus didn't trust him, he was far too keen to prove himself, not to mention he had a motormouth on him, bragging to the entire crew how he was going to earn himself some brownie points with the silent partner of The Stags, which by the way, Riley, if you haven't figured out already, it's me."

A blinding satisfied smile took over his face as if he had revealed the world's best kept secret. His big reveal was wasted though, I didn't give a shit who the silent partner of The Stags was, it meant nothing to me, he should have saved it for Kai.

Ignoring my lack of response, Max's smirk dropped. "You know, I was all for killing Toby and not bothering with his suggestion to lure you away from Kai, I damn well knew it wouldn't work. But once again, Hendrix stepped up to the plate. Hendrix, tell Riley about your cunning plan."

Hendrix stepped forward so he was standing next to Max. The smug look on his face made my blood boil so much that I was pretty sure it would erupt out of me like a volcano.

"Kai had been deliberating about letting Danny take you to Sapphire, he didn't like the idea of the poor princess being cooped up," he said in a mocking tone. "Naturally, I encouraged him, telling him it was a great idea when really, I saw it as an opportunity to see what Toby was made of. Either he would succeed in figuring out a way to get you to meet him without Kai knowing, which would have gone in our favor, or Kai would have caught him, which again, would have gone in our favor. It was a win-win situation. Of course, you know how that ended."

My lips pressed into a thin line as he sneered at me. I closed my eyes to shut out the image of his face. Sadly, he was still grinning at me when I opened them again.

"We may as well cover the ambush seeing as Kai isn't here yet," Max said, taking back the limelight. "He's taking his time, isn't he? Maybe he doesn't give a fuck about you after all."

I bit my cheek to stop the retort from coming out, the sting in my cheek from the first slap had only just started to fade.

"I'll hold my hands up and accept Kai got the better of me at the ambush. Actually, I should say *Miles* got the better of me. He shouldn't have cracked the phone as quickly as he did, from one hacker to another, I can admit the man has skills. He was supposed to do that once I had you under my control, not before." Max started pacing again, his eyes glossed over as he lost himself in the memory. "I had everything planned to a tee. As soon as Kai arrived at Isaac's office, Hendrix made the call to Danny and told him to get you and Angel to a safehouse-"

"Actually," Hendrix interrupted. "I told him to move only you, but the idiot insisted on bringing Angel, so you can thank him for her being involved. Oh wait, you can't," he chuckled. My fists clenched again. I couldn't fucking wait to see Hendrix get his comeuppance.

"Right, right," Max said. "I'd been contacted by a gang following my ad on the dark web, they were confident they'd be able to kidnap you. Hendrix gave them access to the tracker on Danny's vehicle, it was all so perfect. Until Miles cracked the phone, and then it went to pot. Shame really," he shrugged, "it drew a huge amount of attention to Hollows Bay, and it would have been such an incredible show of feat to take you from right under Kai's nose."

"But you were shooting at the men!" I blurted, glaring at Hendrix when I remembered Miles telling me about the shootout that happened when he and Kai arrived at the crash.

The bastard laughed, a cold, humorless laugh that sent a chill down my spine. "I was, I couldn't blow my cover at that point, could I? But I didn't take any of the gang down, I happened to have a terrible aim that particular day," he grinned. "Although strictly speaking, that's not quite true. I did shoot one man. Poor Frank didn't see my bullet before it blew his head apart."

He killed Frank?

Jesus, this man's betrayal knew no end.

The events of everything that had happened over the past few weeks flashed through my head like a montage of images. There was so much deceit, betrayal, and hurt caused by the men standing in front of me, all for the purpose of ruining Kai.

When an image of Danny's smiling face paused in my head, I couldn't stop the question from falling from my lips.

"Why Danny? What did he ever do to deserve being set up as the one to betray Kai?"

"I'm glad you asked, Riley," Max said, a devious grin spreading on his face. "I did it as a favor to John. You see, John and Danny had been in a care home together before John was moved to Florida. Danny bullied John, he was mean to him, and he turned other kids against him. It was something John always remembered, so when I found Danny working for Kai, I promised John I would get the retribution for the time Danny made his life hell."

My eyes flashed to John's dead body again as another wave of sympathy washed through me. I hated bullies, even if they had just been kids. But did that mean Danny deserved to die? No, of course it fucking didn't. Danny may have been a bully as a kid, but he grew into a decent man.

Before another word could be spoken, a beep echoed around the room. Max pulled his phone out from his pocket, tapped at the screen, and was silent for a moment while he read whatever the message said. After a few seconds, he put the phone back in his pocket.

"Kai has pulled into the docks. Wait outside and bring him to me," Max ordered Hendrix. "And send in two of the others, I don't want anything going wrong this time."

He dismissed Hendrix without waiting for any acknowledgment. I may have imagined it, but I was sure Hendrix's jaw clenched at the way Max spoke to him.

Interesting.

He composed himself quickly though and stepped over John's body. "See you in a bit, princess," he said, throwing a wink at me before he disappeared.

Urgh.

I sincerely hoped Kai plucked the eyeballs from Hendrix's head before he killed him.

My eyes widened in alarm as Max stormed toward me, pulling a knife out from the sheaf under his jacket. Fear pooled in my belly as he reached the chair and I braced, anticipating that he was about to lodge the knife in my gut. But to my surprise, he started hacking away at the cable ties that held my hands down.

"It's in your best interest not to try anything dumb, Riley, I would hate to shed your blood before Hendrix has had a go on you, he's been desperate to fuck you for months now."

I didn't have time to respond. As soon as my hands were free, Max yanked me out of the chair, spun me around, and pulled my back to his front. His thick arm held me across my chest, the tip of the knife in his other hand pressed against my throat. He moved so I was covering the length of his body, and it dawned on me that he was using me as a human shield.

"Now the fun can really begin," he whispered menacingly in my ear.

Chapter 29

Kai

I pulled into the docks, the black van that had been following me since leaving East Bay also turned into the street that would lead to the warehouse Thorne had directed me to.

The irony wasn't lost on me. The docks was where Theo was killed, where this all began. Now it would end. One way or another, it would end today, and only one of us would walk away the victor.

I didn't care anymore, so long as I got Riley the fuck out of there and somewhere safe, nothing else mattered.

As I turned into the parking lot Thorne had directed me to, I was met by twenty men, all armed with MP5s, and all of them aimed at me. I rolled the car to a stop, and the second I did, the biggest asshole I'd ever had the misfortune of knowing swaggered out from between the armed men.

The sight of Hendrix made my hands twitch with the need to shed his blood, my mind running wild with new and inventive ways of what I could do to him to make him hurt.

To make him pay for every lie he told.

For every plot he made behind my back.

For killing Danny.

For touching Riley.

When the time came, whether it was today or some point in the future, he would pay, and it would be fucking beautiful.

He waited for me to get out of the car, his hands on his hips, and an arrogant smirk on his face. Underneath his suit jacket, he had a gun in his holster, but he didn't hold one in his hand, he evidently felt he didn't need one with all the men around him. I opened the car door and stepped out.

"Slowly, Kai. And hands in the air," Hendrix called like a little fucking pussy.

I lifted my hands, my jaw ticking as I went against everything I'd ever been taught. It was an alien concept, going into a battle without at least one weapon concealed on me, but I wasn't going to risk it. I wouldn't give Thorne or Hendrix any reason to hurt Riley.

Instead, I prayed to whichever god was out there that Miles would come through for me.

Miles had been too busy smashing up the pew to hear Thorne tell me to walk out of the church, meaning he had someone watching us. That's why I had to go apoplectic on Miles' ass. I had to make it look real, that I was really telling Miles I was going alone.

The van following me from East Bay only confirmed that we were being watched. But thanks to Miles' insistence of our phones being encrypted, I could talk freely to him once I was in the car without fear of someone hacking into our call.

Once Miles' calmed down from his brush with death at my hands, we devised a plan. He was also being followed, so he had one of Jack's men drive him, and they were going to attempt to lose The Stags that were tailing him. The rest of the plan was going to boil down to perfect timing. There was so much that could go wrong, but it was the only choice we had if we wanted at least one shot of us walking away unscathed.

As soon as I was out and away from the car with my hands up, Hendrix nodded to one of the men who came scurrying over to me. I memorized his face. He was a dead man. They all were, but this one would be a death I enjoyed.

He patted me down, his grubby hands running all over my shirt, under the collar, and down my pant legs. As he did Hendrix stared at me, the smirk ever present. I glared right back, letting him see the venom I held for him. It was a battle of wills, neither of us backing down.

The little bitch feeling me up pulled my phone from my pants pocket and threw it on the floor before stomping on it. I didn't care that he'd damaged the phone, it wasn't like anyone could track my location. What pissed me off was that there was a picture of Riley on there. I didn't make it a habit of taking pictures on my phone, in fact, this was the only one.

It was from the night we got married when she was fast asleep. Her hair had been spread over the pillow, her beautiful lashes fanned over her cheeks, and her lips were pulled into a contented smile.

I always thought Riley was the most beautiful woman I had ever seen, but in that moment, she looked like a fucking angel. One I did not deserve. I took her picture so whenever she wasn't with me, I could look back on it and remind myself of what I had waiting for me.

The cunt was going to suffer for destroying that image.

"He's clean, Boss," the little bitch said, returning to his spot with the other men.

Hendrix's smirk pulled into a wide grin. "I thought you'd try to smuggle at least one weapon in," he chortled. "She really has made you weak."

I bit my tongue, refusing to let him rattle me. His grin grew wider, and then he threw back his head and laughed. If Riley's life wasn't hanging in the balance, I would have taken the opportunity to wrap my hands around his throat, twenty armed men be damned.

"Come on, Kai. Max is waiting for you, and believe me when I say he is desperate to reveal his secrets to you. It's been a long time coming." He held his arm out as if he was welcoming me into his home instead of a warehouse used to torture people.

It was one of my warehouses, opposite to the one where Blaze's body would currently be rotting. I hadn't used this one for a while, I had plans to convert it into another drug manufacturing warehouse when a deal I had been working on was finalized. Hendrix knew I hadn't been inside it since the day I took ownership of it almost six months ago. I stepped toward him, every single man keeping their guns trained on me.

As soon as I was in front of Hendrix, he whipped his glock out and held it at me. "I'm warning you, Kai, don't fucking try anything or your little bitch pays." All joking was gone from his tone, and if I wasn't mistaken, it had been replaced by a hint of fear.

He was right to be fearful, he knew I could be unpredictable, especially when my girl's life was at stake.

"Or perhaps I should say, *my little bitch*, I've already told Riley that she belongs to me now, and I can't tell you how much I'm looking forward to claiming her once and for all."

Despite myself, a growl rumbled from my throat, and I took a step toward him. The air echoed with twenty guns cocking as Hendrix pressed his into my gut.

"Now, now, Kai. Max will never forgive me if I blow a hole in you, and if he takes his anger out on me, I'll have no choice but to take it out on her."

His eyes danced with mirth as my fists clenched. The image of Riley tied up, and him touching her flashed in my mind. The urge to kill him was unbelievably overwhelming but where did that get me?

I could reach out and snap his neck in the blink of an eye and be peppered with a thousand bullets. But where would that leave Riley? In the hands of Thorne, that's where, and that was not a risk I was prepared to take.

Hendrix must have realized I'd come to that conclusion because he let out a chuckle and pulled the gun away. The men around me reset their weapons but kept them aimed at me in case I had a change of heart.

"Take me to her," I hissed, speaking for the first time since I arrived.

Hendrix glared back at me, once again the two of us facing off. After a tense minute, he stepped aside and waved his hand to the warehouse door. "After you."

With his gun jabbed in the base of my spine, Hendrix pushed me through the door, and into the warehouse. The warehouse had been used by an international company to import coffee beans, but they'd gone bust a year ago. The powerful smell of coffee still hung in the air as Hendrix guided me to a door on the other side of the reception area.

"You know, you should have done better with teaching Riley to turn off her humanity," Hendrix said, his voice echoing around the empty space. "I almost thought she wouldn't come out of the panic room when I first got there and threatened to shoot Jacqueline, and you know what, she *almost* refused to come out, was prepared to see Jacqueline's head splattered everywhere."

My jaw twitched. I hadn't thought about Jacqueline since I had the call from Thorne, something in the back of my mind told me that it was too late for my loyal maid.

My heart broke for Riley though. She would have tortured herself before reaching the decision to stay put, so what was it that convinced her to open the door? I didn't have to wait long for the prick to answer the unspoken question.

"No, Riley was quite happy to send Jacqueline off to meet her fate, it was the threat against her old work friend, and her little daughter that convinced her to open the door. Silly girl. It wasn't a threat though, if she hadn't opened the door, Kendra and her daughter would have met the same fate Jacqueline met. Let me tell you, Riley didn't like seeing Jacqueline's brain blown everywhere."

It took all my strength to not turn around and wrestle the gun from him. Not just for killing Jacqueline, but for making Riley witness her death. It was only for the fact I didn't know where in the warehouse or how Riley was being held that I didn't.

As we reached the door, I grabbed the handle, but before I could pull it open, I paused and turned my head to look over my shoulder. "Make sure you enjoy your final moments on this earth, Hendrix, because I give you my word. *I'm coming for you*. For everything you have done to Riley, and for everything you have done to me, I'll be coming for you, and I *promise*, I'm going to enjoy every single minute of dismembering you," I hissed, letting him hear the threat in every word.

He didn't flinch, instead, he leaned forward with a maniacal grin on his face. "You really think you'll be walking away from this, don't you, Kai? I've got news for you, buddy. When Max is through, no one will remember you. He'll be sitting on your throne, I'll be by his side, and no one will give a fuck who you once were. Now get your ass in there and say goodbye to my girl, because when this is done, I can't wait to get her out of here and finally taste her sweet cunt."

Blind fury coursed through me, and before I knew it, Hendrix was pinned against the wall, my hand locked in a death grip around his throat.

He knew me too damn well though and saw it coming. We'd sparred together since we were young kids, the two of us evenly matched in fights. He blocked my attempt to disarm him, managing to lift the gun up and rest the nozzle against my beating heart.

He glared back at me with a crazy-ass grin on his face and a wild glint in his eye. "Come now, Kai. Don't do anything rash. You've been warned enough times about what will happen to *Star* if you try anything."

He was pushing every single one of my buttons, and it took every ounce of control I had not to fight back.

I would.

Just not yet.

Seeing resignation in my eyes, Hendrix moved the gun away and reached over to pull the door open. "In you go."

Giving him one final glare, I stepped into the room. My eyes immediately landed on my wife who was held by Thorne, a knife pressed to her throat. On her face was a mixture of pure terror and relief. I wanted nothing more than to go to her, to yank her from Thorne and take her far, far away from Hollows Bay.

Assessing the rest of the room, my gaze fell to the dead body of John Anderson. The gaping hole between his lifeless eyes was still oozing fresh blood. What the fuck had he done to wind up dead? Not that I gave a fuck, it was one less prick I would have to deal with.

On the other side of the room were two armed men. The control over my temper was already hanging by a delicate thread, but upon seeing Jacob, one of *my* men standing there, the thread tore just that little bit more.

"Kai, *brother*, how lovely to see you again," Thorne sneered from behind Riley, like the fucking coward he was. "Ah, I see the penny has dropped that another one of your men has come over to the other side, or maybe I should say, the winning side. You'll be amazed at just how many of your men have turned their backs on you to join me."

Don't rise to the bait.

Don't fucking rise to the bait.

Taking a steadying breath, I tore my gaze away from Jacob, who hadn't been able to meet my eye. When this was over, I was seriously going to have to clean house.

"Baby, are you hurt?" I asked instead, focusing on how the hell I was going to get her away from Thorne.

"I'm okay," she replied, her voice raspy. I raked my eyes over her body, not believing her, and white-hot rage coursed through me when I saw the bruise forming on her cheek.

"Thorne or Hendrix do that to your cheek?"

Thorne huffed. "Does it fucking matter? It's not like you are going to be alive to do anything about it."

It did fucking matter. Both of them would die, but whoever hurt my girl was going to suffer the pain of a thousand deaths.

Instead of replying with what I really wanted to, I asked my own question. "What do you want?"

"What do I want?" Thorne replied. "What do I fucking want? I want what is owed to me!" he roared. As he grew angrier, Riley winced, and it was only when I noticed the dribble of blood running down her neck that I realized he'd pierced her skin with the tip of the knife.

Fuck, I had to get her away from him.

"Twenty fucking years I've waited for this moment, Kai, since the time I was rejected by our father when I was fifteen fucking years old!" Thorne roared, digging the blade in again.

My brave girl squeezed her eyes closed, and when they opened, they were filled with tears, but she didn't let them fall. In fact, she took a calming breath, and with sheer determination, refused to show any pain.

My brave, strong, wife.

"Jacob!" Thorne barked. Jacob snapped to attention, waiting for his orders like a pussy. "Come here and hold Riley."

Jacob obediently crossed the room, avoiding the daggers I was throwing his way. When he reached them, Thorne shoved Riley into his arms.

"Keep your gun pressed to her head, and if she so much as makes one move to get away, blow her fucking brains out."

The muscle in my jaw twitched from where I was grinding my molars so damn hard. I sincerely fucking hoped Miles was getting the information he needed from the drone Jack had deployed to track me to this location, and I fucking hoped like mad it wouldn't be long until Miles called the strike.

"Here's how this is going to go, brother," Thorne said, taking a few steps away from Riley, the knife in hand now hanging down by his side. I swear, if he called me brother one more time, I was going to rip his tongue out. "I'm going to talk, you are going to listen, and you aren't going to make a sound. Understand?"

"What makes you think I give a fuck about anything you have to say?" I replied because quite frankly, I couldn't care less about anything that was about to come out of his mouth.

He smiled at me, a wicked smile filled with malice as he stepped back towards Riley. My lips curled into a snarl as he lifted her hand, her eyes growing wide in fear, but once again showing just how brave she was, she didn't try to pull away.

"Oh, you'll listen. There will be consequences if you don't." The sound of the bone in Riley's pinky finger snapping echoed around the room, followed by her anguished scream.

"Motherfucker!" I boomed. I lifted my foot, prepared to launch myself at the cunt, but the sound of Hendrix's gun cocking against my temple stopped me. My chest heaved with adrenaline, and my hands shook with pure rage, especially when I looked at Riley, tears streaking down her cheeks as she cradled her hand to her chest.

"It'll be her shoulder next, I bet she remembers just how painful a dislocated shoulder can be," Thorne said, stepping away again.

I snarled at him, bearing my teeth, ready for the wolf within me to come out and rip apart its prey. I needed Miles to hurry the fuck up and then vengeance would be mine.

"May I start, or would you like me to break any more of your girlfriend's bones?"

Girlfriend?

My eyes snapped back to Riley where I caught her wedding ring on her other hand. My eyes met hers and she gave me the slightest of headshakes, indicating that Thorne didn't know she was my wife. It was a smart move on her part. If Thorne had any idea she was now a Wolfe, she would be dead already. It was by sheer luck Thorne or Hendrix hadn't noticed the black band on my ring finger, and I subtly moved my hand behind my back.

"I'm listening," I growled as I turned back to him.

"Good. I've waited a long time for this moment, Kai, and I won't have it ruined."

Only, it was going to be ruined. Because at that very moment, gunfire erupted from outside the warehouse, dragging all our attention away from what Thorne was about to say.

Chapter 30

Riley

"What the fuck have you done?" Max roared at Kai, pointing his knife at him while it sounded like World War Three had just started outside. My little finger throbbed like a bitch and my pulse thrummed in my throat where Max had cut me with the blade. But for the first time since Kai arrived, I had a glimmer of hope.

I knew my husband wouldn't come here without a plan.

"Nothing to do with me," Kai rumbled, keeping his face neutral. He was always good at keeping a poker face.

"Don't fucking believe him, Boss, I told you he would have something up his sleeve," Hendrix hissed.

"How the fuck do you think I've managed to do anything?" Kai shot back, glaring murder at Hendrix. "You didn't give me the location until I was close by. You made me rip the tracker off my car, and you know damn well I left Miles behind in East Bay, so how the fuck do you think I've managed to coordinate whatever the fuck is going on outside?"

Max stared at Kai, his face contorting into a snarl. "If I find you've had anything to do with this, I'll gut your little bitch and fuck her corpse! Hendrix! Go and see what the fuck is going on, and take Karl with you."

Hendrix gave Kai one last death stare before he turned on his heel and stormed out, the other guard, Karl, following in his wake.

"I swear to you, brother, if this is an attempt to stop me from taking what's rightfully mine-"

"And what, exactly, do you think is rightfully yours?" Kai interrupted.

He stayed where he was standing, but in the last few seconds, somehow he'd made his presence bigger. The cold hard killer he kept locked away inside of him had come out to play. It was terrifying to witness, and yet here I was, rooting for Kai to unleash the devil inside of him.

"Hollows Bay!" Max bellowed, tugging at his hair with the hand that didn't hold the knife.

Christ, he was losing the plot.

"Tell me, *Michael,* what makes you think Hollows Bay belongs to you?" Kai said, remaining eerily calm.

Jacob's grip on me tightened as Kai took a tiny step forward, missed completely by Max who was too wild with rage to notice as the gunshot's echoing around the warehouse grew louder.

"Because I'm the rightful heir! I was born first, Hollows Bay belongs to me, and I've waited too long for it to be ruined now!"

I gasped when he whipped out a gun from behind his back and aimed it at Kai. Kai though, he didn't flinch. Didn't show any signs of fear that he had a gun pointed at him. In fact, what he did next made my brows rise so high they almost disappeared into my hairline.

Kai laughed.

He let out a chilling cackle that echoed darkly around the room. "You're not going to shoot me," he hissed, taunting Max and taking an obvious step forward. There was now just a couple of feet between Kai and Max, and if Max did decide to shoot, there would be no way he'd miss.

"And what makes you think I won't shoot?" Max growled back, cocking the gun.

"Because you've waited too long for this moment. You just said it yourself, you've waited twenty years to reach this point." He took another step forward, and I held my breath, waiting for the gun to fire. "Tell me, Max, are you really going to throw away twenty years of plotting and planning my downfall with a single bullet? Without me knowing the details of what you've endured all this time?"

Max snarled at Kai. "I am going to fucking kill you!"

Kai opened his arms, widening the target. My heart stopped where fear gripped me. I wanted to scream at him, to tell him to stop being so fucking stupid, but I remained still and placed every little bit of trust in Kai, trusting that he knew what the hell he was doing.

"Do it then. Shoot me." When Max could only growl incoherent words, Kai dropped his arms. "I tell you what, Max, you want Hollows Bay? It's yours."

What. The. Fuck.

He wasn't serious, right?

"Don't take me for a fucking fool, Kai," Max barked. But he lowered the gun, and if I hadn't been looking directly at Kai when he did, I would have missed the flash of triumph in Kai's eyes.

Thoughts churned in my mind. If Kai managed to disarm Max, what should I do about Jacob? I hated being the damsel in distress and thinking that I needed Kai to rescue me, but with a gun pressed against my head, I didn't really have any option.

I wanted to catch Kai's attention to get a subtle clue about what the heck he wanted me to do, but he was focused solely on Max, his dark eyes filled with murderous intent.

"If you want Hollows Bay, put your gun down and fight me like a man, not a pussy hiding behind a weapon. Prove that you're a true Wolfe," Kai hissed, low and deadly.

My mouth dropped open in surprise. Even Jacob's hold on me loosened the slightest at Kai's words. Max's entire body stiffened, and even though I could only see his side profile, it was clear as day the cogs were churning.

I had no clue what Max was like in a fight, hell I'd only met the man for the first time less than an hour ago. I didn't know whether he had any professional training or if he even knew how to throw a punch. I mean, he was a police officer so he must have had some form of self-defense training, but would it be a match for Kai?

"Come on, Max. Prove your worth. If you're going to kill me, at least *earn* your right to the throne," Kai said, smirking.

It was the final straw. Max tossed the gun and the knife to the corner of the room, they clattered as they skidded across the concrete, coming to a stop out of anyone's reach. With his teeth bared, and a roar that echoed around the room, Max launched himself at Kai, but Kai was prepared and met him halfway.

The two of them clashed in a fit of fury. Max grabbed Kai around the waist, but Kai countered the move by smashing his elbow into Max's back and twisting out of his grasp. Punches were thrown from both men, followed by grunts and groans from within the room and gunfire from outside. My heart raced, and I couldn't tear my eyes away from the brutal fight between the two brothers.

Jacob's grip loosened a fraction as he became fixated on the wolves fighting in front of us. It was like watching two wild pack animals fight to the death. Blood sprayed from Max's mouth, and a tooth landed on the floor after Kai struck him with a lethal punch. But Max gained the upper hand when he landed a strike to Kai's gut, winding him.

The pair were evenly matched, and for the first time, fear took root that Kai might not walk away from this. I couldn't bear to think about what that would mean if he didn't.

The two men roared at each other, limbs flying everywhere as they fought to get control, and echoes of punches reverberated around the room. Never in my life had I seen such a savage fight, and every time the men broke apart, each one had a new injury to their face.

But after a few minutes, Kai's powerful fist smashed into Max's face, his nose exploding, and the hit dazed him.

Seeing an opportunity, Kai struck.

He grabbed Max's body and launched him against the wall. Max crashed against it with such force that I was sure I heard bones crack. He collapsed into a heap, but Kai wasn't done. He marched over to Max's broken body and yanked him up by the collar. Max tried to rip Kai's hands away, but he'd lost his strength.

"This is for Theo!" Kai smashed his fist into Max's face, and another tooth flew from his mouth. "This is for hurting my girl!" He punched Max again. "This is for thinking you could ever fucking destroy me." Another punch, only this time, Max's hands fell to his side.

"Fucking hell," Jacob whispered from behind me, his body rigid.

"Bet you wish you hadn't switched sides now, huh?" I hissed back. His grip loosened completely and he dropped the gun from my head as he audibly swallowed.

I kept my cool, not wanting to risk this one opportunity to get away. "If I were you, Jacob, I'd get the fuck out of here before Kai turns his attention to you, there's no way he'd let you walk away given that you had your hands on me. And you know what? That looks like it hurts."

I didn't need to say anymore. Like the little coward he was, Jacob turned and ran from the room as Kai pounded another fist into Max's distorted face, his eyes both swollen shut and his nose busted. His body was slumped, only held up by Kai's hand gripped around his throat. The only way I could tell he was still conscious was from the garbled noise he was making.

"You are not my brother," Kai snarled, his voice deadly, and I knew he was about to make his final strike. "You took my only brother from me, and now you will pay for your sins."

And then time stood still.

My attention caught on a figure stepping into the doorway. Hendrix had his gun raised, and my body immediately tensed. It took him less than a second to assess the situation, Kai holding Max in a death grip, about to deliver the final blow, and me, pressed against the wall, unguarded.

To my sheer horror, a menacing smile spread over his face as he pointed the gun at me and cocked it. I couldn't stop the piercing scream emitting from my throat which grabbed Kai's attention.

He spun around. "Riley, get down!" Kai yelled as he dived in front of me, right at the very moment Hendrix fired two shots.

Kai slammed into me and I took the full force of his weight as we landed on the hard concrete, his body knocking the wind out of me. In the few seconds it took for me to catch my breath, I watched Hendrix drag a barely conscious Max out of the room.

"Baby, are you okay?" Kai asked. He was wheezing but I thought it was from where he had been fighting.

That was until I felt his warm blood seeping through my clothes.

"Kai! You're hurt," I shrieked, pulling myself out from underneath him. As I did, I rolled him onto his back and my heart froze in an instant.

Blood poured from the two wounds he'd received protecting me.

Tears sprung to my eyes, panic bubbling up. "Kai, no, no, no, no!"

My hands flew over his chest trying to find the source of the blood. There was a wound to his left side that was oozing blood, but the wound that worried me more was the hole so close to his heart. That wound was pissing blood, pumping it out every time his heart beat.

I used both hands to cover the wound, plugging the hole as much as I could, but within seconds, the blood seeped through my fingers.

"Riley, it's okay, baby. You're safe," Kai whispered, looking up at me with glazed eyes. One of his cheekbones was already starting to bruise as a result of the hits Max managed to land.

"I don't know what to do, Kai, there's too much blood," I sobbed.

Footsteps dragged my attention away, and for one horrible second, I feared Hendrix was coming back to finish the job. But relief flooded me when Miles and Jack ran into the room.

"Fuck!" Miles cried when he saw the mess. They both ran to my side to help me.

"We've got to get him help, Miles," I cried.

"I don't think we can move him," Jack said, cool as a fucking cucumber as life seeped out of Kai.

"If we don't move him, he is going to die," Miles choked out. I barely heard their words, so focused on trying to plug the wound, but failing miserably.

Jack paused for a split second before jumping to his feet. "I'll get the car and the team to help." He ran back out, and it was only then that I realized the gunfire had stopped outside.

"Kai, please don't die," I whispered, tears streaking down my face.

I was numb.

Completely numb to the sight before me.

Kai blinked up at me, his black eyes filled with nothing but love and adoration.

"He's not going to die, Riley, he's going to be just fine and will be back to being the controlling pain in our ass that he always is in no time," Miles whispered. He was ripping bits of his shirt off and using it to try and control the bleeding, but the material was soaked in blood faster than Miles could rip it off.

Less than a minute later, a team of men were in the room lifting Kai and carrying him out to the waiting car. Blood trailed as they ran out of the warehouse with him. Miles and I followed behind, and as soon as we reached the car, I got in the back with Kai and two men from Jack's team.

Kai was laying across the back seats, bleeding everywhere. As carefully as I could, I lifted his head and placed it in my lap. The two men who had got in the back with us had a medical bag, one started pulling equipment out of it, while the other continued to press cloth against the hole in Kai's chest. Miles jumped into the passenger seat and Jack gunned the engine, speeding us out of the compound.

"We need to get to Dr. Harris' place. He's got a private hospital not far from here, I'll call him and tell him we are on our way," Miles said.

I blocked out his call and whatever the other two were doing to stem the bleeding, focusing on holding Kai.

Tears cascaded down my cheeks as I stared down at my husband, his eyes were half closed, and his breathing labored.

I refused to acknowledge the truth.

That my husband was going to die.

With what must have been monumental effort, Kai slowly lifted a hand and wiped away a tear, but in doing so, he smeared his blood across my cheek.

"I love you, Riley. I'll always love you," he whispered.

I squeezed my eyes shut as my heart began to implode in my chest. "Why does it feel like you're saying goodbye, Kai?"

He smiled then, only a little tug of his lips, but it was still there. "It'll never be goodbye between us, Star. You and I, we're for eternity."

I couldn't hold back the sob that echoed around the car as I leaned down and rested my forehead against his.

The journey seemed to take a lifetime, but in reality, it was only a few minutes with the way Jack was driving. Dr. Harris was waiting outside his surgery with a gurney and a nurse. As soon as the car door opened, his face paled.

"Christ," he whispered, staring at Kai, whose eyes were now closed.

Jack, Miles, and the other men, whose names I didn't know, started to lift Kai out of the car to put him on the gurney. As they were doing that, another car pulled up and more of the security team got out to help. Once he was on the gurney, Dr. Harris, Miles, and the nurse took off on a run toward the little hospital building.

Numbness seeped into every inch of me, right down to my bones.

Without conscious thought, I started walking toward the building, and when I looked down to see I was covered in Kai's blood, my legs gave way. One of the guards caught me before I hit the ground, and carried me into the little waiting room of Dr. Harris' private surgery.

It was pointless bringing Kai here. He needed a fucking hospital, not a little surgery. He needed a team of medics, and a shit ton of blood to replace what he lost.

I wanted to barge into the room they disappeared into and tell them to get him to the city hospital, but instead, I collapsed into a chair. It would be pointless demanding they took Kai to a hospital.

In my heart of hearts, I already knew.

I don't know how long we sat in silence, neither I nor any of the other guards who had come to the waiting room spoke a word. When Miles finally emerged from behind the door, he was as white as a ghost.

His eyes met mine, and they were filled with tears.

"Riley," he croaked. I didn't want to hear anything else from him, but the words still came as my heart imploded violently in my chest. "Riley.... I'm sorry.... Kai, he didn't make it. Kai, he's dead."

To be continued.....

Acknowledgements

So, that ending sucked, right? Sorry about that! I'm sure there are a heap of unanswered questions but all will be revealed in book 3, I promise!

I really hope you have enjoyed this chapter of Riley and Kai's story, I had so much fun writing it, even if I did get mad at myself at certain times.... I had to re-write Danny's chapter several times because I just couldn't bring myself to bump him off!

There are a few people I want to take a minute to thank. Firstly, my Alpha reader, Sandra, who chews my lady-balls off if I don't provide her with chapters on a regular basis. Thank you for your feedback, suggestions, and encouragement.

To my beta readers, April & Whitney, thank you for all your words of advice and encouragement. Without you, I'd probably be sitting quietly in my writing cave giving myself reasons as to why I shouldn't publish my books. Your kind words and support have been the driving force to push aside any self-doubt and get on with it!

To my street team, thank you for helping to spread the word and get both Collide and Implode known in the big wide world. I am learning that social media is an absolute minefield, but with your help, you are really helping me to navigate through it.

To my mum. She is my biggest supporter and my best critic (even if I don't want to hear it sometimes). Thank you for always being there for me.

Thank you for believing in me, and thank you for never discussing those sex scenes with me!

To my husband who puts up with so much of my shit, and never grumbles…. well, okay, sometimes he grumbles, but it's usually justified! Thank you for all your support, I wouldn't be writing this today if it wasn't for you pushing me out of my comfort zone. I know I don't always show it, but I love you from the bottom of my heart, and I am so incredibly grateful to have you in my life.

Finally, to every person who picked up and read Collide and Implode. Thank you. Your support means the world to me, and I have truly been overwhelmed by the number of people who have reached out to tell me that they have enjoyed Collide or taken the time to leave me reviews. I sincerely hope you enjoyed Implode just as much. If you have enjoyed it, please leave me a review, I can't tell you how important they are to a newbie author!

Book 3 in the Hollows Bay Trilogy is a work in progress and will be released in the coming months. If you want to be kept updated with how it's progressing, get exclusive sneak peeks, and take part in giveaways, then please join my social media groups:

Facebook: Hunter's Pack

Instagram: e.k.hunterauthor

If you have any questions, please get in touch with me via my website: www.ekhunterauthor.com

About the Author

Elizabeth-Kate lives in Oxfordshire with her Husband and two Sprocker Spaniels. She spends a lot of time with her nose in a book, usually the kind with morally gray characters and feisty female leads! When she isn't reading, you'll find her in her writing cave dreaming up new ideas for plots and characters.

Elizabeth-Kate likes to take her Spaniels, known as the Smelly Weasels, on long walks. She can't start the day without coffee otherwise she turns into a monster, and her party trick is devouring a pack of cookies in one sitting!

Also By

Hollows Bay Trilogy

Collide

Implode

Book 3- Coming soon!

Made in the USA
Middletown, DE
17 March 2024